I0818004

THE BOND WE
FORGED

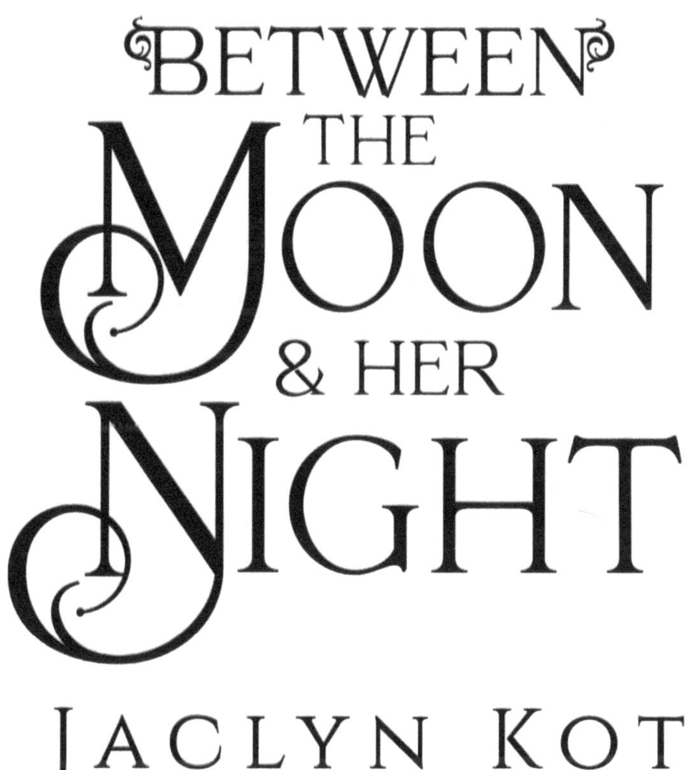

JACLYN KOT

Between the Moon and Her Night
Jaclyn Kot

Editing by Jessica McKelden
Proofreading by New Ink Book Services and Veerie Edits
Cover design by Gigi Creatives
Formatting by Imagine Ink Designs
Map by New Ink Book Services
Chapter art by Steven Rice

Intended for Mature Audiences

This book is a dark fantasy romance that contains content that could be triggering.
Please visit www.jaclynkotbooks.com for more information.

MYSTERY.ARTIS

For my readers who have been waiting oh, so patiently for some Von and Sage action.
Are you ready for your reward?
If so, turn the page.

Good girl.

Prologue

Aurelia

I was created just over three hundred years ago.

The heart which beats inside my chest was a sacrifice made on my behalf, something that was necessary for my body's creation. It was taken from the God of Life, rinsed in the Selenian Sea, then planted in the womb of my mother moon. When this body was strong enough to house the divine, my soul was placed in it, and from there, I was born.

Fully made as a woman and delivered into the embrace of the God of Life.

Aurelius. Son of Sol and the King of the New Gods. The Lord of Light, and I, *his* lady.

For a time, we loved one another.

At least . . . I thought we did.

You see, even though my husband carried the title of king, I was never addressed as queen. I wore a crown, yes, but my status never surpassed that of princess. I was always expected to stand beside his golden throne, never to sit beside him as an equal. I was never allowed in court meetings or given any role that was of any importance in serving the two realms Aurelius ruled over.

I had but one job—produce heirs for my king.

And at that, I failed. I couldn't even give him *one*. Quite the predicament for the so-called Goddess of Life.

But my failure was not my own.

Before my creation, before Aurelius's, there was another god who ruled, a much older, stronger, more sinister one—the God of Death, King of the Old Gods. He was the first king of the Three Realms—the Immortal Realm, the Living Realm, and the Spirit Realm—but under his control, they started to deteriorate. So, the omnipotent Creator removed two-thirds of the God of Death's kingship and gave the Immortal and the Living Realms to Aurelius. As one could imagine, this did not sit well with the God of Death, and like a venomous snake, he coiled in the shadows, waiting for his moment to strike.

On the day of my making, I was given all the parts a woman needed to create a child, but when the God of Death caught wind of my creation, he stole me into his night. There, he placed his massive hand, adorned with black ink and silver rings, upon the flat of my stomach, and with a wicked gleam in his starless eyes, he cursed me with his touch of death.

Like frost kissing the petals of a delicate flower, my womb began to wither. Not only this, but so did my ability to create any other forms of life—no animals, no plants, nothing. The God of Death stripped me of all that I was, and then he forced me to crawl back to my husband, to tell him that I was barren.

For years, I believed that was the day that the first fracture was made in our seemingly perfect marriage, but I was blinded by love and unable to see that it was full of hairline cracks that had been there all along.

As time continued, and I was unable to fulfill my divine duty—to create—I became sick with a horrific fever. It felt like my body was strapped to a pyre, eternally burning, the flames never ending, never ceasing. Not once. Aurelius tried everything to help me, whether it be procedures like bloodletting or drugs like dwale to drag me under, but nothing helped to end my torment.

At least, not until the darkness returned to my side, sweeping me into his strong, steely arms and taking me away with his shadows. Amongst my screams of pain, I found a sliver of solace—his cool rings were euphoric against my blazing skin.

I awoke lying on the floor of a cabin, the mountainous God of Death seated in a chair beside me, an apple in one hand, a knife in the other. As he cut the red fruit, he told me that he would make a deal with me to end my suffering. He would give me an apple seed so that I could create life with it. I was so desperate for relief that I accepted. But his deal was conditional. Whenever the fever returned, he would give me a seed to plant, but I was to plant it directly outside of the bed chambers I shared with my husband. It was a diabolical plan, because whenever Aurelius looked outside, he would be forced to see the trees I had planted, created from what the God of Death had given me. It served as a silent reminder that Aurelius was ruling land that once belonged to the God of Death.

Years swirled into decades, and decades caved to centuries. Thousands of seeds stretched up from the soil, growing into tall, mighty trees, until a grand orchard stood outside our bedchamber, spanning for miles in swaths of glorious green laden with ripe reds.

And so, instead of children, I had given my husband thousands of trees. Trees that were born from the God of Death's seed and my labor. As they grew tall and fruitful, Aurelius's affections for me withered. If that had been the God of Death's plan to destroy our marriage, well, he succeeded. In truth, though, Aurelius had played the bigger part in its demise, by never treating me as a woman deserves to be treated.

But before I realized that, before I realized my worth, the God of Death brought war to our doorstep. Aurelius and I put our marital problems to the side as we looked to defend his kingship.

The Immortal War spanned decades.

When it was over, our side had lost.

The God of Death enslaved the New Gods, one by one, leaving me to be imprisoned last. On the day he came for me, I was still fighting on the battlefield, unaware that our side had fallen, until the bastard stole me from the warzone and told me that we had lost. There, on the cliff of the mountainside, I made my final stand against him. I gathered what little strength I had left, and I shoved my blade into his stomach—targeting the same place he had touched when he stole my ability to create. Blood, as red as a mortal's, seeped from his nasty, deep wound. I couldn't believe what I was seeing, for I was no stranger to the rumors—

The God of Death *could not* bleed.

And yet, somehow, he was.

The face he made was one I would never forget. Surprise. Confusion. And something much, much darker. Something . . . possessive.

He told me he was calling off the war.

Disbelieving, I asked him why, and that was when he said, "Since the dawn of time, I have spent millennia searching for an answer to the empty void inside. And now, at last, I have it. How fitting that she should be the very thing that can kill me."

Then . . . he left. One black feather was rendered in his wake. It was the first of many that would eventually find their way to me.

True to his word, he ended the war.

Our people celebrated, believing a false lie fed to them by the court that we had won and defeated the monster—the God of Death and his army. One could imagine the horror upon their faces when he showed up at the victory celebration with Aurelius in chains and another deal on his wicked lips. He would free Aurelius, give back the two realms, all in exchange for one thing . . .

Me.

I was to go with him and live in the Spirit Realm where I would become his bride.

Seeing Aurelius reduced to his imprisoned state, it tugged at my fragile, biased heart, and I made the deal.

Later that night, when every immortal with any knowledge tried and failed to break the bonds that the God of Death had imprisoned Aurelius in, I tried to comfort him. But in his jealousy, he turned cold towards me. I crumbled, never having felt such disgust from him before, a male whom I thought I loved. When I picked myself up from my broken state, I charged into his court, demanding to speak with him.

That day was when *everything* changed.

Aurelius told me that he was going to gather the children of the Old Gods and have them Cleansed from existence with iron and flame, the two elements necessary to end a Demi God's life. But that wasn't the worst part of it all, no. You see, fire needs wood, and there was one place nearby where wood was in abundance—

My orchard.

The only thing that was *mine*.

The orchard that I had tended with such love and care throughout the years was going to be weaponized, used to take innocent lives. I had thought the God of Death was wicked and cruel for stealing my ability to create, but his actions paled in comparison to what Aurelius was going to do.

. . . What he *did*.

One by one, my trees were cut down, but as they fell to the ground, I did not shatter.

No. Instead, I rose.

Because finally, I had found my voice.

My courage. My *worth.*

I tore off my wedding band, telling him we were over.

Angrily, he took the ring, forced it back on, and then snapped my finger to the side, the broken bone locking the gold band in place. As he did that, he told me that he would never allow me to leave him. Before he could hurt me further, I let my light take me to the only person who could help me—

The God of Death.

I went to the Spirit Realm, greeted by the fall of black snowflakes and a looming, haunting castle. Inside, I found the male who I once thought my enemy, but when he took my broken finger and healed it, I started to wonder if I had been wrong about him. He told me he would help me free the Demi Gods and give them a place to live in the Living Realm—Edenvale. There, he would gift me a wall of endless mist that would surround the continent and protect them from Aurelius.

When I asked him what he wanted in return, knowing he never made a deal without wanting something in exchange, his answer shocked me.

Nothing.

The maker of deals wanted *nothing* in return.

And to me, that meant a great *something.*

But would it be enough for me to move forward from our treacherous past?

That, I didn't know, but I supposed I was going to find out.

Chapter 1

Aurelia

The Selenian Sea sprayed her cool mist on my face as I gripped the wooden banister, fighting the urge to vomit—a battle I had consistently lost ever since I boarded this blasted knarr.

The ship, made from a hard wood, in a grain pattern I did not recognize, was stained an inky black. That same color was mirrored on the large, square-rigged sail that stood proudly above, catching the breath of the wind. A raven-headed prow was carved into the front, guiding us ahead. It was one of fifty ships that had been provided by the God of Death to help the children of the Old Gods escape Aurelius's vengeance. Those who had wings flew above us, their silhouettes momentarily blocking out the sun every once in a while. The waters were violent, constantly assaulting the cargo vessel as we fled to safety—to the continent of Edenvale.

Apart from my unworthy sea legs and brewing stomach, I felt a hairsbreadth of relief the further we sailed. Despite that sliver of ease, I did not let it water down the direness of our situation. There was a good chance that Aurelius would come after us, especially once he learned that his dungeons were empty, and so were his coffers. I had used Aurelius's own precious gold to buy the guards' silence and compliance, thus helping the Demi Gods escape. Aurelius had destroyed my trees, so I took *his treasure*—he wasn't the only one who knew how to weaponize something of great importance.

At any given moment, Aurelius's army could emerge on the horizon, descend upon us, and try to drag us all back. But the Demi Gods would not go willingly, not when they knew what awaited them in the Immortal Realm—a spiked iron collar and a hot, ravenous pyre.

And so, they would fight.

As would I.

I would not go back to a life of slavery. Of mistreatment and abuse.

No, I knew my worth now. And no one, not a soul, would ever take that from me.

"Excuse me, Lady Light, but might I offer you something to help with your nausea?" asked a friendly female voice to my left.

White-knuckled, I held firm to the polished banister, shifting my weary, watery eyes to look at her. Brown-haired, blue-eyed, and young—not much older than eighteen, I would think. A light dusting of freckles and a pinch of blush warmed her otherwise cool complexion. She was pretty, in her own way. Some features—her nose, for one—were more pronounced than others.

She swept her hand out from underneath her tattered cloak, offering me view of what lay in her palm—a small, black vial, corked at the top. The opaque glass prevented me from seeing the contents within.

I raised a questioning brow. "What is it?" I asked, my voice as wobbly as my legs. How strange that the sea was a part of my making, and yet when placed on a boat, it made my stomach bubble like a forgotten pot left over the fire. It was just one more thing that my divinity lacked.

"It is a mixture of different ingredients, but the primary one is ginger. It will help you," she replied with a soft smile, tilting her head to the side ever so slightly. Her long brunette hair had a gentle wave to it, falling well past her waist. "Go on, take a sip."

Take a sip, princess, a regal, male voice demanded of me. Aurelius.

I bristled as an uneasy feeling stirred the contents of my stomach, but it wasn't from my seasickness. It was from a memory—of Aurelius's ichor spreading across my tongue. The way it would claim my thoughts, my mind . . . my body.

For years, that, to me, was love.

But now I know that it wasn't. Which begged the question—what *was* love?

I shook my head. "I appreciate the offer, but—"

I was cut off as the boat struck a wave, and the bow was lifted into the air. When it came back down, smacking against the water, the limited remnants of my stomach rose into my esophagus. I retched over the side.

Afterwards, I looked at the young woman, sucking air like a fish out of water. "I appreciate the offer, but I'm alright for now." I dried my mouth in the nook of my elbow, a few hundred years of propriety and manners all but forgotten.

"You don't look alright," she pointed out, her hand still extended in offering.

"I will be once we make land."

"We won't reach Edenvale for a while. Are you sure you want to suffer that long when you could simply take a small sip of what I am offering and have your symptoms cured?"

For an eighteen-year-old, she was awfully confident in her tonic-making abilities. Curiously so. I didn't sense any type of grand divinity coming from her. If anything, she appeared more mortal than Demi God. What a peculiar girl.

"You seem rather confident," I challenged. "Do you possess earth magic? Is that how you were able to make the ingredients for the tonic?"

"Something like that."

I unclenched my hands from the banister, the joints in my fingers groaning in relief. Turning around, I propped my elbows against the railing, leaning on it to help relieve my quivering sea legs. I glanced at her sidelong. "You are not a Demi God, are you." It wasn't a question, so I didn't ask it like one.

"I'm not." A small pause. "No."

"Then what *exactly* are you?"

"I am what you are." She flashed her teeth in a cheeky smile.

"I am a goddess," I pointed out, questioning if she really understood what she was implying.

"You are . . ." She nodded in agreement. "And so much more too." She chuckled to herself, as if she knew something I did not. "Tell me, you could light walk directly to the continent we are traveling to and save yourself from this—" She gestured at my sorry state, "—and yet, you do not. Why is that?"

I was a bit surprised by the girl—by her bluntness.

Brown brows lifted, her eyes twinkling as she said, "Well, are you going to answer?"

Creator above, she was pushy too.

I decided to bite on her question. "Because I feel a responsibility to protect those who sail on these ships. If I light walk to Edenvale, it will mean leaving them all behind. Should Aurelius show up, they might need my protection. That is why I stay and endure."

"But they are not *your* people, so why should you care?"

"Do you think I'm a monster?" I retorted, shaking my head.

Was that what people thought of us gods? That we only cared about our own? Was that what Aurelius's leadership had reduced us to? Or . . . was I the anomaly?

Regardless—

"Is not *all* life precious?" I asked, glancing past her to an old man whose crooked legs looked to be fairing no better than my own. He had obviously gotten more mortal blood than Demi God blood when he was being knitted together in his mother's womb, which meant that he, too, aged like the mortals did. He dipped a mop into a wooden bucket as a child ran past him, chasing after a small ball made of twirling wind and leaves. He looked up, laughing softly as he watched the young boy play. When the child collected the ball, he turned back towards him and exclaimed victoriously, "I got it, Grandfather!" Words of encouragement fell from the elderly man's lips before he returned to his task.

I shifted my gaze back to the girl. "Is not all life worth saving, regardless of age, sex, or belonging?"

Her smile grew, as if I had just told her the very words she had been wanting to hear. And for the briefest of moments, I was shown a small glimpse of the incredible divinity that did indeed live within her—something she had purposefully let slip through, judging by the twinkling, mischievous look in her eyes.

And it was powerful. Breathtakingly so.

"You *are* a goddess," I said, equal parts surprised and astonished. "And yet, you hide it. You appear . . . mortal."

The boat struck another violent wave, and water sloshed over the side, misting my back and my arms with the cool tears of the inconsolable sea. Was she angry that we were sailing on her, using her for our own gain? I understood that feeling all too well. Despite the cool droplets of water wetting my skin, it did little to neutralize the prickling heat radiating throughout my body from my seasickness.

"I suppose I am a bit of both." The girl beamed, offering me the vial once more.

"How do I know it's not poisoned?" I asked, glancing at it. In the castle, prior to Aurelius and I eating any meals, our food was always tested. Especially after the one incident with his brother—a story for another time. Yes, we were immortals, but that did not mean we couldn't get sick by ingesting something that did not agree with our bodies.

"You don't." She flashed me a closed-lipped grin, her eyes squinting shut.

An odd one, indeed.

I sighed and took the bottle, popped the cork, raised it to my nose, and took a delicate sniff. I made a sour face as I quickly shoved the cork back in. "That *does not* smell like ginger."

"It is as I told you before. Ginger is one of the primary ingredients, but not all of it." She tucked her arms behind her and began to rock in place, the motion not helping with my already swaying state.

My stomach heaved. "Can you not do that?" I asked, warring with my rising bile.

She gave me a half-hearted apologetic look and stopped.

Thank the Creator.

"Well, anyway, I'll leave that with you." She nodded to the vial. "Whether you take it or not, *the choice is yours*." Then she turned and began to walk away, the hem of her brown cloak darkened from the wet deck.

I clutched the vial as I called out to her, "Wait. I didn't catch your name."

"My name is Ezravaynia," she said over her shoulder, but she did not stop walking. "But you may call me Ezra."

Ezravaynia. That name.

"Wait!" I shouted after her, my eyes going wide. "Are you the Goddess of Free Will?"

She stopped and turned to look at me over her shoulder. "That is up to you to decide."

And then she was gone.

Later on, when the celestial stars peppered the dark night sky, my nausea became particularly bad. Desperate for any form of relief, I popped the cork on the vial, pinched my nostrils closed, and drank some of the bitter contents down.

Surprisingly, it worked just as Ezravaynia had said it would.

It quelled my nausea instantly. My curiosity, however, not so much.

In the past, I had searched for the elusive Goddess of Free Will, but I had never been successful in finding her. So why had she shown up now, offering me aid?

And why did I feel like that wouldn't be the last I saw of her?

Chapter 2

Von

My boot heels scuffed against the worn, sizable dock as I strode ahead, my steps performing a countdown, ticking down the seconds until *she* arrived. Those who stood in my way parted quickly, scampering backwards in fear as their eyes stretched wide as if they had seen a phantom. Perhaps, they had. The wind's violent breath whipped my black cloak behind me while gliding its fingers over my face, brushing back my hair and whispering in my ear a message that heated my cold, bloodless veins—

We're bringing her to you, my king.

In response, my shadows flickered hungrily around me, swarming in anticipation, latching on to that truth. Tasting and lapping at it, feeding the predator within. If I were a good man, I might have the slightest reservation about holding her to our deal, but that was just it, wasn't it?

I *was not* good, nor was I some fickle mortal man.

To my right, a humble, weathered fishing boat was tied up to the dock, bouncing up and down on the turbulent waters. Two men sat in it. Despite the vast number of years between them, they bore a great resemblance to one another. Grandfather and grandson, I presumed. Their hands were full of blood, scales, and chunks of fish as they worked on filling a bucket with chum. Despite how strong my winds were—something I had purposely done to quicken her journey—the stench of cut-up fish assaulted my nostrils.

Fish. I detested it.

Unless we were talking about the female variety. Then that was different.

The older man's weary eyes met mine, a bolt of panic shooting across them. The rusty hinges in his jaw sprung open, the color chased from his skin—painting him ashen.

Claaaack.

He dropped his knife.

That got the attention of the young man who was seated across from him. "Grandfather, what is it—" he asked, his words trailing off into stunned silence.

Although I was past them now, I didn't need to look back to know the younger one's eyes were fixed on me, and it wasn't because of my handsome good looks. I presumed he wore a similar expression to his grandfather's. It didn't matter if they were living or dead, mortals all wore *that* same expression when they saw me—

Terror.

"Relax, old man," I chuckled as I continued forward. "I have not come for *you* today."

If he said something in return, I didn't catch it, for something else had caught my attention.

Across the white-capped waters of the Selenian Sea, hundreds of my ravens emerged on the horizon. The left corner of my mouth twisted upwards—the wind was telling the truth after all. Reaching the end of the dock, I slipped my hand into my pocket, the twist in my lips spreading to the other side as I spied what the horizon presented to me—a fleet of fifty knarrs, one of the ships carrying precious, precious cargo. Their square-rigged sails were painted with my insignia—a raven standing on top of a skull with a glass orb in its beak.

"Look, there! What is happening to the horizon?" shouted one of the port workers, reminding me how poor mortal eyesight was.

His words spread like a festering infection, claiming a dozen tongues, getting them to repeat a similar message of concern. Slowly, hundreds of working hands stilled. Some people began to pray, asking for aid and mercy from the New Gods.

Should the God of Life hear their prayers, that could make this situation . . . interesting.

I glanced ahead, speaking to my wind—

Bring her to me. Quickly.

Like a good soldier, the wind answered with a mighty, continuous gust. Fifty sails flexed, stretched beyond their means, and the ships began to pick up speed. My ravens called out to me, the wind carrying their caws, amplifying them. As they came closer, those who stood behind me began to abandon their prayers as a wall of black descended upon us. Some began to run back into the city of Katlegin, seeking shelter from something they could not understand. The curious ones remained behind, watching. Waiting.

My ravens flew over top, their talons stretched out as they landed, one by one, along the irregular rooflines, etching them in a line of black. There was no rhyme or reason to the placement of the various shacks, stretching along the waterfront—a testament to how old this part of the city was. It had existed long before streets were created.

Flying above the ships, wings spread out, were the descendants of the Old Gods—otherwise known as Demi Gods. Those who did not possess the gift of flight sailed below. Although I ruled over the Old Gods, I did not consider their children my people. This was in part because I no longer held dominion over the Immortal Realm, where most of the children of the Old Gods lived. When the God of Life decided to imprison all the Demi Gods and *Cleanse* them from the lands, I heeded it little mind.

But then *she* came to me with a pretty plea on her pretty pink lips and I couldn't help myself.

I told her that I would aid her in her rescue mission by providing transportation to a place of refuge. Although I could not bring the living to the land of the dead, I could carve out a small part of the Living Realm for them. And so, I told her to bring them here, to the self-sustainable continent of Edenvale.

That was one of two reasons why I was here right now.

"Do you see them?" cried out a woman from somewhere in the distance, her voice ringing out like a bell, full of wonder.

"What are they?" panicked another.

I rolled my eyes. Mortals were such a jumpy, anxious species.

"I don't know," said a man. "Could they be . . ."

"Are they gods?" chipped in a young boy.

"Why would gods come here?" snarked another.

I smirked.

"Creator above, what if they are demons?"

Their hysteria continued to grow, but I heeded it little mind, because that was when I saw her—

Aurelia. The Goddess of Life.

She stood at the front of the lead ship, silken strands of her long, white hair whipping around her. She wore a gown the color of fresh-fallen snow. A band of gold metal armor molded around her petite torso, drifting into a "v" over her sex. The fabric was slit all the way up to her hips, and when the wind would hit it just right, it showed off a hint of her porcelain skin and wealthy thighs.

Even in the daylight, her divinity radiated with the glow of Luna.

Striking eyes, the color of a clear-blue sky, met mine. Her brows tugged slightly together, her expression shifting, its meaning foreign to me.

So much about her was foreign, and yet *so much* was familiar.

The way her adorable, useless canines tugged at her bottom lip whenever she was thinking. Or the way her nose tilted upwards, ever so slightly, when she smiled. The sounds she made during the middle of the night, when she was alone, pleasuring herself. Ah yes, I had heard those husky moans as I hid in the shadows outside her bedchamber's window, felt them like a summoning to me, to come and take control over that strumming hand of hers, to chain her wrists above her head, and claim her pleasure for my own.

Since the dawn of her creation, I had been obsessed with her.

But our history had been written in darkness, and I was the one who held the quill. I had stolen her ability to create, ruined her marriage, and tormented her to no end. And as for the latest of my sins against her, I had forced her into a deal I would never allow her to escape from.

"She's beautiful," remarked a woman behind me.

"She must be a goddess," whispered another.

As the ship made port, one of the crew members leapt from the boat, his boots thudding on the dock. Horrific scars, the flesh swollen and raised, wrapped around his neck and wrists. To the mortals, the scars would be invisible, but to me, I could read the language of the dead.

A coil of rope was tossed onto the dock, and he began to reach for it, but when his brown eyes flicked up to mine, he instantly dropped to one knee and dipped his head. "My king." His voice crackled with fear.

"Rise," I told him. "Continue what you are doing."

He nodded, picked up the rope, and began to tie it to a wood post laden with a rim of slick, green algae.

I felt something pull—an invisible chain of sorts, tugging on me. Just as it always did whenever she was near. No better than a slave, shackled to her, I obeyed its command.

My gaze met those incredible blue eyes, clear and vibrant and watching.

I sauntered casually over to the side of the boat and held out my heavily inked hand, my silver rings glinting in the light. Smirking, I asked, "How was your journey, Little Goddess?"

She looked at my offered hand as if she expected it to be laced with poison. Her throat bobbed as she swallowed. Then she did something that surprised me—she placed her small hand in mine, accepting my offer.

Her touch set fire to my nerves, stirring them awake.

Using my hand to stabilize her, she gathered her skirts and rose onto the dock. By mortal standards, she was tall, but by immortal ones, the reverse was true. I peered down at her, watching as her teeth feathered her lip. Temptation seeped into my bones, urging me to snatch her face and do it for her. How badly I wanted to feel what it would be like to have my teeth in her skin.

Soon enough, I reminded myself.

"The journey was fine, thank you," she said, her voice all regal and poised. I detested it. That wasn't her. That was centuries of her being forced into a mold she was told she needed to fit, because that was what her ex-husband wanted.

I would free her of it.

Aurelia pulled her fingers from mine and began smoothing her gown, giving them a job as if they were needed elsewhere, but the fabric was already wrinkle-free. She didn't fool me. I knew when people were uncomfortable. Her actions showed me that she was no different. Luckily, we had eternity to work on that. In time, I would train her to enjoy my touch—to yearn for it.

She glanced to her left, taking in Katlegin while I took her in.

My perfect little female, so untainted and so . . . innocent.

That wouldn't last for long.

As another ship ported on the other side of the dock, people began to file off the one that Aurelia had been on. Cautiously, they walked forward, holding on to their loved ones. They all wore the same concerned look, unsure of this new land that they were expected to make a home of.

"Do you think . . ." Aurelia paused, a hint of worry threading into her royal tone. "Do you think they'll be alright here?"

There it was again, that *same* incessant pull, begging me to reach out, to take her, to lock her in my arms and never let her go.

For my own calculated reasons, I didn't.

Instead, I slid my hand into my pocket and followed her gaze.

The people who stood on the shoreline looked like they didn't know what to make of the situation. I had chosen this city for a reason—it was old and secluded. The people who lived here were relatively peaceful folk. Had it been any other city, one more accustomed to raiders or war, they would have reacted much differently upon seeing an unannounced fleet of ships sailing towards them.

Horns would have blasted. Weapons would have been raised.

Blood would have been spilt.

But not with the people of Katlegin, no.

Instead, they stood there, watching as strangers unloaded on their docks—somewhat mesmerized. Their reactions made sense, considering the strangers were Demi Gods. Droplets of divinity had been embedded in their makings, which made them taller, stronger, more pleasing to the eye. Why wouldn't the mortals be mesmerized? For the people of Katlegin, I doubted many of them had ever seen a Demi God before. I would wager the same could be said for the rest of Edenvale. The continent was so far excluded from the outside world that it was often forgotten about, another reason why I chose these lands to offer refuge to the children of my people. Even during the Immortal War, Edenvale had remained untouched.

Azure eyes flicked to mine, brows lifting expectedly. "Well?"

Ah, there it was, a crack in the perfect, regal tone. That was better.

"I cannot say what the future holds for them," I answered the impatient little female. “But I can tell you that this is much better than what Aurelius had planned for them.”

White lashes swept over rosy cheeks, her gaze dropping, momentarily, at the mention of his name. I hated that he still held that control over her. Hated that it was not a tangible thing that I could wrap my fist around and rip from her, so that she could be free of those feelings, of *him*.

My ravens, which had been mostly silent up until now, began to caw loudly.

Something was wrong.

I looked to the horizon, taking in what was flying straight for us—

An army of immortals, dressed in ugly golden armor.

Led by the pompous little shit himself—the *so-called* King of the New Gods.

I rolled my eyes.

Chapter 3

Aurelia

My heart struck a mighty blow against my chest, as if it were trying to crack through my ribs, all so it could get back to *him*. To the male who had abused its keeper—Aurelius.

He was coming for the children of the Old Gods.

He was coming for *me*.

"Little Goddess." Like a well-sharpened blade, Death's voice cut through the tidal wave of emotions threatening to drag me under, anchoring my attention to him. I met his steady gaze. His otherworldly eyes were a bottomless black, so deep I wondered if souls got trapped in them. "We need to form the barrier, now."

"How?" I asked, shaking my head. "We won't have enough time."

People rushed past us. Those who had been unsure about leaving the ships mere moments ago were now moving much faster, fear written in their eyes, in the whites of their knuckles as they tugged their loved ones off the dock.

"Sure, we do," Death replied with a cocky smirk. Large hands bracketed my shoulders, and in one swift move, he spun me to face the end of the dock, towards the hundreds of soldiers, led by Aurelius, that were flying towards us.

The hairs on the back of my neck prickled as Death stepped in closer behind me, his vast shadow blotting out the sun. My body's reaction to him wasn't out of fear—no, that so-called ship had sailed.

This reaction was *different*.

It was like how I felt that day he showed up unannounced at the celebration ball after the Immortal War had ended, looking the epitome of dark and divine as he swept me around the dance floor—the sparks between us enough to start a fire that would burn the realms to ash.

"Hold up your hands, palms towards the sky," he instructed me, his voice low, commanding, in my ear.

I did as he asked. "Like this?"

"Mhm," he rumbled in that chest-deep tone. "You do so well with commands, Kitten."

My cheeks tingled with heat.

He let out a low chuckle—the sound chock-full of male arrogance and unbridled seductiveness.

Creator above . . . *this* male.

Focus, Aurelia. Focus. There's an entire army coming for us. Now is simply not the time to start thinking about the tall, broody, tattooed, muscular—

Fuck! I was doing it again.

Focus, damn you.

I turned my annoyance to him, or at least I tried to.

"Hurry up," I snipped, as if it was his fault for making my body feel so attracted to his. Come to think of it, it *was* his fault. If he wasn't so much, so much, well . . . *him*, then this wouldn't be an issue. So damn him. Damn him and his sex-god body.

"So very bossy," he mused as he placed his hands over mine, keeping them about a foot apart. A spark of heat transferred into my palms, as if two stones had been struck against each other. Then, that flicker erupted between us, producing a strength of magic that felt like it could fracture the earth in two.

The power that exuded from him . . . it was intoxicating. Like alcohol being poured directly into my veins. It was overwhelming. Incredible.

This was the unparalleled power of the King of the Old Gods, and he was sharing it . . . with me.

Freely.

"You have all you need to create the barrier," he said, keeping up that continuous, potent flow of energy.

I didn't need to ask how to do it because suddenly I just knew. I looked past the ships that waited to dock to the army quickly approaching. I chose a spot between the two.

My lungs drew in a breath, and then I released everything the God of Death had given me. Bolts of black, void of light, shot forth from the turbulent sea, arcing and racing upwards at an unfathomable speed. The strikes of shadow magic veined and webbed across the azure sky, expanding into each other. It gobbled up the horizon, painting it in a stretch of never-ending black fog that wrapped around the continent, cutting off Aurelius and his soldiers from reaching us, cutting off Edenvale from the rest of the world.

When it was done, people whispered behind us, questioning what they had just witnessed. It was not long before three words began to pass from tongue to tongue.

The Endless Mist.

I lowered my hands to my sides as I stared at the massive black wall we had just created. "How long will it last?"

"It will last as long as you need it to," Death answered.

"And Aurelius won't we be able to get through it?" I spoke over my shoulder.

"He will not, unless you allow him to."

"So then, it obeys me?"

"Essentially . . . yes."

"Good." I nodded once, looking forward.

"Now then, about our deal, Little Goddess."

Our deal.

It had haunted me ever since the night of the celebration ball when we had made it. There were times where I considered going through with it, wondered what it would be like to wake up in a bed with his muscular, inky arms wrapped around me. Then there were times I couldn't fathom it because I had just gotten out of a marriage and the last thing I wanted was to be forced into another one.

But at that moment, when I had to decide, I knew my answer.

It was the safe one. The one that protected me from any further harm that would come at the hands of another male.

"I'm sorry, Death. But I cannot," I whispered as my light wrapped around me, taking me from him.

Away from Edenvale.

Chapter 4

Aurelia

One Month Later

I pulled the hood of my cloak over my head, ensuring my features were hidden as I weaved my way through the alleyway in the bustling metropolis of Veylandria. People, a mosaic of ages and races, stood up ahead, clogging the alley like the archaic outhouses I had recently come to learn about. Back in the Immortal Realm, where magic was in abundance, we had indoor plumbing. But here, in the Living Realm, a land with very little magic, they were one step above wiping with a leaf.

I spared a quick glance behind me, ensuring I hadn't been followed. I didn't know if I was becoming paranoid, but over the past month, I had certainly seen a lot of ravens throughout my travels. Were the Reapers watching me, reporting back to their king about where I was? I hoped not—hoped it was just a coincidence, although my gut told me otherwise. I stepped into the back of the line, if it could even be called that. People were scattered all over the place, facing each other in conversation.

Off to my right, a man held his spouse upright, cradling her trembling frame as she coughed into a rag—the yellowed cloth splattered with red. "You'll be okay, my love," he promised her, his concerned expression stating otherwise. She nodded somberly before she was overtaken by another coughing fit.

Standing to my left, slightly ahead of the couple, was a trio of girls. They looked to be around seventeen.

"Do you really believe that the potion maker will have something to help us find rich husbands?" asked the one who stood in the middle, her head bobbing between the two who flanked her.

The shorter girl, whose dark, cropped hair framed her wide eyes and sternly set brow, shook her head. "I think this is a bad idea. For all we know, the potion maker could be a—" She glanced around. I slid my gaze to the side, trying not to get caught eavesdropping. She lowered her voice, "—a witch."

"Stella," the taller blonde hissed. "Don't be such a stick in the mud."

"I'm not." She crossed her arms over her chest. "I just don't think this is a wise idea."

The one in the middle opened her mouth to speak, but the blonde raised her hand, silencing her, and said, "So then what *do you* think is a wise idea?"

"I . . ." Stella trailed off, her arms loosening, along with her rigid posture, as she searched for an answer to their money woes.

"I'm waiting," the blonde snarked.

The one in the middle started, "Irena, I think that—"

"Look." Irena, the blonde, cut her off, something I was beginning to suspect she did a lot. "I don't know about you two, but I'm tired of being poor. I'm tired of folding sheets and sweeping floors and living in these—" she grabbed hold of her dingy, brown skirt, the hem tattered and worn, and shook it, "—these rags." She leveled the other two with her gaze. "I don't care if the potion maker gives me rat piss to drink, I'll do it if it helps me get a rich husband."

I was tempted to tell her that wealthy husbands weren't the key to happiness. I'd lived in a palace made of gold bricks and I'd been miserable. But judging by Irena's stance, a stranger wasn't about to change her mind. I glanced back at the couple who stood on the other side, noting the bags that had formed under the man's eyes as he supported his wife. *That* was the kind of man a woman should want to end up with. Someone who cared.

Just then, the line shifted ahead.

Irena huffed, turned on the back of her heel, and stomped a few paces forward. Her friends looked at one another, exchanged a silent conversation, and then followed after her.

My gaze leapt from person to person, until I reached the end up ahead—nearly sixty feet away. There were *so many* people, and the line had barely budged since I'd arrived. At this rate, I wondered if I'd even get into the apothecary before the potion maker closed up shop. And then what? I'd be forced to either stay overnight and hold my place in line or come back tomorrow.

And by tomorrow, it could be too late.

I rolled my head back, stretching my neck as I massaged my tightly woven muscles and looked at the night sky. It was full of brilliant, twinkling stars. It wasn't even five o'clock yet, but here in the north, the days were short.

But not nearly as short as they were in the Spirit Realm.

That was one of two places I did not want to be.

And if Death found me, that's exactly where I would end up.

The piercing cry of a raven sounded from somewhere up above, making my hair stand on end. Someone tapped me on the shoulder and my divinity nearly leapt from my bones.

I swirled around, my hand shooting out, ready to summon my blade and ram it into *his* stomach, just like I did that day on the battlefield. Yes, I did feel something for the Blood King, but I was choosing myself for once. I had spent too many years under a man's thumb, and I had no desire to be stuck in that same position again—feelings or not. When I was fully turned, instead of finding a tall, brooding, dangerous male, I found an elderly one who was more mustache than body. His shoulders were curved like a hawk's talon, his legs like crooked sticks.

He looked up at me through kind eyes, blinking. "Excuse me, miss, I didn't mean to startle you," he said. "I was just wondering—" He scratched the back of his head as he glanced around, "—is this Barbas alley?"

"It is," I told him, softening my gaze and defensive stance.

"Thank the gods. I made it after all." He beamed gleefully, looking ahead. He squinted, taking in the river of people before him. "Are *all* of these people waiting to see the potion maker?"

I nodded. "They are."

His shoulders sagged. "How long have they been waiting for?"

"A while, I imagine. The line doesn't seem to move very fast. At this rate, I can't see many more people getting in to see the potion maker before the shop closes for the night."

"Then I fear I've made a mistake in coming." His voice crackled with emotion as he withdrew a plaid scarf from an inside coat pocket. He held it to his heart.

I made a puzzled face. "What do you mean?"

"My son was born with a condition that the healers have no name for. He has spells that come and go where he can't breathe. It has robbed him of having a natural life. He's never been able to attend school or get married or even have children of his own. A few months ago, it started getting worse. Now, it has become so bad he is confined to his bed. We've had the town healer in to look at him and . . ." His eyes clouded over. "He told us that there was nothing he could do and that our son was not long for this realm—that he would be lucky to survive the week." The elderly man paused, lowered the scarf from his heart, his gaze falling to it. His trembling, aged hands held it with such care. Such love. "My wife wanted us to be together, as a family, for his remaining days, but like the stubborn old fool that I am, I was not willing to let my son go. And so, I gathered the little coin we had saved and used it to travel here, where the great potion maker lives. It has taken me four days to get here, and I worry, if I do not get back in time, I—" He broke. Tears started racing down his hollow cheeks.

My heart, already broken and bruised, ached for him.

I placed a gentle hand on his shaking one. "I'll get you in," I whispered.

He looked up at me, his weathered face slick with tears. "How?"

"Like this." A glow spread around me, connecting to him through our joined hands.

I light walked us through the stone buildings, inside the apothecary.

Rosemary, mint, lavender, and some other scent permeated the air. I breathed in, trying to pinpoint the fourth smell, but no answer came. The apothecary was dark inside, a few hanging lanterns providing the only light. The ebony-stained wood floors matched the shelves lining the halls, full of vials, bottles, salves, and various other tinctures. In the corner sat a small bed with a quilted throw placed over top, and a wood stool beside it. Down from it, was a set of steep stairs, leading up to what I imagined must be the second floor.

The old man gawked at me. "How did you do that?"

"I'm a goddess," I told him, not seeing any point in lying.

The rusty hinges in his jaw sprung open, well-oiled by my honesty.

Footsteps sounded from the floor above, garnering our attention. The older man's mouth slapped shut like a bear trap.

"Yes, yes, drink it two times a day," a slightly muffled female voice said through the floorboards.

"And that will help me with my . . . problem?" asked a man, his voice equally muffled.

"It will, although there might be a few *minor* side effects," the female replied, her voice sounding slightly familiar. I tried to place it.

"Any I should be concerned about?" he asked.

"Oh no," she chuckled. "Nothing that won't remedy itself in a day. Or two. Maybe three. Possibly four. If it takes five then come back. Tonics for side effects are complimentary."

"Alright . . . then." The man didn't sound very confident. Wood screeched upon wood and then a few of the old, wide-plank floorboards above us groaned, protesting the heavy weight that had shifted onto them. Substantial footsteps sounded, joined with much lighter ones.

The old man's eyes widened even further. Frantically, he whisper-shouted at me, "I don't think the potion maker will be too keen on us being in her apothecary without her permission."

I shrugged a shoulder, the act hardly visible due to the thickness of my cloak. "There's only one way to find out."

The stairs creaked at the top. The elderly man's eyes darted between me and the steep stairwell in such a way I could practically hear the warning horns blaring inside his head.

"All will be well," I assured him, although I wasn't entirely certain about that. I had seen dozens of healers and potion makers over the past four weeks, but not one of them had been able to help me. The majority didn't even want to try, especially once they heard I wanted to break a deal with the God of Death. They would usher me out of their shop, tell me never to come back, and slam their door in my face, time after time after time.

In truth, I was beginning to lose hope that I would ever succeed at my task, but here I was, trying one more time. *Please let this one be different,* I prayed to the Creator.

A pair of button-up ankle boots emerged from the stairwell, followed by a brown skirt that soon gave way to a lacy blouse and then . . . familiar blue eyes set in a familiar freckled face.

"What took you so long?" Ezravaynia asked me with a great big smile.

Chapter 5

Aurelia

"*You're* the potion maker?" I gasped as I flipped my hood down.

"That, I am." Ezra performed an eccentric bow before she spun on her heel towards the man who stood beside her and said to him, "Before I forget. I have one more thing for you." She patted her skirt's pockets, looking for something. When she found whatever it was she had been searching for, her face lit up with a great big smile. She withdrew her hand and offered it to him, palm facing up. In it—a pebble.

I nearly fell over.

"Put it under your pillow when you sleep," Ezra told him as he took it from her hand.

"I will," he replied as he looked it over, his expression equal parts confused and mesmerized.

"I'll be with you two in a moment," she told us as she walked the man to the front door. She gave him a few more instructions and then bid him goodbye. When he was gone, she turned to me and said, "Now, would you like to tell me why you are trying to outrun the God of Death?"

The elderly man beside me turned a ghostly white, his wide eyes darting up to mine. "The God of . . ." He stumbled over the last word, unable to say it. Slowly, he stepped away from me. It was an acceptable response, considering not a soul alive wanted anything to do with the keeper of the dead.

Ezra's piercing eyes landed on him. "Oh, for goodness' sake, don't be so dramatic. You'll give yourself a heart attack at your age," she scolded, placing her hands in the crook of her hips. She huffed at him before she glanced at me. "I'll speak with you first." She looked back at the man. "And you, after."

"O-o-okay," he stuttered, his hands clutching tightly to the scarf, which I was beginning to suspect belonged to his unwell son.

"Perhaps you should attend to him first?" I asked with a degree of uncertainty.

Ezra paused for a moment, glanced at the scarf, and then back to me. "No. You first." She started for the stairs, calling over her shoulder, "Come along, goddess."

Before I walked behind her, I gave the elderly man a final glance, finding only fear written in his eyes. I could only imagine what he would do if I were to tell him I was Death's runaway bride.

He'd probably soil his pants. And rightfully so.

When we were upstairs, I walked around the room, taking it in.

The space wasn't large by any means, but it wasn't small either. Wood beams supported the slanted roof, vaulting to a high point in the middle. There was a table and four wooden chairs positioned by the only window in the room. It was small and round and locked closed with a brass latch. In one of the corners, two cozy but worn-looking chairs sat in front of a small, crackling fireplace. The fire gnawed away on a few logs of wood, chewing them up and spitting them into ash. Mirroring downstairs, shelves full of tonics and salves lined the north wall, as well as a small working station that had jars and vials scattered all over it, various ingredients strewn about.

"Busy day?" I asked her, eyeing the messy counter.

"It always is," she answered with a sigh as she walked over to the table and sat down. She placed her hands in front of her, folding them together. "So?" She looked at me expectedly, the question she asked downstairs still standing.

"I made a deal with him. I exchanged Aurelius's freedom for my own, but I cannot go through with it," I expressed, walking over to the table. "I've spent my immortality appeasing one male. I refuse to spend any more of my time in servitude to another."

"I cannot blame you for feeling the way you do." She gestured to the seat across from her. I took it. "But the deal you made is not one that you can go back on. Tattooed bargains, as you know, do not work that way. Not to mention you made one with *the* God of Death, of *all* immortals."

"I refuse to believe that, and that's why I have traveled all this way to speak with the *great* potion maker." Softly, I shook my head. "Little did I know that it was you I would actually find." I chuckled. "Irony seems to have a sense of humor."

"Meaning?" she asked.

"Well, I have come to the champion of freedom, asking for my own."

She took a deep breath, slender shoulders rising. "I am sorry, dear, but as I said before, the deal between the two of you is not one that I can break." I opened my mouth to protest, but she continued, "I'm not finished. Although I cannot break it, that doesn't mean I won't help you, child."

Any mortal would have found a girl who looked to be no older than eighteen calling her elder a child strange, but to me, it made sense. Ezra and her sisters, the Goddess of Fate and the Goddess of Destiny, were said to be very, *very* old—even by immortal standards.

"So then, you *will* help me?" I asked, a shimmer of hope tinting my words.

She nodded. "I will."

"That's wonderful. But . . . how?"

She leaned forward, her eyes darting over my arms, as if she was searching for something. Then, she asked, "Has the rotting started?"

I gave her a funny look. “What do you mean by *rotting*?”

“When the God of Death decides to call in your deal, if you choose not to accept, your skin will begin to rot, starting where the tattoo is. That is the price one pays if they do not deliver on their end.” She reached across the table and unfurled her hand, revealing a silver tin small enough it could fit in my palm. “Should that happen, this will help with the pain, as well as slow the spread.”

I took the cool tin, feeling its light weight in my hand. Looking up at her, I asked. “So then because I have seen no sign of . . . skin rot, that means he hasn’t called in the deal yet?”

“That is correct.”

My brows wove together. “Why do you think he hasn’t?”

“Who knows.” She shrugged, pulling her hands back and placing them in her lap.

A sliver of hope trickled through me. “Do you think he has decided to let me go? To forget the deal?”

She cracked a smile and then burst into laughter. “Oh, I highly doubt that.” She shook her head. When her giggles trailed off, her tone became serious. “Death will *always* yearn for Life. It is the natural order of things.”

“So then . . . I will never be free of him?”

“No. No one is.” She reached across the table and patted my hand. “Don’t look so glum. You have your freedom for the time being. Perhaps you should find a way to enjoy it.”

“Enjoy?” I repeated. I hadn’t really thought about my own

enjoyment in . . . well, I couldn't remember the last time it had crossed my mind.

"Yes, enjoyment. You know. Drinking. Dancing. Eating." Her gaze pinned mine. "Slipping between the sheets with a man. Or woman. Or both. There is no greater pleasure than the pleasures of the flesh."

I shook my head. "I can't."

"You can," she cut in. "I see no ring on your finger. Nothing stopping you from living as you should. What happened to the goddess who, a few minutes ago, said she no longer wished to live in servitude to a man?"

She had me there.

"I will show you how to enjoy yourself and to live as a free woman. But first—" She pointed to the floor and then stood up. "I should help that poor man."

I rose as well. "Are you going to be able to save his son?"

"That is a simple enough question, and yet the answer is nothing of the sort. Mortal conditions are not always easy to treat, and sometimes, the soul has a will of its own. If the unwell person is not able to make the journey here, then I ask whoever is coming to bring a treasured item on their behalf, so that I can get a feel for their will. If someone no longer wishes to be in this realm, then I will not prohibit them from leaving."

"That's why he brought a scarf," I thought out loud.

"Yes," was all she said.

A small passing of silence lingered for a moment.

"What do I owe you for this?" I raised the tin, pinched between my thumb and forefinger, and shook it softly. It felt awfully light to be full of salve.

She looked at it and then me, a mischievous twinkle in her eyes. "A night out. Where are you staying? I'll have a carriage pick you up tomorrow, around eight."

"At the Sitting Duck Inn." It was one of the only rooms available in the entire city, and believe me, when I read the wood sign on the front of the building, swinging in the breeze, rusty chains snickering at me, I had aggressively rolled my eyes. To the point they felt like they were going to get stuck in the back of my head.

She gave me a peculiar look and then burst out laughing. "That's about the size of it."

Chapter 6

Von

Beads of sweat pooled on my skin, joining together before they rivered down my heavily inked torso, catching on the lip of my pants. There was fire in my lungs, heating my muscles, expanding my broad chest, filling my bloodless veins with adrenaline.

I stood in the arena of my gothic-inspired amphitheater forged from volcanic materials. The behemoth structure spiraled towards the amethyst sky, tall enough it could rival the mountains in the distance. It stretched across ten acres of land, the circumference so large one could get lost in it. The arena itself was split into quarters, each part used for a different purpose, for a different form of entertainment. The section I stood in now was a span of black sand, used predominantly for gladiator battles.

On any given day, the amphitheater seated tens of thousands, but today, the stands were empty. All because I was a gracious king, and I would spare my brother's fragile ego from public humiliation as I kicked his ass.

Like I said. Gracious king.

Folkoln stood across from me, blotting his torn bottom lip with the back of his hand. He was missing a thin pie-shape from it, the pierced flesh now lost to the sands. In his other hand, he held a dagger forged from a dark metal, a glistening, emerald gemstone set in the pommel.

"You've been spending too much time at Hard Spirits, brother," I taunted him, inspecting my own dagger, saturated in his golden ichor. Immortal veins always wept gold, and yet, on that fateful day when the Goddess of Life had slit mine open, it was as red as the mortals'.

I didn't know what to make of it.

"And you haven't spent enough." He smirked, eyes as black as a viper's scales meeting mine. The left corner of his mouth twisted upwards, the severed bit of flesh sewing itself back together. "Haven't you heard? The war is over. We should be enjoying the spoils of defeat. You know, drinking, smoking, enjoying a warm pair of thighs."

"I have no desire to bed any of the women here." I twisted my wrist, rotating the dagger as we began to circle one another, much like vultures about to square off over a scrap of meat. The scrap of meat being bragging rights for the winner, which would last until our next sparring session when the board would be wiped clean.

"Of course not. The one you wish to bed is in another realm, playing runaway bride," he chuckled, stepping one combat boot over the other. "Explain something to me, will you? You made a deal with her, so why don't you just go get your new pet? Or call the deal in? It's not like you to not collect on a bargain."

"You're not wrong," I told him, studying his movements just as carefully as he studied mine.

"So then, why don't you?"

"If I collect her or call in the deal, it's going to make it that much harder to win her over, especially if her skin begins to rot. She's as stubborn as a newborn filly determined to learn how to walk. I can only imagine how well that conversation would go over with her."

Folkoln raised a questioning pierced brow, his tone sarcastic. "*Win* her over?"

"It is what I intend to do."

"Saphira won't like that."

"That's her problem, not mine."

If my sister had it her way, she would have the Crown of Thorns placed on Aurelia's head the moment she got here, thus ending her immortal life. Yes, I had made the crown which was crafted from the root of a tree that possessed white leaves. That nameless tree, which was located in the Golden Palace, was said to be Aurelia's weakness—the very thing that could kill her. And yes, I had fully intended to use the crown, but then things had changed. Aurelia showed up at my castle, asking for my help, and I knew right then and there that I would never be able to let her go.

Now, I hungered to take her life in a completely *different* way.

One way or another, she would be *mine*.

She already was, she just didn't know it yet.

Folkoln slit the air, marking it with an "X." Black fire engulfed where he cut, and it shot towards me. I swung my blade, producing a shield of wind to blast against it. Then we charged, right through the middle of wind and flame.

With a mighty swing, he drove his dagger in my direction, extending his arm above me. I stepped into him, catching his arm in the air before he had a chance to complete the follow-through. I forced his hand upwards while I tried to fire my dagger into his ribs, but all it caught was a skiff of smoke.

He emerged behind me.

I twisted around, blocking his attack.

We went at it again, looking for a way to break one another's balance, but each time, we both came up short. We were constantly moving around the arena, searching for that one misstep in the other's movements, that fatal error that either of us could capitalize on. Every once in a while, one of our daggers would find a bit of flesh to chew into, but nothing to tip the fight in one another's direction.

"So then, what *is* your plan with your little pet?" Folkoln gritted, his teeth clenched so tightly it triggered a muscle to kick in his jaw. We were caught in a deadlock, my strength pitted against his. "I know you must have one."

"Trying to throw me off my game, brother?" I asked.

"Maybe. But I am genuinely curious."

I shoved him back. "Once Aurelius learns that Aurelia is not in the Spirit Realm, he'll send his men to look for her. When they find her, they'll demand to take her back to the Immortal Realm, which, considering what Aurelius did to her, is the last place she'll want to be. When that does happen, my ravens, who are watching over her, will alert me to go to her. I'll simply step in, remind her of our deal, and she'll be forced to choose."

Slow clapping sounded from the stands, echoing amongst the obsidian arena.

"Bravo, brother, you truly are a grand manipulator," Saphira purred, her condescending tone gilded in fake admiration. Piercing, emerald eyes swept to mine. "Donning the skin of a shepherd, pretending to protect his precious, stupid, little sheep." Her lips twisted into a poisonous smile. "When in truth you are the starving wolf. It is a grand charade."

Folkoln and I exchanged looks with one another, acknowledging our sparring session was over for the time being.

Saphira released a mocking, breathy laugh as she continued. "But what will happen when she learns the truth, that you were the one who whispered into the wind where the goddess is hiding, sending the information straight to Aurelius?"

I raised a brow in challenge. "Who says I was the one who let the information slip?"

"I do," she said as she descended the stairs, heels clicking against stone, the hem of her black gown trailing behind her. "Because I *know* you. Just as I know that you will tire of her eventually, just as you have with all the others. Mate or not. And then what, brother? Will you come to your senses and realize that you traded two-thirds of our kingdom for some New God bitch?"

Her words, intended to cut like a scalpel, had the impact of a butter knife.

Yes, I had traded the two Realms for Aurelia, and I would do it again if given the choice. But I did not have to explain my actions or decisions to my sister, something she had clearly forgotten.

I quirked a black brow, my gaze sliding to Folkoln's. "Do you see a crown upon our sister's head?"

Folkoln gave me a look that seemed to say he didn't want to be dragged into this. Still, he said, "I do not." His flat tone furthered his stance.

"Neither do I," I mocked, grinning. I ran the flat of my blade against my thigh, wiping away Folkoln's ichor. I switched to the other side of the dagger, repeating the action. "And yet, she acts as though *she* is the sovereign of all." My eyes flicked up to hers—a challenge in them. "Tell me, Saphira, who is the monarch of these lands? Is it you, or is it me?"

She stopped her descent. Her lips twitched, her nostrils widening as she inhaled a frustrated breath. Those small tells told me that I'd struck a nerve. Good. I wasn't finished.

When she didn't respond, I bore down. "If you wish to be queen of this realm, then prove yourself worthy and fight me on these black sands. If you best me, I will hand over my throne and leave you to rule the Spirit Realm as you please. And if I win, which we both know that I will, you will agree to return to your place as my commander, and never challenge me again. Do we have a deal, sister?"

Her sour expression turned honey sweet. "You know me, brother—I have no desire to replace you, I merely want what is best for you." She dipped her head. "I'll leave you two to it."

Shadows slithered around her, taking her away.

"What are you going to do about her?" Folkoln asked, his fingers running over the healed part of his lip. I could see the cogs turning in my brother's head—he was itching to pierce that part of himself again.

I sighed. "I haven't quite figured that out yet."

Saphira was impossible to break once she got stuck on something, and right now, me calling off the war—and my reasons for doing so—were her latest obsession. Eventually, I would have to figure out a solution for how to handle things with her, as they were only bound to get even worse. Especially once I brought Aurelia back here.

A moment that could not come soon enough.

The thought of her being out there, away from me, caused tension to drill into my muscles, stringing them taut. I swung my blade and turned to Folkoln. "Again."

"Alright, but the loser buys at Hard Spirits tonight," he said, taking a step forward.

"Deal."

Chapter 7

Aurelia

"What, in the name of the Ancient Ones, are you wearing?" Ezra asked as I stepped out of the carriage, championed by two mahogany-brown Clydesdale horses—their manes neatly braided, and trimmed hooves well-maintained.

An hour prior, I'd had plenty of time to study them as I peered out the window of the small room I was staying in at the Sitting Duck Inn, debating if I should go or not. Ezra had helped me on the boat, yes, and then she had offered me a salve to use if Death called in our deal and my skin began to rot, but ultimately, I did not know her. She was a whimsical goddess who danced on the current of mischief and wonder, elusive and hard to nail down.

Naturally, I had found myself wondering . . . was Ezra someone I could trust?

I decided there was only one way to find out, and that's why I was here—

A twenty-minute carriage ride away from the city, tucked in a dense grove of caragana bushes and slender poplar trees, standing in front of a stone path that led up to a humble two-story home forged from a combination of brick and mortar. The steep roof was tiled, which was quite different from the thatch roofs I had seen back in the city.

Ezra caught my gaze, tracing it all the way to the roof, as if she were following some invisible line. "The tiles are made of ceramic. They don't catch fire like the straw ones do."

"Catch *fire*?" I asked, my curiosity getting the better of me.

"Well, when you are combining all sorts of potions, some tend to get a wee bit . . . explosive." She giggled, her head swiveling back towards me. She batted a hand. "Anywho, never mind that. Let's get back to what you are wearing."

I glanced down, plucking at my white tunic, inspecting it. "Is this not what the mortals typically wear?"

"It is, but where we are going, you will look severely underdressed," she said with a grin. She gestured to what she was wearing. It was a lovely little number, the body-length dress dyed a deep red. It clung to her body, fitting her in all the right places, emphasizing her femininity, while leaving some places left to be discovered. It reminded me of something a courtesan-turned-princess would wear—sultry yet refined. "You need to wear something like this."

"It's a lovely gown, but I own nothing of the sort," I said, shrugging one shoulder.

When I left the Immortal Realm with hundreds of freed Demi Gods on the run, packing a bag hadn't exactly been high on my priority list. So, all I had to my name was the clothes I was wearing and a few more that I'd left at the Sitting Duck Inn. The white gown I had donned when I arrived in Edenvale had been fashioned by my personal seamstress. I'd had it made a few days before I released the prisoners. The seamstress had given me a peculiar look when I told her what my vision was for the dress, as it was far from the stuffy, vice-grip gowns she was used to making for me—dresses that Aurelius liked to see me in. The sleek, white gown was glorious, yes, but once I spent a few days among the mortals, I realized that it made me stand out. And standing out didn't exactly seem like a wise idea, all things considered. So, a few weeks back, I traded the sumptuous, luxurious silk for a few basic white tunics, two pairs of brown breeches, and a cloak.

"Then call me your fairy godmother because I'm about to expand your wardrobe." Ezra gave me a wink. Spinning, she started for the house. "Come along, let's find you something sexy to wear."

I stood there, wondering if I had made a bad decision in coming here.

Sighing, I decided to embrace the moment and followed her inside.

Chapter 8

Von

In architecture, Hard Spirits resembled a gothic cathedral more than a drinkery. Intricate, stained-glass windows provided a moody slash of red, spilling like blood on the onyx-tiled floor. It was the most renowned tavern in the Spirit Realm. It didn't matter what day of the week it was, people lined up for miles outside, hoping for a chance to come in, just to get a taste of the God of Chaos's famous liquor—

Spiritberry wine.

Despite its name, that shit packed a punch. Especially to those who had not built up a tolerance to it.

It was a thief of propriety, guaranteed to reduce the most high and mighty into depraved animals—guaranteed to get them on their fours, whether it be to purge their guts or *have* their guts purged. Some would be granted access to the basement below, the entire level devoted to making the most primitive of desires come true. People referred to it as *The Dungeon*. My sister had something similar in the underground chamber of her temple, though hers wasn't quite as . . . depraved as Folkoln's, but what more could one expect from the God of Chaos?

I sat on a slightly curved, leather settee in a private area on the second balcony, shrouded in darkness. Black velvet curtains were pulled to the sides, giving me view to the main floor, which was packed full of dancing, twirling bodies. I could see them, but they couldn't see me.

In the middle of the floor was a polished fountain made of hematite. The body of a naked woman was carved into the stone, a sash tied over her eyes—a small hint to what waited underground. She was so very lifelike, from the dimples in her back, to the veins in her forearms. Her hand reached above her—a fine nozzle embedded in her palm. From it, spiritberry wine sprayed into the air, creating a waterfall effect around her. People gathered all around the fountain, raising their cups and filling them with the dark purple substance. Whatever wine didn't find its way into a cup drained into the reservoir beneath, and then circled back up through the statue, repeating the cycle again and again and again.

My long legs stretched out before me, eating up the space between the glass oval table and the settee. Tonight, I'd slipped out of my dark lord attire and donned something much more casual—a partially unbuttoned black tunic tucked into leather pants. Everyone else was wearing their finest, sexy attire, dressing up in hopes of finding someone to go home with—or perhaps to go downstairs with if the invitation was presented. But that wasn't why I was there. I was there to down a bottle or two and attempt to relax my high-strung nerves.

"Your winnings, brother," Folkoln said as he placed a bottle on the glass table, along with two cups.

Leaning forward, I snagged the bottle, popped the cork, and poured some into a glass—the pitch of the gentle stream's note increasing as I filled it. I raised it to my nose, inhaling the fruity, vanilla scent. "Spiritberry wine is not what I had in mind when I told you to bring me a bottle of your finest."

"Don't be such a liquor snob," Folkoln said as he dropped onto a chair, adjacent to me. He snatched the bottle by the neck, his rings clanking against the glass, and poured himself some. "This isn't like that watered-down shit I have running through the fountain. This is the good stuff. The *real* stuff. Guaranteed to soften the stick you've got wedged up your ass." He gave me a shit-eating grin, tipped his cup to me, and then tossed it back.

I smirked, rolled my eyes, and brought the cool glass to my lips. But just before I was about to drink, I stopped, because I felt a familiar pull. One that captured my gaze and tugged it to the dance floor—right to *her*.

"What is it?" Folkoln asked, and then, "Well, I'll be damned."

I slid the untouched glass onto the table, got up, and walked over to the balcony railing, looking down below. My greedy eyes raked over the white-haired goddess who was being tugged through the densely packed, shoulder-to-shoulder crowd. The Goddess of Free Will was at the helm, steering them both towards the fountain, empty cups in their hands.

Free Will might have brought her here, but I could feel the taste of Fate in the air, the power of Destiny. All Three Spinners were weaving this part of our story, placing her in my path tonight.

And Creator above, she looked divine.

Thin fabric hugged her body, serving up her feminine curves like a Sunday buffet. I bit my bottom lip. The dress was a light lilac color, making her stick out like a sore thumb in the sea of black that surrounded her. It complimented her skin tone while highlighting her lovely snow-kissed hair—the tips swaying across the upper shelf of her peachy bottom as she walked.

I took note of all the heads swiveling her way, committing their faces to memory. It didn't matter if they were man or woman—I'd treat them equally if they got *any* ideas about touching what belonged to me.

"What are you going to do now?" Folkoln asked.

"I don't know." I blew out a breath. "Try not to destroy your tavern, I guess."

"I'd rather you didn't. I'm lucky it's still standing after what happened last week with Asher and Carosena." He sighed. "Do you want me to have her removed from the premises?"

"No, don't do that." I watched as she walked up to the fountain and raised her cup, her smile mesmerizing. "Let her have her fun for tonight."

I pulled away from the railing and went to sit back down. My hand floated over the cup and went straight for the bottle. I grabbed it and chugged a third of it. It was like drinking liquid candy, sugar exploding across my tongue.

Folkoln glanced to his right and raised his hand, motioning for someone to come into the private area. A redhead walked in, scantily dressed, with a circular tray in her hands, a folded cloth napkin placed on it. "Put it there," he told her, eyes flicking to a spot on the table in front of him.

I recognized her as one of his workers, but her name was lost to me.

She lowered the tray onto the table and then looked at him and asked, "Will that be all, my lord?"

"No, doll." His lips twisted into a malicious smile. "I want you to do it."

"I-I-" she stuttered. "I can't."

Light flashed across his dark eyes. "You can."

"You know I can't stand needles," she whimpered.

"I'm well aware, that's why I want you to do it." He grabbed her wrist and tugged her into his lap. She squealed in both delight and terror. He nuzzled his nose against her neck, breathing her in. "You know your emotions are my favorite to feed on."

"Yes, but you know me and needles don't mix," she breathed, her arms wrapping around his neck. Her lips said one thing while her actions said another.

"That's exactly why you are going to do it." He nipped at her nose. "I'll take you downstairs later if you do."

"Quit playing with your food," I growled at Folkoln, my nerves shot.

"This is technically your fault," he said, shooting daggers at me. With the redhead in his lap, he reached forward and flipped the sides of the napkin over, revealing a thick needle and a piercing—one that matched the one I'd slit out of his lip earlier in the arena. He pointed to the healed part of his lip and then to the other side which still had a piercing in it. "I'm uneven now."

"I could cut the other one out," I offered with a smirk, taking another swig from the bottle.

Folkoln didn't respond. Instead, he said to the girl, "Go on."

With trembling hands and eyes that looked on the verge of popping out of her head, she reached for the needle. When she picked it up, her face turned a ghastly white.

"This is painful," I groaned before I pounded the rest of the bottle. I tossed it on to the settee, walked over to them, snatched the needle from her hand, and grabbed my brother's bottom lip faster than he could react. "Hold still," I snarled as I pulled his lip out and shoved the needle through it. Ichor bubbled to the surface, trickling down his chin. Folkoln didn't so much as budge, his attention transfixed on the redhead who looked like she was going to vomit.

She scrambled off him, falling on the floor with a loud *thump* as she covered her mouth—dry-heaving on the spot like a cat with a fucking hairball. *Why had I agreed to come here tonight?*

I tossed the needle onto the tray, grabbed the piercing, and shoved it through his lip. I slapped the side of his head. "You're even now."

As I had absolutely no desire to watch the girl wretch on the floor, I left the private area, my shadows dissolving Folkoln's ichor from my hands. When I descended the polished stairs, I met a familiar face, but it was not the one I was hoping to see.

"Ezra," I greeted, my voice tepid.

"Von," she said with a big smile. "It's been a while."

I couldn't care less for pleasantries. "Why did you bring her here?"

"The poor thing has never had a *real* night out in her entire life," she replied with a mischievous twinkle in her eye. "What better place to do that than Hard Spirits?" She gestured to our surroundings with her free hand, the glass of spiritberry wine in the other.

"She shouldn't be here," I breathed, my voice a spark, ready to ignite.

"Why shouldn't she? Did I miss a big sign saying that the Goddess of Life is not allowed to be here?" Theatrically, she looked around.

My lips thinned. "You can cut the sarcasm."

"Only if you cut the bullshit."

We stared each other down.

Then Ezra said, "She has spent the majority of her life locked up in a cage. I know what she is to you, but that does not mean you need to lock her up too. Why not free her of your deal with her? Why not let her live as she chooses? When she is ready, she will come to you, but at least allow her the chance to experience life on her own terms first. She has been robbed of that for far too long."

"Release her from our deal," I scoffed. "Our deal is the only thing she has to protect her right now. If she does not come to live here in the Spirit Realm with me, then Aurelius will eventually find her. And then what? She'll be forced to go back to the world she ran from."

She huffed a laugh. "You weave your words with such a careful tongue that I almost buy into what you are trying to sell, but you and I both know there is a simple answer to all of this . . . you could let her live in Edenvale. The Endless Mist would be enough to protect her from Aurelius."

I nodded. Once. "That's true, I could let her live in Edenvale. If she meant nothing to me, then that's exactly what I would do, but the fact that she is my bonded changes things. She belongs by my side, on my throne. In my bed. You and I both know that. So whatever game you are trying to play by bringing her here tonight, know that it will not change my mind. The Little Goddess will be *mine*."

"You are a stubborn old god," Ezra snipped. She looked down at her glass, peering at the contents, shaking her head. "Worse than a mule."

I narrowed my eyes at that.

A moment passed, filled with the sounds of merriment, drunken conversations, and music.

Ezra sighed. Blue eyes lifted to mine, and she said, "She came to me, you know. Asking for my assistance in helping her break the deal between you two, but I know the only one who can free her from it is you. That is why I brought her here tonight, in hopes that you would see her dancing and enjoying herself, and find it somewhere within your rotten, black soul to give her a chance to have more than just a taste of freedom, but a lifetime of it."

I knew that Aurelia was trying to break our deal—my ravens who had been following her over the past so many weeks had reported as much—so that really didn't bother me. And the fact that Ezra had come up with a plan to try to appeal to my humanity, well, it was laughable.

I had none.

I slipped my hand into my pocket, tipping my chin up as I narrowed my gaze on Ezra. "Why do you suddenly *care* so much about her?"

"I have my reasons," she said. "None of which I will divulge to you."

"I find that rather suspicious. Perhaps I should be wary of you and your intentions for *my* mate."

"Ha!" she laughed out. Then did it again, even louder, as if the first obnoxious laugh wasn't ridiculous enough. "My intentions are a lot more noble than yours," she snarled as she poked me in the chest.

"I'm skeptical of that," I muttered as I rubbed at the spot she poked, surprised by the strength in her dinky finger—stained green at the end. All of her fingers were like that. I had heard of the potions and tonics she spent her days making, something her sisters didn't seem too keen on. They were convinced she wasn't pulling her weight—spinning futures with them. Although, what could one expect from the Goddess of Free Will—forcing destiny and fate upon the mortals clearly wasn't something she was interested in.

No wonder she was telling me to free Aurelia of our deal.

We were both self-serving immortals.

Ezra shrugged and said, "Skeptical or not, I don't really care what you are, but I will tell you something, free of seed payment, or whatever arrangement it is you have with my sisters."

I waited, not sure if I wanted to hear another premonition because I barely knew what to make of the last one I had been told. The Goddess of Fate's voice echoed in my mind—*But heed this warning, and heed it well—your mate's life is linked with the very male she is destined to kill.* Was I the male that Aurelia would end? All things considered, it made sense. She was the one and only thing that could make me bleed—that could bring my long life to an end. And yet, that seemed too simple. Which begged the question—if not me, then who?

Regardless, the thought didn't sit well with me.

"Sage's happiness will come at the cost of your own." Ezra's voice brought me out of my private thoughts.

"What?" I asked, replaying her words, chiseling them into the eternal stonewall of my memory, right underneath the last premonition I had been told. "Who is *Sage*?"

"She is," Ezra said as she took a step back, her head turning to look out at the pulsing floor. There, surrounded by one too many males, was the Goddess of Life, dancing away.

I had never seen a more beautiful creature.

Out of all the things I expected to happen tonight, I did not expect the drunk Little Goddess to lean over the marble-top bar and steal a bottle of spirits before she left. And yet, that's exactly what she had done. With an amused smile on my lips, I told Folkoln to add it to my tab, patted him on the back, and then I followed her and Ezra to the Living Realm.

I glanced up at the swinging wood sign, kicked back by the force of the natural wind—

The Sitting Duck Inn.

I grinned. Yet another thing to be amused about.

Keeping a careful distance, I waited for Ezra to leave before I strolled inside, protected from view by the cloak of my umbra. I followed the pull of Aurelia's tattoos, tracking her through them.

The hallway to her room was narrow and dingy. The place smelled of must and mold. It was too small for my liking—too crammed. Too mortal. Why she had decided to stay here when she could live in the comforts of my castle was beyond me.

I could offer her so much more than this.

She would understand that soon.

A smile touched my lips, but it quickly flattened when I walked up to the wood door that looked like it was one swift kick away from falling off its wilting hinges. *That* was what was protecting my mate? No, that wouldn't do. I ran my hand over the door, sinking my shadows into it, forging an invisible barrier that would protect her from any intruders—well, excluding myself.

When I was satisfied with my work, I listened in.

Her breathing was slow and even-paced, telling me that she was asleep.

Perfect.

I materialized on the other side of the door, taking in her slumbering frame. A small window allowed a bit of moonlight to spill into the room, its fingertips brushing over her skin, painting her in a soft glow.

When she turned her head to the side, my eyes narrowed in on her neck—on the thrumming veins laced beneath her ivory skin.

My fangs throbbed. My cock too.

What I wouldn't do for a taste of her.

I stepped closer, unable to help myself. With my eyes on her closed ones, I watched for any signs of her waking as my fingers slid across her neck, tracing the vein that was calling my name. Summoning me to take. To feed.

"Soon enough, Little Goddess," I promised her, as I retracted my hand. My silent steps carried me back, into the swirls of darkness.

Tonight, I would let her sleep.

But tomorrow?

Tomorrow, she would be *mine*.

Chapter 9

Aurelia

My tongue felt like I had spent the night licking the bottom of a barrel, but it was the pounding ache in my head that promised I had. Whatever Ezra gave me to drink last night knocked me flat on my royal ass.

I rubbed my eyelids, forcing them open.

A painting of rolling hills peppered with fluffy sheep greeted me, nailed to the wall at the end of the small mattress I was laying on. The lumpy-bumpy bed, probably infested with things I didn't even want to know existed, was a sure sign that I was back at the Sitting Duck Inn.

I dusted off the cobwebs of my memory, trying to figure out how I'd gotten back here. One sprung free. It was of two wobbling women as they zigzagged drunkenly through the hallway, laughing themselves to tears. Me and Ezra. Once my fumbling fingers had found the right key to get into the room, we burst inside, hushing each other to keep quiet, but doing a poor job of it. The last thing that I remembered was falling on the bed, and then . . . well, that was that.

Grumbling, I propped myself up on my elbow. I smacked my lips, evaluating their insufferable dryness.

Creator above, I needed something to drink.

Glancing over to the dresser, I spotted an unknown bottle of whatever I had brought home with me from last night's adventures. Shoving the blankets back, I staggered out of bed and snatched the bottle from the dresser. I brought it to my nose and sniffed.

Coughing, I shot my arm forward, jerking it as far away from my face as I could.

Nope. I was not about to tango with whatever *that* was again. The bottle made a *thunk* when I sat it back down.

I walked over to the chair which housed my cloak, threw it on, and decided to head downstairs to see if I could find something else to drink—a gallon of water would be preferable. I locked the door behind me, tucked the skeleton key in my pocket beside the tin Ezra had given me, and then headed for the stairwell.

When I reached the main floor, I bristled at what I saw—or rather, *who* I saw.

Quickly, I stepped back and peeked around the corner.

Two tall males stood in the foyer, at the front counter, talking to the innkeeper. Their voices were heavily accented—one quite charming, the other brash and impatient. I recognized both of them. They had the same proud posture as Aurelius. The same white hair color and handsome good looks. His two brothers—Malachai and Nicholas.

I knew why they were here.

Fuck, I mouthed, not daring to even whisper the word, knowing full well their immortal hearing would pick up on it.

Slowly, I backed up, my mind threshing out a plan. If I light walked out of here, the tinge of magic left in my wake would alert them immediately. Not only that, but Nicholas was able to track light walking trails, which would lead him straight to me wherever I went from here. That meant I couldn't use my powers to get me out of this situation—I'd have to use my two feet.

I glanced at the doors ahead.

I could do this.

I. Could. Do. This.

I inhaled a quiet breath, trying to calm my rampantly beating heart. When I felt my lungs were set at an even pace, I flipped up my hood and then I moved. On quick, silent feet, I briskly walked towards the door, not daring to look back.

When I was just about to reach the exit, the innkeeper broke off her conversation with them and called after me rather sternly, "Ah, miss, I'm going to need you to pay for your room if you want to keep it any longer. It's been two days, and I haven't seen a single coin from you yet."

Thanks a lot, lady, I snarled internally.

My hair raised on the back of my neck as I felt two sets of immortal eyes bore into me.

Wasting no time, I grabbed the handle of the door, flung it open, and then I ran like Death's hounds were nipping at my heels. The leather soles of my shoes pounded on the brick-paved road as I raced past an oncoming carriage. The horses nickered in annoyance at me, their coachmen chiming in with a few curse words. Reaching the other side of the road, I glanced behind me as I ran, my heart leaping into my throat when I saw that Aurelius's brothers were gaining on me.

"Princess!" Malachai shouted in his regal tone. "We do not wish to harm you."

Malachai might not, but that didn't mean Nicholas was of the same mind—or Aurelius, for that matter. I had not only left him, but I'd also freed the prisoners he had planned to kill and used his precious gold to do it. And if that wasn't bad enough, I had allied myself with his enemy, the God of Death. There was no telling what Aurelius would do to me if his brothers took me back.

Something I'd rather not find out.

"Aurelia!" Nicholas yelled angrily. His voice was so much like Aurelius's, it had me picking up my speed. I darted around an elderly woman, trying my best not to knock her over.

"Princess, please," Malachai tried again. He had always been the kindest of the trio. Had it just been him, I might have stopped, but the fact that Nicholas was with him? There was *no* fucking way I was going to do as he asked.

"This is your last warning," Nicholas snarled from behind. His voice was like a whip against my skin, opening old wounds, causing buried emotions to brim. I shoved them down.

Keep your head, dammit.

I wove around a corner, into a slender back alley.

My heart sank as I realized I had picked a dead end, leading right into another building, which meant I was going to have to light walk through it.

"Nicholas, don't," Malachai shouted at the exact same moment I heard the twang of a bowstring let loose, followed by a *thwishhhhh* coming straight for me. I fumbled for my groggy powers—

Thunk.

"That wasn't very nice," purred a deep voice, steeped in ancient, brutal power. *That* voice, unlike any other, conjured a shiver to skitter across my bones. Heart pounding and lungs heaving, I came to an abrupt stop.

Slowly, I turned around, knowing full well who I would find . . .

Darkness personified stood behind me, his broad-shouldered back facing me. The edge of his cloak broke off into tendrils of shadow. A skull, dipped in silver, sat on his one shoulder—forever keeping watch.

The God of Death.

He stood there, radiating his casual arrogance as he inspected the long, slender arrow. My jaw sprung open—he'd caught it midair, kept it from burrowing into my back. Although it wouldn't have been enough to take my immortal life, it would have hurt horribly had it found its target. I winced at the thought of it.

"Did a toddler make this?" Death asked, ticking the arrow from side to side, drawing attention to it. "I'm only asking because I've never seen such shitty craftsmanship before." He tossed it over his shoulder, but before it had a chance to hit the ground, his shadows darted around him, devouring it in midair.

"Blood King," Nicholas snarled as he conjured another arrow, made from a light wood and tipped with silver.

"No, brother," Malachai growled, placing his hand over Nicholas's bow, shoving it down. Malachai looked at the Blood King, raising one hand in deference. "We do not wish to fight." His tone was diplomatic.

Death chuckled darkly. "Then I'd advise you two to tuck your tails between your legs and run back home to your master."

"You son of a bitch," Nicholas snarled, his temper flaring.

Malachai cut in quickly, his tone as calm as the glass top of a morning lake. "We have a duty to return the princess to her husband."

"Oh, well, why didn't you say so?" Death asked as he stepped to the side, rolling his wrist as he gestured to me like I was some grand prize waiting behind a curtain. I curled my upper lip. "Go on, then. Take her."

Nicholas and Malachai exchanged confused looks.

"What?" I hissed, taking a protective step back.

Death looked over his shoulder, his lips twisting into a cocky grin. "Your ex-husband's men have come to take you back to him. Considering you seem to have no interest in keeping your deal with me,

I can see no reason why I shouldn't hand you over to them."

"Are you serious?" I seethed, disgusted.

"I am." He turned towards me. "Unless—" starless black eyes met mine, "—you come back to the Spirit Realm with me. Now."

"She does not belong to you," Nicholas sneered, taking a step towards us.

Death heeded him little mind as he extended a tattooed hand towards me. "Well, Little Goddess, what will it be? The Spirit Realm or the Immortal Realm?"

"Neither," I snarled as I conjured a dozen levitating daggers behind me and let them fly.

I didn't bother to wait and see who they hit as I let my world explode in light.

Chapter 10

Von

My answer came in the form of a glint of azure and an onslaught of pain.

Her daggers, much like ice in structure but not temperature, hit their mark, two of them embedding in my torso, while the rest flew past me. One lodged in my chest, the other in my stomach.

And then she was gone.

"Fuck," I grimaced as I leaned against the brick building, using it to stabilize me. I wrapped my hand around the handle of the dagger that had punched its way into my left pectoral and pulled it out, the veins in my neck threatening to burst out of my skin. I moved on to the one in my stomach. The muscles in my forearms flexed as I extracted the blade, the wound squelching, as if it didn't want to give up the dagger—something that was of her.

I inspected the small weapons, lacquered in my blood. The last time I had seen one . . .

I was transported back to that day when I had stolen her from the battlefield, when she had driven her sword straight into my stomach. The ice in her eyes as she did it, my beautiful, lovely creature. In that moment, without realizing it, she had condemned us both for eternity.

For that was the day when everything changed.

"Fucking bitch," Nicholas's pained tone growled from behind me.

"Hold still, brother," Malachai demanded. "Let me help you."

I glanced over my shoulder, just in time to see Nicholas, who had been knocked flat on his ass, shove his brother's proffered hand away. His bow laid on the ground beside him.

"Piss off. I'll do it myself," he grated as he grabbed hold of the dagger and tore it out of his leg, roaring as he did. The weapon clattered when it struck the cobblestones. Chest heaving, his dark-gold eyes flicked upwards, looking to my seeping wounds and then to the daggers I still held in my hand.

Malachai followed his brother's gaze, his brows hooking together as he, too, tried to make sense of what he was seeing.

Understanding lifted Nicholas's contorted features, and he burst out laughing.

Fuck.

"You've been holding out on us." His mouth twisted into a

sardonic smile. "Brother, how many times have we faced the Blood King in battle, only to find out that he does not bleed?"

"Too many to count," Malachai confirmed, crossing his arms over his chest.

My shadows swirled around the daggers, swallowing them whole. Abdomen contracting, I pressed off the wall, masking my pain with a flat expression.

"And now the Blood King bleeds before our very eyes," Nicholas stated, his immortal flesh slowly beginning to stitch his injury back together, unlike my wounds, which were healing much slower than usual—all because of her. He rose from the ground, brushing back the tendrils of hair that had fallen over his forehead. A dark chuckle rolled out of him. "What do you make of it, Malachai?"

Malachai tilted his head to the side, assessing. Then, he said to me, "There is something I could never understand. You waged a war that lasted years to get your lands back from my brother, the king. You were so close to winning, to reclaiming all your kingship. But then you traded my brother's freedom, and the Immortal and Living Realms, in exchange for her. Now—" he glanced at the injury in my chest, "—I understand why you did it." His eyes shifted back to mine, conveying he knew more than he had said.

He knew *what* she was to me.

Nicholas cut in. "She is your weakness. The one and only thing that can end your immortal life."

Ah, yes, she was that too.

And so much more.

I looked at Malachai, expecting him to divulge what else he had just learned, but for some reason, he didn't. For that, I was grateful.

"I believe the Goddess of Life's worth just grew to an exorbitant amount," Nicholas said with a malicious grin.

A muscle kicked in my jaw.

The thought of what he might do to Aurelia, just to use her against me . . . my dark power rumbled protectively beneath my skin—for her sake, not mine.

Nicholas continued, "Can you imagine what our brother will do when he finds out that his wife is the very thing that can kill his greatest enemy?"

Wife. That one little word that Nicholas used to link her to Aurelius grated on my nerves.

But I was too old to let him win at *my* game of fuckery, for I was the master of it.

I saddled a grin on my lips and said with a chuckle, "Funny, when she was here a few moments ago, I didn't see a wedding ring on her finger. Did you?" I gestured behind me, to where she had been standing before.

They exchanged confused looks.

My lips flattened. "Tell me, did you do anything to help her when Aurelius broke her finger? Oh . . ." I dragged out the word. "That's right, you did nothing." Nicholas opened his mouth to speak, but I cut him off. "I have one question for you. Do you smell anything with this?" I tapped my nose. "Or has it been wedged up Aurelius's ass for too long?"

"You bastard." Nicholas's temper flared as his hand whipped out to the side. Like a magnet, his bow shot into his palm, he nocked it with an arrow, and took aim. All of it was done in the blink of an eye. He had speed on his side—but that was about the only thing he had going for him.

"Go ahead," I said, letting a hint of my lethal power brim to the surface, giving them a taste of the dark beast that lingered beneath the confines of my tattooed skin. "We'll see who is left standing afterwards."

"Brother," Malachai warned between clenched teeth. "Lower your weapon."

Nicholas sneered. Then, like the good pup he was, he did as he was told.

"Ah, I see you understand basic commands," I said. "You're smarter than I thought." My tone fell flat. I was growing disinterested in this little exchange. I handed my thoughts over to what did interest me—

Her.

Right now, she was under the impression that she could run from me, because I had allowed her to do so one too many times. All of this was my fault, because I believed that once push came to shove, she would choose a life with me over Aurelius.

But I had been . . . wrong.

The headstrong goddess didn't choose either—she chose herself and fired a barrage of daggers at me in the process. I looked down at my stomach, at the freshly healed wound. Although the skin had mended itself, the tattered cloth and blood remained—serving as a reminder of what she was willing to do to escape me.

I couldn't fault her for it, no more that I could fault a frightened animal for biting the hand that reached for it. It was a natural survival instinct. But now that Nicholas knew that she was my weakness, that *changed* things, which meant my hand was forced to do more than reach.

Chapter 11

Von

When I stepped out from my swirling umbra, a moonlit, woodland canopy swelled over top of me, forged from the towering reach of ancient oaks. Their gently rustling leaves were a rich tapestry of colors—yellows, golden browns, and vibrant reds. They were a few weeks shy of letting go of their respective branches and falling to the forest floor where they would rot and decay and be returned to the soil they were made from. Just as all living things must do eventually. It was the natural order of things. No one escaped death. Not even *her* . . .

I glanced around, my brows raising ever so slightly—I *knew* this forest.

Quite well, actually.

I knew that if I tracked east through the oaks, I would find an effervescent lake—long forgotten by this world. One that was fed with an underground stream of heated water. If I continued onwards from there, I would find myself at the foot of Orion's Peak. And if I were to fly to the top, I would see a stretch of untouched land, and a bay of water that fed into the Selenian Sea.

Of all the places she could run to . . . *this* was the spot she chose—

A nameless forest in the land of Edenvale. It meant nothing to her, but it meant something to me. Because this was where I would come when I needed to think, when I needed a moment away from the Spirit Realm, when I needed not to be king.

I shook my head softly, a grin piercing the corners of my mouth—of course Fate would lead us both here. Although I didn't understand the mechanics of it, it seemed fitting, somehow. And deep down, on some molecular level, I could feel that things were about to shift between us. In what direction I didn't know, but I was determined to find out.

I ambled forward.

The world was quiet—too quiet—as if it had taken a breath upon my arrival and was now holding it. Even the crickets had fallen silent.

The only thing that made any sound at all was the rapid beating of her heart.

Ba-dump. Ba-dump. Ba-dump.

It called out to me, just as it did that day on the battlefield. She had been so courageous then, facing off against me. What happened to that creature who had iron in her spine and ice in her veins? Where was she now? Hiding among the trees like some frightened animal?

No. That wasn't her.

And I didn't buy it for a second.

"Come out, Kitten," I purred as I prowled ahead, my combat boots crunching the twigs and leaves beneath them. "Show me those pretty, pretty claws, won't you?"

The breath of my wind floated towards me, carrying her scent with it—fresh, crisp citrus and gentle, airy sea salt. Tracing its origins, my feet stilled, and I looked to my left, over to a towering tree. Its leaves were a lovely, moody red, much like the color of my blood on her daggers. Much like the color her flesh would be when I forged the bond between us—her ivory skin flushed and pearled with sweat.

Above, the light of the moon faded, painting the woods in darkness as a barrage of heavy-bottomed clouds began to roll in over top—a storm was coming.

I started towards the tree, the beast in me licking his lips at what was hiding on the other side of it—no better than a starving wolf closing in on a little rabbit. I circled around the wide trunk. She wasn't there.

Schhrringg.

A cold, hard, blade pressed against my neck, its sharpness biting into my skin.

"Free me of our deal—" Aurelia demanded from beside me, "—or I will do it myself."

Her voice was firm. Confident.

Ah, there she was. *That* was my girl.

I smirked, my canines sinking into my bottom lip before I let it slip free.

Thunder rumbled in the distance and the natural winds began to pick up, blowing around the heavy-topped trees, shaking their branches violently.

"Do it," she snarled, but her words were all bark and no bite. She was threatening me, yes, but if she really wanted me dead, she would have done it already. Instead, she continued our game of cat and mouse.

"I won't," I answered her. My shadows snaked around me, licking at her sword, if only to get a taste of her. I looked over my shoulder, down at her. "I will *never* free you of our deal."

Two clouds struck each other, causing a blast of thunder and a flash of light that arched off the blade that was held to my throat. Nature's waterspout cranked open, bringing an onslaught of heavy, heavy rain, pounding down on us both.

"Why won't you?" she hissed, her voice so cold it rivalled the frozen wastelands of the north, and yet, the irresistible pheromones she had begun to emit spoke a great deal otherwise—something my divinity all too eagerly picked up on. She might as well have been a cat rubbing herself against me, her tail in the air, flicking back and forth like a waving white flag. Did she enjoy the visual of her blade against my throat? Or was it the adrenaline she felt rushing through her veins, knowing that I was hunting her in these dark woods? Regardless, her sweet scent was like a summoning, calling to my primal nature, begging me to strip her of her clothes and attend to her needs.

"I asked you a question," Aurelia snarled, ignoring her desire.

Did she not realize I could scent her body's reaction to mine?

A sigh, born from deep within my chest, rumbled past my lips. "Because I am no better than a winged insect who has lived for an eternity in darkness. I've gotten a glimpse of your light and I cannot help but be drawn to you, regardless of if I am destined to burn in your flame. I couldn't care less. I am obsessed with you in every possible way a god can be, and I will stop at nothing until I have consumed you, just as you have done to me. So you can fight me all you want, but there is only one way this is going to end—with you on your back and my tongue tending to that little problem of yours between your legs."

Her mouth popped open.

Seeing my chance, my hand shot up, wrapping around her blade with such strength that it squealed beneath my grasp. The sharp edges bit into my skin, conjuring blood to the surface. The light sting was nothing compared to how good it felt to bleed—to feel . . . alive.

That was what she did to me.

And that was why I would never give her up.

"So what will it be, Little Goddess? Will you be a good girl and go down willingly?"

A mighty crack of thunder rumbled the ground beneath my feet, charging the air with electricity.

Her mouth snapped shut, a V forming between her brows. "You are such a bastard."

"A bastard, am I? Is that why you are dripping wet for me?"

"I am not," she growled out the lie, baring her adorable little fangs.

I grinned, showing her my wicked canines in return. "Your pheromones say otherwise, darling."

The blade dissolved and my hand clamped shut, misting my blood into the air, infusing the droplets of rain as they fell to the forest floor. Aurelia leapt backwards, conjuring another sword. Her cloak parted, revealing a white tunic beneath, clinging damply to her heaving breasts.

The sight of her like that—my wild, weapon-wielding beauty—it was enough to make this proud, unkneeling king *tempted* to drop to his knees.

But I wouldn't do her such a disservice.

I would give her what she wanted, so that her precious ego could take solace in knowing that she did not go down without a fight.

I rolled my wrist and summoned my sword—Death Weaver. It was made of Vischordian black steel—one of the strongest metals known to immortal kind and nearly impossible to find. Bones were etched into the handle, a screaming skull crowning the pommel. I rotated my wrist, swinging my sword, as I asked, "What will you give me for winning, Little Goddess?"

"You won't," she snarled.

I let out a low laugh. "We'll see about that."

Then, like the warring clouds above, we collided.

In a flash of obsidian and azure, our blades found each other in a *clang* so loud that it rivalled the blasts of thunder. The energy produced was like lightning, obliterating the trees surrounding us. She tore her sword from mine and swung again. I parried her attack. Twisting, she pulled back, her movement graceful, elegant. She spun to the side, her heavy, soaked cloak failing to keep up, and fired another shot, one my sword eagerly answered. Stepping out of range, she pulled the string on her cloak and let it fall to the side, unburdening her body from the weight of it.

I lifted a lone brow, shooting her an arrogant, crooked grin. "Undressing yourself so early?"

She bared her teeth at me and attacked again, my laughter filling the air. Our blades became hung up on one another. I had to admit that her swordsmanship was better than I expected it to be, a skill she must have earned during the Immortal War.

"Aren't you going to thank me, darling?" I purred, blowing water from my lips.

"For what?" she grated, shoving against me with her sword, her eyelashes soaked and clumped together.

I didn't budge. If she wanted to make any ground here, she was going to have to retract her blade from mine. Or try something else.

"For getting you out of that dreadful palace," I told her. "Into the real world, where you could do fun things . . . like fight in a war."

She gave me a peculiar look but didn't bite as we remained deadlocked, both of us too stubborn to move. That was fine by me—I quite liked her body's proximity to mine.

Tauntingly, I said, "Had I not started the war between our people, your swordsmanship would not be what it is today. Admit it, you enjoyed bathing in my men's blood. I know it appealed to some part of your divinity."

"I didn't," she growled as she conjured a shield and sent the lip of it flying for my abdomen—aiming for my freshly healed injury. I caught it before it could connect, and it groaned under my crushing grip. "I hated every second of that fucking war."

I smirked.

Long gone was the *proper lady* she portrayed herself to be, replaced by the unpolished, raw version.

That was the *real* her.

Dredged to the surface after centuries of being buried deep. Underneath the layers of etiquette and decorum and what she was told she needed to be. I would do everything within my power to free her of those personality-numbing expectations.

"I don't believe that for a second, sweetheart," I told her. "I saw you on the battlefield that day, covered in mud and blood and high on adrenaline. You were no longer the lifeless, pretty doll who stood by her window, night after night, wondering when her husband would remember she existed. No, with a sword in your hand, you were alive. Just as you are now."

Her lips parted, but her dangerous tongue was dormant for once, telling me more than her useless lies ever could. I had found the crack in her proud armor—I was getting through to her. A moment passed between us as we stared into one another's eyes, firmly deadlocked as the thunderstorm raged around us.

"How do you know about the window?" she asked, the malice gone from her voice.

The air shifted between us—that incredible pull tugging with all of its might.

One look at her, and I knew she had to feel it too.

"Because I was there, outside, every night, waiting to catch a glimpse of you." I let go of her shield. Lowered my voice. "All the time that you spent longing for him, I was there, longing for you."

"I—I didn't know." Her gaze drifted to my lips, lingering there.

Too long.

I grabbed her chin and hauled her mouth to mine through the cross of our blades. Lightning exploded around us, eclipsing the darkness of the night—celebrating our kiss, centuries in the making. My shadows swallowed my sword, freeing my hand so that I could grab her weapon. I took it from her and tossed it to the side while I kissed her senseless, my mouth branding hers as *mine*.

And for a fleeting moment, she kissed me back.

That small taste of her desire was all she gave me before she rammed her shield into my chest with every ounce of her immortal might. Caught off guard, I was thrown backwards, my body smashing through tree after tree after tree, shattering them upon impact like wooden fireworks going off in the night. My fingers shredded through the soggy ground beneath me, anchoring me to the earth.

When I came to a stop, I grunted as I stood up—

Fuck, that hurt.

My body spat out the wood shards that had slivered their way inside, leaving dozens of little wounds on my lower back. Apart from that, I was covered in mud, grass, and bits of weeds, but it was my pauldron, the left shoulder forged into a skull, that had fared much worse. It was full of cracks and missing pieces that were now lost to the forest. I yanked on the strap that held it in place and it fell to the ground.

My rabid eyes locked on her as I growled, "That wasn't very nice, Little Goddess."

She dropped her shield and took a hesitant step back, and then another—that one quicker than the last.

"Do not," I warned.

And then she did . . . she turned to run, light blooming around her.

She was fast, but my shadows were faster.

Chapter 12

Aurelia

Something wrapped around my ankles, crushing them together, and then the world was yanked out from underneath me. I landed with a wet smack on the drenched soil, the air shooting out from my lungs as my mouth filled with bits of mud. The side of my face and body were plastered in it. I spat out the gritty, soggy texture, strings of spittle slinging over my bottom lip and dripping down over my chin. Wheezing, I jerked my head to the side, looking to see what was locked around my ankles—

A chain, stronger than iron, forged from shadow.

Awkwardly, I kicked my legs, as best as one could when they were hogtied like a damn animal. It didn't budge.

I traced the chain back to Death, his hand held out in front of him, holding on to the bonds. Black, impenetrable eyes were fixed on me, shadowed by his wet, dark hair. Lightning struck behind him, etching out his masculine silhouette. Every bit of his towering, warrior-derived frame looked menacing. Terrifying.

A nightmare brought to life, come to possess me.

To *own* me.

"Do you know what your first mistake was?" he grunted as he started to pull on the chain, tugging me towards him, through the mud. "You should have slit my throat when I gave you the chance."

Scrambling, I clawed at the doughy, slippery ground, trying to grab hold of anything that would give me a bit of leverage. A rock. A root. *Anything.*

Panic rode me hard as I realized my time was running out. Once Death got a hold of me, he would take me back to the Spirit Realm against my will, forcing me to make good on our deal, forcing me to become his bride.

Water gathered at my fingertips, and I forged it into a dagger. With both hands, I drove the blade into the ground, all the way to the hilt, and for a second, it was enough.

The pulling stopped. The chain slackened.

"And do you know what your second mistake was?" Death purred in his rich timbre, his voice so deep I felt it in places it had no business being right now. *Damn him.* "Thinking you could outrun me."

The chain tightened, my blade snapped, and he dragged me

backwards as I thrashed like a fish out of water. When I was within his grasp, he flipped me onto my back. Muscular thighs, forged from steel, locked my legs in place, while his massive hands grabbed my wrists and shackled them above my head.

Death straddled me in the mud as the sky fought above us.

"You are such an asshole," I seethed, fighting against his unbreakable hold, my chest heaving from exertion.

He smirked at that, as if he took pleasure in it. His wickedly sharp fangs poked out from his top lip, and I was reminded that I was trapped underneath an ancient predator—chiseled with muscle, adorned in ink—temptation and danger all wrapped into one.

Every inch of him was lethal.

Seductive.

His black lashes lowered as he raked his gaze over me, his lips parting and his tongue rolling and pressing against his bottom row of perfect teeth. Slowly, his eyes lifted to mine, pinning me there. "Do you want to know what your third mistake was?"

"Not really," I said, adrenaline coursing through my veins. The kind that made my skin feel flush. The kind that made my heart stampede with anticipation.

"Well, that's too bad, because I'm going to tell you anyway." He licked his lips as if he were savoring the last remnants of a meal he had just finished. He sucked the bottom one, tugging his teeth across it for good measure, as if he couldn't get enough, and then said with a low, sexy groan, "You kissed me back, Kitten."

"It was a mistake."

"Was it?"

"Yes."

He brought his mouth to mine, close enough I could taste the word. "Liar."

A shiver skittered across my bones, all the way down to my desperate, traitorous core.

I breathed deeply, inhaling his amber and sandalwood scent, made sweet with the addition of his ichor, all of it somehow still present even though he was drenched from the rain. We both were.

A crack of thunder sounded, charging the air with electricity.

Or maybe that was just us.

"Do you want to know what I think?" he said, pulling back, just a little.

"What?" I asked, my lungs suddenly short on air as I peered up into his eyes, spellbound by those starless pools of divine obsidian. I should have been out of my mind with fear. The God of Death, the ruthless Blood King who was feared by all, had me in a state of submission with my wrists locked above my head and my ankles bound in his chain.

But right now? I wasn't afraid—

I was *aching*. For *his* touch. For him.

All of him.

"I think that you like running from me, that you want me to chase you, to capture you, and force you to submit—to show you that you are the epitome of my desire, because that was something he never did. I think that you want to be conquered by me, but you are terrified of what that will mean . . . of what will be left of you." His thumb tugged my bottom lip to the side. "Tell me I'm wrong." He released it.

"You are." My voice cracked, snapping the lie in half.

He leaned in, hovering his mouth over mine, his proximity taunting, driving me wild. "Then tell me to stop."

But I couldn't.

I couldn't tell him to stop because I didn't want him to.

So I did the very thing I had been dying to do for decades now—

I kissed the insufferable, sexy bastard.

Chapter 13

Von

Her kiss was the striking of a match, setting me on fire. Even as the rain fell from the heavens, I was being burned alive as her ravenous lips moved against mine. Releasing her hands, one of mine landed beside her head, mud squishing between my fingers, while the other wove into her hair, the long strands clumped with wet earth. I held her there as my lips coaxed hers open and my tongue slid inside, weaving my black magic into her mouth, binding her to me.

I'd claim every inch of her.

And even then, it wouldn't be enough. With her, I'd never have my fill.

Never.

My chains slid from her ankles, releasing her. At the same time, her hands moved to the hem of her tunic, eager to remove her wet, muddy clothes.

"No." I caught her wrists, stopping her, and pulled back, sitting on my haunches.

She looked up at me with those pretty blue eyes of hers, confusion swimming inside of them. "Why are you stopping me?" she asked, frowning. "I thought you wanted this."

"Because, Little Goddess, undressing you is *my* job now. And indeed—" I ran my gaze down her torso, her clothes dissolving in my wake, revealing her sensual, naked body to me. She gasped when she realized what I had done. My wind danced across her flesh, brushing over her hardened nipples, sweeping down to her sweet little sex. "—I want *all* of this."

"How did you do that?" she asked, her skin pebbling with goosebumps.

"Party trick." My gaze roamed over her supple valleys and mouthwatering peaks. She was like a piece of perfectly ripe fruit, begging to be devoured. I couldn't wait to get my teeth in her, my cock in her . . . my cum *in* her.

I lifted her arms above her head, pinning them there with one hand. She regarded me with curious eyes. With my free one, I swept my fingers through the mud, coating the tips. Between the swells of her breasts, I drew one letter on her rain-slickened flesh. My hand drifted down and I painted another. And then another. And another.

Until it said—

"Mine," she read the word out loud, her chest quivering, eyes watching as I lowered my hand.

"All fucking mine," I purred darkly, possessively, as I marked her lower abdomen with an X. "And when I'm buried *deep* in here, and you are screaming my name, you'll understand that."

"Death," she whispered, her voice caught in her throat.

"Mmm. Just like that," I mused as I cupped her breast, my cool rings biting into her heated skin—marking her with my massive handprint. She let out a needy little whimper, a plea for more. "But I'm going to need you to sing my praise much louder than that. I want the entire world to know who you belong to."

I guided her face to the side as I kissed my way across her jaw, nipping at her skin, leaving little bite marks, not enough to break the skin, but enough to leave a mark. She rolled her head back when I moved on to her neck, giving me the length of it, her breasts thrust up towards me—my hand still working the one. Her powerful ichor thrummed throughout her veins, begging me to bite her, to taste her, to drink from her.

Tempted to oblige, I scraped my fangs over her throat, hard enough to raise the skin. Her body went still, like a rabbit at the end of its life caught in the wolf's iron jaw. I could hear her blood rushing through her veins, hear her heart hammering in her chest—not in fear, but in . . . anticipation.

Saliva pooled in my mouth. I ran my tongue over the spot where my teeth had just been, marking her neck as something I would return for later. Because right now, I wanted something even more than that—

I wanted to taste the sweetness I scented pooling between her legs.

I kissed and nipped her soft skin, trailing my way down to her breast. I sucked the perky, pink bud into my mouth, flicking my tongue over it. Her soft moans urged me on, and I suckled her harder. Her hips rolled, begging for a bit of friction. In answer, I pressed one leg between hers, allowing her to rub herself on my heavily muscled thigh.

As I released her hands, I trapped her nipple between my teeth, biting down just enough to inspire a whimper between her moans. Releasing it, I suckled and licked my way down her torso until I reached her sex—the only part of her that wasn't positively filthy at the moment.

I stole a glance at her, finding her wide eyes on me.

"What are you doing?" she asked, her voice breathy. Husky.

"I think it's rather self-explanatory, Kitten. I'm going to eat your cunt."

"Wait . . . what?"

"Do not tell me that you have never had your sex licked before?"

She shook her head and I had to do everything within my power not to let my jaw spring open. When one lived to be as old as I was, very little surprised me, but *that* did. If anything, it only served to confirm something I already knew—the God of Life was one dumb little shit.

"Right," I said as I lifted her legs and placed them on my shoulders. "We remedy that now." Wasting no time, I delved between her thighs and began sucking on that sweet little ball of pleasure, nestled underneath a protective bit of flesh.

"Oh," she rasped, her hips lifting from the ground, rolling and chasing after the rapture I was giving her. Her hands fisted in my hair, pulling at it, testing the roots.

I growled in approval. I was going to teach her so many, *many* things.

My fingers pressed against her sex, parting her for better access. I released her swollen bud and swept my tongue along her wet little slit. Tasting her for the first time.

Fuck, she tasted divine—sweet and crisp and—

Just like an apple.

My mate *tasted* like a fucking apple.

I was no stranger to the nectar between a woman's legs, but not one of them had ever tasted like this—I licked her again—tasted like they were made for me—and again—tasted like their arousal was my own personal brand of endless addiction.

A predatory growl rumbled from my chest. Pulling back, I captured her gaze as I licked her wetness from my lips, not willing to part with a single drop. "I will be the first and last to eat you like this, yes?" I wasn't asking, but I needed to hear her say it.

"Alright," she said, wiggling her hips for me to continue.

Alright? No. That wouldn't do. That juicy little cunt belonged to me now.

Hand bracketing her leg, I bit her thigh and she let out a yelp. "With meaning, darling."

"Yes, okay," she agreed, all hot and breathy and needy.

"Good girl," I praised, going back in, eager to drown in her nectar. I drove my long, powerful tongue into her while my fingers swirled her clit.

She threw her head back, writhing beneath me as she cried out, whimpering and moaning as the storm raged above us. Hearing her sexy little sounds made me harder than steel.

I flattened my tongue inside of her, stretching her while tasting her. I ran it along her sleek walls, branding her in the scent of my saliva. I pulled my tongue out to the tip and then I plunged back in. I did that, again and again, until she started to squirm—her body telling me she was close. I pinned her wiggling hips, locking her there, forcing her to take the pleasure I was giving while my fingers strummed her and I fucked her with my mouth.

She trembled as she came on my tongue. An animalistic growl broke from my chest as I feasted on her sweet release. I swept my tongue along her slit, licking her clean, before the rain could wash away a single drop.

Her eyelids were at half-mast, her trembling body dazed from the aftermath of her climax. Seeing her like that, drunk on pleasure—it made the beast within me purr deeply.

What I wouldn't do to keep her like that for the rest of eternity.

My cock strained against my leathers.

I left fresh, muddy handprints on her legs as I pulled them from my shoulders and lowered them to the ground. My heat washed against her skin as I crawled up her body and kissed her deeply, driving my tongue into her mouth.

She sucked on it, a throaty *mmm* falling from her lips.

Pulling back, I asked her, "Do you like the taste of yourself in my mouth?"

"Yes," she mewled, her fingers pulling lightly at my tunic. "But there's something else I need more."

"What is it, Kitten?" I needed to hear her say it.

"I need to feel you inside of me," she said. Desperate.

Fire filled my veins, burning away my last tendril of restraint. I didn't know if the New Gods put as much of an emphasis on the bond as us Old Gods did.

I didn't even know if she knew what the bond was.

A good man would ask her if she knew. A good man would warn her that when we mated, it would weld the bond in place between us. That it would chain her to my side for the rest of her immortal life.

But I wasn't a good man . . .

I was—yup, you guessed it—

A bastard.

Chapter 14

Aurelia

Dark, obsidian, lose-your-soul eyes met mine and my breath hitched in my throat. The way Death looked at me just then, I had no words for it. That look. It belonged solely to him, a look that no one else could replicate. It was primal and intense.

Possessive.

And it had my body *trembling* for him. I needed his skin on mine. Needed to feel the weight of him. Needed to feel him *inside* of me.

“Take them off,” I demanded softly as I hooked a finger on the lip of his pants, feeling the smooth leather on one side and the hardness of his body on the other.

“So *very* bossy,” he teased as he leaned back on his haunches.

I propped myself on my elbows, feeling them sink into the muddy ground. His shadows swept around him, eating away at his clothes until nothing was left.

I swallowed, my gaze raking over the hardened planes of his incredible body. Rain beaded together, forming small rivers, washing some of the mud from his tanned skin. Inky markings lapped over each other, drawn on a canvas that was running out of room, painting his massive, muscular frame in splendor and sin.

Every inch of him was so damn . . . lickable. My gaze lowered down his carved, rigid abs. When I saw *it*, I realized a depraved truth—

I was going to be ruined.

Mind. Body. And soul.

I imagined that was how mortals felt when they watched an oncoming tornado chew up the world as it came for their home, knowing full well it was going to destroy all their cherished things and leave them trembling and wide-eyed, and left with nothing.

Creator above, every bit of this male was *massive.*

And rock-fucking-hard.

His wicked length bobbed against his stomach, reaching *all the way* to his belly button. It was corded with powerful, thrumming veins, matching the rest of his unlawfully chiseled physique. Built to dominate. A quarter of the way down was a tattoo—a feminine pair of lips. I thought back to the bite mark he had given me when we made our deal, and somehow, this felt connected to that, which meant—

"Are those *mine*?" I asked, eyes flaring wide.

"Yes." His voice was a deep, dark purr.

White-hot heat pooled low in my belly—that truth had no business being as delectable as it was. My lips forever etched on his proud length.

"Why *there*?" I asked.

The corner of his mouth twisted upwards. His sexy smirk was criminal. "So you know where to put your mouth."

My lips parted, my gaze sweeping up to his.

He chuckled, those heavy muscles contracting as he positioned himself over top of me. One hand landed beside my head, stabilizing his body over top of mine. He was so much larger than me, it seemed unreasonable. And yet, I didn't fear him like I had before. No. Now, like this, I felt protected. It was strange yet familiar, and it made very little sense, but when his mouth lowered to mine, it suddenly made *all* the sense. Our tongues intertwined, caught in a playful war—taunting and tasting each other.

Large, calloused fingertips brushed down the length of my body, stirring my flesh to bloom for him. His hand trailed between us, his fingers finding that sensitive bud—swollen and throbbing, his touch the cure. He twirled it, playing with it until I was moaning into his mouth, whimpering for more.

He pulled his lips from mine and brought his fingers to my mouth. "Open for me."

Slowly, I parted my lips, and he slid three of his massive, long fingers inside, his skull ring scraping against my teeth as he pushed them as far as my throat would allow. The taste of arousal and earth exploded across my tongue, bits of sand and grit releasing in my mouth.

"Suck them clean," he purred, while his fingers playfully slid in and out of my mouth. Heat ripened my cheeks as I realized he was literally fucking my mouth with his fingers. "Get them nice and wet."

I did as he said—I sucked and lapped and licked, cleaning every inch of his fingers, *even* his silver rings.

"Always so good for me," he groaned, pulling the wet digits from my mouth and lowering his hand. His finger dipped into my wetness, pressing deep inside of me. When he sank it all the way to his knuckle, my toes curled into the mud.

"Fuck, you are so tight, Kitten." His eyes darkened, turning blazing hot. "It's a good thing you are so wet for me."

"Yes," I cried out as I tipped my head back. A husky moan fell from my lips as his finger curled inside of me. My hands wrapped around his arms, feeling the steel etched beneath his skin—feeling the wealth of his incredible power.

"I want you, Death," I mewled, living up to the nickname he'd given me.

"And you will have me," he stated, adding a second finger, stretching me.

I clutched on to him as his wondrous fingers drove any tangible thoughts to extinction. All I could think of was him, and the way his hand felt between my legs. The things he did with it. An animalistic sound escaped my lips when he added a third. I had never been filled so wonderfully before. His fingers stroked that mind-shattering spot inside of me. When I was on the cusp of another orgasm, his fingers slid out, swiftly replaced by something much, much broader, nudging against my entrance.

My heart drummed loudly, my attention focused on our bodies, at this moment before we were fully connected. I wrapped my leg around him, locking him to me, a silent plea written in my gaze, relaying just how much I wanted him.

I took a breath.

Then the King of the Old Gods *conquered* me.

Powerful hips pressed forward, and he started to slide himself in, inch by incredible inch, never breaking eye contact. Fire brimmed as he stretched me beyond reason, forcing me to accommodate him—bend or break. Pain and pleasure mingled together, dancing underneath my skin, and a husky moan fell from my lips, carried away on his wind.

Death claimed me so slowly, so intimately, I forgot how to breathe.

Forgot how to function.

"You feel so fucking good," he groaned as his cock exorcised my soul from my body. Had he not slid himself back, leaving just his thick crown in me, I might not have returned to my trembling frame.

He kept me there, pinned beneath him, as his mouth lowered to mine, his kiss to my lips so heartbreakingly sweet, before he trailed down to my neck. Those soft kisses disarmed me. A lure of trust, coaxing me to relax.

"I claim you as mine," Death growled as his hand on my hip turned crushing. Lightning struck in warning as he angled his head and his fangs plunged into my neck, ripping through sinew and nerves at the same time he drove his cock back in.

I screamed as white heat enveloped my body, stars dancing behind my vision, as my body was torn between two worlds—pleasure and pain. Seconds was all it took for the former to win out as the venom from his fangs and the feel of his cock stitched rapture into my veins. His hand released my hip and intertwined with mine, pulling them both above my head, pressing them into the muddy earth as he drank from me.

He scattered my thoughts, tethering me to him—to where our bodies were connected. His heavy sack tapped against my bottom each time he slammed into me. With each rhythmic thrust, I could feel him go deeper and deeper and—

"Fuck," I rasped, my lungs rattling in my chest—my world was being torn apart.

I had sex before, but it had *never* been like this.

Never this . . . euphoric.

As his fangs slid from my neck, he rolled us over in the mud and the rain, flipping us so that I was on top of him. My knees landed on either side of his hips as my hands fell to his muscular chest, stabilizing me.

Goddess divine, he felt so much *deeper* now.

"Ride me, goddess," Death commanded, his hand slapping my bottom. I let out a low, surprised yelp. "Show me how good my future queen can take her king's cock."

His hips teased mine, and suddenly mine were moving on their own accord, dancing with his in perfect rhythm—never breaking contact as I absorbed each powerful thrust while his hands bracketed my hips. Our eyes were fixed on one another, staring deeply into each other's souls as our bodies spoke a language of their own.

He lifted his hips, angling them, hitting that sacred spot inside, repeatedly.

I cried out in pleasure, my fingers digging into his strong, sturdy pectorals, carving little half-moons into his slick, inked skin. The fine cuts pooled with his divine blood.

"Drink from me," he commanded, his voice husky.

Leaning forward, I ran my tongue over the small wounds, keeping my eyes locked with his. I wanted him to watch me drink from him. Just as I had watched him feast between my legs. A rich, slightly honey-sweet, metallic flavor spread across my tongue. Power seeped into me. His power. And it was intoxicating.

Magic scented the air, as if a spell were being performed. Like the celestial spirits, beyond the swells of the thunderclouds, had been planning this moment between us for millennia.

That's when I felt it . . .

A fusing of sorts, of two broken halves being welded back together. A give and a take, in a grand payoff etched with cataclysmic bliss that came in the form of the strongest orgasm I had ever had. It wasn't just me reaching it—it was as if Death had forced his hand into me and was pulling the immense pleasure from my body like a thief in the night.

Stars burst throughout my vision, dancing and twinkling.

My body trembled with each earth-shattering wave as I rode out my release, while Death found his.

"Take every drop," he said roughly. He held me to him as he filled me with his seed, branding me in his essence. A silver light illuminated from within his skin, passing to mine, unlike anything I had ever seen before.

I blinked in my half-dazed confusion.

When I looked into his eyes, when I thought I saw the inky color of them begin to disappear and be replaced by another, my vision turned cloudy. My body swayed and I collapsed on top of him, losing myself to the realm of dreams.

Chapter 15

Aurelia

A cool draft whispered through my subconscious, luring me from the embrace of sleep. That same light touch of air strolled across my bare shoulder as if someone were walking their fingers over it. The sensation changed from light to something harsher—like a cold bit of metal was being run along my sensitive, heated skin. The touch was intimate. So intimate it sent a shiver skittering down the span of my back, straight to my sex.

I was suddenly all too aware of the molten heat building between my thighs, accompanied by a dull, nagging ache.

"Are you dreaming of me, Kitten?" purred a primal voice.

Startled, my eyelids flickered open.

Sitting on the ledge of a ceiling-scraping, arched window, directly across from me, was the masculine silhouette of a predator.

Amethyst light bathed his bare, heavily muscled shoulders, teasing a small glimpse of the inky markings that lingered on his skin. It caught on his onyx mane, tugged up into a warrior's top knot, while cloaking his features in shadow. Leather pants hugged his muscular thighs, accompanied by a pair of combat boots. A nearly devoured apple sat in his palm. He raised it to his mouth, his teeth slicing into the ripe fruit as he severed off the last chunk. Even though I couldn't see his eyes, I could tell they were fixed on me.

While he watched me, I surveyed my surroundings.

I was in an enormous bedchamber, dimly lit by a crackling, roaring fire, bathing obsidian walls in a sensual red. The fireplace was forged of bones—skulls, femurs, and ribs, encased in a layer of silver. Surrounding it was a settee flanked by adjacently placed wingback chairs, a coffee table sat in the middle. My gaze swept back to the canopy bed I was lying on, large enough to fit a pair of expanded wings. Onyx-dyed silk hung from the canopy, the same fabric mirrored in the luxurious sheets that surrounded me. A bar area was to my left, the shelves behind it lined with unmarked bottles—most likely full of spirits.

Spirits . . .

My eyes darted from one window to another. Finding the same answer repeated over and over again. Outside, there was an ominous, dark, moody sky. A sky that was not forged of azure—no, it was of a foreboding amethyst.

"You brought me to the Spirit Realm," I snarled at him, jerking up onto my elbow.

"I did," Death replied.

"Unbelievable."

"*You* made a deal," he reminded me, as if that were reason enough. It wasn't.

"One you forced me into," I bit back, my tongue a blade, sharpened and ready to cut.

He scoffed. "I forced you into nothing. You agreed of your own volition."

"What choice did I have?"

"You could have said no," he teased in that cocky, arrogant tone that made me want to punt him out the window.

"As if it were that simple! I *thought* I was doing the right thing by trading my freedom for Aurelius's."

Death flashed his white canines. "And how did that work out for you, sweetness? You traded your soul to the King of the Spirit Realm just so that worthless asshole could crawl back to his. And what did he do to repay you? Oh, that's right, he cut down your orchard."

My blood boiled beneath my skin, my head feeling like a dried-up pot that had been left too long over the fire, ready to explode. But I held it in, reasoning that I didn't have to put up with this—*or* him. The arrogant jerk.

My eyes shifted around the room, landing on the balcony doors.

"Don't even think about it," he warned. "The Living Realm is no longer safe for you now that you pulled that little disappearing act of yours and wounded me in front of Nicholas and Malachai. They know that you are my weakness, something Nicholas will tell Aurelius. When he does, Aurelius will stop at nothing to get you back. From now on, you will stay here, under my protection."

When I flung those daggers and ran, I knew that there was a chance I might be exposing the truth to Nicholas and Malachai, but I had been shoved into a corner and forced to decide within seconds. And so, I chose—I chose myself, damning the consequences in the process. And yes, it might have been stupid and brash, but I was desperate. And desperate people did desperate, stupid things.

Was that why he was adamant about keeping me here? So that I couldn't be weaponized against him? It was a question that begged to be asked.

"Confining me here . . ." I looked at him. "Is that for my safety or yours?"

"Yours."

"And if I choose to leave?"

The air shifted.

"Then I will hunt you down and drag that fine little ass of yours back here," he said slowly—as if he wanted me to taste each word. The way he made it sound—an invitation and a warning.

I swallowed, trying to find my backbone—which tended to disappear all too easily with him. "So I'm a prisoner then."

The dark god snorted in mockery. "Although I quite enjoy when you are in my chains, no, you are not a prisoner here."

"So then, what am I?"

"My future bride."

"And if I don't want to be?"

He shrugged a large shoulder. "It's a bit late for that."

I huffed. *Insufferable male.*

Pressing off against the window, he strolled towards me—his gait a lazy, powerful prowl. He tossed the apple core over his shoulder. Shadows swam abound, chewing up the remnants of fruit—seeds and all—before it had a chance to touch the ground.

I shot upright, the silk sheet drifting down my body—grazing against my sensitive skin. A desperate little sound bloomed on my tongue, a whimper that was more animal than human. A plea.

I was horrified. Confused.

What in the Spirit Realm was that? my inner voice asked.

The tips of Death's long canines snatched my attention as his lips twisted into a smile.

It's your body's way of summoning mine, his chest-deep voice answered inside my head.

My breathing became erratic, his voice conjuring liquid heat to pool low. I bit my bottom lip, trapping the next desperate sound before it could escape. I swallowed it down.

What is happening to me?

"Why can I hear you inside my head?" I asked, snatching up the sheet and covering myself with it—ignoring the feel of it against my skin and how my body was screaming for more friction.

Friction that only *he* could provide.

His massive hands, full of ink and rings, propped on the bed as he leaned forward. The shadows parted from his face, revealing—

His *eyes*. They were no longer a bottomless black.

They were full of the most incredible color I had ever seen.

Like leaves in late spring, after the rains had come. A beautiful, opulent, vibrant . . . *green.*

"*You can hear me because we are bonded, Little Goddess,*" he purred, reaching for a tendril of my hair, trapping it between his thumb and forefinger. "We are now connected through an ever-flowing channel—a private river vein that belongs only to us, where we are able to communicate silently with one another."

My heart thumped against my chest. *Bonded*?

"That's impossible." I shook my head. "Aurelius said that the bond didn't exist." As soon as the words fell out of my mouth, the aftertaste of deceit blossomed on my tongue.

I was an idiot. A gullible, stupid idiot.

After Aurelius and I consummated our marital life, he had been nothing but frustrated after. As it was my first time and I hadn't completely understood the pleasures of the flesh, I thought that I had displeased him. He assured me that I hadn't. The following day, he had a group of healers brought into our chambers to run a variety of health checks on me. I couldn't make a lick of sense from their poking and prodding. After they left, Aurelius brushed off my questions with a kiss to my forehead. He told me that he was *only* concerned about my health due to my deal with the God of Death. And like a love-sick puppy dog, I licked his lie right up. After that day, I didn't see Aurelius for a few weeks, and when he finally returned, he told me that he had been busy working with council members, as they were making crucial amendments to the laws of the Immortal Realm, but I was never told exactly *what* for. It wasn't until a few months later, when I overheard some ladies gossiping in the halls about the new rules regarding the bond. It was not to be spoken of anymore and doing so would result in arrest.

Now, it all made sense. Aurelius's frustration. The change of law.

He was angry that the bond had not formed between us, but now . . .

I looked at the deliciously handsome god who was preoccupied with a ribbon of my hair—void of mud, sparkling white, *and* brushed.

Had Death *bathed* me? *Brushed* my hair? I should find that thought revolting, considering I had been unconscious, and yet I didn't. I felt . . . cared for. Never mind that, there were more pressing matters at hand like—

That's what the constant pull was between us. Like a rope tethered to us both, always trying to bring us together. Even when I hated him, the feeling had been there.

Fated.

Bonded.

Complete.

His green eyes met mine, and just seeing that color there made me swell with pride and—

"You are my mate," I choked out, equal parts dumbfounded and astonished at this revelation. I couldn't understand why I hadn't realized it before. Tears pricked my eyes, blurring my vision.

He let go of the tendril of hair and sat on the bed beside me, long legs stretching out. Strong arms pulled me onto his lap with ease. Rough fingertips tipped my chin up, bringing my gaze to his. "As you are mine," he said, his thumb brushing over my bottom lip.

His body felt so good against mine. His muscles. His warmth.

His dark, unparalleled masculinity. Speaking of—

I could feel his erection pressed firmly against my bottom.

That familiar hunger began to build. Not one of the stomach—no, it was one of the flesh. And like a wildfire feeding on acres of dead brush, it began to consume me.

Control me.

Before I knew what I was doing, I was turning around, straddling myself on his lap. My legs spread wide on either side of him, aligning my sex with his—his pants were the only thing that separated us. My hands started wandering all over his phenomenal body, exploring his hardness while my lips found his strong, sturdy neck. He tipped his chiseled jaw upwards, giving me better access while his fingers wove playfully in my hair. I lapped and suckled, feeling the powerful swell of veins beneath—*filling* with blood *for me*.

The Blood King would bleed for no one else, only me.

I scraped my teeth along his skin, right over the rose tattooed on the side of his neck.

Drink from me, he spoke through our bond.

My canines elongated and—

My canines elongated!

I jerked back, my eyelids flaring wide.

Death's black brows knitted together. "What's wrong?"

I covered my face as I scampered off him, off the bed, and raced to the doorless frame that led into the bathing room. The room matched the dark aesthetic of the monstrous bedchamber, complete with twin sinks and a bathing pool large enough to fit ten people in it. The gently moving waters reflected on the glass-top ceiling, painting it in a wavy, blue glow.

I peered at myself in the mirror, flipping up my top lip and inspecting the sharp incisors. I poked at my lengthened canines.

In my hundreds of years of being a goddess, *that* had *never* happened before.

Chapter 16
Von

She was standing at *the* sink, the sink I *never* used.

The sink that I had installed when I was a hopeful young god who dared to wish that I might someday find my mate. The same sink that I had grown to hate over time, because whenever I looked at it, I was reminded that the other half of my soul was missing. That, perhaps, I would never find her.

That was the sink she was standing at.

At that moment, my knees did something they had never done before—they buckled. They buckled at the sight of her—the Goddess of Life, *my bonded, my mate*—standing at the sink I had installed for her long before her creation.

It was *always* meant to be hers.

And if someone would have asked me if waiting all those years to see her standing there was worth it, without hesitation, I would have said yes.

A *thousand* times over.

I took in her naked, beautiful frame—appreciating her and all that she was.

My Little Goddess.

My gaze ran over the curvature of her sexy little bottom, ripe and swollen and oh so fucking bitable. The tattoo of my teeth marks lingered there.

I bit my bottom lip, half inclined to give her a matching nip on the other side.

Slowly, my gaze drifted upwards, lingering on the adorable twin dimples set in her lower back. I traced her spine, all the way up to her slender shoulders. She had her face glued to the mirror, pulling up her top lip as she tapped the sharp point of her canine.

What are you doing? I asked across our bond.

Her eyes met mine in the mirror, and then she dropped her hands, a light-pink hue tinging her cheeks. "I—" She swallowed and then turned to me, her supple breasts snagging my attention. She walked towards me.

Oh yes, I'd bite those too. I'd sink my teeth into every inch of her. Sink *myself* into every inch of her. Until she was consumed by me. Just as I was with her.

My fingers slipped under her chin and I tipped her face upwards. "What is it?"

"My teeth." She lifted her upper lip, showing me. "Something is wrong with them."

"Wrong with them?" I chuckled softly, the sound more breath than laugh. I shook my head. "There is nothing wrong with your teeth. All New Gods' fangs elongate when they wish to feed." That was one of the differences between Old Gods and New. Ours remained permanently long and sharp. The space between my brows crinkled. "Don't tell me you have gone this long without your teeth ever doing so?"

I couldn't fathom that.

The life essence of another, whether it was blood or ichor—terms that were linked to either mortal or immortal yet were sometimes used interchangeably—was necessary for us immortals. Although we would not die if we went without it for a long period of time, we could grow incredibly weak and frail, to the point we would lose bodily functions.

But here she was, standing before me. Sure, her ribs were a bit more prominent than I would like, but she seemed perfectly healthy otherwise.

"I know that New Gods' teeth lengthen when they feed," she huffed at me. "Aurelius's would when he drank from me."

Jealousy, potent and raw, vibrated throughout my body at the mention of that fucker drinking from her. Immediately, I regretted not leaving him locked in my dungeon with Marishka, my monstrous tarantula, after the Immortal War ended.

Aurelia made a strange face, as if she tasted something funny on her tongue. She shook her head, her expression returning to normal. "But mine don't do that. They never have," she said, her hand shooting up as she began to press the pad of her thumb against the sharp tip of her right incisor.

"Then how did you feed?" Surely, she had to. I caressed her cheek, my hand dwarfing her face. I marveled at the size difference between the two of us, at the way my inked hand looked against her porcelain skin.

It was a visual I would never get enough of.

She quit tapping her tooth. "Aurelius would typically have his ichor infused in my food and wine. On rare occasions, he would bite his wrist or dig his claws into his chest and have me drink from him, but I never actually *bit* him."

Something about what she had just said did not sit well with me. I didn't like the idea of him putting his ichor in her food and wine any more than I liked the idea of her drinking from him. Whether that was due to my own territorial nature or if it was something more, I wasn't quite sure.

"Is this the first time your canines have lengthened?" I asked.

"It is," she confirmed with a single nod.

As much as I wanted to revel in this new information—that my mate's canines had lengthened for the first time when her lips were against my neck—I couldn't. It wasn't normal for an immortal's teeth to take hundreds of years to erect. Pair that with the fact that her divinity seemed dormant as fuck when her body needed to heal, I felt even more uneasy.

Sometimes, her body acted more mortal than immortal, and in some ways, that scared the shit out of me.

Eyes as deep as the sea met mine. "How do I make them go away?"

A smile tugged at my lips. Damn, she was adorable. "Why do you want them to?"

Her brows pressed together. "They look ridiculous."

"I disagree."

She shot me an unimpressed look, pushed me away, and went back to the mirror.

The chain between us gave a gallant pull, but I ignored it, letting her have her space for the time being.

"Why don't you like them?" I asked, crossing my arms over my chest.

Her eyes met mine in the reflection of the mirror. "Because . . . they are barbaric."

"Barbaric?" I snorted. "They are a way of life for us, a means of ensuring good health."

"There are other ways to feed."

"Ah yes, through a gilded goblet. You New Gods are such refined, well-mannered beings," I teased.

"We are," she said with a playful smile—unintentionally showing me her lovely little fangs again. "Unlike you uncivilized Old Gods."

"We are an exceedingly brutal species," I agreed, circling behind her.

"Primitive too," she added in a sultry tone, eyes tracking my movement.

"Heathens to the core." My shadow draped over her as I placed my hands on the counter, on either side of her, locking her in my cage.

"Ruthless and cruel." She stole a shaky breath of air, as if I had chased it from her lungs.

"Possessive of what is *ours,*" I purred before I lowered my mouth to her skin, kissing the tender spot between her neck and her shoulder where I had bitten her yesterday. The wound was now healed, courtesy of hers truly. Mouth busy, I pushed a question across our private channel. *Do you like it when this heathen's teeth are deep in your pristine flesh?*

Her lips parted ever so slightly.

I nipped at her playfully, pushing another thought across. *Perhaps*—I pressed my hardened length against her—*you would like this heathen's cock instead?*

She gasped—the sound feminine. Sexy. A small tease of what was to come—

And by that, I meant her.

Her desire-filled eyes met mine in the mirror's reflection as she purred through our bond, *And if I want both?*

"Then both you shall have." I twisted her sleek, white hair, roping it around my heavily inked arm, using it as leverage as I guided her forward against the counter. She gasped as the cool glass touched her skin. "Spread your legs for me, Kitten. Show me if you are wet enough to take my cock."

She paused, hesitant at first, but then she obeyed, widening her stance, giving me better access to her.

I looked down, eyeing her pretty, swollen sex—

So fucking breedable.

"Mmm," I growled in approval, biting my bottom lip.

I sank a ringed finger into her for further inspection. When I pulled it out, it glistened in her arousal.

"Such a good girl," I praised. "Getting yourself ready for me."

She watched through the mirror as I brought my finger to my mouth, sucking on the sweet, crisp taste of her, sampling her like an appetizer. She tasted just as she did in the forest, like an apple—my favorite thing to eat. Even her arousal was designed to appeal to me.

She was a lethal trap. One I was eager to feel clenched around me.

I was thankful for her incredible long legs bringing her sex so close to mine. It required a bit of angling on my part, but nothing I couldn't work with.

"Your body was made for mine," I said, running my hand over her ass, giving it a playful swat before I guided her back up. My pants and boots were dissolved by my shadows, revealing my naked body behind hers. Blue eyes raked over what she could see in the reflection of the mirror. Her scent became even more potent, and my mouth watered in response.

"Please, Death," she pleaded, the sound driving me wild. I could hear her blood pounding beneath her skin, singing for me, begging me to take it.

"My desperate little mate. So in need of me," I mused as I reached for my length.

Within seconds, I had my cock and teeth buried in her as I took her against the sink that was always meant to be hers. I swallowed her sweet ichor in greedy mouthfuls, pulling it from her veins. Two rivers of gold blood dribbled down her neck, my fingers sweeping over them, smearing the gold across her breasts, dirtying her pristine little body.

I wanted her filthy—*thrust*—I wanted her shaking—*thrust*—I wanted her to understand that now that she'd let me in, she'd never get me out.

Her eyelids were drooping, weighed down by the intensity of her lust and the blood I had taken from her. Her lips parted, panting and moaning as I drove inside of her again and again and again.

She was a work of art. A thing of beauty. One that I simultaneously wanted everyone and no one to see. It was a conflicting feeling. On one hand, I wanted everyone to know that she had been claimed by me—how pretty she looked when she was writhing on my cock. How it turned her into this carnal creature, stripping her of all her proper bullshit and reducing her to *this*—

My needy little female.

But then, the thought of anyone else seeing her like this was enough to make me want to destroy every living, breathing thing—to rip all other life to shreds and mate with her in the ashes just to prove a point of who she belonged to.

I slid my fangs from her neck as my hand clasped her cheeks, lifting her face. I pulled her attention to herself in the mirror. "Look how beautiful you look when my cock is inside of your tight little cunt, making you writhe, making you moan," I purred in her ear. "Look how beautiful you look when I'm fucking you."

"Yes," she moaned, blue eyes meeting their own reflection. She clenched around me.

Her eyelids threatened to close as her body tensed underneath mine. She cried out for her salvation as I stole it from her, wrenching her orgasm out of her with my deep, powerful thrusts. As she pulsed around me, shaking and screaming, my cock swelled and I released my seed, drowning her quivering sex.

When we both came down, I pulled out of her, her sweet little walls clenching tightly around me, refusing to give me up. I smirked at that, but my lips fell flat as I watched my seed leak out of her.

I clicked my tongue in disapproval. "Although that is a pretty sight, that simply will not do."

"What?" she asked in her dreamy contentment.

I spun her around and lifted her onto the counter.

"What are you doing?" she asked softly, her voice sultry and sedated. Curious.

I swept my fingers along her slit, gathering my cum. "Putting this back where it belongs, sweetheart." I pressed my fingers into her core, pushing my seed up as far as my fingers could reach. I worked her like that, over and over, until she was moaning again.

Until she was climaxing again, coming on my fingers.

Afterwards, I lifted her from the counter. She clung onto me like I was the last thing tethering her to this world, her body shaking, fading. I carried her towards the wall, lowering her back down on her feet.

"Death," she said, her voice soft—sedated. Her head bobbed, her eyelids threatening to close. I hadn't taken that much of her ichor and yet she seemed almost intoxicated right now—drunk on blood loss and the aftermath of her lust. The way her body was behaving reminded me of a mortal's.

How peculiar.

Gently, I lifted her head. "Feed, from me, little one." I held my wrist to her mouth in offering. "I'm not done pleasuring you yet."

Her wet tongue pressed against my arm and then her canines sunk in—the pleasure of it far exceeding the pain. My powerful blood thrummed to the surface as she began to drink. Her desperate hands swarmed to my forearm, keeping it there as her suckling became more ravenous, her energy returning to her. A toxic mixture of pride and satisfaction swarmed in my chest as I fed her my blood—something I had never experienced before until I met her. I had no idea providing for her would feel like this . . . feel *this* good.

Fuck.

My length turned to granite.

"Good girl," I grunted in praise as I captured her thigh and lifted her leg, eager to be joined with her once more.

Chapter 17
Aurelia

A slick sheen of sweat coated my body as Death had me pinned up against the bathroom wall, my one leg hitched over his hip, held there by his hand. His eyes were on mine as he weaved his wicked magic into me—it came in the form of deep, long strokes and unbroken eye contact. His pace was a dangerous, dangerous thing.

"Just like that," he rasped in his deep baritone. "Just like that." His hand was placed at the base of my neck as he dominated me so thoroughly, I knew I'd be ruined from ever wanting to ride another again.

He wasn't just having sex with me—he was *possessing* my soul.

My body trembled as I tracked towards my third orgasm. The last one felt like it had shattered me at the seams. And judging by the way I was feeling right now, this one was going to destroy me completely.

My hips rolled with his, absorbing each thrust—the contact between our skin never breaking. Not once.

"Come for me," he purred, his voice smooth leather and oxygen-stealing smoke.

His command, the *feel* of *him*—they worked in tandem, shoving me over the edge of a mountainous cliff and plunging me into the abysmal depths of oblivion.

"Death," I cried out his name, my head tipped back, my eyes rolling towards the heavens like the possessed thing I was.

"Uh-uh." His hand clasped my chin and he pulled my face to his. "Eyes on me, Kitten. I want to watch your soul leave your body as you come on my cock."

Eyes on his, I let him watch. Let him watch what he did to me as the world was swept out from underneath my feet and I floated amongst the stars.

At the same time, his hand crushed the wall beside my head, bits of shattered rock raining down to the floor. He climaxed right along with me as he angled his hips, his molten seed filling me, my greedy sex draining him of every drop.

After, when we both started to come down from the ecstasy of our joining, he said, "The next time you come, I want you to call me by my name."

"Draevon?" I asked, my voice breathy.

"No, baby girl." He grinned in such a way it made my knees wobble. "Von."

"Von," I murmured, tasting his name on my swollen lips. It was the first time I had ever said it.

. . . *It was the first time I had ever said my mate's name.*

My eyes rounded at the corners as realization hit me square and center. Days ago, I had been running away from him, and now, I couldn't get enough of him. Literally. I needed him everywhere. What had changed between then and now?

The bond. That's what.

"Pull out," I told him, pushing against his broad chest.

Thick black brows knitted in concern. "What's wrong?"

He did as I asked, the evidence of us all over his huge length, roped in thick, prominent veins, tattooed with my lips. My core throbbed at the sight of him—he was *already* getting hard again. The Blood King's appetite was insatiable.

And apparently, mine was no better.

I was tempted to jump back on him—to ride him again.

No. That *wasn't* me.

Sure, I had a healthy sexual appetite, but it had never been like this before, which meant—

"Is the bond making me *like this*?" I asked, the words rushing out of my mouth at the same time I strung the thought together.

"I mean, I like to think it's because I'm, well—" the dark god gave me an arrogant grin as he motioned to himself, his frame stacked with enough muscle and ink that I momentarily lost my train of thought, "—me. But to answer your question, yes, it is partly to do with the bond. It's not uncommon for mates to stay locked up *in* each other for weeks after the bond is forged. Sometimes months."

I crossed my arms over my chest. "So then how do I know that I even want this and it's not the bond making me like this?"

"You don't." He shrugged those big shoulders of his and then walked over to a shelf housing a stack of folded black towels. He snagged two and then strode over to the bath. The view of his muscular backside—forged for endless thrusting—spawned a dozen unholy thoughts. "Come, Little Goddess. Let me clean you."

I shoved my thoughts and his offer to the side.

"How can you be so nonchalant about this?" I snipped, chasing after him.

He hung the towels on separate hooks. "Because I knew what I was getting myself into."

"You knew what you were getting yourself into?" I repeated with a degree of question. And then it hit me like a potato sack chock-full of bricks. I stumbled backwards. "You bastard! You knew! You knew we were mates, and you consummated the bond while knowing that I had no idea. You *forced* me into this."

With feline speed, he turned to face me, his expression animalistic. "Yes, I knew. And I'd do it *again* if given the choice. If forging the bond is what keeps you locked to my side, where you have *always* belonged, then so be it. Besides . . . you seemed *more* than willing yesterday."

"I was willing to have sex with you, yes. I was not willing to pledge myself to you for all of eternity," I snarled back—my power yearning to be unleashed, my hand aching for a weapon. One that I could ram right through the deceitful jerk.

"Well, darling, it's a bit late for that," he said with enough sarcasm to last me a lifetime.

Anger shredded through me, but before I accidentally killed the big oaf, I beckoned my light to take me from here—away from this Creator-forsaken realm.

But it didn't answer.

I tried again.

Nothing. *Nothing.*

I didn't understand. The wards that surrounded the castle—the ones I had seen the first time I came here when I had asked for Von's aid in freeing the children of the Old Gods— prevented light walking. But after Von had agreed to help, I was able to light walk back to the Immortal Realm, as I was no longer considered an enemy of the realm, or so he had said at the time. But now, that part of my power was as dormant as a seed buried in frozen grounds, under five feet of snow.

Had he done something to the wards to make it so I could not light walk at all?

Von's knowing eyes met mine and he smirked. "Like I said, Little Goddess, I'll do anything to keep you." The towering predator stepped into me as he grabbed my chin roughly. Ancient, lethal power crackled as he growled dominantly, "You are *mine*."

His. I was his. My knees buckled and my core ached—

No!

It was the damn horny-ass bond again.

The insufferable bastard had just admitted that he'd neutered my ability to light walk. I held on to that, feeding it like coal to my fiery anger.

I slapped his hand away from my face as I stepped away from his intoxicating presence. "What did you do?" I demanded, forging as much venom as possible into those four words. "Did you do something to the wards?"

"It is not the wards, no. I might have been the catalyst, but I'm not entirely to blame." His arrogance was unfathomable. "Now that your divinity has found its equal, it has no desire to aid you in running from me at the moment. In fact, it has other plans."

"Meaning?" I snarled, my molars ground so tight my jaw began to ache.

He continued, "The bond increases sexual appetite between newly formed mates, and then periodically at other times. Nature has made it that way to ensure a successful breeding. That is why your divinity won't allow you to light walk away from me. And that is why your body craves mine so intensely. It is no different than a feline in heat."

"The *bond* wants me pregnant so that's why I can't light walk?" Fury, potent and raw, coursed through my veins. "Shit," I gasped, thinking of all the times we had had sex over the past so many hours. With Aurelius, I had never been able to conceive because of Von's curse, but there was one little caveat to it that I had all but forgotten these past few days—

I *could* get pregnant, but only with *his* seed.

Fuck. Fuck. Fuck.

Why had I not thought of that earlier? I knew the answer—it was the damn bond pulling the proverbial wool over my eyes.

"Is that what you have been trying to do?" I hissed.

His lips thinned. "No. Whenever I have spent my seed inside of you, it has been null and void. One of the perks of being the God of Death." His eyes darkened. "I will never treat you like breeding stock, Little Goddess. I am *not* him."

If he thought that was enough to redeem himself, he was sorely mistaken.

"Says the deceitful male who forged the bond between us and took *my* choice away. No, you might not be him, but there are similarities." Done with this conversation, I strode out of the bathing room.

Death followed. "Where are you going?"

"I'm getting away from you," I snarled over my bare shoulder. "Clothe me."

"Good luck with that," he said, not bothering to do as I requested.

I raised my hand, flipped my middle finger at him, and then walked out the door into the hallway, making sure to slam it behind me. At the same time, a simple but elegant black dress wrapped around my body, trailing to the floor. It was a lovely bit of black silk that hugged my curves and plunged perilously low between my breasts—which were no longer smeared with my ichor.

Party tricks, indeed.

I took a step forward and walked straight into a wall of unyielding steel.

"Leave me alone!" I shoved against Von.

Except, it *wasn't* him.

It was the smoke-yielding, pierced version of him—Folkoln.

Although I didn't know him, I knew *of* him, at least what gossip had trickled through the rumor mill. None of which painted him in a very good light. People feared him just as much as they feared his brother.

Folkoln had one hand tucked in his pocket and a bottle in the other. He leaned in, inhaled a deep breath, and then he flashed his sparkling-white canines at me like a dog with a bone. "Have you tired of my brother so soon, little dove?" His sinister grin grew. "Perhaps you'd like something a bit more . . . chaotic."

"Ugh," I said, repulsed—*did he just sniff me*? I darted around him.

"Ouch," he snickered.

I didn't bother to wait for him to say something else as I raced down the hallway, eager to get away from Von and his pierced lookalike.

Chapter 18

Von

Cursing under my breath, I clothed myself and swung the door open, finding my smirking brother standing on the other side.

"You two seem to be getting off to a good start," he snarked, shoving a clear glass bottle against my chest as he strolled past me and into my private chambers as if he owned the damn place. The insolent bastard.

Reminded me of myself.

"Not exactly," I said, fighting the bond and its incessant need to be near her. That pull had gotten even worse now that we were mated. It was like a chain wrapped around my ankle from me to her—the further she got, the more it pulled. Sighing to myself, I made the split-second decision to let my little runaway have a head start; it wasn't like she would get very far anyway. Not with the bond working against her, my ink on her skin, and my scent all over her—*in* her.

The latter I had made sure of.

Not just so that I could find her, but so any curious immortals who got any unwise ideas would know who she belonged to. I'd marked her with my seed. And I planned to do it every chance I got like the territorial asshole I was.

I pulled my thoughts from her and pushed them on to the bottle, surveying the color of the spirits inside. The amber liquid was a hairsbreadth darker than it usually was. To the human eye, the difference would be undetectable, but to mine, it stuck out like a sore thumb.

I turned around, facing my brother. I raised the bottle and asked, "What is this?"

He shoved his hand in his pocket, his smirk growing. "A gift for the happy couple."

"That wasn't what I was asking." My expression remained flat. "If you have come here to be a leech, you can see yourself out."

"Relax, brother, I'm just screwing with you. Also, I spent the morning feeding off Saphira's emotions so—" he patted his stomach, "—I'm full. By the way, she's pissed about you not going through with the plan. Come to think of it, I don't think I've ever seen her this angry."

The plan. To use the Crown of Thorns to end Aurelia's immortal life, thus freeing me of the risk to mine. It had been Saphira's idea, and for a moment, I had considered it.

Now? The thought of going through with it curdled the contents in my stomach.

"You should probably go speak with her," Folkoln tacked on.

I raised a lone brow. "Do you think it would do any good?"

"Probably not." His broad shoulders bobbed. "But it might be worth a try."

I sighed.

If anyone possessed the ability to stay stuck on something for an eternity, it was Saphira. Navigating her persistence would be a challenge, one I'd have to figure out sooner rather than later.

I walked over to the private bar—forged of black stone and darkly stained wood. Shelves, full of liquor, lined the wall behind it. Six tall stools sat in front, specially made for my long legs. Sitting in squatty-ass stools got old real fast when you were my height.

Folkoln started, "I'm going to be away in the Living Realm for a while. I quite enjoyed my time there during the Immortal War, but the taverns they have are atrocious, so I'm going to open a string of new ones just like Hard Spirits."

I plucked two glasses that were turned over, neatly stacked on top of a clean cloth.

"The God of Life is going to be pissed when he finds out you are setting up taverns in his realm," I said, smirking. Aurelius would see it for what it was—a royal fuck you.

"I'm counting on it," Folkoln stated with a twisted grin as he walked over and slid onto one of the stools.

"How long do you plan to be gone?" I popped the cork on the bottle and poured a few fingers' worth inside the glasses.

"That's a good question," he said. "It depends how much time it takes to get permits and build the structures, but I plan to work around the clock until the taverns are finished. I'll pop back in every once in a while to check on Hard Spirits, but my primary focus will be on getting the new establishments up and running."

I nodded and slid one glass across the bar top, over to Folkoln.

"Thanks," he said, nodding once. "Looks like the mating bond was successful. Your eyes have changed."

"They have." I picked up my glass.

He smirked. "They remind me of Saph's now."

I rolled my eyes and he laughed.

Bringing the rim to my nose, I breathed in the spirits. Like the color, the scent was off too.

"Do you remember that one experimental batch you made a few summers back?" Folkoln asked.

Over the centuries, I'd made *a lot* of barrels, and drank myself to oblivion on a good portion of them. They all tended to blur together. "Not really."

"I figured. I found this barrel tucked *way* in the back, covered in a few decades' worth of dust. You know me—I'm willing to try anything once—so I tapped into it."

"And?"

"Drink up and see for yourself." He clinked his cup against mine. "To forgotten barrels and pissed-off females."

"Creator have mercy on us all." I shot the glass back.

Chapter 19

Aurelia

I ran my fingertips over the cool, obsidian walls, my bare feet padding down the length of black rug, embossed with intricate swirls of silver. It stretched out before me, spanning the entire corridor from end to end. Dozens of banners made from a heavy, luxurious-looking cloth hung on either side of the hall, twinning one another in placement. A matching emblem—a raven standing on top of a skull—was stitched into each banner. Black metal torches, forged to look like skeleton hands, lit the hallway. A purple flame burned in them, tinting the dark walls a glowing amethyst.

Wandering castle hallways was something I had grown rather used to over the years. Following my creation, when I was lovesick for

Aurelius, I used to do it in hopes that I would be able to catch a glimpse of him during his back-to-back meetings or constant travels. Knowing that he was working hard for the good of the realms, I never pried about his whereabouts or insisted that he spend more time with me. Instead, I roamed the halls like a ghost, silently longing for him, keeping my loneliness to myself so that he could be a good king.

I was doing my duty.

Or so I blindly believed.

But now, I realized how stupid I had been.

Aurelius had never loved me; he loved the idea of me. I fed his ego. Nothing more. Nothing less.

When I reached the end of the hall, I was granted a few options—I could either go to the left or the right, or I could take the coil of tightly winding stairs straight ahead of me.

Something tugged—*the bond* tugged—begging me to forget the other options and return to *him*.

Although the bond's pull was strong, my anger was stronger.

"Stairs it is," I said to the ghosts of this place.

I cursed the bond and Von the whole way down.

The sound of bubbling, sputtering pots, light conversation, and the rhythmic tapping of knives against cutting boards gathered my attention. The slight acidic aroma of fermenting dough and savory, stewing meats followed shortly after.

My mouth watered and my stomach grumbled.

That was one more thing I had in common with the mortals—I

hungered frequently, unlike my immortal counterparts who could go months without eating. Not me. A day or two without food not only made me ready to gnaw my arm off, but it also left me in a sour mood.

Following the allure of the delicious smells, I quickly tracked ahead.

Stepping into the huge kitchen, I was greeted by a waft of heat and delicious spices, and the upturn of a few heads. Some offered me a warm smile or a nod before they went back to what they were doing—chopping, mixing, or kneading, while chatting with their neighbors. Rows of tables sat beside each other, providing the large kitchen with ample preparation space. Stools lined the tables, about a quarter of them occupied by the kitchen staff.

The hearth, large enough to fit a small carriage in, was placed in the center of the far wall. Two people stood in front of it, one of them stirring a bubbling pot, while the other preheated a cast-iron griddle.

"Excuse me, lass," wheezed an elderly male from behind me—his tone heavily accented in a string of soft vowels and hardened consonants.

I glanced over my shoulder, finding four tiers of crates, a pair of skinny legs, and a set of weary eyes peeking around them.

"Sorry," I apologized, quickly stepping out of his way.

"Dinna worry," he said, his shaky legs carrying him ahead. Reaching the end of the table, he dropped the crates on top, a loud *thunk* sounding in the process. I guessed him to be somewhere in his seventies, but considering he was down here, who knew how old he truly was.

A sturdy-looking woman, who had been drizzling chocolate on some type of puffy, golden pastry, stopped what she was doing and hurried over. “Is that all the apples ye were able to get?” she huffed at the man, her hands dissolving in the wealth of her hips. She possessed the same accent as him, which made me wonder if they had been born in the same lands in the Living Realm before their souls were brought here to live out their afterlife.

“Creator’s sake, lass, what do ye mean *is that all*? I nearly blew my back out carryin’ those blasted crates in,” he declared, his hand reaching behind him, massaging away.

“Well,” she sighed, “I reckon they’ll have to do.”

“Aye, I sure hope so,” he said as he sat down on one of the stools.

“It’ll be your hide if they are no’ enough, not mine,” she teased him. “Maria, Rosa, can ye two lasses work on peeling these?” she spoke to two girls who were seated at a table, dicing vegetables—the scars on their cutting boards telling of the many, many meals prepared on them.

“Yes,” one replied.

At the same time the other one said, “Of course.”

“Very good. Ye can pull Rosalia from cellar stockin’ duties if ye need an extra hand,” the woman said.

“Okay,” one of the girls responded pleasantly as she reached for the top crate. With some difficulty, she carried it, waddling her way over to the table like a woman who was nine months pregnant. The other girl grabbed the next one. She didn't fare much better.

The woman watched them for a moment, before she turned back to the man and asked, "Have ye eaten yet today?"

"Nay." He shook his head.

She patted his hand. "I'll get ye a bite then." Kind blue eyes swung up to meet mine, time-stitched crow's feet webbed at the sides. "D'ye want somethin' to eat as well, dear? Ye have the look of hunger in your eyes."

I nodded, my voice a bit croaky as I said, "That would be wonderful. Thank you."

She gestured to the seat across from the man. "Please have a seat, then. I'll be a few moments as the stew isna done yet. I can assure ye'll be in good company with Early here."

Early gave me a wink and motioned for me to come sit.

And so, I did.

"I dinna reckon I've seen your face before," Early said as I slid onto the stool across from him while the kind woman headed off to fetch us some food. "Face like yours—" he nodded, "—I'd be sure to remember it." His eyes grew wide. "Ah, sorry, lass. I dinna mean for that to come across any type of way. It's just that ye are very bonny."

"Thank you," I said, shrugging softly. "A compliment is always nice to hear."

He smiled at that. "Do ye have a name, miss?"

I opened my mouth to tell him, but then I paused. I paused because my name didn't really feel like my name anymore. Aurelius had given it to me on the day I was made, but like the heart beating in my chest, it was of him, not of me.

And so, I looked at Early and said, "You know, I'm not entirely sure I do anymore."

He gave me a knowing look. "Aye, I understand. Sometimes we outgrow the names that were given to us. My parents didna call me Early, but the folks around these parts know me as such. Never on time, but always Early." He gave me another wink.

A soft laugh fell from my lips. "Well, it's a pleasure to meet you, Early." I extended my hand over the table.

He took it and I had to do everything within my power not to jerk out of his soft grasp. Because his hand was not made of flesh, but cold, cold bone. Although it took me by surprise, it was not jarring. Because I had felt another hand like that once before—it belonged to the captain of the floating boat that transported people to this castle.

He gave my hand a gentle shake. "As it's a pleasure to meet ye as well, Snow."

"Snow?" I asked warmly as I retracted my arm, the feel of his bony fingers lingering on my skin.

He tapped the small remnants of hair that clung to the sides of his head. "Reminds me of the color of the snow in the Livin' Realm, unlike the black stuff that falls here." A reminiscent smile tugged at his lips.

"Ah, I see," I replied, thinking for a moment. "Do you miss it?"

He shot me a confused look.

"The Living Realm."

He shook his head. "Not the Livin' Realm itself, nay. The people though, I do. Although so many years have passed, I doubt they are even there anymore." He nodded to the kind woman who had offered me food. She was standing at the hearth, unloading a cutting board full of vegetables into a bubbling pot. "Davina, over there, is one of the only people I know from the Livin' Realm. We grew up together."

That explained the matching accents.

"She seems very kind."

"Aye, she is."

"So, then—" I flicked my eyes to Davina, "—are you two together?"

"Goodness, nay. We're just friends." He paused for a moment, the light in his eyes fading. "My wife passed before me, but when I showed up here, I couldna find her. She's in a different tier in the Spirit Realm."

Ah yes, I had heard of the different tiers that people were sorted into, based on how they acted in the Living Realm.

"Why don't you request to be placed in her tier? So that you two can be reunited?"

"Och, I have tried. Every Monday for the last thirty years, I have stood outside the throne room, hopin' to see the king or one of his advisors so that I can put in my request. But every time, I'm turned away."

"The God of Death won't approve your request?"

"That's not the problem. Nay, it's that there are so many people waitin' to put their own request in that they end up closin' the doors before I can get to the front of the line." Early's voice became hoarse. "What I wouldna do to be reunited with her. She was the love of my life. Still is."

"I might be able to help you," I said, watching as a young girl came over to us with a tray in her hands. On it sat a few cups, a glass teapot, cream, and sugar.

"Would either of you like a cup of tea?" she asked, her voice sweet and bubbly.

"Please," I answered.

Early nodded. "Tea would be wonderful. Thank ye, lass."

The girl placed the tray on the table, metal sounding against stone.

As she dished the cups out to us, Early looked at me. "I appreciate the offer, truly, I do. I dinna mean to sound ungrateful or rude, but I've done everythin' I can to get back to her without any luck so how are ye goin' to help me?"

The girl began to pour the tea into my cup. As it filled, I looked up to Early and said, "I'm going to get you a private audience with the God of Death."

The only downside about my promise? It meant I had to talk to the bastard.

Chapter 20

Von

After we'd emptied the bottle and Folkoln left, I gave in to the aggravating chain yanking on my ankle—the damn bond and stubborn female were going to be the end of me. I tracked her to one of the castle's five kitchens, but just before I walked in, my foot paused mid-step—

Aurelia was *laughing.*

It was rich and breathy. Infectious. I couldn't help but smile.

I needed to see for myself . . . see what my mate looked like when she was laughing. I cloaked myself in my shadows and stepped inside the kitchen—feeling an immediate change in temperature due to the continuously lit hearth, steaming pots, and cooking foods.

Aurelia was sitting at one of the many tables, an empty plate and bowl resting before her. She clapped her long, elegant fingers together. An elderly looking man with blue-pale skin sat across from her. He waved his arms around in the air, telling some grand story. But whatever it was about was lost to me, because all I could hear was her beautiful, decadent laughter.

When the man finished his tale and she began to dab at the tears gathered on her lower lash line with the back of her finger, I wanted to materialize and command the old man to tell another story just so I could hear her laughter again.

I wondered what it would be like to hear her laugh *like that* for me.

Leaning against the wall, I watched her. Just as I had done countless times before when I stood outside her bedchamber's windows, watching as she brushed her hair while she overlooked her orchard. She had been so proud of it, of all that she had created. And what had that prick Aurelius done with something she took so much pride in?

He had gone and cut down every one of her trees.

As much as I wanted to rip his throat out for hurting her so deeply, his actions were the catalyst that drove her into my open, waiting arms. Now she was in *my* castle, not his—where she belonged.

A woman who was covered in vicious burn marks walked over to the table, her scars telling me that fire had most likely been her end. She began to gather the empty plates and bowls while asking in her heavily accented voice, "Can I get ye two another bowl of stew? Perhaps another biscuit?"

The man who sat across from Aurelia shook his head. "Thank you, Davina, but I canna have another nip. Ye outdo yourself every time."

I eyed his blue, pale skin—

Sailor's Plague.

It became rampant on ships about a century ago, spreading quickly through contaminated drinking water. It made the mortals unable to control their bowels. As their bodies became racked with dehydration, their blood would thicken, thus starving the infected of oxygen and turning their skin a sickly blue. It wasn't uncommon for them to be dead by nightfall. Although the plague became dominant on ships, it soon spread inland, claiming even more lives.

The Da'Nu had risen rather impressively during that period, although it wasn't nearly as bad during the Death Plague. That one had delivered me thousands of souls, the worst plague in mortal history. I felt a tinge insulted when I learned they had named the sickness after me. If I wanted to take mortal lives, I could rack up a tally much higher than some silly little plague ever could.

When the Sailor's Plague ended, the mortals needed someone to blame, and so they placed it on the sailors. The Goddess of Sickness had rolled her eyes at that and decided to release a new virus for good measure.

The woman—Davina—turned to Aurelia and asked, "And how

about ye, love? Can I get ye anythin' else?"

Aurelia's eyes darted to the empty bowl, thinking over the woman's offer.

Davina chuckled, a joyful, hearty sound. "A blind person could see ye've still got the look of hunger in ye eyes. My goodness, lass, how long has it been since ye ate last? Never mind that, I'll fetch ye another bowl and a biscuit."

My lips thinned—

I certainly was not blind, and yet, I had not seen that my mate was . . . *hungry*. My ego felt a bit wounded by that. It was a strange feeling. One I didn't particularly care for.

Aurelia was an anomaly. I had fed her my blood a few hours ago, and yet she was still hungry . . . for food, it would seem. Once again, her body was proving itself to be more mortal than immortal. Such a curiosity, my mate.

Perhaps that was why she was quick to anger before.

She certainly seemed to be in better spirits now.

Aurelia thanked Davina. The woman gave her a warm smile, gathered the remaining dishes on her tray, and then hurried over to one of the sinks. It didn't take very long for Aurelia and Early to strike up another conversation. Occasionally, something he said would bring a twist to her lips and she'd bless him with a smile.

I was both thankful for the old man and jealous of him. Thankful that his stories could make her laugh, jealous that I wasn't the one earning her breathtaking smiles. Although I had known Aurelia for centuries, there was so much about her that I had left to discover. It was something I could easily commit myself to, because she was the other half of my soul. The female I had waited millennia for.

It didn't take very long for Davina to return. She unloaded a bowl of steaming stew and a plate with a lightly browned biscuit from her tray, setting them before Aurelia.

"Thank you," she said, smiling.

"Of course," Davina replied before she returned to her duties.

Then, I watched as my future queen's poised and perfect manners were abandoned, all in the name of food. She inhaled, and I mean fucking inhaled it. And when I was certain she was done, she used her thumb to clean up the breadcrumbs, popping it in her mouth and sucking it clean.

A grin touched my lips—I'd found her weakness.

Food.

After Aurelia said her goodbyes, she stepped out of the kitchen and into the hallway. Hidden in my umbra, I stood behind her, her body a breath from mine. My fingers itched at my side, tempted to reach for her, to drag my knuckles down her arm and watch her responsive skin prickle in my wake.

She glanced to her left, to the stairwell that would take her back to my bedchambers, and then to her right, to a path that would lead her further away. Head swiveling, she looked back to the stairs and my breath faltered—was my headstrong little female thinking of returning to me?

As if the question had been spoken out loud, she shook her head and went the other direction.

A muscle kicked in my jaw as I ground my molars together. Headstrong *indeed.*

I stalked after her.

She tossed her head over her shoulder. "I know you're there." Her voice could have rivalled the throes of winter—it was a bitter, bitter cold. The kind that ate away at one's nerves and turned their skin a deathly purplish black.

My shadows peeled away as I stepped through them. "How did you know?"

"The bond has relaxed. It does not pull like it did before," she answered, her long legs keeping up their quick pace. "So I figured your bastard self had to be close."

"Clever goddess," I mused.

"Not clever enough to stop being tricked by you," she snarled, her sourness an emotion I could taste on my tongue.

Ah yes, I had heard of that, too, that as mates we could feel each other's emotions when they were running high. And right now, hers were being shoved down my throat. That was going to take some getting used to.

"I did not trick you," I stated. "I claimed what *belongs* to me."

Her feet came to a sudden stop as her rage barreled into me like a wall of flame chewing through a buffet of dead bushes. That was all the warning I had before she turned around and thundered towards me, her hair defying gravity as it swirled around her.

"I am not an object to be claimed!" she shouted. Her voice was like a whip, striking against the castle walls. And although she had not struck me, it felt like she had. This anger of hers, it was visceral, raw, and it cut deep.

I *knew* that she was not an object, nor did I view her like one.

That was not what I had meant. She belonged to me, just as I belonged to her. We were two halves of the same star, finally returned to one another after centuries apart. We were inevitable. And yet, the idea of it, it made her feel as if she were an object. Something to be placed on a shelf and admired.

Because that's what the fucker had done to her.

I didn't know the entirety of what went on between her and Aurelius, but I knew enough about how he treated her. About the rigid clothes he made her wear and the limited love he showed her. How he made her act like someone she was not. That was all she had known, and now her understanding of belonging to someone had been severely damaged for it.

My gaze softened. "Is that how *he* made you feel?" I asked, although I already held the answer.

Her mouth popped open, and then it clamped shut. She shook her head. "I'm not having this conversation with you."

When she went to turn around, to walk away, I grabbed her arm and pulled her back towards me. “Ah, ah, ah, love.” I snatched her chin, angling her face to mine. “You can run from things all you like, but eventually, they will catch up with you.”

She tore her jaw from my fingers. “You, of all people, do not get to give me advice.”

“If not me, then *who,* exactly?” I challenged as I peered down at the stubborn little creature. “Because the last time I checked, I’m the only soul in the entire Three Realms who gives a damn about you.”

“Fuck you!” she growled as her hands shot for my face. Before she connected, I caught her wrists and swung her so that her back was against the wall. She landed with a soft *thud*, her pretty pink lips parting as the air escaped from her lungs. I pressed her arms beside her head, keeping her pinned there. The heat of her body mingled with mine, electricity shooting between the two of us in a storm of anger and . . .

I could taste something sweet and crisp blooming on my tongue.

It tasted just like an apple—just like her.

This was what her lust tasted like.

Her words repeated in my mind, *Fuck you.*

I couldn’t help myself.

“Do I look cheap?” I asked, the intensity of her desire drawing my lips just above hers. “At least buy me dinner first.”

She glared daggers at me.

Then her lips smashed into mine.

Chapter 21

Aurelia

My lips crashed against his as his body pressed against mine, keeping me firmly locked against the glass-like wall as he feasted on my lips. His tongue dipped in, swiping around my mouth as if he were trying to claim every inch of it.

I bit down on the strong, muscular organ as a bolt of anger shot through my lust. A sweet, metallic flavor bloomed on my tongue, and my eyes rolled back at the taste of it—of him. Von's blood was powerful. *Incredible.* Like a forbidden fine wine, aged to perfection. Saliva pooled in my mouth—I *needed* more.

Von released my wrists and my eager fingers swam around his torso, tracing the hardness of his muscles, mapping out his potent, thrumming veins.

He pulled his tongue from my mouth, his shadows twisting around us, taking us back to his dark, dimly lit chambers. Icy metal bit into my jaw as he tipped my face to his. "Do you like the taste of me in your mouth?"

I nodded, my eyelids at half mast, drunk on my arousal and the taste of him.

His hand lowered from my jaw, his pointer finger tracing downwards, between my breasts, down my torso, stopping at my sex. He played with the fabric there, black lashes lowering as he looked down. "And what about when I'm deep in here?"

"Yes," I rasped, my voice suddenly parched. I rolled my hips, begging him to just touch me. My actions and my emotions were all over the place, and I knew it was because of the bond, but right now, I didn't care. Logic and anger be damned.

"Then you best be a good girl and quit running from your problems," he said, dropping the fabric and pulling away from me.

I gaped. Flat out gaped.

My disbelieving eyes watched as he turned his back to me and started for the bar area.

"If you aren't going to have sex with me, then why did you bring me back here?" I snarled angrily, my toes nipping at the backs of his boots, stopping when he went behind the bar.

"Because you have issues you need to work through—" he said while his fingers walked over the tops of various sized bottles and decanters, lined on a glass shelf anchored to the wall, "—and the hallway didn't seem like a good place for us to do that."

Us? He was delirious if he thought I was going to confide in him.

He selected a sizable bottle of spirits and began to walk towards the seating area, the epitome of smug arrogance rolling off him in heady waves.

In a split-second decision, I grabbed the bottle from him before he passed by me.

His chuckling reply only irked me further—Creator above, he was intolerable. If anyone was going to need a drink, it was me. I popped the cork, brought the cool glass against my lips, and tipped the bottle back.

Fire. Vicious, horrific fire scorched my mouth, sending my tastebuds screaming.

I blew out the liquid in a spray of amber mist, sputtering and coughing. "What in the Creator's name *is* that?" I gasped, wiping at my mouth.

He let out a low chuckle. "Seventh Tier Whiskey. It's got *a bit* of a burn to it, doesn't it?"

"*A bit*?" I bellowed. One brow quirked. "Why is it called that?"

"Because the Seventh Tier is made entirely of flame." He snatched the bottle from my hand, glanced at the floor, and in a twist of his wrist, he'd cleaned up my mess. He sauntered over to the sitting area and sat on the settee. Shining green eyes met mine. "Tell me something. Your body lacks the ability to heal itself, your teeth took hundreds of years to elongate for the first time, you have a ravenous appetite much like the mortals, and you require sleep *every* night. What else does your divinity lack?"

That got me and my inner goddess to glare daggers at him.

The left corner of his mouth shifted upwards as he threw his muscular, inked arm over the back of the settee, his free hand still holding the bottle. There was that unbridled arrogance again.

Unwilling to play his big cat, little mouse games, I decided not to answer.

"Alright, if you won't bite on that, what will you bite on? Silly me, I suppose I already know the answer to that." He parted his lips and rolled his tongue against the back of his teeth, drawing emphasis to it—the look was highly seductive. I knew what he was referring to—the kiss we had just shared in the hallway, when his tongue had been invading my mouth and I'd bit it.

He was *taunting* me.

Goddess Divine, I wanted to throttle him—

And climb on his lap and ride the big boy like a Clydesdale stallion.

An ache formed between my legs, the lady equivalent of blue balls beginning to take hold. Damn him and the blasted bond. *The bond . . .*

It affected him the same way it affected me.

A potent thought occurred, spilling like a bottle of dye, staining my thoughts. Perhaps I should play his game after all.

I walked over to him, his eyes watching my every move. I lifted my dress and crawled on top of him, lowering myself strategically on his prominent rock-hard bulge. I bit my bottom lip then slowly released it. "Silly me . . . I'm not wearing any underwear."

When I felt his length twitch beneath me, I knew I was on the right track—for having sex? Really? Was that the goal, here?

The bond assured me, yes, yes it was.

You could hate someone and still want them at the same time, and the way he looked right now, sitting there with that seductive *I own all I survey* look that belonged solely to him, well, it made me want to grab his head, shove his face down, and drown the asshole between my thighs.

His black shirt fit him like a second skin, his sleeves rolled back, exposing the inky markings on his forearms. Forearms that were forged from steely muscle and iron bone, and roped with thick, masculine veins. It was a hint at what lingered beneath the rest of his clothes—of that powerful warrior's body, built to rule anything he touched.

And right now, his fingers were on me.

Drawing irregular, light shapes on my inner thigh, making my center pulse with every electrifying graze of his rings. His touch was like ice against my skin, making me shiver with need.

"Did *he* ever touch you like this?" he asked, his voice throaty. Deep. Intimate.

I eyed him suspiciously—was he trying to get me to talk about

Aurelius or was this some dominant male dirty-talk thing? There was only one way to find out . . .

"In the beginning, he did." I draped my arms over his broad shoulders, using him to stabilize me.

"And then?"

"He quit."

His fingers ran up the length of my thigh, drifting under my bunched dress which pooled around my hips—he was *so close* now.

"Why do you think he stopped?" he asked.

When I didn't respond, Von stilled his hand.

I growled, flashing my teeth like some desperate, deranged animal.

As soon as I heard myself, I cut the sound off. I sucked in my pressed lips, clamping them shut with my teeth. *Who was I?*

Amusement lit his eyes. "I'll continue when you answer my question."

Well, that answered that. He was using his touch to pry my past out of me. Something I had no desire in discussing. *Especially* with him.

Huffing, I untangled myself from him and stood up.

"Running again, Kitten?" he purred darkly.

I rolled my eyes, turned away from him, and strode over to the bar. I rifled through the various bottles, popping corks and sniffing the contents—some smelled so potent, I swear my nostril hairs curled up and died. When I finally found one that didn't smell like it would cause necrosis of my insides, I took it with me over to the wingback chair and plopped in it. I crossed my legs and glared at Von.

He smirked. “Making yourself at home, are you?”

“Hardly,” I grumbled. “I am merely making the most out of a bad situation.” I brought the top of the bottle to my lips, tasting the fruity contents—much better than the molten acid he was drinking. The wine sloshed inside the bottle as I set it down on the floor, a light *clink* sounding.

“Oh, come now, is it all that terrible?” Von asked, one black brow raising—the one with the slit in it.

“Horrible,” I replied flatly.

“And yet you sit here, in my company, drinking my alcohol. If you find all of this so abhorrent, why haven’t you tried to leave yet?”

“You said it yourself—the bond prevents me from light walking.” I tossed the quick answer at him, hoping he wouldn’t press any further.

Of course, the persistent male wasn’t finished. “You have feet for walking, wings for flying, yes? Those seem like two reasonable options.”

I pulled my gaze from his, glancing towards the twin glass doors that led out onto the balcony. Beyond them, a sky of amethyst sprawled for miles.

My heart stumbled a tick.

“What’s that about?” he asked, his gaze so piercing I felt like he was taking a dagger to my chest, cutting me open, and peering at my insides. *No one* should be able to look at anyone like that.

"Nothing," I said.

"It was definitely something."

I narrowed my eyes at him.

He shot me a look, as if to say *I'm waiting*.

I decided to ignore his question and said, "I have a favor to ask of you."

"Pray tell, little one."

"I met a man in the kitchen today. He has been split up from his wife for many years and has tried to attend your throne meetings to request to be moved to his wife's tier but has never been successful. Will you help him?"

Von thought it over for a moment, before he said, "I will."

I was surprised by that, how easily he agreed.

"On one condition."

Ah, there *it* was.

"What is it?" I asked, already disliking where this was going.

"Tell me what that little flicker of sadness was about." There was that slice-open-and-inspect-your-insides look again.

"Fine," I sighed. "You asked me why I haven't tried to leave. It's clear that the bond demands we be close to one another so if I were to run, you'd feel it. Considering you have made it abundantly clear that you will bring me back here, running seems like a waste of both my time and yours. Which means I'm stuck here, which makes me sad."

"Although that is an answer, it is not the one I'm looking for and you know it," Von said. "Also, you are a terrible liar. Now fess up. Or else I'll come over there and use my tongue to pry the answer out of you." He gave a wicked smirk.

"You're unbelievable," I growled, pretending his words didn't make me feel like my bones were turning to jelly.

"You're evading," he stated.

Indeed, I was.

"Little Goddess."

Creator above, he was pushy.

"I don't have a full set of wings, okay?" I blurted out. My proud shoulders caved, as if the façade of pretending to be whole had been holding them up all this time.

He was quiet for a moment. Thinking. And then he said, "That's why when I took you from the battlefield, you didn't fly away . . . you couldn't."

"Look, I don't need your pity," I said, standing up, taking the bottle with me.

"I wouldn't do you the disservice," he answered in his deep, dark tone, fixing his eyes resolutely on the far wall.

"Good." I was eager to move on from this topic. "So then, now that I've told you, will you help Early?"

"I will. But you have to do one more thing for me."

My brows collided. "You said *one* condition."

"I lied." He raised his hand, swirling his tattooed finger, the one with a "k" on it, signaling for me to turn. "Show me."

I stared at him. I had never shown *anyone* my wings before.

For most of my life, I thought I didn't have any. I simply chalked it up as one more thing that made me incomplete—adding it to the list. But then one day, when I was in my orchard, standing on the top rung of a ladder and reaching for an apple, the ladder tipped, and I fell. Although it was not a far fall, it was enough to brush the air against my back, instinctually conjuring forth my wings. Although they somewhat cushioned my fall, I'll never forget that feeling of reaching behind me—of feeling the silky soft feathers on one side, and nothing but bones on the other. Lightweight and sturdy, but featherless. Useless.

Incomplete.

Von sat there, waiting.

"Fine," I sighed. "But no more conditions. You do what we agreed to—you help Early."

"Deal," he said.

I squinted at him, at *that* word. It was the whole reason I was here.

He smirked, pleased with himself and his god tier of mass fuckery. Then he swirled his finger once more.

Unwillingly, I turned around. Drawing a deep, deep breath, I revealed my wings, pushing them all the way out—feeling that strange, unfamiliar tingle throughout them—like a foot gone to sleep. I hadn't stretched them in years. I spanned the one wing, full of white, glorious feathers—smooth and uniform and perfect. Then the other decrepit one—sad and useless.

Throughout the decades, I had shed a great deal of tears over my incomplete wings, but time dampened emotions, and now, I mostly felt numb towards them. The only time I felt that immense sadness return was when I looked to the sky and was reminded that I would never know what it was like to fly. I would never feel the wind beneath my wings, guiding me higher in a sea of azure.

I felt Von's dark shadow fall over me, then his fingers as they hovered over the wing made of bones. Not enough to touch, but enough that I could feel the static flowing between us—a steady, intimate thrum of power and warmth. It caused a shiver to sink beneath my skin, skittering across my bones.

"I'm well aware it's quite ugly," I said, staring at a random spot on the rug as I bathed in my numbness.

"On the contrary, I find it quite sexy," he mused, his hand drifting slowly, as if he were memorizing every detail.

"Says the God of Death," I quipped flatly.

Von chuckled, but it didn't seem sincere. It seemed like charity, doled out for me in my time of vulnerability.

Some time passed and then he said, "You and I are like yin and yang—complete opposites, forged to balance one another, to complete the cycles of life and death. But just as yin has a bit of yang in it, yang also has a bit of yin. I believe your wing is like this because of your connection to me. It is that small part of me that has been instilled in you."

I didn't exactly know what to make of all that. It was a theory, at least. One I could dive deeper into, but right now, I craved lighter conversation. So I asked with a teasing smile, "If that is so, then what part of me are you carrying around with you? A stray white hair in that raven mane of yours, perhaps?"

He let out a low chuckle, then said, "No white hairs, but that does give me an idea—"

On my feathered wing, I felt a quick, sharp sting, like a hair being plucked.

My wings snapped back into hiding as I turned around and hissed at him, "What was that for?"

"Souvenir," he stated as he studied a small, white feather—*my* feather—his thumb and forefinger pinching the quill. He conjured a tie, grabbed a tendril of his long, black hair, and secured the feather in place at the end. Upon his canvas of black clothes and swirls of ink, it stood out like a sore thumb.

"*Killers* collect souvenirs," I pointed out.

He smirked. "Now you're catching on."

Chapter 22

Aurelia

Later that night, I sat at the far end of a long table in a massive, enchanting dining hall. Three-quarters of the room were surrounded by tall, ominous windows, giving view to the night sky outside, twinkling with brilliant, shimmering stars. The gothic chamber was sparsely furnished other than the floor candelabras and banners that were placed throughout. Pillar candles in a variety of sizes were placed down the length of the table, their wicks emitting a purple flame.

Von sat at the other end, a silver goblet locked in his ringed fingers—his eyes on me. *Always* on me.

I cracked a peanut into my palm. Two nuts fell out and I tossed them into my mouth. I discarded the shell in the small bowl sitting before me, full of peanut remains and that weird brown papery stuff that the nuts grew in—the stuff that got stuck in the back of your throat if you swallowed it funny.

I wasn't entirely sure why I was eating. It wasn't like I was hungry.

A rather impressively sized dinner had been delivered not too long ago—silver platters full of savory meats, steamed vegetables, and baked breads dripping with herb butter. It was a mouthwatering spread. Happily, I dished up a plate and dug in. The entire time, Von had seemed interested in watching me eat more than anything. So I made a good show of it, just to taunt him—making all the *mmm* noises and licking all my fingers in the process.

Why did I do it?

Earlier, he had left me sexually frustrated when I wouldn't open up to him about Aurelius, so it felt fitting that I returned the favor. In truth, I liked toying with him. It gave me some sort of satisfaction, knowing that the mere swipe of my tongue over my fingers was enough to drive the most powerful god in all Three Realms wild with lust.

Apart from our games of cat and mouse, I think a small part of me was beginning to accept that I was going to be stuck in this realm for the foreseeable future, so I reasoned I might as well make myself comfortable . . .

"If I am to stay here, then I would appreciate my own chambers,"

I said, pushing the peanut bowl away from me.

"No," he replied, without giving my request any thought.

"No?" I repeated incredulously. "It's not like I'm asking for anything big. You *own* the castle, *don't you*?"

"I do, but the answer is still no." He leaned back in his chair, the candlelight painting him a hundred shades of wicked. A hauntingly beautiful nightmare brought to life. His sleeves were rolled back, exposing the black ink etched into his tanned skin. Heavy, chiseled muscle carved out his powerful forearms—forearms that could crush a man's head like a watermelon *or* keep my legs pried wide open as his tongue wrote his dark stories between my legs.

Focus, I reminded myself.

I shoved the intrusive thought to the side, along with the bond, and said, "Why are you being so stubborn about this?"

"It's all quite simple really." He set down the goblet, his piercing green eyes flicking to mine. "I could give you a chamber of your own, but it would be a waste of both my time and yours, because every night, I will have you in my bed."

His proclamation stole the air from my lungs. *Damn him.*

I wet my lips. "But it is customary for royals to have their own bedchambers." At least, that's what Aurelius had told me when I found out he had private chambers of his own.

"That is a ridiculous custom, forged by pathetic males who make it a sport to cheat on their partners." A breath later, I could feel the dark god standing behind my chair, his shadows breaking off from him, licking at my skin. He lifted my chin, angling my face to his. "I have been a bachelor all my life, but now that you are here, I have no desire to share my chambers with anyone else but you, Little Goddess."

I should be angry with him, for denying my request, but I failed to feel anything but . . . moved.

Von only wanted me. He only wanted me—

Until he doesn't, said some imposter voice.

The light feeling I had felt grew heavy as I repeated the words in my head.

Until.

He.

Doesn't.

"I will do something for you, something I should have done a long time ago," Von said, pulling me from my thoughts. Silver rings sparkled in the firelight as a massive, inked hand was placed in front of me.

I eyed it for a moment, before I hesitantly took it.

He pulled me up from my chair, spinning me towards him. How easily he made my body move for him. His hand spread across my stomach, spanning the full width—my silk dress being the only thing that separated us. Eyes filled with the lush colors of an ancient canopy met mine as he said, "I withdraw my curse. I withdraw my touch of death from you."

Like winter bowing to its usurper spring, the frost within began to recede. And with it, I could feel what had withered inside begin to bloom.

Tears welled in my eyes.

I raised my palm and conjured from the well within. In the cradle of my hand, a tiny sprout shot forth with one single leaf.

I laughed softly, wiping at my tears as I watched it grow, awestruck by my very first creation that was entirely of my own making. When it was about a foot high, a voluptuous green bud swelled at the end, weighing it down. I concentrated, pushing harder. The green gave way and it unfurled into a rose, its plush petals taking on a soft, milky white.

"Beautiful," Von remarked softly.

I looked up, expecting to find his eyes on the flower, but instead, they were fixed on me.

"You're not talking about the rose," I spoke softly.

"No." A whisper of a smile. "Although it's lovely too."

Gently, I plucked it from my palm, pulling the tiny roots out with it, and offered it to him. He took it with heartbreakingly careful fingers, as if it were made of glass, littered with invisible hairline cracks. He brought it to his nose and inhaled its honey-sweet, floral scent.

My heart galloped wildly in my chest.

The villain of the realms, viewed as a merciless and unyielding god, who stood nearly seven feet tall was spellbound by a tiny, fragile, living thing.

Death was spellbound by a rose.

My rose.

And it did something to me—to the bond. A fiery heat scorched across my skin, awakening my nerves.

I clasped his forearm, my touch conjuring his attention. He peered down at me, his attention drifting to my lips, then back up to meet my gaze.

"I'm still angry with you," I said, as I leaned into him.

His hand slid across my cheek. "But?"

"But—" my voice was sultry, "—I have *needs*."

He brought his mouth close to mine. "Show me how you want me to tend to them."

"Show you?" I asked curiously.

He smiled his sexy smile, his fingers trailing up the length of my thigh, running over my sex as he whispered in my ear, "Lay down on the table and show me how you want me to touch you."

Moments later, that's exactly what I was doing.

I was reclined on the table, my feet resting on the arms of his chair and my legs spread as my fingers stroked in and out while he sat there, silver goblet in his tattooed hand, the one that said *king,* as he watched me pleasure myself.

When the dark god could take no more, he tossed the goblet carelessly to the side, grabbed my hips and dragged me to the edge of the table. Ringed fingers slung my legs over his broad shoulders as he lowered his face to my sex, his tongue running over my slit in one dominate, animalistic lick.

Then he ate. And ate. And—*oh fuck*—he ate.

High on ecstasy and orgasms, I had no qualms as Von lowered me into the spacious walk-in tub in his private bath chamber. With a washcloth, he cleaned my skin with meticulous care, as if he was polishing something that was of great importance to him. Occasionally, he would lower his head and nip or kiss my skin, stirring a squeak or a soft moan out of me depending on if he used his teeth or lips.

After he dried us both off, he conjured a short, black nightgown over my body and carried me to the bed, setting me down. The mattress dipped under the weight of the mountainous male as he maneuvered behind me. He gathered my hair, pulling it back, and then—

My breath hitched in my lungs when I felt a gentle tug at the ends of my hair—

Death was *brushing* my hair.

"I used to daydream of doing this for you," he said as he worked on one section, utilizing soft strokes. "All those years when I would stand by your window, waiting to see you. You would show up with a brush in your hand as you looked over our orchard. It took you a great deal of time to brush your hair, and I wondered what it would be like to do it for you."

"And? What is it like?" I asked, my voice barely above a whisper. The number of times where I felt cared for over my three hundred years of life were far and few between, but right now, with my heart beating at a slow, steady pace, that was exactly what I felt.

"Like I could do it every night for the rest of my eternal life," he said, placing a soft kiss against my shoulder.

After I crawled into bed, I waited to see what Von would do. I knew that he didn't have the same sleep patterns as me, but a *tiny* part of me hoped he would join me regardless.

"Would you like me to stay the night with you?" he asked from his spot beside me. He had one long, muscular leg hiked up, an arm thrown over top his bent knee as he casually reclined against the headboard. His head was tipped to the side, black lashes lowered as he gazed down at me.

A small part of me whispered yes, but my stubborn, proud lips said, "You don't have to." I tucked my hand under my pillow, looking up at him.

Forest-green eyes drifted to mine. "Are you sure?"

"Yup." I popped the *p* to cover up for the fact that I wasn't sure at all. All of this was new.

A moment slipped past before he replied, "Alright, then. Well, good night, Little Goddess."

"Good night," I answered, watching as his shadows stole him away.

Despite what my lying lips had said, I was a bit disappointed that he had left, but it was nothing compared to the tantrum the bond was throwing. It let me know by placing its invisible vines around my ankle and pulling on it. I tried my hardest to ignore it, as best as one could when it felt like their leg was being torn off.

The bed itself was positively divine—soft yet supportive. Still, sleep would not put me out of my misery. I tossed and turned, flipping this way and that, as I tried to push thoughts of the raven-haired god out of my mind, but no matter how hard I tried, it was futile.

Finally, I said across the private bridge that linked us, *Where did you go?*

It took a moment, and then . . .

Do you miss me already? the dark god purred in response.

A question for a question, used as a means of deflection—I had grown to recognize that tactic of evasion because it was one Aurelius used frequently. When Aurelius was not in our bed—which was often—it was because he was finding comfort in another's or in his private chambers, which I was not allowed in.

Was that what Von was doing right now? Had he gone to be with *another* female?

Insecurity, rage, rejection, frustration—all those emotions slammed into me with a force unlike I had ever felt. At the core of it . . . jealousy. Made a thousand times worse by the damn mating bond.

Molten fire scorched over my skin, lighting me on fire.

I jerked upright, looking to my arms, expecting to find them charcoaled, but finding nothing of the sort. They were normal, and yet the feeling persisted.

Whoa, Little Goddess, Von spoke calmly through the bond. *As much as I enjoy the thought of you being territorial over me, I can tell you it's not what you think.*

His words soothed me, or perhaps, they soothed the bond, because the fire that had been lit under my skin began to dissolve.

How did you know? I asked.

As your mate, I can feel your stronger emotions. You will be able to feel mine too.

I thought about what he said for a moment, then remembered the funny flavor I had tasted on my tongue earlier today, when we had been speaking of Aurelius giving me his ichor—it had tasted of . . . jealousy.

That potent emotion had belonged to Von.

Well, on the plus side, at least I wasn't the only one fighting my demons. Speaking of—

He *still* had not told me where he had gone off to.

I turned back to our personal channel. *So then, where are you?*

I'm in the Living Realm, he answered, *making an acquisition.*

What are you buying?

If you must know, it is a gift.

For?

You. I could hear the smirk he wore by the way he said that one little word.

You are buying me something? I asked, a smile touching my lips. I couldn't remember the last time someone had purchased something for me.

I am, he answered, sounding pleased with himself.

What is it? A pretty necklace? A little lap dog? I laid back down on the bed.

Always so curious, Kitten, he laughed softly. *If I tell you, it will ruin the surprise.*

I twirled a tendril of my hair as I continued fishing. *Oh, I know—an actual gown, perhaps.*

I'm not telling you.

I ignored him, asking, *Am I aiming too high? Some new hair oils, then?*

Go to sleep, Little Goddess.

But I didn't. I continued to push different gift ideas through the bond, while he continued to refuse to tell me. Eventually, when my eyelids became heavy and I was certain I had exhausted every possible gift idea, I fell asleep.

Chapter 23

Von

The morning kitchen staff gawked at me. Busy, working hands stopped what they were doing. Instantly, stools screeched and utensils clattered as the staff began to drop onto bended knee—one by one.

I strode over to a crate of apples, plucked one and said, "By all means, continue what you are doing."

A few heads swiveled, shooting each other confused, wide-eyed looks before they quickly dove back into their kitchen duties. Knives chopped, spoons stirred, and tongues were rendered immobile—not a peep being spoken amongst them. They worked determinedly, as if it were their first day on the job. Quite the opposite of what I had seen just yesterday, as they chatted with one another while working at a leisurely pace. Mortals were a funny breed like that, such diligent workers when under the eye of authority.

The woman whose skin was stamped with the lick of flame walked over to me, her movement slow—cautious. "A-a-apologies, my king, but might I help ye with somethin'?" she asked, her tongue tripping over itself like two left feet.

"You are the head chef of this kitchen, correct?" I peered down at the lush, red apple, deciding where to bite it first.

"Aye, I am." She swallowed so harshly, it made *my* throat hurt.

Peeling my eyes from the apple, I looked at her and said, "You need not fear me, woman."

She nodded, but the way her hands wrangled her apron was telling in itself—she didn't believe a single word.

I sighed. "I have come to speak with a man by the name of Early." When her eyes shot wide and her lips parted, I raised a hand, stopping her from sputtering out her pleas not to harm him. "I mean no harm to him either. I have been asked to reunite him with his wife, and so that is what I plan to do. I merely need to know where to find him."

"Ye are truly goin' to return him to his Amelia, my king?" she asked, her expression softening—full of wonder.

"I am."

Her face lit up, eyes too—like my words had sparked a flame within her. "He is goin' to be one happy man. One happy man indeed," she exclaimed. "I dinna ken where he might be at this moment. When he isna workin', he goes fishin' sometimes. Other times, he likes to sit at the market, people watchin', always searchin' for his sweet Amelia's face, but ne'er findin' her." She paused for a moment, thinking. "He has a house in the Ferva village, though. So I reckon ye'll find him there later tonight."

I nodded. "Thank you."

"Is that all, my king?" she asked, smoothing her apron.

"Not quite. There is one more thing." I grinned. "I want you to teach me how to make those biscuits you made yesterday."

Her mouth flopped open before she sputtered out, "Of course, my king. Anythin' ye wish."

"Wonderful." I sank my teeth into the apple's crisp flesh and tore off a chunk.

Aurelia was still asleep when I returned to our bedchamber, a covered silver tray in my hands. Underneath the lid, a spread of freshly prepared foods, a small pot of steaming tea, and a plate full of golden-brown biscuits. Freshly made by hers truly. On silent feet, I sauntered over to her side of the bed and gently placed the tray on the bed stand, my movement purposefully soundless, as I had no intentions of waking my slumbering mate.

Mate.

The word echoed through my thoughts, causing a grin to pluck at my mouth.

I rolled my wrist, conjuring a folded piece of paper with the words *Little Goddess* written on it and set it on top of the tray.

My gaze shifted to the white rose she had made, growing on the bed stand, its roots hooked around the ledge, helping keep it upright. It had done a great deal of growing since she created it just last night. At the base, slender vines had emerged. They stretched a few feet up the obsidian wall—the greenery contrasting with the black glass.

Out of all the things she could have created, she had decided to make a rose.

Were they of significance to her?

Palm up, I held my hand in front of my chest, conjuring a seed. The seed sprouted, blooming into a rose of my own. I modelled it after hers, but it ended up being a bit larger in size, its voluminous petals stained an inky black. Magic was a bit like a fingerprint, unique to its person, which is why mine didn't completely match hers. I placed it on top of the tray, beside the piece of paper, my gaze shifting to her.

Her slender shoulders raised with a soft inhale, deflating peacefully on her exhale. Her white hair, like veins of a river, cascaded across the starkness of the pillowcase. My black sheets contrasted against her fair skin, highlighting her body like a moon nestled in the darkest of nights.

She was perfect.

She was mine.

And there was *nothing* I wouldn't do to keep her as such. To protect her.

Which meant there was something I needed to do—something I should have done a long time ago.

Inky swirls swam around me as I stepped into the hidden stone chamber in the underbelly of my castle. It was the place I went to bury things—things I never wanted to be found again. The crypt was full of precious items and materials, religious relics long lost to the world, things that both man and immortal kind didn't even know existed.

It spanned thousands of square feet. When one had lived for as many years as I had, you tended to gather quite the collection. I strode forward, passing under one stone arch after another, listening to the ghosts of this place as they whispered to me in dark, eerie greetings—

"Hello, my king," said a haunting female voice.

"Good day, sire," stated a resonant male tone.

"Death has returned to us at last," sighed another.

Their voices were enough to make one's hair stand ramrod straight.

But I had gotten used to them over the great span of years. Some appeared as orbs, while others took on their earthly silhouettes, their forms spun of a translucent white mist.

When their flesh was still warm and filled with life, they had become so obsessed with material items, they could not give them up—not even in death. And so, their souls had bound themselves to the items in their possession, meaning my reapers could not extract their souls and place them in the Da'Nu. On rare occasions, a soul would come to me and ask to be released from their imprisoned state, however, more times than not, the souls remained attached to their earthly possessions. In truth, it was a shame, because so many of them could be reunited with loved ones, but instead, they chose an eternity of isolation.

Mortal greed at its finest.

I turned to my left, ducking under a tiny, arched doorway before I stepped into a small room, not much bigger than a pantry. My legs carried me a few paces before I stood in front of a pillar stand, about five feet tall. The obsidian column with a flat, square top was flanked by standing candelabras. On it—

The Crown of Thorns.

I picked it up, my regret building the more I looked it over. I had been a fool in forging it—the very thing that could take my mate's life. My fist wrapped tightly around it, the tiny thorns pricking my fingers as I carried it out of the room.

"Thief," decreed an eerie voice, mirrored by a dozen more. Hands swarmed around me, swirling and dissolving as I walked through them.

I continued down the center of the crypt until I came to my workshop. It was a grand chamber, filled with various tools I had crafted throughout the centuries, as well as furnaces and anvils. At the far end sat a cement altar and a wood stool. I made my way over to it, tossing the crown on top of my workstation as I sat down.

"Thief! Thief! Thief!" the voices continued, getting louder and louder.

"Enough," I snarled at them all. The word echoed around the chamber, silencing them instantly. I exhaled a breath. "That's better."

I hovered my hand over top of the crown, purple flames emitting from my fingertips. They licked at the edges of it, tasting and lapping, before they began to wrap around it. The roots writhed and twisted, trying to escape their impending demise. My teeth clenched together as I poured more of my power into my flame. I didn't know how long I did that for, but eventually, the white vine began to turn charcoal black before it disintegrated into ash.

A current of my air swept up the crown's remains, scattering it into oblivion.

I took a deep breath. Now that I had completed that task, it was time for me to move on to another. Carefully, I untethered the white feather from my hair, laying it down in front of me.

Then I got to work.

Chapter 24

Aurelia

Out of all the things I expected the Spirit Realm to be, I did not expect it to be so quiet. Yet, that was exactly what it was. It wasn't a bad thing. If anything, it was peaceful. Calm.

The Golden Palace, in the Immortal Realm, had been quiet, too, but that was a different quiet. That quiet was lonely. The kind that amplified your thoughts in the worst of ways. The kind that robbed you of sleep and left you pacing the floors back and forth, feeling like a locked-up animal, stuck in a cage.

A cage.

That's exactly what I thought the Spirit Realm would be like, but here, I was reclined on a lounge chair on Death's expansive, sprawling balcony, my skin warmed by the peculiar giant star that floated above in the amethyst sky, surrounded with black, fluffy clouds. The luminescent ball was not yellow like the sun, but rather silver like the moon.

Despite how bright it was, it didn't hurt my eyes to look at it. I had been studying it for some time as I casually picked at the tray of food I had found on the bedside table when I awoke earlier, accompanied by a small card that had *Little Goddess* written on it and a beautiful black rose. With a hunger in my stomach and a yearning in my soul for fresh air, I decided to bring the tray with me outside. Apart from the raven that was perched on the balcony railing, I had no qualms about my choice.

I broke off a piece of the flaky, fluffy biscuit, a few crumbs falling onto my lap, and said to the bird, "Are you the same one that was watching me while I was in the Living Realm?"

The raven didn't respond.

"I'm guessing you were." I tossed the freshly baked goodness into my mouth. Like butter, it melted on my tongue. I reached out my arm, offering the raven a chunk. "Would you like a bite?"

It didn't so much as move.

"Suit yourself," I said with a shrug, popping it into my mouth.

When the silence stretched on between us for a while longer, I decided to try another approach. "I can't imagine you would be none too pleased with your master, with him shifting your duties and all—having you keep watch over me instead of collecting souls. A grand reaper reduced to a babysitter."

The bird side-eyed me.

I chuckled. "Ah, I have your attention now, do I?"

Sandalwood and amber enveloped my senses as an umbra fell over me, shrouding me in its darkness. I realized then that I hadn't gotten the bird's attention after all—it was interested in the tall, *tall* drink of muscles and masculinity that stood behind me.

I tilted my head up, eyeing the smirking male.

"Enjoying yourself?" Von asked.

"As much as I can be," I huffed, wondering if today was the day he would call in the next part of our deal. I decided to ask. "Have you come to claim me as your bride today, Death?"

"Not today, Little Goddess. Today, I have other plans for you."

"Like?" I asked, eyeing folded clothes in his hand. "What are those for?"

"They are fighting leathers." He tossed them to me.

Instinctually, I recoiled when they landed on my stomach, an "Mmph," squeaking past my lips—the element of surprise conjuring it forth.

"What for?" I asked, gathering the smooth, impenetrable fabric in my hands as I sat up, swinging my feet onto the obsidian floor.

"For training, of course. You cannot expect me to have a queen that does not know how to hold her own in battle." He stepped around the chair.

Who didn't know how to hold her own in battle?

I shot daggers at him. "I'm insulted."

"Good." His lips twisted, his large hands bracketing his hips as he towered over top of me. He wore a set of tight-fitting leathers that had my gaze roaming and my mind swirling with dirty thoughts. His raven mane was subdued in a fighter's top-knot. "Let that be the fire that forges you into a grand warrior."

Green eyes lowered to my torso. The clothes evaporated from my hands, and the next thing I knew, they were on me—my body wrapped in tight, form-fitting leather.

"Starting today, you will come to train with me and a few others every morning," Von said as he glanced at my bare feet, conjuring a pair of knee-high leather boots, much like the set he was wearing.

I looked up at him, placing my hands on the chair to steady me as I leaned back. "Must you dress me every day?"

"I must," he said with a single nod. "It's either that or leave you naked and chain you to my bed so that no one can see what is mine." He shrugged a broad shoulder. "Choice is yours, little bride."

"You are unbelievable."

"Indeed, I am," he purred. Light reflected off his rings as he held out a hand for me to take. "Come."

I eyed it suspiciously. "Only if you agree to give me a closet *and* return my clothes to me, the ones that you dissolved that day in the forest—as well as my cloak," I stated, knowing bargaining was a language he understood.

"I can agree to that," he replied. "There is a room across the hallway. You'll find your cloak and beloved peasant rags in there, as well as a plethora of clothing for you to choose from."

Peasant rags. I narrowed my eyes at that.

"Oh, I almost forgot. The man you inquired about, Early. He has been reunited with his wife, as you requested."

"Really?" I asked excitedly. "That was fast."

Von nodded. "His wife had been placed in the Second Tier of the Spirit Realm, which made the transition fairly simple. Their children, grandchildren, and so-forth are there as well. It's the best tier to be in for mortals. Many equate it to paradise. I can take you to visit them someday if you'd like."

My heart warmed at this happy news.

"I would like that," I said before I placed my hand in his.

"What is this place?" I asked as my boots sunk into the soft, shifting black sands as I walked ahead, taking in the grand structure that circled around me, made entirely of molten glass.

"It is my amphitheater, and what we are standing in is the arena," Von answered. He stood off to the side, watching me as I took it all in. "Predominantly, it is used for entertainment purposes, gladiator battles and such, however, in the mornings, I close it to the public and use it for training."

"It's . . ." I looked around, trying to find the right word, but nothing seemed to do the spectacular, monstrous structure justice, so I settled on the best one I could find. "Breathtaking." I glanced over my shoulder at the tall warrior king, his defined forearms laced loosely over his broad chest. "You *made* this?"

"I did," he answered with a single nod. The white feather—*my* feather—woven at the end of his slender braid caught my attention. The rest of his hair was pulled back into a ponytail. His leathers clung tightly to his muscular, massive frame—trapping my gaze.

"Where did you get the idea to build such a structure?" I asked, momentarily unsure *which* structure I was referring to. Peeling my eyes off his ridiculously climbable body, I looked up, meeting his emerald hues.

"No one has ever asked me that before. To be honest, it just came to me, almost like a distant memory." He blew out a breath of air, more chuckle than exhale. "I couldn't get it out of my head, to the point it became like an obsession. Just like you."

I rolled my eyes.

A wolfish grin twisted his lips before he continued, "So I worked on it every hour I could, getting everything perfect until it was finished, a year later."

Perfect was a good word for it. The meticulous attention to detail was etched into every inch of this place. The fact that it took him only a year to build it was . . . unfathomable. I had to hand it to the big guy—he really put the god in god.

"I've never seen anything like it before," I said, looking around, marveling at it some more. I couldn't even fathom how many people must be able to fit in the sprawling, never-ending rows of seats, how deafening their cheering and roaring must be when the place was packed full.

"It is the only one of its kind in the Three Realms, although beyond our realms, in other lands, more exist."

"There are other realms beyond our own?" I asked curiously, tilting my head to the side.

"Indeed, hundreds of them. Have you heard of the Ancient Ones?"

I started to shake my head, but then stopped. I *had* heard those words spoken once before. "Ezravaynia said something about the Ancient Ones, but I didn't really understand what or whom she was referring to."

"They are a much older civilization. One that vastly predates the creation of the Three Realms. They were the first to come up with structures such as this one—using them for their own entertainment. They would throw different souls into the arenas and have them participate in trials, some that were of the mind, others that were to show off strength or skill."

I took a moment to take all that in. Turning to him, I asked, "How is it that you know so much of these . . . Ancient Ones?"

"I have one locked in the lowest level of the Spirit Realm," he said with a simple shrug.

The hinges in my jaw sprung open. "Sorry, what?"

"A story for another time. We've got company." His gaze shifted to our left, towards an open arched doorway.

Chapter 25

Aurelia

A stunning couple, dressed in fighting leathers, stepped out onto the black sands, making their way towards us. The male's arm was wrapped around the female's back as they moved in stride with one another. Both possessed considerable height and rich, dark skin.

They were immortals—of that, I had no doubt.

The male was rife with heavy muscle and eyes so stunning I found it hard to look away. They were like bottled bits of fire—a canvas of bright orange with flecks of sparkling red. His proud jaw was carved with a neatly trimmed, short beard. He had *that look* about him, like when he smiled, you knew it was going to take your breath away.

And then there was his partner. She was gorgeous, her body curvier than the Da'Nu. She moved with the sleekness of a panther—a sensual, confident roll to her hips as she walked. Her hand, marked with intricate, white flames, rested on her stomach—a small bump noticeable there, just beginning to swell with the gift of life.

A smile touched my lips.

"Little Goddess, I would like you to meet two of my closest friends," Von said, his deep voice like a hook, snagging my attention and pulling it up to his eyes. He gestured to the female. "Zahra, the Goddess of Companionship."

She smiled warmly and tipped her head.

Von motioned to the male. "And Dameon, the God of Protection."

"It is a pleasure," Dameon said, his voice a contradiction—smooth in some places and rugged in others. I could see why his partner had picked him—with a voice like that and eyes like those, I wasn't surprised that she was with child.

"This is the Goddess of Life." Von gestured to me with one large, tattooed hand. His skull ring caught my attention, and my cheeks flushed at the memory of where *that* ring had been last night. My teeth feathered my bottom lip as the bond stoked coals it had no right stoking while I was trying to act like a civilized immortal and not a heat-ridden animal.

I could feel Von's eyes on me—watching. I was certain that if I looked at him, I'd find a hint of a smile ghost across his full, lush lips. Those lips of his were like catnip to me, always summoning me to him.

I ignored the bond, ignored him, and said to Zahra and Dameon, “It is nice to meet you both.”

“As it is you,” Zahra replied, her voice as enchanting as her partner’s. Her lovely brown eyes shifted to Von’s. For a moment, her lips parted slightly, surprise raising her dark brows. Then her expression softened, her mouth growing into a *knowing* smile. “I can see why you were willing to call off the war for her,” she said to Von, her gaze returning my way. “You are a great beauty.”

“She is,” Von purred beside me. I could feel a gentle caress amble down the length of my spine, like knuckles gliding against my flesh, sizzling the molecules awake. And then it was gone, a great absence left behind.

I looked up at him, finding that sensual, toying smirk splayed across his mouth, just as I knew I would. I sunk my teeth into my bottom lip.

“How did things go with the healer?” Von asked, pulling his gaze from mine. My fingers twitched at my side, half inclined to grab his face and force his attention back to me.

I blinked, surprised at myself.

But that wasn’t me, was it? No, it was the bond, making me into something I was not. I forced my fingers to relax, took a breath, and looked at Zahra.

Lovingly, she stroked her belly as she said, “It went well. The babe is in good health. Although Dameon is none too happy.”

"On the contrary, my flame, I am filled with joy," he argued softly, those incredible orbs looking to Von for backup as if they were soldiers on the battlefield. "I am just concerned about the prophecy."

"I can understand that," Von said, his shadows drifting over me, covering me in their protection. A strange taste bloomed on my tongue, its origins foreign, but the flavor not unknown. It tasted of concern, but the emotion was not my own—it was Von's.

Zahra started, "You two worry for nothing. The Spinners speak in illusive riddles that sometimes never come to fruition. We must not let their twisted words take away from our happiness." If her shifting eyes were any indicator, her message was meant for both of them. Then she turned to Dameon, gathered his big hand, and placed it on her small bump—connecting the three of them. "It might not be twins, but the child within me is strong. You will see. All will be well."

Dameon nodded softly, but the act did not meet his eyes. His irises, which had been vibrant mere moments ago, were now dull. Whatever the Spinners had prophesized had laid a deep claim on him, one not even his partner's affirming words could break him free of.

They looked at one another, lost in private conversation.

Zahra sighed, her shoulders lowering on the exhale. She let go of his hand and then looked at me, giving me a half-smile. "Well, shall we leave these two men to brood while us women actually get some training done?" She proffered an arm.

"Sounds good to me." I chuckled as I took it, deciding I liked her already.

We walked over to a random spot—a good fifty feet away from Von and Dameon.

"My flame recognizes the one in you," Zahra said as she slipped her feet out of her shoes, stepping into the sands. The same white flames that were tattooed on her hands were also placed across the tops of her feet. "Do you use the gift very often?"

"No, not really," I replied. "Aurelius is well known for his use of flame."

"So?" She spread her feet shoulder width apart. "That doesn't mean you can't use yours."

She had a point.

I realized that after the words fell from my lips, how ridiculous they sounded. I had chosen not to use the element of fire for hundreds of years because my warped little brain didn't want to insult Aurelius, as that was *his* primary element. And even now, after everything, I was still stuck in the same thinking pattern.

Not anymore.

"Will you teach me how to control it?" I asked, taking a step forward.

"Of course." She grinned, her smile so bright that I was certain Aurelius would be jealous. "When Von asked me to come train with you, I was more than happy to say yes. Also, I'm hoping that we'll be able to get to know one another better. I think that you and I will make great friends."

Friends.

The concept was a bit foreign. Especially considering I was so used to other goddesses not liking me. But here she was, offering an invitation to be just that . . . friends.

Although Von was the initiator in all of this, her offer felt genuine.

My heart warmed.

"I'd like that," I told her, sharing a smile of my own. I glanced over my shoulder, finding Von's green eyes peering back at me. He and Dameon were standing over by a weaponry table.

He offered me a wink.

I rolled my eyes, warring with the smile tugging at my lips, and then turned back to Zahra. "Where do we begin?"

"We begin with stretching and warming up our muscles, removing the tightness from them so that the flame can move freely throughout our bodies." She gestured for me to come stand beside her, which I did. "I will be altering my stretches because of the baby. I'll walk you through the ones I cannot do. But before we get to any of that, take your shoes off so that you can feel the heat from the sands. It will help to ground you."

I nodded, unlaced my combat boots, and stepped into the sand. It felt incredible against the bottoms of my feet, warm and slightly abrasive, like a gentle massage.

"Place your hands on your stomach and take a deep breath in," she said. "Feel your muscles awakening there. Exhale slowly, feeling your abdomen contract, the power within this incredible muscle."

I did as she said, following her instructions, tuning myself to the movement of my body. We went through various exercises, focusing on different muscle groups and slowly waking them up, or lengthening them, as she sometimes liked to say.

About ten minutes later, when my muscles were warm and flowing with energy, Zahra said, “Before I start walking you through some basic movements, I think it might be best if you show me how you bend water.”

“That works for me.” I nodded.

A shadow flickered above, pulling at my attention. I looked up, finding a sleek, black feather floating down towards me, carried on the gentle breath of the wind. I placed my hand in front of me, palm facing towards the sky, and the feather fell directly into my hand, just as they always did.

Zahra beamed. “Your bond has been blessed.”

I glanced up from the feather, looking to her. “What do you mean?”

She smiled warmly as her hand lovingly circled her small bump. “When a pair of mates find one another, the male will begin to gradually shed some of his feathers. Most males don’t even notice when it happens. Dameon didn’t when it started. He still doesn’t.” She let out a soft laugh. “Over time, the feathers are delivered to the female so that she may collect them.”

Collect them? That’s exactly what I had done, unknowingly.

I thought back to the little chest I had hidden in the back of my closet at the Golden Palace, where I stored the other feathers I had received. I knew that they were Von's, but I never knew why I got them or why I felt compelled to collect them. In truth, I felt a tad guilty for leaving them behind now—not that I'd had time to go get them, all things considered.

I frowned, wondering if Aurelius had found them. If he did, he would have them destroyed. The thought caused my stomach to knot. "Why do we feel a need to collect the feathers?" I asked. "Is there some purpose for them?"

"It is naturally ingrained in us to do, just as it is for birds to build nests for their offspring." She tipped her head, her voice soft. "When you conceive, your baby will not be born with wings. So you will take the feathers you have collected and weave them into a set. Then you and your mate will gift them to your baby upon their birth."

Warmth radiated from my chest. I had never heard of such a thing, but I found it . . . endearing, and sweet. Not that a baby was something I was even close to considering at this point in my life, but I could appreciate the whole idea from afar.

Afar being the keyword there.

Chapter 26

Aurelia

For the next month, something ate away at me, and as time went on, it only seemed to be getting worse—

It was the damn *feathers* that I'd left behind at the Golden Palace.

Ever since Zahra told me what they were for and that it was our job to collect them, some unknown instinctual part of my brain had been switched on and now retrieving the feathers was all that I could think about. Day and night. Night and day. It didn't matter if I was training with the group, trying to sleep, eating food, *or* being eaten by Von—the feathers haunted me.

I suspected it had something to do with the bond.

Was it driving me insane? Yes.

Was that why I was standing outside of Zahra and Dameon's chambers, knocking on their door in the middle of the night? Also, yes.

It wasn't like immortals slept regular hours anyway. Von sure didn't. In fact, I didn't know *when* he slept, or *if* he slept at all. Some nights he would stay for a while, wrapping me up in his big strong arms, stroking my hair as his touch lulled me to sleep, but he never stayed the full night with me. I had a feeling that he was waiting for me to ask him to, but I . . . I just wasn't there yet. Although with each passing day that need to ask became stronger.

I breathed a sigh of relief when Zahra opened the door, one hand on the handle and the other holding a book, her finger marking the spot where she left off. A dark-emerald dress embroidered with white flames adorned her sensual frame, her curly hair pulled back into a bun.

Her brows furrowed when she saw me. "What's going on?"

"I need to talk to you about something," I said, my body vibrating with urgency. This whole *protect the feathers* need was detrimental to my impulse control, and I was already impulsive enough.

Nodding, she took a step back from the door. "Come in."

Swiftly, I stepped inside.

Their private chambers were huge—like a mansion had been stuffed inside. There was a large foyer that fed into a sitting area, warmed by a crackling fireplace. Various doors lined the interior walls, accompanied by a plethora of hallways that led to other living spaces. I imagined one probably led to their nursery.

The feathers! snarled that interior voice that would not leave me alone.

Fuck. Shut up. I'm working on it, I scolded it, wondering if I had finally gone insane.

Zahra closed the door and then gestured to the sitting area. "Make yourself at home. Can I get you something to drink and then we can talk?"

"I'm okay, thank you," I said as I walked over to a chair and forced myself to sit. My knees started bobbing.

"Alright then," she answered before she settled into the chair across from me. She marked her book with a piece of paper and then set it down on the end table beside her. She looked at my jumping knees.

I slapped my hands over top of them, forcing them to stop. *Goddess divine, this whole thing is ridiculous.*

"I thought you seemed a little weird earlier today during training. What's going on?" Zahra asked, her voice soft and warm.

Indeed, I had been. I could barely concentrate as we went through our routine, Von's stupid plumes on the forefront of my mind.

I took a breath. Creator knew, I needed it.

"Is Dameon here?" I glanced around.

"No, he's at his temple, recharging. It's just us. You are free to talk. Tell me what's on your mind."

"It's the feathers," I blurted out. "I can't stop thinking about them."

"Okay, I mean, it's not uncommon for mates to feel protective over them. They are rather important, after all." She shrugged a shoulder.

"No, that's not it. Back in the Immortal Realm, I had a small, wooden chest that I kept them in. I knew they were connected to Von, but I didn't understand their meaning. When I fled the Golden Palace, I didn't have time to go get them. Now, there's this internal voice that is demanding that I do just that." I forced myself to take another breath. "I kept the chest hidden in the back of my closet. I'm worried what will happen if Aurelius finds them—if he hasn't already." My teeth tugged at my bottom lip.

Zahra was quiet for a moment before she said, "Your bond is new, which means you probably can't light walk right now. Is that correct?"

"That's right." I nodded my head, surprised she knew that. "Did it happen to you too?"

"It happens to all of us females, but not our male counterparts. It's a bit primitive, isn't it? Clipping our ability to port far away from our mates, while the bond makes us crave them desperately. No wonder I ended up like I am." Her eyes shifted down, pointing to her belly before they returned to mine. "Anyway. So you need me to shadow walk you to the Immortal Realm so you can retrieve them, don't you?"

"I couldn't ask that of you. It could be dangerous, and I don't want to put the two of you in jeopardy."

"Nonsense. We'll be quick. In and out," she said without

hesitation. She paused for a moment, thinking, and then, "Can I ask you something?"

I nodded.

"Why not talk to Von about this?"

"We're just . . ." I looked for the right words. "Not there yet."

"But you two are bonded." She gave me a strange look like she didn't quite understand my reasoning, like the bond should trump everything else.

"I didn't choose the bond though." I gestured to the walls around us—to the castle. "I didn't choose any of this."

"Word to the wise, love, none of us choose the bond—it chooses us on the day our souls are woven into the stars," she said with a soft smile. "I know it can be scary at first—it was for me, but had I not taken a chance on what the universe had planned for me, I wouldn't be where I am today. Dameon is the other half of my soul, the one who completes me, and the love of my immortal life. Just as Von is yours. You just need to take that leap of faith first. I promise you, your world will become so much richer for it."

I sat with her words for a moment, letting them sink in. The trust part was easier said than done. I had trusted a male before and where had that gotten me?

Bruised and broken.

And now I was expected to trust another? Letting Von into my body was one thing, but letting him into my heart was *entirely* another.

"Shall we go get those feathers?" Zahra asked, pulling me out of my swirling thoughts.

I raised my brows. "Are you sure?"

She grinned. "I'm always up for an adventure."

Moments later, we were standing in my old bedchambers back at the Golden Palace in the Immortal Realm. My room was just how I had left it. I wasn't sure if Aurelius would have trashed the room in his rage when he'd found out I had fled. But, for some reason, he hadn't. My traitorous heart—something that was of him, not me—kicked optimistically. I ignored it. That ship hadn't just sailed—it had sunk into the abyss of never again and go fuck yourself.

Zahra stepped ahead, looking around. "It's a bit gaudy, isn't it?"

"Truly, it is." I answered.

The gold-bricked walls were obnoxiously loud, screaming of Aurelius's ridiculous amounts of wealth. Then again, that was him. He always wanted people's eyes on him, to be the center of attention. How I stayed with him for so many years, looking up to him, I did not know.

Zahra continued to walk around as I made my way over to my old closet. Reaching the far end of the room, I dropped to my knees and began reaching behind the densely packed dresses, their scratchy material abrasive against my face. My fingers connected with a small wooden chest. I pulled it out and opened it up. In it were Von's feathers.

All of them.

Safe.

Happy now? I asked the voice inside.

When it didn't reply, I took its silence as a good thing.

I closed the lid, grabbed the chest with one hand, and stood up. I started walking towards the door, but stopped in the middle of the room when I reached the slender column that spanned from floor to ceiling.

Fingerprints were etched into the stone pillar. I ran my fingers over them—

A perfect match.

"I told you to hold on," snarled a woman's voice in my ear.

"I . . . can't . . . breathe," I huffed as I gripped the column, my body on the verge of passing out.

Still, she pulled on the ties of my corset, stitching my lungs closed with each merciless tug. "Well, if you'd quit spending so much time in that damn orchard and more time waist-training, we wouldn't be having this problem, now, would we?" she growled, her voice as kind as a dagger against my throat. "No wonder the king doesn't visit your bedchamber anymore."

I snatched my hand back, breaking free from the memory. There were thousands more like them, some much worse. I stepped away from the pillar, looking around at the room I had spent so much of my life in.

It was filled to the brim with stuffy dresses and rib-breaking corsets. Hundreds of clothing options and not one was tailored to be comfortable. They were meant to restrict. To conform. I realized then how much I hated those clothes. They were the uniform of my oppression. The façade of a perfect, doting wife. A smiling face and an empty head—just how Aurelius wanted me to portray myself to be.

Well, that person was gone now.

But I realized I had never had a funeral for her—for Aurelia.

I ran my fingers over the clothes as I walked, letting my ravenous fire seep beyond the surface of my fingertips. Dress by soul-crushing dress, I lit that fucking room on fire, leaving no piece of fabric untouched.

Like a phoenix, I was born anew as I strode out of the flames that engulfed the chamber, with the small box, full of Von's feathers, tucked safely under my arm.

Zahra's gaze roved over me. She stood with her hip cocked, her arms loosely threaded over her chest. "I don't know what that's about—" she eyed the flames coming from the room, "—but I know what a woman looks like when she just laid something dark to rest. So whatever it is, I'm proud of you."

In truth? I was proud of myself too.

After I finished thanking Zahra for her help, I returned to Von's pitch-black bedchamber. Squinting, I made my way over to the bed, my hand swiveling in front of me as I felt for it. A hand wrapped around my wrist, tugging me into a mountainous torso.

I screeched. My heart kicked up its pace, slamming into my ribs like a war drum at the end of its song, seconds before the clash of swords and shields.

Piercing green eyes, sharp enough they cut through the darkness, peered down at me.

"And where did you scamper off to, Little Goddess?" purred a deep, sexy voice as *his* divine masculine scent of sandalwood and amber enveloped my senses. The voice. The smell. All of it—him—was intoxicating. He let out a low chuckle. "I thought I put you to bed hours ago."

"I was with Zahra," I panted. Now I had two reasons for my lungs to stumble for breath—having the living daylights scared out of me and the delicious, dark god whose muscular arms were wrapped firmly around me.

Although I couldn't see it, I could feel it as Von lifted a ribbon of my hair. He inhaled softly. "I rinsed your hair with lavender tonight, and yet it smells like smoke." He let the tendril go. Slowly, his knuckles brushed down the length of my arm, over my hand that held the small chest.

Tap. Tap.

His fingers thumped against the box. "And what might this be?"

The spell was broken. Embarrassment crawled across my cheeks, turning my ears red. I was no better than a mortified child whose secret about who they fancied had been shared with the other children, so naturally, I blurted out the truth of it. "It's your feathers, you big brute."

Smooth, my inner critic seethed.

Swiftly, I tried to shift the topic. "You nearly scared me to death when you grabbed me like that."

"That's an interesting choice of words," he remarked, pausing for a moment, lowering his face to mine. "My feathers? Have you been collecting them, little mate?" I didn't need light to see it—I could *hear* the smirk he wore.

Of course he would find this entertaining.

I pressed off of him. "If you must know, yes, I have been."

"You know what that means," he said sensually—so sensually I was certain my ovaries kicked out an egg.

I snarled—the bond was ridiculous.

"It means nothing." I dropped onto my knees and shoved the chest under the bed, stashing it under there like a squirrel stocking her cache with food. Except this wasn't food. This was a box full of feathers destined for a babe I did not plan to have. All of this served me no purpose, and yet here I was, obsessing over them, protecting them like some lunatic . . .

Damn bond!

A raspy chuckle. "I wasn't going to say *that*."

"Then what were you going to say?" I looked up at him, just

barely able to make out his masculine silhouette, my eyes *slowly* adjusting to the darkness.

"I was going to say that a wise female once told me that killers collect souvenirs. Which leads me to wonder . . ." He lowered his voice. "Are you plotting my murder, darling?"

"Most definitely." I stood up.

He let out a soft laugh and I couldn't help but grin.

His hand wrapped around my lower back as he guided me between his parted legs. "I need you to promise me something."

"What?"

His thumb and forefinger clasped my chin, tilting my face up to his. Even when he was sitting and I was standing, I had to look up at him. "The next time you go to the Immortal Realm, you let me know so that I can accompany you."

If he hadn't been holding my chin, my mouth would have fallen open. "How did you know I went there?"

"I followed you."

"Why? Did you think I was running from you?"

"No. You are too content with me and my cock right now to run." An unbridled amount of swaggering arrogance infiltrated his words.

I had to give it to him—the bastard wasn't wrong. But he and his legendary-sized ego didn't need to know that. "I'm sorry to tell you this, but I think it might be the latter that is doing the heavy lifting there."

He let out a low chuckle. "Oh, really?"

"Mhm," I teased, nodding. My smile faded as my thoughts returned to the whole point of this conversation. "So then why did you do it? Why did you follow me?"

"I followed you because I was worried about you. Now that Nicholas knows what you are to me, the Immortal Realm is not safe for you anymore. So if you feel the need to scamper back there again, to find some long-lost something or other, I ask that you come to me first, so that I can go with you. To protect you."

"Oh." His words touched a soft spot. A spot that made me want to smile, because his admission made me feel . . . good.

He lowered his lips just above mine. "Promise me."

"Fine," I spoke softly, a smile caressing my lips. "I promise."

"Good girl," he praised in that voice that made me want to strip off my clothes and race him to the sheets. "Now . . . do you need me to put you to bed again? Tell you a little bedtime story?"

I draped my arms over his broad shoulders, one by one. "Only if you write it with your tongue."

"Done." His fingers played with the fabric at my waist, twirling it softly. "What do you want it to be about?"

"Hmm." I thought for a moment. "About the wicked, sexy, tall, tattooed villain that everyone fears."

"I like how this is starting. Go on."

"And the princess who is trapped in a palace. She stands by her window every night."

"She is a beautiful creature." He tucked a tendril of hair behind my ear. “Just standing there, waiting to be taken. Then what happens?”

“He watches over her for a time, until one day, he decides to steal her away, taking her back to his dark castle.”

“And what does he do with her once they get there?”

I whispered against his lips, “That’s your part of the story to tell.”

“With this, yes?” He swiped his tongue across my lower lip. The act was so primal, so territorial, like he was marking me. I ate it up.

“Yes,” I groaned softly, pulling my lip into my mouth, sucking on the taste of him.

“Mmm.” A sensual, deep purr. One that I felt rumble all the way down to the apex of my thighs—*Creator above, this male*.

Without another word, he pulled me back onto the bed with him, my excited squeal getting lost in the night.

Chapter 27

Von

The following morning, my gorgeous little mate looked positively divine, dressed all in white as we walked down a lengthy corridor. Her long legs stretched out from the twin hip-high slits in the silky fabric, teasing me with each stride.

I'd cut her training short this morning, sweeping her back to our bedchamber so that she could get ready for today. When she found the luxurious, sexy dress laid out on our bed, she gave me a curious look. I told her that I had designed it to look like the one I saw her wearing the day that she arrived in Edenvale. It was unlike anything I had ever seen her wear before, so unlike the ridiculous, rigid clothing she had worn when she lived in the Immortal Realm. She had run her fingers over the fabric, exclaiming that she loved it. With a smile on my lips, I'd asked her to put it on. So, while I sat in my chair, watching her, that's exactly what she did. With every deliberate sweep of her hand across her skin, she made the act of undressing and dressing a knuckle-biting affair to watch.

We rounded the corner, walking into a much wider corridor, the dark walls full of artwork—paintings of the Old Gods. At the bottom of each was a silver plaque, stating who the picture was of.

She looked at the first painting—

The Goddess of War was adorned in her light armor and wicked leathers, her brow deeply furrowed, and a snarl on her painted red lips. She held her wicked blade out in front of her, pointing it at the viewer. A black viper coiled around her free hand, its mouth propped open, hissing in warning.

Saphira had hundreds of paintings of herself spread out all over the castle, while I only had the one—which just so happened to be at the end of this hallway. She had roped me into it many years ago, and it had been the first and last one I had made. Unlike her, I had no desire to have my likeness painted and placed all over the castle—my good looks were already etched into the minds of every soul in this realm, as if they needed the reminder.

"I've been wondering about something," Aurelia said softly, pulling me from my private thoughts.

"Pray tell, Kitten. What is it?"

"Are there quite a few people who are not able to be with their loved ones because they are split into different tiers?" she asked, pulling her gaze from Saphira's likeness, and looking to the next one, which belonged to the Goddess of Storms.

"Unfortunately, yes. There has been such a large influx of souls over the past couple centuries, it is hard to keep up with them. Quite a few slip through the cracks."

She glanced to the other side of the hall, finding the portrait of the God of Lust. The male lived up to his title—inspiring the affections of both sexes. I noted that her step slowed, and her eyes took their sweet time taking the tall, handsome god in.

I narrowed my eyes.

"What sorts the people and decides where they go?" she asked, steps slowing so she could spend a bit longer with the painting.

I decided it would conveniently go missing tonight.

Answering her, I said, "The Da'Nu river decides what tier to place them in when they first arrive here. The ravens drop their souls in the rushing waters. Based on their past, it decides where they are to go. However, it does not consider their loved ones, it only looks at that soul's specific behavior."

"So then . . . how does one get moved to a different tier?"

"Such a curious little kitten," I mused, smirking. "They have to request it during one of the throne meetings."

"And then?" She looked up at me.

Creator above, those wide, blue eyes were going to be the end of me. "They make their request and then I decide if I will grant it or not."

"So, all of these people have to rely solely on you to either approve their request or deny it?"

"Yes."

"That sounds like a rather poor system."

I chuckled at that. "If you saw how things were before, you would find the old ways even worse."

"What were the old ways?" she asked, her tongue lingering on the last two words, drawing attention to them.

She was such an inquiring thing, and as always, I was more than happy to indulge her.

"Originally, the Spirit Realm was made up of three tiers. For centuries, I left the mortals to do as they pleased in their own tier." I shrugged. "I figured they had gotten along in the Living Realm, why should it be any different in the Spirit Realm? But as it would seem, having eternity on their side accompanied by no repercussions for bad behavior, well, it led to moral rot. Because of it, living conditions became abhorrent. I do believe my blindness to what was happening down here is why the Creator dethroned me from the Living and Immortal Realms and gave them to Aurelius while forcing me to rule over the realm I'd allowed to run amok."

She shook her head, her brows knitting together. "I thought that all three realms were in a state of decay and that's why Aurelius was made?"

"That was a grand stretch from the truth—one that Aurelius fed the realms. All so he could portray himself as the redeeming hero and I the destructive villain. It was just the Spirit Realm that had gone to shit. The other two realms were in good standing."

She was quiet for a moment. Too quiet.

I had a feeling it was to do with my lackluster replacement—a topic she had made abundantly clear she did not wish to speak about. But just because she didn't want to talk to me about him, that didn't mean she wouldn't open up to someone else. In truth, having her train with Zahra, Dameon, and I wasn't just because I wanted her to become a stronger warrior. I wanted her to have a friend, someone she could confide in. Who better for that role than Zahra, the Goddess of Companionship?

"Is that why you went on to create the nine tiers? To redeem yourself?" she asked, pulling me from my private thoughts.

"Not quite." I glanced down at her, finding her eyes on me, as curious as ever.

I sunk my teeth into my bottom lip—it was all I could do to stop myself from backing her against the wall, taking her pretty little face in my hands, and kissing her until her knees grew weak.

"So . . ." Softly, she shook her head, as if this was some perplexing riddle she couldn't figure out. "Why did you do it then?"

I let out a rumbling breath, my voice husky. "I made the tiers because I met someone who cared deeply for the mortals, who saw their worth, while I was blind to it." I paused for a moment, my gaze holding hers. "I made the tiers because of you, Little Goddess, because I wanted to honor what you treasure."

Chapter 28

Aurelia

My feet slowed.

I was *the reason* he'd created the tiers.

I didn't know why—maybe I was a fraction too gullible—but . . . I believed him.

For once in my immortal life, I was at a loss for words. I didn't know what to say or how to feel. All I knew was that a part of me that had hardened myself to him, it had started to soften.

Was that how it would always be with us—a mixture of bad and good?

Was that what relationships were meant to be like?

Because for so long, all I had known was bad.

Whether that be my relationship with Aurelius or my interactions with Von in the past. Both males had hurt me deeply—one stole my worth, while the other stole my purpose. But the thievery of my power to create was steeped in grays—unlike what Aurelius did to me, which was as stark as black and white. Von's reasons for doing so had been multifaceted. Complex. I was the wife of his enemy. A means of getting his lost realms back. But Aurelius? *I was his wife*, the woman he had given his heart for, and he still chose to mistreat me. To abuse me.

But now the circumstances had changed.

Von was trying to make the living conditions better for the people of this realm. On top of that, he had come to my aid, helped me free the prisoners, without question or demanding payment. I looked down at the beautiful dress I was wearing. He hadn't made it because it appealed to his tastes, he had done it because he thought it appealed to mine. Because he thought that *I* would like it. And I did.

All of that was the good. Von was being . . . good to me.

Because to the rest of the world, I am the villain, but to you, and you alone, I no longer wish to be. His words replayed in my head, pulling me back to that memory. Of when he had healed more than just a broken finger. He had healed a part of my broken spirit that day—I just hadn't realized it at the time.

Now, I did.

"Are you coming?" he asked over his shoulder. His stroll had that casual arrogance to it—unperplexed by the giant, meaningful thing he had just told me and the shifting that was beginning to occur inside of me—separate from the bond.

"Yes," I said, blinking away the bits of mist that had formed in my eyes. I quickened my pace and caught up with him.

Neither of us said a word as we walked in silence down the rest of the corridor.

When we reached the end, we both took pause.

Giant sconces, lit with violet flames, flanked the sides of the very last painting.

This one was a sight to behold.

An intricate pattern of vines and bones were carved into the wood, a heavy layer of black lacquered over top. Within the painting was the God of Death himself, wrapped in all his dark, ancient splendor—an unmatched warrior king. His floating crown above his head, an apple in one ringed hand, a smirk on his lips, and—

My brow furrowed.

Four slashes were slit directly across his neck, causing the painting to sag a bit.

"Wild guess here, but I'm thinking it's not supposed to be like that," I pointed out.

"No," he sighed. "Although I have a good idea who did it."

"Who?"

"More than likely, it was my sister, Saphira." He shrugged his broad shoulders and then turned to the right, starting down the hallway.

I stole one more glance at the wickedly handsome male in the painting, and then chased after the real thing. "Why would she do that?" I fell into step beside him.

"Because she is angry with me for trading the realms and Aurelius in exchange for you and so she has become like a child and is acting out."

"So what are you going to do about it?" I asked with a degree of seriousness.

"I'm not entirely sure. My sister can be rather bullheaded at times."

"It must run in the family."

The corner of his mouth twitched upwards into a sly grin as he purred, "You have no idea, Kitten."

"I think I have a fairly good grasp."

"Do you now?" he teased in a deep, dark rumble. Three little words had never sounded so good. Like an invitation to take a sip of something you knew was going to rot you to the core, but regardless, you drank anyway—just so you could know what it was like to feel alive.

I opened my mouth to say something back, but the hallway suddenly ended, caving into a set of ominous stairs that disappeared into darkness. Something sinister ran its fingers down the length of my spine, causing the hairs on the back of my neck to raise.

"Go on," Von purred from behind me, and I realized that the touch had been his. But it had felt different than it usually did. It felt . . . cold.

Hard. Unnatural.

I turned to look at him. "Von, I—"

My words died on my tongue as my heart launched into my throat.

The right half of Von's face was as I had always known it to be—achingly handsome. But the other half was—

Horrifying.

On the other side of his face, the flesh and muscle were . . . gone. Revealing nothing but bone. Bone that was not of ivory, but of polished, dark silver. Like metal. The only thing that remained was his eye—still a vibrant green.

"What is this?" I gaped, my brows pressing together as I stepped away from him, away from the stairwell and whatever lurked down there.

"Need I remind you that I am the God of Death, sweetheart? This is who I am." He extended his hand to me in offering. I peered down at it, finding nothing but silver bone, the knuckles stamped with the word king. His rings hung loosely, yet gravity held no dominion over them as they stayed firmly in place. Loyal to him.

His eyes shifted to his right, towards the stairwell.

I followed his gaze. "What's down there?"

"Your future," he answered, retracting his offered hand. He turned to the stairwell, beginning his descent. "Come along, Little Goddess. We have left them all waiting long enough."

Them all?

With a harsh swallow, I hoisted my skirt, hesitantly following after him.

When we reached the bottom, a hallway spanned before us, dimly lit with flickering candlelight.

The air felt different. Ominous.

It reminded me of what it felt like when I'd taken the captain's hand to step onto the floating boat. There was no flesh or muscle or sinew, only cold, hard bone. That's how it felt, but far more concentrated—like the threads of life had been stolen from the tapestry of the world.

Chapter 29

Aurelia

Moments later, I was seated on Von's lap, overlooking a grand throne room, its black, opaque, glass-like walls lit with the dancing flicker of purple flame. Chandeliers, forged from bones so large they must have once belonged to a giant, hung from the arched ceilings, dozens of feet above us. Matching sconces were placed around the walls, alternating with banners that held Death's sigil on them. Incense coated the air, scenting the vast room with the deeply earthy, musky smell of patchouli.

The mountainous chamber was *full* of immortals, humans, ravens, and creatures. Creatures that I had never seen the likes of before. They made my blood run cold. Some looked like they were . . . rotting, their skin hanging unnaturally from their bones. Like worms were chewing on them from the inside, slowly causing them to decay.

Some individuals wore matching black cloaks trimmed in silver, their hoods up. Skull masks with prominent beaks sat on their faces, concealing their identities. Ten of them stood at the front of the room, on either side of the dais, facing the crowd. Their cloaks were different, dyed with a deep amethyst. In their skyward facing palms, they held small, glass-like spheres . . .

Souls.

Despite the amount of people in this room, the temperature was not warm. If anything, it was quite cold, like fall on the cusp of winter. The only thing granting me any form of heat was Von.

Both of his legs were full of muscle, as was his torso, which made me wonder how much of his body matched the left side of his face. His fingers, the ones with flesh on them, drew small circles on my elbow. The ones made of bone rested peacefully on the arm of his throne.

An eerie silence lingered in the vast room. It was so quiet, I could have heard a pin drop on the polished, obsidian floors. So, when I heard something sliding against the floor, my attention jerked to the right, looking to find the source. Stepping out into the light was a cloaked figure, their hunched shoulders wide like a boulder. They dragged their leg as they walked, the tattered remnants of their cloak sliding behind them. From this angle, I couldn't see their face, but something in my gut told me that I wouldn't want to.

"Bow to your king and future queen," rasped the male voice. It sounded as if his throat had been filled with gravel, making his vocal cords hoarse as he spoke.

Future queen.

My lips parted ever so slightly. Sure, Von had said that's what I would be, but to hear it spoken by a stranger, it was just . . . different. Not good or bad. Different. Real, even.

All at once, everyone but those wearing the purple cloaks lowered onto bended knee. Even the dozens of ravens that were perched all around the room dropped their heads in respect. They stayed like that, frozen in place—waiting to be told otherwise.

I had spent a great deal of time in a throne room throughout my lifetime, but I had never seen a crowd who was so obedient. Not even Aurelius could get them to behave like this. So what had brought about such subservience? Was it fear? Or was it respect?

Perhaps, it was a bit of both.

Von's fingers ran up the length of my arm, sweeping across my neck to my jaw. His thumb and forefinger plucked my chin, pulling my attention towards him. "Command them to rise."

"What?" I asked, my eyes rimming at the corners as I took in the monstrous side of his face. My gaze drifted to that one vicious, sharp fang. Without gums, it looked even longer now. Even more menacing. I was fairly certain that if he were to bite my wrist, the porcelain incisor would go all the way through it.

"They will not rise until they are told to," he said. "Command them."

"What makes you think they will listen to me?" My gaze shifted from his fang, tracing along his prominent cheekbone. My fingers itched in my lap, tempted to touch that side of his face—something that frightened me—just so I could feel the adrenaline of doing it.

"Because I have told them to," he said, his voice low. "I meant what I said . . . You are to be my queen, which means you will rule alongside me, as my equal." He guided my face to look out at the crowd, his hand releasing my chin. He lowered his head and whispered in my ear, "This throne, this realm, these people. My cock and my sword. All of it is yours, Little Goddess."

My gaze flickered over the crowd, leaping from one kneeling person to another.

To know that one word from me was all that it would take to make them stand, well, I had never felt such power radiate from within me. The goddess within, she licked her lips, starved of this for so many centuries.

All I had to do was say one little word.

When I spoke, it was her voice, not mine. "Rise."

I watched in amazement as they did—they rose for me. Hundreds of eyes lifted, falling on me and the dark king whose lap I was seated in.

The hunched male with the raspy voice turned towards us and I bristled—

The man's face looked as if it were engorged, like too much fluid had built up beneath the skin. In some places where it wasn't as swollen, those parts were lined with deep wrinkles and sagging flesh. His lips were painted in a smear of black, like he feasted on the blood of monsters.

I could feel a silent laughing breath come from Von, skittering across my skin—turning it to gooseflesh as he asked, “Does Ithar frighten you?”

Ithar bowed to us, and then he turned back to face the crowd.

“What is he?” I whispered to Von over my shoulder, watching as the strange male limped across the floor, speaking to the crowd.

“He was an oracle, but he lost his gift of sight many years ago.”

“How did he lose it?” I asked, watching Ithar as he took a silver bowl from a cloaked, masked figure who walked up to him.

“He insulted the Goddess of Fate, claiming that her prophecies were not accurate. It struck a nerve, so she broke his legs so that he could not swim and threw him into Lake Thersha, a body of water that can leech the power from one’s bones. Sure enough, the waters dragged him down into its stomach, swallowing his ability to see the future. Then it spat him back out.” Von paused for a moment. “Although his gift was beneficial, he now has other uses.”

I had heard of the power-thieving waters of Thersha before in the books I had read, but it was painted in a more mythical light because no one had ever found it. There was speculation that it was in the Immortal Realm, but no one knew where exactly. I couldn’t help but wonder if Von knew where it was. Considering he had been here since the dawn of the Three Realms, I suspected he did.

"What do you mean by other uses?" I asked as Ithar walked to the front of the throne, his leg dragging like an anchor behind him. He stood there with his back turned to us, the bowl raised above his head for all to see. Everyone else in the room was silent.

"So many questions, my curious one," Von mused. "Because he has been stripped of power, the Ancient One that I have imprisoned has no interest in eating him as his soul would be of no substance to her. So he is the one who goes to feed her. He is the first who has been able to walk out of her prison alive."

His answer conjured a dozen more questions—primarily about the Ancient One *eating* people—but instead of asking, my tongue stilled in my mouth as I watched the scene play out below, my curiosity piqued.

Ithar lowered the bowl in front of him. One by one, the purple-robed figures began to walk up to him, discarding the orbs into the silver bowl, glass striking metal. A total of ten times. When it was full, he turned towards us and laid the bowl at the bottom of the dais. Then he got onto his hands and knees, lowering his face to the floor. "I humbly ask you to bless this sacrifice, my king," Ithar said, his voice as pleasant as a metal fork scraping against teeth.

"You have my blessing," Von answered casually, as if Ithar had asked to fill his wine goblet, much less give his blessing to a *sacrifice*.

Ithar scrambled to his feet, the process a painful ordeal to watch. He grabbed the bowl from the ground, bowed his head to us, and then began walking to a doorless arched frame that was tucked into the back of the room—where it led to, I did not know.

I sat there for a moment, churning the melting pot of thoughts rolling around my head. Ithar, the oracle who had lost his sight. The only one who could *feed* the Ancient One. The bowl of gathered orbs—ten, to be exact. And a blessing for a sacrifice.

My stomach turned heavy, filling with lead.

I swung my head, looking up at Von through my lowered brow. "You feed the Ancient One *souls*?" I hissed under my breath.

"It is a necessary evil."

"A necessary evil?" I repeated in disbelief. "Those souls are somebody's someone."

Von's eyes burrowed into mine, and the hairs on the back of my neck stood on end. "*Those souls* are abusers and rapists, and they deserve so much worse than being fed to the Ancient One. They deserve to burn in the fires of the Seventh Tier for the rest of eternity."

"So then why don't they? Why feed them to this . . . Ancient One?"

"Because it is the bare minimum to keep her alive. If she were to die here, her people would seek revenge, and I can assure you that would be much worse for all of us," he answered, his gaze lifting from mine, drifting over the crowd, until it stopped.

A muscle feathered in his jaw on the flesh side of his face, his teeth visibly clenching on the other.

I looked to see what had caught his attention, what had caused his reaction—

And that's when I saw her.

The Goddess of War.

Chapter 30

Aurelia

The painting I saw earlier *did not* do Saphira justice—she was even more fearsome in person. She did not stand with the crowd, but off to the left side of the room, a stride away from an arched doorway that was painted in shadow.

A tight leather dress, dyed onyx, wrapped around her tall, lithe frame. One manicured hand was raised beside her head, a black snake coiled around it. Her sleek hair hung loosely, cascading like a waterfall, all the way down to her waist. Even with the scowl on her face, she was devastatingly beautiful.

Much like her brother.

A loud metal *click* sounded, garnishing my attention towards the far end of the room. A set of massive doors, inlaid with ornamental vines, parted, opened by two stone statues thrice the size of mortal men. Their movement was stiff as they walked the door open, their footsteps as loud as thunder.

Hundreds of people waited on the other side, shoving against one another in desperation. They stretched on like a river, disappearing into the grand hallway behind them. There were *so* many. Their lips were moving as if they were talking, but I could not hear a whisper of sound. Despite their pushing and shoving, not one of them was able to step into the chamber, even though it looked like they were trying to.

Briefly, my gaze flicked back to where Saphira had been standing, only to find the spot empty. She reminded me of a serpent, popping its head out of its hole only to retreat into darkness again.

A curvy female, whose brown hair was slicked back into a bun that looked so tight it made my head hurt, strode towards the people on the other side of the door. Just through her movement alone, I knew that she was an immortal. She pointed to a few people in the crowd, selecting about twenty, and then turned to face us.

"That's Ismay, my assistant," Von said, his fingers still rubbing those small, teasing circles against my arm. "I will have to introduce the two of you."

I nodded, looking the pretty, *pretty* female over. My lips pressed together, forming a flat line. As if he had to pick someone *that* good looking. I blinked, surprised at myself.

I wasn't jealous of her.

. . . It was *the bond*, I lied to myself.

A low, rumbling chuckle sounded behind me as Von said, "You have nothing to worry about, Little Goddess."

"I don't know what you're talking about."

"Mhm," he purred.

Ignoring him, I looked back ahead, towards the set of grand open doors.

As the people stepped over the threshold, the air rippled, distorting the view of those who stood outside the throne room, like a droplet of water striking a glass-topped lake. The lines waved towards the frame of the door, and then the air returned as it was moments before.

A barrier.

That's why I hadn't been able to hear them, why they hadn't been able to come in.

I suspected that the goddess who was now walking down the long stretch of aisle towards us with powerful, confident strides had something to do with it.

Heads turned, watching as the goddess led the people towards us. When she reached the end of the aisle, she bowed her head. Then she turned to the others who had lined up behind her and said, "Your king will hear your requests now."

The first, a man with wide eyes, stepped forward. He removed his cap in respect, nervously wrangling it in his fingers. His knees struck the obsidian floor, one at a time. Then he made his plea. "My king, my wife and I have been separated from our daughter for close to fifty years. We humbly ask to be reunited with her in whatever level she has been placed."

Von shifted behind me so that he was leaning on the left of his throne's arm, his skeleton thumb tucked under the iron bone of his jaw, a finger snaking up the side. "What is your daughter's first name?" he asked, his voice steady, powerful. A king speaking to his subject.

"Andromeda, my king," the man replied, voice trembling.

Von was silent for a moment before he answered, "Your daughter's soul is no longer as you once knew it to be. When she walked amongst the living, she traded her humanity for material wealth. But no matter how rich she became, it was never enough. Eventually, her greed for coin consumed her in such a way that her flesh turned green and her eyes fell from her head. She now wanders, aimlessly in the eighth level, amongst her monstrous brethren."

"No," the man choked out, tears falling down his cheeks.

"For that reason, I decline your request to be reunited with her," Von ruled.

"Please, Your Majesty, she is our only child," the man begged through sobs.

"My ruling still stands. Even if I were to send you and your wife to be with her, she would no longer recognize either of you."

"We could try talking to her," the man pleaded.

"Your breath would be wasted, just as I am wasting mine now," Von said, his tone bored. He raised a hand, gesturing for two guards to come take the man away.

I angled my torso, turning to face Von. "Why not let him try?"

Like this, seated in his throne, he seemed even larger somehow. Green eyes lowered, meeting mine. "Because I have allowed others to try before, and it has only ever made things worse." His fingers drifted across my jaw, his intimate touch robbing me of my concern and replacing it with desire. "Some souls simply cannot be redeemed."

"Are you one of them?" I breathed, studying the skull side of his face—it made my heart pound, made my pulse quicken. It was frightening, and yet . . .

It was arousing.

Did I like this? Did I like seeing that dark side of him?

He cracked a smile, both terrifying and beautiful, all rolled into one. His words infiltrated my mind. *Part your thighs for me and decide for yourself.*

You can't be serious, I scoffed softly. *There are hundreds of people in here.*

I'll tell them all to leave. His heated breath washed over my skin, like a dragon breathing over *his* gold. *As if I would ever allow anyone to see what is mine.*

Von. Fire licked at my cheeks.

Do you not believe that I will? he asked, his hand, which was drawing lazy circles on everywhere *but* the one spot I wanted him to touch, making it hard to concentrate.

When I didn't respond, Von commanded from behind me,

"Everyone out." His voice was filled with immense power—power that my divine feminine recognized, and it had her licking her lips at the intoxicating taste of it.

No one said a single word as they were commanded to leave. They simply bowed and then began to walk out. As soon as the throne room was empty and the doors clicked shut, Von's thumb and forefinger trapped my chin as he angled my face to the side, guiding me to look up at him.

"Your scent is driving me wild," he growled softly, his voice like heavy smoke, a silent thief in the night, stealing the oxygen from my lungs.

"*You* are the one who has been *teasing* me the entire time," I reminded him.

He grinned, his expression painting him as the perfect example of unbridled male arrogance. "I suppose I have been, haven't I?"

I turned around, positioning myself so that I was straddling his lap. I placed my hands on the hardened muscle of his chest—strong and sturdy and dangerous. It wasn't the only thing. I could feel his erection beneath me, just as hard as the rest of him.

"So what are you going to do about it?" I asked, wetting my lips.

"Give me a kiss and find out." His fingers, the ones made of bone, tapped his bottom lip.

A shiver strolled through me—

His mouth was half flesh, half teeth and bone.

Sharp.

Dangerous.

Terrifying.

My heart pounded in my chest, pushing adrenaline through my body as I hesitantly reached for his face. Slowly, I ran my fingers over the skull side—more metal feeling than bone. That was what he was made of—not some flimsy, easy to break bone, but cold, hard steel. It was unnatural. Frightening. And yet, there was something about it that made me feel . . . protected. Like no one could touch me, harm me, while sitting on the God of Death's lap.

My lashes fluttered down as I eyed where he wanted me to kiss.

Slowly, I lowered my lips against his.

It was the strangest feeling—his plush, soft lips on one side, and nothing but teeth on the other. His steely fingers held my chin, keeping me there as he kissed me back.

His shadows drifted around us and then I was sitting on the throne while he stood over top of me, his tongue dancing with mine.

Those cold, cruel fingers released my jaw and he raised to his full height, bathing me in his darkness.

My breath hitched in my throat as I watched his shadows sweep away his clothes, revealing his sexy torso derived from inked skin and rippling muscles. Besides the skull side of his face, skeleton hand, and a bit of his forearm, his body was just as I knew it to be—completely and irrevocably *him*. Slowly, my gaze crawled down his prominent, defined abs, drifting over the mouthwatering v-cut, halting at the weapon between his legs—erect and ready and huge.

My body quivered at the sight of him.

My clothes were the next to go. Cool air wafted over my skin, chased away by the heated way he looked at me.

"So fucking beautiful," he praised in that deep, chest-rumbling tone of his. His hands grasped my legs, and he pulled me lower in the throne, so that my bottom was close to the edge. He leaned forward, bringing his mouth to mine as he lifted my legs up, placing them over the throne's arms. Something wound around my legs, locking them there. I broke the kiss, jerking my head back so I could see what it was—

Shadow chains.

"Trust me," Von purred with a sinful grin as he lowered onto his knees.

His skeleton hand pressed against my stomach, holding me there. The second his tongue swept along my slit, he groaned deeply. He laved at my sex, licking it relentlessly.

"Von," I whimpered as his tongue found my core, plunging inside.

The sight of his half-skull face eating me out was the most horrifyingly erotic thing I had ever seen. He did it like he was famished, like he had been starving for decades, and I was his first *real* meal.

Pulling his tongue from me, his molten mouth latched on to my clit. At the same time, his fingers entered me—the bone hard and unforgiving as they drove all the way to his knuckles. A raspy moan escaped me as I tossed my head back, my hands fisting in his black hair.

I had never felt more powerful as I orgasmed again and again, chained to Death's monstrous throne as he knelt before me, worshipping me with his tongue.

In the deep hours of the night, Von and I sat in his spacious private bath. I leaned against his broad, sturdy torso, watching the swirls of steam as they danced from the surface of the shimmering pool. Water trickled as Von raised a washcloth from the water, his large hand squeezing the cloth until more dribbled out. In a soft, slow motion, he ran it over my shoulder, down my arm, until it disappeared beneath the water again. I'd lost track of time, unsure how long he had been washing my skin, not that I had any qualms about it.

"Am I clean yet?" I asked in a quiet, joking tone, a small smile touching my lips.

"You are," he said, his chest rumbling as he spoke, causing a hint of a vibration at my back. "But what I am doing now—" he brought the cloth up and ran it over my skin once more, "—is not for the purpose of washing you."

"No?" I mused, enchanted by the softness of the cloth as he ran it above my breasts, taking his time. I closed my eyelids, soaking up this moment, feeling the fabric as it brushed across my flesh.

"Your body is a temple, and it deserves to be praised and adored. This—" he ran the cloth over my sensitive nipples, pulling it under the water, down my torso, "—is me showing you that."

My heart stumbled, missing its beat. I lifted my arms from the water, lacing them around his neck as I gave him full access to the rest of my body, should he want it. Looking up, I angled my head so that I could see his beautiful face, now returned to normal. I had a question I had been wanting to ask him for some time now. "Von?"

Eyes as green as a canopy of leaves, framed by lashes so black they looked to be naturally rimmed with kohl, met mine. "Yes, Little Goddess?"

I nibbled on my bottom lip, released it, then asked, "Will you stay with me tonight?"

A smile dawned on his lips. "I've been waiting for you to ask me to." He dropped the cloth in the waters, cupped my cheek, and brought his lips a breath above mine. "Of course, I will."

Chapter 31
Von

A thick, black fog rolled in last night, resulting in a blanket of heavy dew come the next morning. Condensation gathered on the top lip of the window, forming lush, fat-bottomed droplets. They hung on until they could no longer. Bowing to gravity, they let go and hit the small ledge below with such force, they splattered back up on the window—giving the illusion it had been raining.

Had I not spent the last eight hours watching the fog roll in and the condensation gather, I would have thought it had. Why had I spent so much time watching something so monotonous, one might ask? Well, the first was because I *rarely* slept—I avoided it. The second was because my slumbering mate was lying on my arm, and like a pet owner with a cat nested in their lap, I did not have the heart to wake her.

Or to move, for that matter.

Plus, the feel of her plump little rear shoved against me was positively divine, although it did not aid in my wandering thoughts of all the different ways that I would enjoy waking her up. But considering how exhausted she had been after we'd broken in every inch of the throne room yesterday—I knew I should let her sleep.

Besides, there was something I needed to do. Alone.

Slowly, carefully, I pulled my arm out from underneath her, my shadows replacing my spot and curling up protectively behind her. I watched her for a moment, my gaze raking over the curvature of her slumbering feminine silhouette.

My lovely little female.

I eyed the fang marks I'd left on her breast, the sheet not quite pulled up enough to cover her. If there was one perk about her body taking a while to heal, that would be it—my markings lasted a pleasantly long time on her flesh. Mortal men liked to see rings on their spouses' fingers, but not me, no. A ring could be removed. The meaning behind a ring changed over time—sometimes for better, sometimes for worse.

But my fingerprints etched into her ass? The meaning behind that never changed.

It meant that I hungered for her. Deeply.

I released a withheld breath of air, then clothed myself in a simple black tunic and leather pants. The bond was none too happy as I shadow walked away from the room, leaving my mate in her state of peace as I prepared for war.

My umbra swirled around me as I entered the subterranean lair, burrowed deep underneath the monumental temple my sister had built in her honor, all the way down in the Sixth Tier. A land void of light, dominated by dust storms and blazing heat. The inferno climate was courtesy of the fiery tier that sat beneath it. Because of it, nothing grew in these desolate lands—not even weeds. Despite the lack of vegetation and high temperatures, Saphira spent most of her time here. Sometimes she would attend the worships up above in the main part of the mountain-sized building, allowing those who celebrated her to feed her divinity with their praise, and other times, she slithered below, where she fed in other ways.

I strolled ahead, over the stretch of marble floor, ducking underneath the Moorish lanterns that hung from the low ceiling. Horseshoe-shaped windows with smoke-tinted glass allowed for glimpses inside the various chambers. All of them were filled with people, saddled up around tables of different shapes and sizes. Cards, dice, and coins occupied their black velvet-wrapped tops. In some rooms, gambling tables were not the only source of entertainment. Some were filled with husky moans and naked, writhing bodies, slick with sweat.

"Would you like a dab?" a naked brunette slurred as she stumbled up to me, her pupils gobbling up her irises. She raised her hand, showing me a monochromatic shell—or rather, the thick, grimy paste within it. Most of it was gone. "You can apply it anywhere you—*hiccup*—want, but I recommend here." She pointed to her sex, a thatch of dark curls.

I didn't show a speck of interest as I walked by her.

I was no stranger to what she was offering, but I had very little desire to live as I used to anymore. There was a point in my life where I was willing to try anything to pass the time, but now that I had my mate, I wanted to savor every second of it.

"Hello, handsome king," purred a man who was on his hands and knees, swirls of gold paint slathered across his freckled skin. "Would you like a taste of me?" he asked, reaching for me as I passed by.

I let a shadow slip free, like a jungle cat on a loose leash, its jaws snapping at him.

He let out a scream and shot back on his ass, crab-walking up to the wall behind him. Drugs or not, since when had I become so approachable to the dead in this tier? It didn't sit well with me.

I let my shadows scare off anyone else who tried to touch me as I continued forward, stopping only when the corridor expanded into a massive room that caved into a circular pit, rimmed with marbled stairs.

What was the pit full of?

Vipers. Hundreds of them. All focused on one task—mating.

In the middle of the giant snake orgy was a raised platform. On it, various offerings, chests, and sacks full of coins, jewelry, perfumes, fabrics, and other riches. They surrounded a green velvet lounger. Reclined on it with a silver goblet in one hand and a young viper coiled around the other was the pain in my ass herself—

Saphira.

Her sleek black hair was tugged harshly into a ponytail, the long strands tossed over her left shoulder. A band of leather wrapped tightly around her chest, matching the tiny skirt she wore. A man stood behind her, holding a platter full of grapes, while a female fanned her with a feather fan made from black ostrich feathers. They both wore a black leather collar that matched my sister's outfit. Nothing else. Their gaunt bodies were full of black and blue splotches, bite marks, and cuts.

"Brother," Saphira greeted flatly. Emerald eyes daggered into mine. A sneer formed on her bloodstained lips. "I see the mating bond was successful."

"It was," I said with a dirty grin as I slipped a hand into my pocket. "Folkoln brought us a bottle of spirits to celebrate."

"Good for him." She didn't bother to hide her disinterest.

I pressed my brows together, feigning confusion. "I was surprised you didn't show up with something to congratulate us."

"And what would you have me give to you?"

"A basket or something." I didn't bother to hide my sarcasm.

"Is that why you have come, to hound me for not bringing you a *mating* gift?" Her hand jerked upwards, raising the goblet beside her head. "More blood!"

The male servant placed the silver tray full of grapes on a small table before he returned to her side. He raised his arm to his mouth, and with his blunt, mortal teeth, he bit into his flesh. He didn't even wince—a testament to the strength of the drugs he was on. Lips stained with crimson, he lowered his arm over her goblet. He cupped his wrist, applying pressure as he wrung out his weeping veins—his expression as blank as if he were just squeezing out a cloth.

Arrogantly, I sucked my teeth, the corner of my mouth twisting upwards. "No, that's not the reason I've come to this cesspool."

The room became quiet. Even the snakes began to still.

"So then, why are you here?"

I leveled her gaze. "I'm going to make *her* my queen and I expect your full support."

"Full support?" she cackled. The young snake slithered up her arm, winding itself loosely around her throat. "You gave the Immortal and Living Realms to one New God, and now you plan to give half of the Spirit Realm to another? You will *never* have my support for that."

I scanned the room, finding a great deal of eyes on us. Watching. Waiting. Good. The more witnesses the better. Let them be reminded who their king was.

I let a ripple of my dark power pulse around us in warning. It was enough to send those who stood watching recoiling back.

"I am not asking, Saphira."

Irritated, she gestured to the male to stop. He stepped back, his hand clamping around his bloody arm. She brought the goblet down, black lashes nearly kissing her cheeks as she peered at the innards of the cup. I knew my sister well enough to know that she was not interested in the contents, but rather, was deciding how to proceed. Saphira was a smart goddess, but she was also easily ruled by her own agenda and ego. This could go either way.

Lifting her head, her thick black brows arched as she asked, "And if I do not give you my support?"

"Then I see no reason for you to live in the Spirit Realm any longer." My voice cut like a lethal blade.

"You would kick me out of my own home?" A flash of hurt raced across her face. "I have been with you since the beginning of our creation. I have been *nothing* but loyal to you." She tossed her goblet to the side, the metal clattering against the marble floors, splattering it in red. Her servants jumped. "And you would toss me out just like that?"

I delivered my response slowly. "If you give me reason to, then I will."

"How dare you!" she screamed, her voice echoing around us. Shadows swarmed around her and then she was standing before me, the black polish on her nails catching the dim firelight as she attempted to strike me.

I caught her wrist, felt her immortal bones groan beneath my crushing grip. "You have forgotten your place, sister."

My winds picked up around us, hurtling into the sides of the temple, shaking dust from every crevice, making the mighty structure tremble. I looked behind her, sinking myself into the minds of the vipers—the creatures I had just as much of a hand in making as her. Although they were a product of Saphira and me, there was one thing I had over her—I was the king of this realm, not her. The sleek, black serpents turned towards us, their mouths stretched wide open as they hissed.

Not at me, but at her.

Even the one that was weaved around her neck had turned on her.

I lowered my face to hers, my tone threatening. "You would do best to remember it."

I let her arm go and she took a protective step back. Her eyes darted around the room, noticing how many more were fixed on her. She tore the snake from her throat, throwing it on the floor as if she had just been told her necklace was made of fool's gold. Her lip curled in disgust, her expression like an open-faced book—one I could easily read—

I had deeply wounded her precious ego.

Reining in my winds, the temple stilled. I released my hold on the vipers and they went back to what they had been doing before, completely unfazed by what had just happened. Although, I could not say the same for my poor sister.

I strode past her, my shadows swallowing me whole as I left my parting words with her, "Consider this your last warning, Saphira."

I hoped that that would be the last of it, although deep down . . . I had a feeling it wouldn't be.

Chapter 32

Aurelia

I placed my hands on my hips as I took a step back, surveying my work. Delicate green vines grew along the black walls, adorned with vibrant, white roses. The flowers were identical to the one I had made all those nights ago, when Von removed his curse. When I woke this morning at the crack of dawn, I had felt an immense need to create, and this was helping to scratch that itch.

"You're up early," Von's deep voice purred from behind me as he entered the room.

"I am," I answered. I glanced over my shoulder, taking in the tall, muscular immortal, who held a silver tray in his hands. Every morning since he had brought me to the Spirit Realm, apart from the very first day, he'd brought me a tray full of freshly cooked foods. On the days when I was awake, he would sit and watch me eat, and on the days where I was still asleep, he'd leave them by my bedside, with a note and a black rose. I thought that eventually he would grow tired of it . . . but he didn't.

"What are you doing?" he asked as he placed the tray down on the coffee table in the sitting area.

"I'm livening our bedchamber up. It's too dreary."

He rumbled in approval. "I like hearing you say that word."

"What word?"

"Our." He made his way over to me.

I blinked. "I didn't."

Did I?

"You most definitely did," he confirmed as his arm wrapped around my waist, pulling me against his muscular frame. Creator above, he smelled good. He glanced up at the vine-covered wall, peppered with white roses, looking over my work. "I love it."

"Do you really?" I asked with a soft laugh, my hands falling over top of his.

"I do," he answered. "I think you should do it to the rest of the place. I want to see your signature written all over *our* castle walls."

"Even in the throne room?"

"Especially there," he rumbled as he swept me up into his arms, carrying me bridal style over to the settee. He sat down, positioning me sideways on his lap. His shadows wrapped around the legs of the table, pulling it over to us. Shadow hands lifted the lid, revealing what was underneath—crisp, sliced fruits, steaming eggs, browned ham, and cubed potatoes, seasoned with rosemary and oregano.

My mouth watered.

"Eat, little mate. For what I have planned for you today, you are going to need the energy."

"Oh?" I plucked a grape and turned back to face him. "And what do you have planned for me?" I asked, my voice sultry. Slowly, I slid the grape between my lips, hollowing my cheeks as I sucked it in.

Von's greedy eyes watched, something dark swimming inside of them. "You'll just have to wait and see."

A slightly tart flavor awakened my taste buds as I chewed. Swallowing, I said, "I've never been the patient type."

A wicked grin. "Then it's a good thing I am."

Indeed, it was.

I turned back to the tray, my fingers dancing over top, debating what to try next. "Davina is such a wonderful cook. I should grow some flowers and take them to her in thanks for all the meals she has sent."

Von chuckled, then asked, "Do you want to know a secret?"

"Sure." I lifted the fork and knife and cut off a small piece of ham. I slid it into my mouth, the sweet, smoked meat making me salivate as soon as it hit my tongue.

"Davina isn't the one who has been making you food."

When I was finished chewing, I asked, "Who has been making it then? Another cook?"

". . . Why do you think I bring you a tray every morning?"

It took me a moment.

"*You* are *the one* who has been making my food?" I gasped, looking up at him.

"Yes." He nipped at my nose.

I had to sit with that for a moment. All of this time, Von had been making my morning meals. He could easily have the kitchen staff do it, but instead, he was making them.

My brows pressed together as I looked up at him. "Why?"

"Originally, I thought it would be a good way to win you over, as you seemed rather food oriented. But in truth—" he captured a lock of my hair, running his fingers down the length of it, "—I do it for the same reason I brush your hair every night. Nothing pleases me more than having the privilege of caring for you."

His words plucked at a tender string.

And yet . . . I was scared to fully let them sink in—because what would happen when he no longer felt that way? When he got bored of me? I knew the answer because I had already lived through that once. I would be left alone, yearning for the way he used to treat me. A ghost of my former self.

I glanced down, my appetite gone.

"What is it?" he asked, his curled finger tucking under my chin, gently lifting my fallen gaze and bringing it to his.

I nibbled on my bottom lip. "When I am no longer the shiny new thing you enjoy pining over? When you grow tired of me? Then what?"

"Ah, Little Goddess." He let out a gravelly breath. Softly, he shook his head. "If there is one thing that I am certain of, it is that I will *never* grow tired of you."

"How can you be so sure?"

Gazing into my eyes, he said, "Because I was used to living in a world of black, but then you came along, and for the first time in my life, everything was painted in rich, vibrant color—from the blue of your eyes to the pink beneath your moonlit skin to the red on your lips. The colors of you follow me everywhere I go. And if this world were to end, and I was placed in another, the colors of you are what I would spend an eternity searching for." His large hand cradled my cheek, swallowing the side of my face. "You have enriched my life in ways I did not know were possible. In ways I did not know that I needed. You are the love of my eternal life, and I will spend the next thousand years proving that to you—even more, if I must."

"Von," I said softly. My heart beating rapidly in my chest.

He brought his lips to mine, whispering against them, "You are the light to my darkness. The moon to my night. I love you, Little Goddess."

Butterfly wings filled my stomach. I took a large, deep, savory breath, committing his words to memory.

And then I kissed him.

When Von said earlier that he had something planned for me, I didn't expect it to be . . . *this*.

"We're certainly not in the arena," I said as we stood on the edge of a cliff, overlooking a sea of pine trees. How they grew on such a drastic incline, I would never know. And yet, they did. Against all odds. The wind whipped around us, howling like a giant, angry wolf.

"No, we're not," Von said as he released me from him. "Zahra was having back cramps today so she wouldn't have been able to train with you anyway. So I decided we should try something else."

"Is she alright?" I asked, worry tugging at my brows.

"Dameon said that the healer said she'll be fine, and that it is a normal part of pregnancy."

"I see. Perhaps I should go see her later."

Von nodded in agreement.

I made a mental note to do just that, then asked, "Alright, well, what have you brought me all the way up here for?"

He smirked. "I'm going to teach you how to fly."

"Von, I only have one wing."

"No, Little Goddess, you have two," he said, holding out his hand. Black swirls danced from his palm, twisting and turning, dipping and churning until they produced—

A wing.

About the same size as my white one, but it was made from his glorious, black feathers.

Tears filled my eyes as my gaze darted from the wing to him, and then back and forth a few more times. Finally, I choked out, "You made me a wing?"

"I did." He smiled. "It is only a prototype so we might have to tweak it as we go, so today will just be a test run, but it should fit over top of yours. You have the bone structure; you are simply just missing the feathers."

I brushed my tears away, stepping closer to him as I dared to run a trembling hand down the wing prosthetic he had crafted for me. The feathers—*his* feathers—were so soft against my skin. "There are so many of them," I said, somewhat astonished. "Do you even have any left for your own wings?"

A cocky, arrogant smirk curled the left side of his mouth as he said, "Have you seen my wingspan, baby? I have plenty to give."

I shook my head, a smile warring at my lips.

"Now turn around, and let's see if it works," he instructed.

So I did just that.

Von held me by the waist as he carried me through the air, flying us just underneath the fluffy black clouds. I could hear it in his voice that he was trying not to laugh as he said through the bond, *Okay, this time, try to flail less.*

That was easier said than done.

We had been at it for hours, and I was failing miserably. I was no better than a baby bird being kicked out of the nest, destined to fall on the ground as my wings failed me. Although I never did hit the ground because just before that would happen, Von would catch me. And when he did, typically he would be laughing, like he was getting some great kick out of my pathetic attempts at flying.

At least *he* was enjoying this. I couldn't say the same for myself.

Okay, I'm going to let you go, he said. The wind noise up here made it impossible to hear one another's voices, which was why we were using our private channel to speak on.

No, wait, I'm not ready yet. I clutched his hands.

You've been saying that for the last fifteen minutes. Wings out, Kitten, he purred in command.

Von, I snarled, looking at the ground—which was far, *far* below. Last time, Von had waited until the absolute last second to grab me and I was certain my body was about to be splattered into smithereens.

No time like the present, darling. Now quit being such a chicken shit. Wings out.

Did he just call me a chicken shit? I scoffed at that.

Do you think that maybe there might be a better way to teach me? Like starting on the ground first?

Baby birds learn how to fly by trial and error, not sitting hunkered down safely in their nest, he replied. *Your body knows how to do this, just as it knew how to throw out your wings that day you fell from the ladder. Trust in your instincts*.

Are you calling me a baby bird?

I am, he purred. *Now, try for me one last time.*

Fine, I said, swallowing harshly as I looked at the ground below.

Remember, spread your wings and find a current, he said, and then he let me go.

I screamed as I fell through the air, the ground coming faster and faster at a bone-smashing speed. I flailed, trying to press my wings out. The left one caught a current, just at the tip, but instead of guiding me upwards, it knocked me off course and sent me spinning.

The world twirled, shifting from green pines to an amethyst sky, going around and around and around.

Wings out, Little Goddess! Von shouted through the bond.

I hadn't even realized I had tucked them in.

The earth was getting even closer. I had seconds left to do something.

I closed my eyes, shoved my wings out, and then—

Something caught me.

And this time, it wasn't Von.

It was my wings!

I'm flying! I screamed through the bond, excitement overtaking me, rendering the entire experience rather short-lived as I flew into a large branch full of green needles.

Later that night, Von and I sat on the bed as he healed the scrapes, bruises, and cuts I had acquired after I lost the battle with the pine tree.

"You did really well today, for your first time," he said as he worked, his fingers sliding over my arm as he raised my wrist to his lips, kissing the cut. It healed instantly.

"Says the male who laughed the entire time," I huffed, side-eyeing him.

A grin pierced his full lips, his heated breath washing over my skin. "You just looked so adorable I couldn't help myself." He kissed another spot, and the bruising began to disappear.

"Mhm," I said disbelievingly.

"Mhm," he rumbled sexily. Playfully.

I nibbled my bottom lip, watching as he continued to kiss away my scrapes and bruises—quite literally. Every other immortal was able to heal themselves, but not me. It was something my divinity lacked. Yet somehow, Von could heal me. Just like my incomplete wings, it was one more broken part of me that he completed.

My gaze turned soft as I watched him work, enjoying every brush of his lips, every caress of his fingers.

After a bit of time passed, I asked, "Can we try again tomorrow? With flying?"

He let my arm go as he lifted his head and nodded. "Of course we can." His gaze shifted to my lips. "I missed a cut."

"Funny, I don't remember seeing one there."

"Oh, it's there." He pulled me into him and his thumb brushed over my bottom lip. "It's just really, *really* small, but still, it needs tending to."

He lowered his lips to mine, kissing me deeply.

Chapter 33

Aurelia

I was a terrible friend.

Terrible.

Yesterday, after hearing that Zahra was unable to come to training, I had fully intended to go visit her, but then Von took me flying, which ate up most of the day, and then after I flew into that tree, he had spent the rest of the night kissing *every* inch of me.

And I mean *every* inch.

Apparently, I had bruises and cuts in places that hadn't even come in contact with the pine. Funny how that worked. Not that I had any complaints.

This morning when I woke up, my thoughts immediately went to

Zahra. Naturally, my conscience was kicking my ass for it. I knew I had to make it right. So, I got dressed, shoveled my morning meal into my mouth as I crafted a bouquet of flowers for her. The roses and peonies came naturally, but the baby's breath took me a few attempts to make. Although they weren't perfect, they were still lovely, so I decided to include them. I finished the bouquet off with some salal and then headed towards Zahra and Dameon's chambers.

My knuckles rapped softly against their door. I heard footsteps from the other side and then it swung open—

Dameon answered, shirtless and sweaty.

He had a towel slung around his neck, one hand holding onto it. His sleek eight-pack was on *full* display. It was well defined, like the rungs of a ladder, asking to be climbed. I imagined Zahra did it frequently. And honestly, good for her.

He smiled with his perfect white teeth, fangs and all. "Good morning, Aurelia."

"Morning. Is Zahra here?" I asked, peeking around him.

"She is," he said, his bare feet padding against the floor as he backed up. "Come in."

I walked in, flowers in hand, my moral compass no longer screaming at me that I was a shit friend.

"Zahra, Aurelia is here," Dameon called out, speaking over his shoulder.

Moments later, Zahra came striding out, her dark-orange gown flying behind her, catching on her quick-paced current. She held two baby outfits, one in each hand. The first was a tiny pair of pants and a matching shirt, and the other one was an adorable little dress. "Boy or girl?" she asked, showing me the outfits.

Dameon stood at her back, wrapping his arms around her, his flame-colored eyes peering down at the clothes.

"What do you mean?" I asked, my gaze flickering between her left and right hand.

"Do you think it's a boy or girl?" she replied. "I'm fifty-fifty right now, so I keep buying clothes for both genders."

I took a breath, inhaling softly as I let her question sit with me, until I felt the answer come to me. "Boy."

"I think it's a boy too," Dameon said, pressing a kiss against her shoulder.

A sunny smile tugged at Zahra's lips as she leaned to the side and glanced over her shoulder at Dameon. "Does that mean you have come around to it not being twins?"

"I only wished for it to be twins because of the prophecy," he said, pressing a kiss against her cheek. "As long as the two of you are healthy, that is all I care about."

I was tempted to ask what the prophecy was—I almost did—but I decided that some things were not meant for everyone's ears, and if Zahra wanted to tell me what it was, she would. But for the most part, she seemed to be dismissive of it. Maybe she didn't want to talk about it for a reason.

That was something I understood.

So I didn't pry.

In a sweet reply, Zahra kissed her mate's cheek.

"Mmm," Dameon purred with a wicked amount of swagger. He bit his bottom lip, as if he couldn't get enough of her.

Zahra laughed softly before she turned her attention back to me, her eyes going to the arrangement of flowers. Dameon's followed.

"They are for you," I told her, holding them up. "Because of your back pain yesterday."

Dameon released her from his arms, and she handed him the little outfits, saying, "Can you take these back to the baby's chambers?"

He nodded and made his way to a hallway that was on my right.

Zahra turned to me, taking the flowers. She looked them over, her eyes twinkling as she did. "These are so very lovely. Thank you for thinking of me."

"Of course. How are you feeling today?"

"I'm quite well today, actually. Sorry about missing training yesterday." She offered an apologetic smile.

"No, no, please don't be." I shook my head. "You are growing an immortal. You have a *valid* reason."

"True," she said, her hand drifting to her belly. "By the way, speaking of training, I was thinking . . . you've come a long way with channeling the flame, so perhaps we could switch things up and have you focus more on earth-bending. I don't know a whole lot about how earthly powers work, but I think Von might be able to help us out there."

My brows raised ever so slightly.

Von could help me . . . earth-bend?

"Why the look?" she asked, peering curiously at me.

"I guess I didn't realize that Von had the ability to hone the powers of earth, but now that you mention it, it makes sense." The apples he was always eating, the seeds he'd given me for the orchard, the black roses he left on the silver tray, the ravens he commanded—he'd made all of those. The castle I was standing in right now, it was forged from hot lava, elements of earth and fire, being swiftly cooled off by . . . rain. I gasped. "Can he command fire and water as well?"

"Yes." Zahra nodded. "He is the only god in the entire Three Realms who possesses all six of the primary powers. And even then, he has powers beyond those six, powers no one else has."

My mouth popped open. "So mind and dream? He has those as well?"

"He does, although because he detests his dream powers, that's why you'll barely find him sleeping. As for the mind, surely you've seen that in action on the daily—he has a knack for getting inside people's heads, knowing what they are thinking."

Indeed, I had *most* definitely seen that. No one could mess with someone's head quite as good as Von. He was, for lack of better words, the king of fuckery.

"I'm just a bit surprised by all of this," I told her, my shoulder bobbing slightly. "Surprised I didn't realize it before."

"Don't be, it's not exactly common knowledge." She looked at the flowers. "Now, I should probably put these in some water. Come with me to the kitchen and we can keep chatting."

Moments later, Zahra and I were in their pristine, private kitchen—it looked like it had never seen a meal prepared in it before. Considering the Old Gods didn't eat regularly like the mortals did, and they could attend the dining halls if they wanted a cooked meal, I could see why the kitchen looked as it did. I sat at a round table, a cup of steaming herbal tea in my hands. Zahra was busy placing the flowers in a silver vase, humming softly to herself.

She broke off the pleasant sound. "How's the tea?"

"It's good, thanks." I peered down at the cup—breathing in the chamomile, ginger, and peppermint.

"I picked it up from the market down in Velosh, in the Third Tier. You'll have to accompany me next time I go. I think you'd enjoy it—there are so many different things to try." She washed her hands and then joined me at the table, seating herself in front of her cup of tea.

"I'd like that," I replied, setting mine down after I had taken a small sip.

Zahra pressed a hand against her tight, springy, dark curls, styling them, her eyes sliding to mine. "So . . . I heard a bit of gossip the other day while visiting with some friends."

"Oh?" I shifted forward, leaning in.

"Apparently—" she rolled her wrist, highlighting what she said next, "—*someone* lit fire to the Goddess of Life's private chambers in the Golden Palace." She paused for a moment, a smile touching her lips. "It destroyed a bit of the bedchamber, but the worst damage was done to the closet, where they suspect the fire was started."

"Hmm." A saccharine grin plucked at my mouth. "I wonder who would have done that."

"That's what the other goddesses were wondering as well." Her head bobbed softly. "I guess the God of Life had a colossal-sized tantrum when he saw that the Goddess of Life's clothes had all been destroyed. From the sounds of it, they were worth a pretty copper."

At the mention of *him*, my body bristled. The smile fell from my lips.

Swiftly, Zahra reached across the table, her hand falling on top of mine. "Aurelia, I apologize. I didn't realize—"

"It's okay," I told her, patting her hand with my free one.

"No, it's not," she said. "I know what it's like to react like that when you hear someone's name and I know what it means."

"Do you?" My voice was soft.

"I do." She paused for a moment. "Before Dameon, there was someone else. Although the bond never formed between us, I truly thought he was the love of my life. In the beginning, everything was great, but there were these subtle little flags, like him not approving of what I was wearing, or him getting jealous when I spent time with my friends. When people started to notice, I brushed it off, making excuses for him because I thought I loved him. Over time, the mental abuse just kept getting worse and worse, until I no longer recognized myself in the mirror. It's peculiar how someone can do that to you—

rob you of who you thought you were." Her eyebrows pressed together. She shook her head, pushing the thought away. "Anyway, one day, when I was at a particularly low point, Dameon came along and he changed everything. He showed me what it was like to be loved by a good man. He saved me."

I couldn't help but apply what she said to my own situation—in so many ways, Von had saved me too. I was just slowly realizing that.

"I'm so sorry, Zahra," I said to her before I took a breath, and then I did something that took a great deal of strength—I uncovered a part of my past that I had never told anyone, a part of my past that I had kept so deeply buried inside of me, I never planned to show it the light of day, but now, I felt empowered to . . .

I wanted to.

"One day, when Aurelius and I were walking through a forest in the Living Realm, we stumbled upon a peculiar tree. It was standing all by itself, as if nothing wished to grow near it. It was a bit larger than a fully grown apple tree, with leaves as white as snow. As we approached it, I became violently ill, to the point I fell unconscious. That's how we discovered what my weakness is, what can end my immortal life. Months later, Aurelius and I got into a disagreement about how much time I was spending in my orchard, which quickly escalated into us shouting at one another. He forced me to drink his ichor so that I would be compliant to him and then he . . ." I paused for a moment, needing a few seconds to form the words on my tongue, to find the courage to let them out. "And then he grabbed me by my hair and dragged me through the courtyard gardens. There, planted in the middle, was the tree we had seen in the forest, the one that made me sick. He had had it removed and brought to the palace, something I didn't know about until that day. When I began to vomit and the world began to flicker in and out, he flipped me onto my back, his hand crushing my throat as he threatened to end my life." I looked down at my lap. "Days later, when I woke up, he was sitting by my bedside. He apologized profusely and I forgave him. That night, we made love for the first time in months, and I was content with him once more."

"Aurelia, that's so horrible. I wish I knew you back then, so that I could have helped you somehow. Abuse is a terrible thing. It really messes with your head and self-worth. I know other women who have gone back to their abusers more than seven times, because they think that is what love is. And it can happen to even the strongest of women." She let out a breath, her hand never leaving mine. "Does Von know?"

"He knows a small portion of it. He thinks there were only two incidents, but . . ." I took a sharp inhale. "There were so many more."

"Do you think it would help you heal if you talked to him about it?"

"I don't want him to know."

"Why not?"

I chewed my bottom lip. "Because I fear what he might do if he knew about it all."

Zahra was silent for a moment. "I understand. Talking to those we are closest to about abuse is one of the most challenging things we can do. It's okay to take your time opening up about it. The important part is that you *talk to someone*. If you like, I can be that person for you, for as long you need. Just as Saphira once was for me."

"Saphira?" My brows tugged together, creasing the space between them. I hadn't expected that name to come up during this conversation.

"As hard as it might be to believe, Saphira and I were once close friends," she replied with a confirming nod of her head, a hint of a small smile tugging at her lips. "She was there for me when I needed her and so I will always hold a special place in my heart for her, even though we are no longer as close as we used to be." Her head dipped as her fingers warmly stroked her belly. "I suppose life has a variety of seasons, doesn't it?"

I nodded.

I supposed it did.

Chapter 34

Aurelia

"You've been perched on that railing every morning for months now. At this point, I think it would be nice to know your name," I said to the raven as I finished my morning meal, wiping my fingers with a cloth napkin. I set it down on the tray and turned to look at the bird.

As usual, it said nothing.

Sighing, I reclined back on the chair, tossing my arms upwards and stretching them over the back.

Suddenly, the bird looked down, over top of the railing, cocking its head to the side as if it were zeroing in on something.

"What do you see?" I asked.

Again, no response.

I rose from the low chair, my black silk robe falling to my mid-thigh, and strode over to the glass-like railing, beside the bird. My hand settled on the cool banister as I looked over it, peering down below—

A treacherous path snaked towards the castle, gradually widening the closer it came, until it molded with the unnaturally flat mountaintop—like a river vein meeting the sea. The sides were steep, plunging into oblivion. I had stood at the bottom of that path once, when I came here to ask for Von's aid in saving the children of the Old Gods. The wards had prevented me from light walking any further and so I had been faced with a choice—walk the miles-long path, or ride on a strange boat that floated on the air itself.

I chose the latter.

On the path, there appeared to be an altercation.

Strange beings who I had come to recognize as castle guards were gathered in a circle. They were tall creatures that were dressed from head to toe in black leather armor—their faces completely covered by metal skull masks, complete with wicked horns that either pointed upwards or curled back.

When I saw who they had surrounded, my heart struck a mighty blow to my ribs.

Standing in the middle of them was a redheaded male adorned in royal, gold clothing, his sword drawn. I recognized him immediately. He was the only friend I had ever known in the Immortal Realm, and now he was here.

Surrounded by castle guards.

"Arkyn!" I shouted.

Striding out from the shadow of the castle was the God of Death himself. His shadow cloak flickered behind him as he thundered ahead, his dark, ethereal crown floating above his onyx mane.

The circle parted, the creatures bowed, and I watched as Von conjured his sword and disarmed Arkyn in all of three moves. The eerie guards grabbed Arkyn by his shoulders, kicked the backs of his legs out, and made him kneel in front of Von.

Von raised his sword.

"No!" I screamed, my light wrapping around me.

One moment I was standing on the balcony, and the next, my bare feet were on the cool, rocky ground, my arms spread out as I tried to protect Arkyn from that fatal blow. I had no time to question how my light walking abilities had suddenly worked after months of ignoring my call, but I imagined it had something to do with the bond wanting me to be closer to Von.

"What are you doing?" Von grated at me, stopping mid-swing. He lowered his weapon immediately.

"What are *you* doing?" I tossed the words back at him. "Arkyn is my friend."

"Aurelia," Arkyn sighed in relief from behind me, his breath ragged. "You are alright."

I glanced over my shoulder and gave him a soft smile. "I am. What are you doing here?"

"Friend or not," Von cut in, his voice summoning my gaze, "the half-breed has New God ichor coursing through his veins. By coming here, he has broken the laws of this realm. In doing so, he will pay with his life."

"The same ichor flows in mine," I snarled. The space between my brows creased. "If that is the law of these lands, then why am I still alive?"

"Because you are different, little bride, and you know that," Von said. He rested his blade against his shoulder and tipped his head to the side—taking in the small bit of silk I was wearing. His expression turned positively sinful. A wealth of lust washed over me, the weight of it damn near buckling my knees. It tasted different than my own—it tasted of Von, and it was insatiable.

"Cut it out," I told him.

"I cannot," he said through a wolfish grin, clearly enjoying this.

. . . I could work with that.

"I'll make you a deal if you spare him," I said, lowering my arms to my sides while I raised a single brow.

Von angled his jaw, those emerald eyes peering down at me like a hawk eyeing up a plump little mouse. "I'm listening."

How about I show you instead? I purred through our private channel.

He laughed and his sword disappeared. Von's hand encircled my waist, and he pulled me into him as he said to the guards, "Take our *guest* to the dining hall so he can have something to eat." He looked down at me, his hand clasping my chin as the rough pad of his thumb ran over my bottom lip. "A feast for a feast. It seems like a good trade."

Heat kissed my cheeks as I growled through the bond, *You did not just say that out loud.*

I did, he replied, flashing a proud grin.

I scoffed at his audacity.

"His life in exchange for—" Von grinned, "—a taste of my female. Do we have a deal, Little Goddess?"

I nodded. "We do."

Then the big brute picked me up and tossed me over his broad shoulder like a hunter collecting his trophy kill of the season—something that he would use to feed him for the long, harsh winter. Knowing Von's immortal stamina and his unappeasable appetite, there was a good chance he'd do just that—he'd take his time devouring me. Use his wicked tongue to pry the very life from my bones, to carve me into submission and drown me in pleasure.

But as good as that sounded to me *and* the bond, Arkyn was here, and I wanted to speak with him. To ask him why he had come.

"Von, wait," I huffed, trying to fight his hold.

Smack.

I gaped as my rear began to sting—he'd *swatted* my ass!

It rang out as clear as a bell—humiliating and . . . arousing me even more.

I decided that speaking to Arkyn could wait for an hour or so.

The bond was more than happy to agree.

Chapter 35

Aurelia

"Aurelia!" Arkyn exclaimed as he jolted up from the window seat he had been sitting on when I walked through the door into the large study a few hours later. The room was spacious, filled with furniture, sprawling rugs, and mahogany bookshelves that ran from floor to ceiling. There was a large, darkly stained table that sat just off to the side, surrounded by chairs.

We rushed towards one another, embracing each other tightly. But the warmth I felt from being reunited was swiftly replaced by a bitter taste on my tongue—as if I had bitten into a lemon peel. I choked on it.

Sputtering, I quickly pulled back from Arkyn. The taste began to recede.

I turned around, finding cruel green eyes locked on me. Their owner had his muscular arms crossed over his chest as he leaned against the doorway, a sinister sneer on his lips.

"Are you alright?" Arkyn asked, pulling my attention back to him.

"Just swallowed funny," I lied poorly then I snarled across our bond, *You are jealous of me hugging an old friend?*

An old friend whose cock practically burst through his pants when he saw you, Von answered with a growl.

You are ridiculous.

Shall I have my shadows dissolve his breeches and show you the extent of his enjoyment in seeing you?

"One moment," I said to Arkyn, smiling softly. I spun on the back of my heel, my lips thinning as I stomped towards Von. I shoved against him, my hands pressing against his iron forearms. "Get out!"

Von snorted, his monstrous frame not budging an inch. His massive hands grabbed hold of my wrists, shackling them. He leaned in, his masculine amber scent washing over me, steady eyes holding mine as he said, "No."

One word from him. That was all it took to make me see red.

With a snarl on my lips, I said, "You egotistical—

"It's alright, Aurelia," Arkyn cut me off, his voice urgent, as if he thought he was protecting me.

I glared at Von.

He grinned in return.

I narrowed my eyes on him, shooting out imaginary daggers. When it only seemed to feed his smirk, I rolled my eyes, yanked my wrists from his oversized mitts, and gave him my back.

I looked to Arkyn—his auburn brows were anchored in concern, shadowing his honey-brown eyes. His eyes had always seemed to glitter, as if there were flecks of gold sewn into them, but right now, they seemed dull. Apart from that, he seemed thinner than I remembered him being, as if something had been eating away at him.

"Why are you here?" I asked as I walked towards him.

He looked past me, to Von.

"He won't leave, so you might as well say whatever it is you have come to say," I sighed with an apologetic smile.

Arkyn clenched his molars, the muscles in his jaw pushing out at the sides. He exhaled a withheld breath, relaxed his mouth, and then said, "Aurelius is not doing well."

My stomach churned at the mention of my ex-husband. The male who had robbed me of so many years of my life. Who had snapped my bones as easily as he had destroyed my trees. Suddenly, I felt Von standing behind me, his shadow falling over me like a dutiful soldier covering its commander on a bloody battlefield.

Under Death's protection, I said, "And of what concern should that be to me?"

A crease formed between Arkyn's brows. "You cannot mean that."

"You *saw* what he did to me."

"Yes, I was there. And he lost his temper with you. He never should have done that. *Any* of it. But he has been broken since you left. He is not thinking correctly, and his divinity is not acting as it should. The New Gods are losing confidence in him, Nicholas as well. I fear what might happen if he does not pull himself together."

"So what would you have me do?" I shook my head, a great hurt welling in my chest. If I had ever wondered where Arkyn's allegiances lay when it came to me and Aurelius, now I was given a blunt answer. Ultimately, he sided with his sire. That small bit of hurt fed the flames of my anger as I raised my voice at him. "Return to the man who betrayed me? Abused me?" I scoffed. "I will do no such thing, and you are a fool to even ask."

"Aurelia, you are not acting like yourself," Arkyn lowered his voice, his eyes darting to Von—suspicion abound.

I knew what that look meant. He thought Von was controlling me somehow. As if I was a puppet and he was the master making me do as he pleased. Making me speak the words I had just spoken as if I was a brainless mouthpiece.

But Von was not Aurelius.

And he had *never* silenced my voice.

Not once.

My divinity brimmed to the surface, filling my voice with might. "I have never been more myself, and the fact that you do not see that makes me wonder if we were ever truly friends. You have wasted your time in coming here. Go back to *your* king, Arkyn."

He looked as if I had slapped him across the face.

I didn't wait for a reply as I turned, strode around Von, and walked towards the door. Von followed behind me.

"Aurelia, wait!" Arkyn cried out.

Aurelia. *That* name. I was so sick of it.

I spun back around and thundered towards him. "Do not call me that."

"What?" Arkyn shook his head, trying to grasp at something he could never understand.

"*That* is not my name," I growled at him, years of bottled feelings pouring out of me.

"If that is not your name, what is?"

"My name is—" I looked around me, my gaze landing on the table to my right. A silver bowl sat there, with an unburned smudge stick in it. Without thinking, I grabbed it and lobbed it at him as I shouted, "—Sage!"

And I'd be damned . . .

The name *felt* right.

As stupid and impulsive as it seemed—it felt . . . like me. And it couldn't have come at a better time—when I was standing up for myself.

Arkyn ducked and that sage stick sailed right on past him, hitting the window behind him and falling to the floor. Wide, honey-brown eyes met mine and Arkyn raised his hands in defense. "Alright, I hear you. I did not come here to anger you and I am sorry for that. That was not my intention at all."

"So what did you expect to achieve by coming here?"

"In truth, I saw all of this going much differently. I expected to find you in chains. I had planned to barter for your freedom," he said truthfully, living up to his godly title.

Von scoffed, his deep voice interjecting. "And what could you possibly have that you think I would trade for her?"

"I wondered if you might have changed your mind. That perhaps the very thing you traded in the first place, the Living and the Immortal Realms, would entice you to strike a new bargain," Arkyn answered, his eyes shifting to Von. "I could make it so that they would be yours again."

Von was silent for a moment. A long moment. "How?"

Betrayal gutted me where I stood. This had nothing to do with my freedom and all to do with getting me back into Aurelius's greedy hands. "You cannot be serious," I said to Von.

But Von didn't reply.

"In his current state, Aurelius is not fit to lead." Arkyn's eyes shifted briefly to me. "If you grant the Goddess of Life her freedom and my father safe passage to Edenvale, where he will be safe from those who might try to harm him, then I, the future king of the realms, will hand them over to you."

Goddess of Life. I couldn't help but notice how Arkyn was unwilling to call me by the name I had just chosen for myself. It struck a sour note.

Von started. “Well, well, well. I did not expect to hear this, of all things, today. However, I’m not interested.” My soul galloped wildly as he walked over to me, taking me in his strong, sturdy arms.

“But you would be king of all Three Realms again,” Arkyn challenged.

Von caressed my cheek, his gaze firmly holding mine as he said, “Without *Sage,* I would be the king of nothing.”

He’d used my name. Not Aurelia. Not Little Goddess. Or Kitten. But *my* name.

He was proving a point to Arkyn—to me.

That he honored me.

Respected me.

At that moment, if he would have asked me to be his queen, I think I might have said yes.

Chapter 36

Sage

A few days later, after Arkyn left, Von's large hand was placed over my eyes, nearly swallowing my face in the process. His scent of amber and sandalwood surrounded me, his masculine flavor appealing to me in ways that made me want to pull his hand from my face and climb the tall god like a tree.

Although I couldn't see, I could hear, and I knew *those sounds* anywhere.

It was the orchestra of churning wooden wheels and clopping hooves striking against brick-paved streets. The sound of busy people working tirelessly as they traveled from one point to the other, trying to make a living for themselves as well as their loved ones.

It was the sound of the living.

A sound I had grown accustomed to hearing during my days where I would watch over the humans from my perch in the Immortal Realm, my thoughts swirling with dreams of being like them someday.

"You can look," Von said, pulling his hand away.

My eyelids popped open and vivid bright light swallowed the darkness from my vision. Pupils focusing, I glanced up to the sky, an ocean of velvet blue, smooth and clear. Not a single white fluffy cloud to be seen.

My body vibrated. I had been right after all.

I turned to Von, unable to contain my excitement. "You brought me to the Living Realm?"

"Yes, but that's not all," he answered, his eyes shifting ahead.

I followed his gaze, turning to face what was in front of us.

The frame of a gothic-inspired manor towered before us, swallowing up the sky, seated on a massive lot. The arched windows were just beginning to be installed. A few workers hoisted the one up a ladder, trying to get it to its destination.

Large homes lingered on either side, a half a mile away.

The manor was being built on a slight hill, which gave us a visual advantage over the neighborhood, as well as a great view of the city. A city that was filled with color, nestled in the gentle embrace of rolling hills.

"What is this place?" I asked curiously.

"This is Belamour, an up-and-coming new city in the northern region of Edenvale," he answered, stepping into me. His heat washed over me, coaxing a tingle to walk down the length of my spine.

"Why have you brought me here?" My attention shifted from the sprawling, playful hills back to the incredible manor.

"Do you remember your second night in the Spirit Realm? You reached across the bond and asked where I was."

"Mhm. You said that you were acquiring a gift for me."

"This is it. This manor is for you. Whenever you find yourself missing the Living Realm, you can come here. My only stipulation is that you bring me, of course."

"What?" Emotion cracked the word in half. I turned to face him, my eyes as wide as saucers. "I can come here whenever I want?"

"Yes," he said with a soft smile. "Because the Endless Mist surrounds the continent, you won't have to worry about Aurelius or his brothers or his men. You'll be safe here."

I stepped into him. "Von, I—"

His hands cupped my cheeks, his eyes shifting between mine. "Say nothing, Little Goddess. This is my gift to you."

My hands wrapped around his muscular forearms as I stood on the tips of my toes and I kissed him deeper than I ever had before. For a time, I was certain that the world had dissolved away, leaving just the two of us and this moment we shared.

Unwillingly, slowly, I pulled back, my eyes searching his. I was no stranger to kissing him passionately, but I had never kissed him like that—so . . . intimately.

What would he make of it?

What did *I* make of it?

"Mmm," he growled in pleasure as I pulled back. "I'm making a note to buy you more things if it means I get more of those."

A soft smile tugged at the corners of my lips. "You liked it then?"

"I like everything that you do." The pad of his thumb ghosted across my lips. "I have one more thing I want to show you."

"Alright," I breathed.

His umbra dipped around us and then—

We were standing—*standing*—amongst the stars, on top of a swath of fluffy white clouds that spanned into the distance.

"You brought me to the sky?" I asked, a bit puzzled. I held my hand out as a star danced over top of it, bits of silver glitter drifting onto my palm.

"Yes, Little Goddess, but not just that. Where we stand now is sacred." His fingers laced with mine and he guided my hand to rest against the middle of his chest. A small smile touched the corners of his lips. "This spot is ours. It is where we once belonged before our souls were split apart."

Light, airy magic drifted around me, brushing across my skin as the universe whispered to me. It did not speak in words, but delicate musical notes. It was like he had lifted the lid to a small locket box, because a soft, beautiful melody began to play—happy and sad, and filled with love and loss.

It was the song of us.

The song of Life and Death.

Suddenly, I was overcome with emotion.

Pain cracked across my heart. How could something so beautiful hurt so much? And why did it feel like I was missing something, forgetting something?

"No," Von said, sweeping the tears from my eyes. "I did not bring you here for that. I brought you here because I wanted you to know where our story started. I wanted you to know that should we ever be split apart again, I will wait here for you, until you return to me."

He lowered his forehead against mine.

I closed my eyes.

Please do not leave me again, Little Goddess, Von's voice cried out, pleading with me. Pained and broken and—

I jerked my head back, my eyes opening wide. "Did you just say something through the bond?"

The place between his brows creased. "No, why?"

"It's nothing." I shook my head softly, trying to make sense of what I had just heard. "I just thought you did."

A pained, horrific growl exploded in my eardrums, threatening to burst them. I placed my hands over my ears. Von clasped my forearms, his lips moving, but whatever he was saying, I couldn't make it out because all I could hear was that horrible, horrible sound.

Like a weathervane caught in a storm, the world spun around and around, and then something snapped, and I fell into darkness. The scent of amber and sandalwood followed me into unconsciousness.

I drifted on the current of nothing.

The vessel that housed my soul was weightlessly suspended in the air. It was as if someone had severed the cord that connected me to my body—but there was something about this place of nothing. Something I couldn't quite put my finger on. A finger I did not need. Nor a hand, nor an arm. Because in the realm of nothing, I didn't need my body.

. . . I didn't need anything.

My eyelids were closed, and yet I could see.

In particular, I could see what was above me—

A plethora of stalactites reached down from the rocky ceiling. The uneven, icicle-like structures were luminescent, glowing a brilliant, effervescent blue on the roof of the cave's mouth. The color pulsed, growing brighter and then dimmer, as if it were breathing. As if it were alive.

I recalled that feeling. I had been alive once.

But when or how, I could not recall.

I admired the sparkling, brilliant, breathing formations.

How lovely. How true.

How true?

It made no sense and yet, it made perfect sense.

I would stay here for the remainder of eternity, drifting on the river of nothing.

Please do not leave me, Little Goddess! *a male roared inside my head.*

But the owner of the voice I could not place.

Hands that were tipped with vicious claws fished me out of the waterless river. They hoisted me onto the rocky bank and began to drag me along. My soul peered at them, taking in the strange, beautiful, enchanting creatures, their skin forged of a charcoal gray and intricate white markings. They were tall and lean, their faces long and finely tailored and so heartbreakingly beautiful. Both of them had large, ethereal wings, tucked neatly in. And their eyes—housed beneath hairless brows—were completely black.

"It's a pretty one," said an ethereal voice, beautiful and soft and . . . male.

"Indeed. The empress did a good job upon its creation," said the other one. The sound was equally lovely, but this one was higher pitched. Female, perhaps?

"Yes, she did," agreed the male as they continued to drag me forward. If they found my body heavy, they didn't let on. In fact, by the way they walked, one would think they were hauling something as light as a pillow behind them.

Weave her another fate! *a masculine voice demanded—the same one I had heard before.*

"Where do you think she will send it to next?" asked the female as she glanced down at me. Her hairless brows lowered, her expression changing to confusion.

"I dare not make a guess. The empress knows things we never will," replied the male in his soothing voice. He dropped my arm, and it slapped against the rocky floor—the sound echoing. "Put her on the table and I'll prepare for the extraction." His clawed toes scratched against the ground as he walked away.

"Nemtuk," the female said as she quickly dropped my hand.

"You know I can't let you perform the extraction," the male—Nemtuk—said. "Not after what happened last time. You nearly destroyed that poor soul."

"No, that's not it. I think it's watching us," the female said, her eyes fixed on mine.

"Impossible," Nemtuk scoffed. "They do not possess the ability to be conscious here."

"I'm serious. Come over here and look," she said.

"Fine. Fine," he sighed. His nails clicked against the ground, growing louder as he approached. Clawed fingers clamped onto my cheeks, moving my head from side to side as he gazed into my blank, lifeless face. He let out a shriek and dropped my head. "We must take it to the empress at once!"

Chapter 37

Von

"Ezra!" I yelled as I rushed into the apothecary with my mate in my arms. Her head was slumped against my shoulder, her body shivering uncontrollably. The color was chased from her skin, turning it an ashen gray.

"Lower your voice, you'll scare the herbs," Ezra scolded as she rushed over, shooting me a stern look before she looked at Sage, her expression shifting from stern to concerned. Her purple-stained fingers washed over the Little Goddess's face, shifting from her cheeks to her forehead. "She's as cold as ice. What has happened?"

"She asked me if I said something through the bond, but I hadn't. Terror filled her eyes and then she just fell," I told her, urgency filling my voice. "Help her."

Ezra gestured to a small bed in the corner of the room. "Place her there."

Quickly, I walked over to it, but when I went to lay her down, the muscles in my body locked up like they'd suddenly taken on a will of their own—as if they were not willing to part with her.

"Newly formed bonds are strange things indeed," Ezra muttered as she walked up beside me. "It knows that she is suffering and does not wish to let her go. It feels . . . she is safer in your arms."

In truth, I felt she was safer here, too, but I knew that Ezra needed to examine her.

I gritted my teeth, trying to reconnect my mind to my arms.

Nothing.

"Von," Ezra said.

Somehow, my neck muscles complied, and I turned my head to face her.

She raised her hand, palm facing the ceiling, brought it to her lips, and blew. A plume of green hit me in the face, followed by a waft of mint. Fresh and earthy.

"Breathe it in now," she instructed.

I grimaced as I drew a breath, feeling the foreign particles pass through my nostrils, down into my lungs. It itched horribly.

"Deeply now."

Scowling, I did as I was told.

Seconds later, my rigid muscles relaxed, like a hand had

massaged out the kinks, the tenseness. Abdomen contracting, I leaned over the bed and gently placed Sage on it. "What was that stuff?" I asked, backing up.

"It's a combination of things, but the main ingredient is catnip." She rubbed her hand on her apron.

Fucking catnip? I shook my head. "Does that work for everyone?"

"No. Not really. Just you, and well, cats."

I snorted at that.

Something moved in my periphery, pulling my gaze towards it.

A fluffy brown and white cat emerged from a crate that had been flipped over, a door cut into it. Slowly, he waddled over to me, his watermelon belly nearly scraping against the floor. He began to rub against my legs—painting my pants in fur.

"Like I said . . . you and cats." Ezra stated as she bent over and began moving her hands over Sage's face. Ezra worked in strokes, as if she were smoothing something out, pulling her hands towards her.

"Mrrrow," said the cat.

I glanced down at it and quirked a brow. It looked up at me and meowed again, showing off its tiny little fangs.

"Don't mind Big Papa," Ezra said. "He's just saying hello."

Having heard its name, the feline meowed again. He continued to rub against my legs as I returned my attention to Sage. My stomach knotted. I hated seeing her like that, hated that I didn't know how to help her.

"Should we cover her?" I asked. "Try to warm her or something?"

"No. We don't know what this is yet," Ezra said as her hands glided over Sage's body. She paused. "That's strange."

"What?" I asked, leaning in. Adrenaline pounded through my veins.

"Her soul . . . it isn't here."

"What do you mean it isn't here?" I growled, taking a worried step forward, around the purring cat.

Ezra shook her head, her hands hovering directly over the middle of Sage's chest. "Her soul walks somewhere else. But where or when, I do not know. I do not know if it is a separate realm, a dream, or a vision that she has gone to. Regardless, she is not here, and that is why her body has grown so cold. It has lost the warmth of her soul." Ezra retracted her hands and turned to me. "You have fed from her, yes?"

"I have."

"What color is her ichor?" she asked, brows raised.

I shook my head, not understanding what that had to do with anything. "It is gold."

"You are sure?" She rushed over to a wood desk full of various jars and tinctures. The cat followed her over, meowing at her. She pulled open a drawer, rummaged around it, and grabbed a small knife with a thin, smooth blade.

"Of course I'm sure." I was growing increasingly frustrated.

"The true color might be hiding from us." She went over to a row of shelves and began looking through it before she settled on a tiny vial filled with a clear liquid and dropped it into the pocket of her apron. Then she scooted back to Sage, grabbed her hand, turned it over, and—

I snatched Ezra's wrist. "What are you doing?" I snarled, my shadows peeling away in fear.

"I am trying to help her. So let me do that." She punctuated her words through gritted teeth.

My nostrils flared, but I let her wrist slip free.

"Territorial male," she grumbled as she turned back to Sage.

The beast inside of me rattled against its cage while I watched her carve a three-inch slit into Sage's hand. Rich, golden ichor pooled to the surface, scenting the room.

Ezra didn't look at me as she stretched out her hand towards me—the one that held the knife. I took it from her, raised it over my shoulder, handing it to my shadows. They placed it on a small table.

Ezra's hand darted into her pocket, and she removed the vial. Using her teeth, she pulled out the cork, spit it onto the floor, and then dumped the contents on Sage's palm. As soon as the clear substance mixed with Sage's ichor, it began to hiss and steam.

Her ichor turned . . . red. Just like the mortals. And then it changed to—

"Silver," Ezra gasped. "Well, I'll be damned. I *knew* there was something different about her." She turned to me, her eyes wide. "Do you know what this means?"

I took a breath—I needed it. "She's not just a New God."

"She's not, no." Ezra shook her head.

"So then why does she bleed gold?"

"I imagine it is because Aurelius's heart beats inside her, however that is not her origin. Silver blood shows that her soul predates the creation of the New Gods, but the red is confusing because that would also make her . . ."

"Mortal," I finished her sentence. It explained a lot of things, like why she needed sleep every night, why she needed three meals a day. Sage's soul was both mortal and immortal, but not in the sense that she was a Demi God. No, this was different. This wasn't half and half—it was two separate but full parts of her, like two sides of a coin.

"What do you make of it?" Ezra asked.

"The fact that *you* are asking me, I find concerning."

"Indeed," she agreed, a crease forming between her brows. "My sisters and I have a droplet of silver blood in our veins, but it is *nothing* like hers. It's all so very curious." Ezra let out a sigh. "But perhaps some secrets are better left hidden."

"Meaning?"

"Meaning we leave this riddle for another day and focus on what matters most—bringing her back to us." She walked over to a shelf that ran from floor to ceiling and began looking through her jars of herbs—glass clinking against its brethren as she searched with little patience. "I suspect that she has had her first vision and it has knocked her soul loose in the process." She turned to face me, a jar in her hand. Some type of brown substance lingered within. "We must give her a reason to return here, to us. And then I will call upon my sisters to help me stitch her soul to her body so that this does not happen again."

I eyed the jar suspiciously. "How are we going to bring her back?"

"I'm not. But you are," she said as she walked over to us. She pointed to me, flicking her pointer finger up and down. "Shirt off, muscles."

I didn't bother to ask why. I just did it.

When I dropped my black tunic onto the floor, I looked up to find Ezra's eyes on me, burning as hot as an iron. She let out a low whistle. "The Creator sure doesn't build 'em like you anymore."

I gave her a look.

She chuckled and then gestured to the bed. "If you would, please."

She didn't have to ask twice—the bond had been pulling me towards Sage ever since I placed her there—begging me to take her trembling frame in my arms. Swiftly, I conquered the short but unbearable distance between us. The bed dipped beneath my weight as I scooped Sage up and maneuvered underneath her. I lowered her so that she was lying down against my chest.

Ezra unscrewed the lid of the glass jar, dipped her hand inside, then ran her fingers down the middle of Sage's face, painting three brown stripes.

The scent of wet soil bloomed in my nostrils. "Mud?" I asked.

Ezra nodded. "It is from the floor of the forest where you two forged the bond between you. When two halves of the same star become one, the magic is immense. It preserves the space as it is for centuries, making it a sacred spot. Now—" she gathered more of the mud and repeated the same act on me, "—it will be the thing that brings her back to you." She screwed the lid on the jar and turned to walk back over to the shelves where she had gotten it from. "The barrier of her clothes must go too. You must be skin on skin for this to work."

I looked down at Sage's dress, and it dissolved away, revealing her ghostly pale skin—covered in strange markings that were an angry red, full of deep crevices and prominent furrows. I ran my hand down her back, expecting to feel the divots, but her skin was . . . smooth.

"What do you see?" Ezra asked me as she rushed back over. Her eyes flickered wearily between mine, as if she were trying to find the answer there.

"I think . . ." I clenched my jaw. I had grown used to seeing the markings and scars of what had taken the lives of other souls and it had never bothered me before. But seeing this, seeing the markings stamped on my mate's flesh? Ice ran like a blade down my spine, causing my bloodless veins to run cold. "I think I'm seeing her death."

"Past or future?" she asked, her voice crackling with concern.

"I do not know," I answered. My gaze shifted to her arm. Gently, I took it and rotated it. The depression in her skin was different there—it looked as if it had been made from a rope.

Sage had either died from whatever this was, or I was getting a glimpse of her future.

The flames of anger consumed me as my stomach twisted, aching to purge itself of its contents. My shadows slithered around me, contorting and twisting as they looked for something to latch on to—to destroy.

"That will not help," Ezra scolded, the knife in her hand once more. She placed it in Sage's palm, wound her hand around it, and then took the blade to my wrist.

I latched on to the pain of the blade slitting my skin, focusing on it over my anger. Crimson bubbled to the surface.

"Feed your mate and call her home," Ezra said as she stepped back.

I brought my wrist to my mouth, drawing a few swallows of blood, and then I leaned forward. I tipped Sage's face up to mine and pressed my lips against her freezing ones, parting them as I released my blood into her mouth.

Come back to me, Little Goddess, I purred through the bridge of our connection.

Her lips began to warm under mine and then . . . she swallowed.

I pulled back, my hand roaming over her cheek.

Slowly, her eyelids fluttered open.

Weary blue eyes met mine.

"Nockrythiam?" she asked weakly, before her eyelids fell back closed.

Chapter 38

Sage

"Don't touch me!" I screamed at the vicious, claw-tipped fingers wrapped around my arm. Bending water, I forged it into a dagger as I shoved it forward, aiming straight for the creature's throat.

"Whoa, whoa, easy now," a male's voice said as a large, tattooed hand wrapped around my wrist, stopping my hand mid-swing. "You're safe, Sage. You're safe."

Familiar green eyes met mine.

"Von," I whimpered his name, my gaze darting to my hand, to the weapon that I held inches from his throat.

Gasping, I dropped the dagger. It fell on the bed between us.

I looked around—obsidian walls were covered in green vines and white roses. Von was seated beside me. Zahra stood at the foot of the bed, her expression full of concern. Dameon was beside her, his arm wrapped around her lower back.

We were back in our bedchamber. But moments ago—

I thought back to where I had just been, a land of nothing. With *those* creatures. My heart began to stampede as my lungs searched for oxygen.

Where had all the air suddenly gone?

Why couldn't I breathe?

A warm hand caressed my cheek. "You're safe," Von assured me. "Take a deep breath, Kitten."

I took a shaky, shaky inhale.

"Good girl," Von praised. "Another one."

I did as I was instructed.

"Again," he said.

We did that for a little while until my breathing returned to normal. When I was finally able to speak, I asked, "What happened?"

"You were fine one moment, and the next you were unconscious," Von replied softly, his hand stroking my hair in comforting, slow movements.

"We've been worried about you," Zahra said.

My brow furrowed as I tried to recall my last memories before I was shoved into *that* place. A place that I hoped was nothing more than a nightmare, and yet, it had felt so very real.

"How long have I been out for?" I asked, my gaze shifting

between the three of them.

"A few days," Von said, pulling my attention back to him. That's when I noticed it—the worry behind his eyes.

He looked . . . tired.

How strange. I had never seen the male sleep once since my arrival, and here he was, looking like he needed a week of it.

Was it because of me?

I ran my fingers over his cheek. "I'm here. I'm alright."

He nodded, but my words didn't seem to meet his eyes. They did nothing to chase away the concern, the worry . . . the torment. Gently, his fingers wrapped around my wrist, and he brought my hand to his lips, kissing the back of it with such heartbreaking tenderness.

Dameon cleared his throat. "We'll leave you two alone."

Zahra nodded. "Yes, I'll stop by later on to check on you."

"Thank you," I said in place of goodbye as they left the room, leaving just the two of us.

"Do you want to talk about it?" Von asked, his eyes studying me with that piercing gaze of his, looking for answers to questions he had yet to ask.

I nibbled on my bottom lip, thinking his request over, before I nodded. I told him about my nightmare—about the weightless feeling I had felt as I floated on a current of nothing, and the strange, winged creatures with the charcoal skin.

Throughout it all, Von was silent, and when I was finished, he pulled me into his arms, holding me so tightly I didn't know what to make of it. My fingers knitted in his black tunic as I lowered my cheek against his chest. I breathed in his scent, warm amber and earthy sandalwood, and my body melted into his.

After a long while Von's arms slid from me as he pulled back, his movement slow. His fingers slid across my skin, down my forearms, taking my hands in his.

"Does the name Nockrythiam mean anything to you?" he asked, eyebrows folding in.

I searched the crevices of my mind, looking for the name, but found nothing. "No, it doesn't. Why?"

Von's chest rose as he inhaled a deep breath. Exhaling, he told me about taking me to Ezra and everything they had done to return my soul to my body. *That* did not sit well with me, considering the nightmare I had found myself placed in—those strange beings. An eerie feeling crept across my skin, like a thousand tiny bugs looking for a place to burrow in. I brushed the thought to the side, swallowed the large lump that had formed in my throat and focused on Von, on the security I felt having him this close to me.

"Ezra called upon her sisters. Together, the three of them stitched your soul back into your body so that won't happen again," he said, his thumbs brushing over the back of my hands in comforting strokes.

That gave me a slight sliver of relief, all things considered.

I was silent for a moment, taking in everything I had been told. After, I asked, "So what does this all have to do with that name you mentioned?"

His hand slid from mine, raising to cup my cheek as he met my gaze. I nuzzled into his touch. Softly, slowly, he said, "Because after your soul returned, you awoke briefly. You looked at me, and you called me by that name—Nockrythiam."

Nockrythiam.

Although the name meant nothing to me, something . . . warm emitted from my chest.

A deep, tender feeling.

One I had no name for.

Chapter 39

Sage

After that day, life drifted into a peaceful rhythm in the land of spirits.

In truth, I was content with my life. Happy even.

I stepped down the stairs into the spacious private bath, the water sloshing as I lowered into the embrace of the steaming waters. I walked to the far side and seated myself on the bench. Tipping my head back, I rested it on the ledge behind me, and sighed—

The heat felt good on my muscles, like a gentle massage working out the kinks.

I had spent most of the day with my arms above my head, working on growing my vines not only up the walls of the throne room, but onto the towering ceiling as well. Typically, Von joined me in the throne room, leaning against the wall with a satisfied grin on his lips as he watched me work, but today, he wasn't there.

Unlike Aurelius, whose whereabouts had always been a mystery, I knew where Von was—not because of the bond, but because he told me that he was going to be in council meetings for the day. He had even asked if I wished to join, but I had decided the throne room needed me more.

I closed my eyes. A visual of an arched ceiling and growing vines appeared on the forefront of my mind, as if I had looked up at it for so long it had engrained its way into my vision.

"I see you've made yourself right at home," said a captivating voice, the honey-dipped words *almost* hiding how poisonous they were.

My eyelids sprung open and I jerked my head up, landing on a pair of cruel green eyes. Firelight reflected off of them, causing them to shine like a predators in the night—

Saphira.

I was tempted to say to her *I see you've finally slithered out of your hole,* but I figured that probably wouldn't make for the best of first impressions. However, considering that I hadn't seen her since that day in the throne room, and she hadn't bothered to come and introduce herself to me over the past so many months, I guessed she had probably made her mind up about me.

I knew how it looked to someone like her. I was the New God who stole her brother and because of that lost them the Realms.

Without a doubt, I was certain she hated me. Disliked me at best.

Well, she could get in line. It was a long one. The number of females who hated me back in the Immortal Realm because they all wanted Aurelius was abysmal. Especially after that dreadful tea party where I nearly drowned a room full of them.

"I suppose I have," I said with a soft smile—fighting her fake sweetness with a bit of my own. "Saphira, I take it."

"The one and only," she said, her heels clicking softly, her hips swaying confidently as she sauntered towards the bath. She raised her thin skirts, slipped her foot out of her heel, and dipped a painted black toe into the water. "Do you mind if I join you, sister dearest?"

I didn't know what to make of her request or how I should use my cards at whatever game she was playing, but I wasn't about to fold right now.

I gestured to the waters in invitation. "Be my guest."

"Thank you," she said as she began to descend into the waters.

It was not uncommon for people to share bathing chambers, but two things set this whole scene apart from what would be considered normal. The first was that these bathing chambers were private. The second was the fact that Saphira didn't take her clothes off—which proved a whole other point. This wasn't about her bathing; it was about her flexing her muscle.

She slid onto the underwater bench adjacent to the one I was sitting on. Casually, she draped her wet arm over the ledge, propping herself up on it. "So . . . when's the wedding?" she asked in a fake, dreamy voice.

"We haven't discussed it."

"Ah, I see," she said in such a way it made it sound like she had just uncovered a juicy bit of gossip. I heeded it little mind, certain she was just trying to mess with my head. Her gaze lowered from my eyes, looking into the waters. "And are you pregnant yet?"

I didn't care for her question. "I do not believe that is any of your business."

"I'll take that as a no then," she said with a saccharine smile.

"Take it however you want," I told her flatly.

Her expression softened, her voice matching as she said, "You know, I've always wanted a child of my own. One that I could raise in my image. Who would be loyal to me."

"So then why don't you have one?" I asked, not really sure where she was going with this. Not really sure where I was going with it either.

She took a breath, her lips twisting into a sad smile. "How much has Von told you about me?"

"I'll be honest. Not a whole lot." Saphira didn't exactly come up in conversation with Von. Ever. Come to think of it, only the one time when Von had suspected that she was the cause of his painting's decapitation.

"I see," she said. "Well, let me tell you a little bit about myself. Six centuries ago, the Creator finally gifted me my bonded. His name was Aryx and he was the God of Love. He was undoubtedly the most handsome god I had ever seen. People would fall at his feet and weep. But he was so much more than just good looks. He was a thinker. He taught me a great deal of things about the world, about myself. On one cold, winter night in the Dupine Forest in the Living Realm, we formed the bond between us, and for a brief moment in my life, I was happy. I thought that we would spend eternity together, but I was wrong." She paused for a moment. "I remember that day so very well. We had been in bed together, trying to start a family. You see, that was our dream. Aryx's brother, the God of Lust, showed up at our door that morning. He told us that a giant had appeared in the Living Realm and that she was literally *swallowing* souls. Draevon, who was the king of all Three Realms at that time, and some of the other immortals were getting ready to go fight her. Aryx agreed to go as well. I begged and pleaded with him not to. We argued. He went anyway. By the time I got there, there wasn't a trace of him left." She looked down, her face slack. Numb.

Although there were no tears in her eyes, it was not hard for me to see that after all this time, Saphira was still mourning for her mate.

She drew a breath and lifted her fallen gaze. "On the day that he died, I pledged to myself that I would never give the life we had dreamed of to another. That included having children, and so, you see, I cannot have a child because of my loyalty to him. I should have gone to protect him on the battlefield that day, but I was too stubborn. And so this is the price I pay."

"Saphira, I am so sorry," I said softly. Although I didn't trust her as far as I could punt a mountain, that didn't mean I couldn't feel for her.

Green eyes flicked to mine, covered by a lowered brow. "I do not want your pity." Her voice was sharp like a wounded animal. "That is not why I am here."

I sensed she was about to tell me her purpose in coming, which was why I didn't blatantly ask.

Sure enough, she said, "I have come to tell you the truth. As my brother clearly has not."

That got my heart going. "The truth about what?"

"Do you not wonder how Aurelius's brothers found you so quickly?"

"I can't say that I have . . ."

"Well, you should." She moved across the waters, slowly coming towards me. Suddenly, I felt like the pool was much too small. "They knew where to find you because *someone* betrayed you and told them exactly where you were."

I shook my head. I could already see the image she was trying to paint, and I refused to believe it.

"Do you know who it was?" she asked, her lips twisting ever so wickedly as she draped her arms over my shoulders.

I bristled at her proximity.

"It was a raven. And you know who commands ravens, don't you?" She blew out a breath of air from her nose, pleased with herself and the lie she had just told.

"I do not believe you." I shoved her arms off me.

"I have no reason to lie to you." She laughed cruelly, the sound like sandpaper against my frayed nerves. "Draevon was the one who sent his raven to tell Aurelius, *your abuser*, where you were hiding. He knew that when Aurelius's men came looking for you, it would force your hand. Although it didn't go as planned, he was still able to forge the bond that day, taking away your choice in the process. He manipulated the entire situation, just as he has been manipulating you ever since. This whole charade has never been about him and you, it's been about his hate for Aurelius, about taking away what matters most to him. You truly believe the heartless God of Death is so doting and loving? Well, I've known him for thousands of years—the notion is laughable. Just as your bond is. Forged on a lie, forged by him betraying you. And to the man who broke you, no less."

"No!" I shouted, bathwater exploding around us as my power surged. It slammed into Saphira and tossed her backwards, out of the pool. Water soaked the entire room, nearly emptying the bath in the process.

Saphira coughed and sputtered as she laid on her side on the floor.

I strode out of the bath and crouched beside the gasping female. "You can spin your lies all you want, but I do not believe you," I snarled before I stood up. I grabbed a towel, wrapped it around myself, and then left the room.

But by then, it was too late. The seed that Saphira had planted had begun to take root.

Chapter 40

Von

My ass fell asleep a good four hours ago.

I'd been seated here, at the head of the table, which housed twenty of my council members, since this morning. I had asked Sage if she wished to join, a part of me hoping that she would, but she was content working on her latest task—decorating the castle with vines and roses. Today's meeting was taking longer than usual, but considering I'd been putting the meetings off so that I could spend more time with her, I supposed that was to be expected.

Now, my ass and I were paying our dues.

Thunk. Ismay, my assistant, dropped *another* stack of scrolls in front of me. "These are the documents he's speaking about." Before she went to return to her seat, her brown eyes flicked to the dark-haired god who was sitting a few chairs down, his person adorned with every sparkling jewel known to man—

Pertheus, the God of Wealth.

Although he didn't show it in appearance, he had taken a big hit to his coffers since I was removed from overseeing the Living Realm. In fact, we all had. When I was king and the people worshipped the Gods of Old, we didn't have to do very much to be praised by them. Mortals would cram themselves, shoulder to shoulder, inside our temples and give up their offerings.

Then the New Gods were made, and all of it went to shit.

People turned to them, and the grand buildings that were built in our honor began to be forgotten about—*we* began to be forgotten about. Now, most of those once proud, incredible structures had crumbled to dust, or were on the verge of it.

When I started the Immortal War, my gods had been so starved of the people's praise, they had chomped at the bit to try to get the Immortal and Living Realms back. During that time, there was a brief insurgence of Old God believers, and it had all given them a taste of what it was like—to be praised by the people once more.

That was a dangerous thing.

But then I called off the war. Traded my mate for the two realms.

Naturally, it had caused a great deal of discourse that I was still dealing with the aftermath of—

I looked at the scrolls, picked one up, and began to unfurl it. Eyes scanning the list, I scoffed when I saw the price circled at the bottom. I tossed the roll of paper onto the table with little care. "It is an exorbitant amount," I said, looking to Pertheus.

"That is what I was taking in during the war and it is what I will require going forward," he replied, propping his elbows on the chair's arms. He steepled his fingers. "It seems like a small price to pay, considering you have committed us all to be forgotten about once more. All for that New God *pet* you keep like a cat on your lap as you sit on your throne."

"Be careful of what you say, Pertheus," Dameon growled from across the table.

"Or what?" he snarled back at him.

Dameon leaned forward, but Zahra raised her hand from her pregnant belly and pressed it softly against her husband's chest as she said, "Or my mate will roast your pompous ass." She offered Pertheus a closed-lipped smile.

The room fell silent.

Zahra's hand returned to rest against her stomach as she glanced around the table. "You all forget that the times have changed and the people do not praise immortals like they used to. Not to mention they have gone and created their own false gods. Even if we had won the war, that does not mean things would have returned to how they used to be."

Some gods nodded their heads in agreement with her, while others remained stone-faced. Their actions, or lack of, said it all, marking the loyal from the disloyal.

Without warning, molten fire scorched its way throughout me—burning me alive right where I sat. I clenched my hands together, fighting the urge to rip someone's head off.

But the emotion was not my own, which meant—

Sage.

Shadows sweeping around me, I went to her. I found my mate storming out of the bathing chamber, a towel wrapped around her soaked frame, speckled with droplets of water. She hadn't even bothered to dry off.

"What happened?" I asked, strolling towards her.

"I just had a chat with your sister," she said, her voice distant.

Every protective bone within my body turned rigid. "Are you alright?"

When I went to reach for her, she took a step back, *away* from me.

She shook her head. "No." Weary blue eyes met mine, pools of hurt swimming within them. "Is it true? Did you send a raven to tell Aurelius where I was just so you could force my hand?"

I swallowed. "You made a deal with me, Little Goddess."

A second passed. Then one more.

And then I felt her heart shatter.

It nearly brought me to my knees. "Sage, I—"

She cut me off. "I don't want to hear it." Her voice was equal parts fiery rage and deep, deep sadness, and I could feel every devastating ounce of it. "On that day I came to ask for your help, you pledged to me that you were done being the villain in my story. But then you forged the bond knowing what we were. You took the choice away from me and didn't give me the chance to choose you on my own. Still, I forgave you for that. But now to find out this? That you were *willing* to feed my whereabouts *to Aurelius*, even after *you knew* some of the things he did to me, all so you could force my hand? You manipulative kings are all the same! You are *no* different *from him*!"

Her emotions were like ash on my tongue, choking me right where I stood.

"I should have killed you that day in the forest," she snarled, and then she went to walk past me.

I caught her wrist. "I fucked up."

"You really did." She tore her arm away from me and pointed to the door. "Get out."

"Sage." I desperately wanted to take her in my arms. To try to fix the damage I had done. I took a step towards her.

She stepped back, turning her head to the side as if she couldn't stand to look at me. "Please. Just go."

I hated this. Hated that she was hurting so deeply, and it was all because of me.

For once, I didn't argue.

For once, I let her have her space and I did as she asked.

Following that day, Sage kept herself locked inside our bedchambers.

I wanted to be there for her, to apologize and console her, but when I shadow walked inside, it only made matters worse. With the use of her blade and the eyes of a heartbroken female, she made it very clear I was to get out.

Zahra, who was one of the only souls Sage would let in, would pat my shoulder when she came out of the room. She would repeat the same message, telling me to give Sage time.

And so that's what I did.

Although I had not realized it back then, I had done the worst thing someone could do to the person they loved. It wasn't just that I had manipulated the situation, it was who I had involved to do so, and now I saw how it looked from her perspective—

I had *allied* myself with the god who'd *abused* her.

That was what had wounded her so deeply. And rightfully so.

Throw on the fact that the bond intensified emotions, and well, I could understand why she was reacting as she was. On top of that, I hadn't just betrayed her—the bond seemed to think I had betrayed it as well. As the bond catered to its own rules, it shut down my ability to speak with her on our private channel. The invisible chain wrapped around my ankle didn't pull anymore. Even her emotions were no longer something I could taste.

Sage and the bond had cut me off.

I did all that I could do to show that I was sorry. I, the God of

Death, spent my days in the kitchen, preparing all her favorite foods. I set the tray by her door, accompanied by a black rose—only to find the food untouched and cold a few hours later.

Sage went days without eating food or drinking any ichor, and although that time would not affect any other immortal, I worried what it might do to her.

One night, while I sat outside of our bedchamber door, my arm tossed over my knee, I realized what I needed to do to make things right, to prove that I was not the horrible monster she had come to see me as.

It was going to be among one of the hardest things I had ever done before.

Chapter 41

Sage

I washed my face with water from the tap, splashing the warm water against my cheeks, chasing away the streaks from the tears I had shed earlier that day. Through the reflection of the mirror, I eyed the spot on the ground where I had thrown Saphira after she told me of Von's betrayal. Wherever that serpent had slithered off to, I didn't know. Nor did I really care. I had enough problems to contend with.

Yes, what she told me was a gutting truth. And yes, it had hurt me deeply.

But I had never imagined my anger towards Von would last this long or be of *this* intensity. Considering the bond had no interest in linking me to him, I couldn't help but wonder if it was also playing a part in my heightened emotions.

I dried my hands on the towel and walked out of the room. I glanced at the door that led into the hallway. I knew what would wait for me on the other side—a meal prepared by him. His peace offering.

One I had no interest in.

A few days ago, he went as far as having Zahra bring one of the trays in. She told me that it had not been prepared by him and had encouraged me to eat.

But it didn't matter if the meal was made by his hands or another's—food had lost its appeal to me. Sure, I'd picked up the fork and poked at it for Zahra's sake, but as soon as the cooked carrot touched my tongue, I'd wanted to gag. That was what the extent of my emotions were doing to me—they were making me sick to my stomach.

I walked over to the room that housed both my clothes and Von's. I rifled through them until I found an old familiar friend—

The cloak I had acquired during my brief time in the Living Realm. I swung it around my back and put it on. Sure, the fabric was stiff and coarse, but it felt comforting for some reason. Perhaps because when I wore it, in those brief moments, I belonged to no one else but me. I was my own person.

I slid my hand into the pocket, finding the tin that Ezra had offered me when I asked for her help in breaking the deal between Von and me. I pulled it out, surveying the small silver container.

A thought bloomed—

Now that the bond had gone silent, Von wouldn't know if I were to leave, and I would be able to use the salve from the tin to keep my skin from rotting because I was no longer honoring our deal.

"Ezra, you genius," I said, smirking to myself. I shoved the tin back into my pocket and then headed towards the door. When I jerked it open, my spine turned rigid—

Black, starless eyes lifted to mine. "Little Goddess."

I reared back, tried to slam the door in his face, but his large, tattooed hand caught it before it had a chance to close.

"No," I growled, backing up a step.

He raised his hands in deference as he stepped over the threshold. "I come in peace."

"I don't really care what you come in," I snarled, my voice not sounding quite like me. "Get out."

"No," he said, and then his shadows swallowed him where he stood. Not even a breath later, hands wrapped around my torso, pulling me against him as his shadows drifted around us.

A sprawling canvas of black sapphire, adorned with twinkling, celestial stars, and a huge crescent moon bloomed above me. A gothic manor towered before me, the architecture incredible. Dark and menacing and breathtaking.

This was the gift he had given me. I shoved away from Von, suspecting him of further treachery. He let me go, although he looked none too pleased to do so.

Confusion swirling, I asked, "Why are we here?"

"When I told you that I was done being the villain, I meant it. But then I fell into old habits. I connived and manipulated, and I broke that oath to you. And so, I am making things right, I am putting your needs above my own." He looked at the massive building. "This manor belongs to you, and you alone."

I was stunned. So stunned that when he gathered my hand into his and pressed a soft kiss against my knuckles, I didn't pull away.

Then, the God of Death said, "I release you from our deal, Little Goddess."

His hand slipped from mine, and then he was gone.

In his departure, a lonely black feather was left behind. Just like the day he had left me standing on the cliff, when he told me that he was calling off the war.

Before the wind could sweep it away, I picked it up.

I had finally gotten what I wanted—

I was free at last.

So why did I feel like crying?

Chapter 42

Von

If I didn't know any better, I would've thought that I had walked into Hard Spirits, but considering the bastard sun shone outside, that was a dead giveaway I wasn't in the Spirit Realm.

One hand in my pocket, I casually walked around the freshly built tavern, rife with the smell of lung-clogging paint, the scent so powerful I wouldn't be surprised if it clung to my nostrils long after I left. The floors and furniture were covered with protective linens that were splattered with black splotches and a few other dark colors. I passed by a mortal who was standing on a ladder, a brush in one hand and a cup of paint in the other. He pressed the brush against the wall, fanning out the bristles as he began carefully, dragging his hand this way and that, painting a unique pattern all by hand. Another painter did the same thing, working on an adjacent wall. Despite them being mortals, their attention to detail was incredible—

"Well, well, well, look what the raven dragged in," Folkoln said with a shit-eating grin, looking up from the countertop he was polishing a few strides to my left. As soon as his eyes connected with mine, the twist of his lips flatlined. One pierced black brow shot up. "That's one concocted mess of emotions you got going on there, brother. Can't say I've ever felt anything *like this* coming from you before. What happened?"

I let out a rumbling breath. "I freed her from our deal. I let her go."

Folkoln quit polishing. He dropped the cloth, placed his hands on the lip of the countertop, and leaned over top of it, his voice serious, low. "Who the fuck are you and what have you done with my brother?"

I snorted at that.

"The God of Death that I know does not free anyone from a deal. On top of that, she's your mate. How do you just . . . let her go?" he asked, taking a step back so he could better survey what was underneath the counter. "I don't know about you, but I need a drink for this." He bent over, slid something to the side, and started fishing around the shelves tucked underneath the bar, glass clinking against glass.

"It's a long story," I sighed as I leaned against one of the pillars that stretched from floor to ceiling.

"Let her go," Folkoln muttered to himself as he retrieved a bottle, as if he was unable to believe what I had just told him. He shook his head again.

In some ways, I supposed I was in disbelief myself. I wasn't exactly known to be a giving god. I was used to taking, owning, and acquiring. Possessing. It was at the very core of my being and the reason I was who I was, the reason I was made.

It was what enabled me to be the God of Death.

I did the dirtiest job known to immortal and mortal kind and I did it without reservation—I was the keeper of souls. The king of the dead. The first reaper of the living.

I was a taker, not some fucking goody-two-shoes giver.

And yet she had changed something in me.

She made me want to give. She made me want to do better, if only for her.

All of it for her.

My chest pinched and I scrubbed at the pain with my thumb.

Amber liquid trickled into a glass, the sound pulling me from my private thoughts.

Folkoln handed it to me. "Start from the top," he said as I took it.

So I did. I gave him the rundown of my ultimate fuckup and how it lost me the female I had waited centuries for.

When I was finished, Folkoln said, "I don't even think what you did was all that bad. You were given a deck of cards, and you played your hand."

"Coming from someone who has less morality than a charlatan peddling fraudulent wares, that means very little, brother."

Folkoln snorted. "Well, at least your humor is intact. But what about your balls? Or did you chop those off and hand them over to her too?"

My lips thinned as I narrowed my eyes on him. "Funny."

"I thought it was," he said with a masochistic grin before he lifted his glass to his mouth. He drank the remnants of it and then set it down on the counter, the cup not making so much as a whisper of sound.

The painters chatted on and off with each other as they worked, filling the void when my conversation with Folkoln trailed off. Sometimes one would laugh at something the other said. Sometimes they'd both laugh. They seemed to work well together, as far as I could tell.

I looked around the tavern—the word seemed like a lackluster way to describe it. Design wise, it would be unlike anything most mortals had ever seen. It would be a popular place once it was up and running.

I glanced back at Folkoln. "When do you plan to open?"

"I'm aiming for the end of the month," he said.

"That's coming quickly."

He nodded. "It is."

"How's construction going on the other ones?"

"Six have already opened their doors. I pop back in to check on those whenever I get a chance."

"Sounds busy," I said, my lips moving on their own accord, but my thoughts were miles away. They were stuck on a white-haired goddess. In the beginning, I had planned to consume her, but in the end, it was she who'd consumed me.

For once in the history of all living things, she had done the impossible—

Life had trumped Death.

"So . . ." Folkoln started as he leaned on the counter, his elbows propping him up. "How are you going to get her back?"

"Fuck if I know," I said. "I gave her her freedom."

"Then let her have her freedom, but that doesn't mean you can't be a part of her life."

"No . . . I suppose it doesn't," I said, rubbing at my jaw, my rough finger pads sounding against the small bits of stubble.

Sage was angry with me right now, but that didn't mean she would be forever. I wanted her, more than anything, and if that meant that I had to wait decades, if not centuries, to have her, then that was exactly what I would do.

I snagged the bottle we had been drinking from—it tasted just like the one he had brought to my chambers to celebrate Sage and I being bonded. I don't know if it was because of that, or because it tasted so damn good that the off-breed whiskey had quickly become my drink of choice. I teetered the bottle back and forth, drawing his attention to it, and asked, "Did you come up with a name for this?"

"Can't say that I have," Folkoln said, reaching for his polishing cloth.

I nodded to the other side of the bar, to the rows of stacked glasses. "Give me two of those."

Folkoln gave me a peculiar look but didn't ask why. He retrieved two glasses and set them on the counter before me. I filled a few knuckles' worth inside. When I was finished, I turned towards the painters, two cups in my hands. "You two, come over and try this."

They looked at me and then to each other, confused. Afraid.

Although not all mortals could sense what I was, some certainly could. Judging by the looks on their faces, they knew.

"Don't piss your pants, boys, it's only booze," I said with a lifeless chuckle.

Slowly, they set their brushes down and cautiously began walking over to us. The one dried his hands on his denim overalls, the blue hidden under years of paint. The other one ran his trembling fingers through his hair, as if he was gussying up to meet his maker.

Mortals were always so dramatic.

"Have a sip." I offered them the two glasses, which they both took.

The one did as I said, sampling a small swallow. But the other one—a good-looking man in his mid-twenties—he couldn't stop himself as he drank it down in eager gulps. The liquid was gone faster than a toupee in a windstorm.

"Impressive," I said to the guzzler. "What's your name, lad?"

He wiped at his lips. “Alexandre Bourbon.”

I turned to the other. “And yours?”

“Dominick Clutterbuck, sir,” he said, still sipping on his glass like it was a cup of fine wine.

Amused, my lips flickered at the sides, but I kept my composure. “Well, Clutterbuck, that’s an unfortunate last name to have.” I turned to the other. “How’d you like to have a new type of alcohol named after you?”

His brows slammed into his forehead as he stuttered, “Are you being serious?”

“I am,” I said, topping him up a bit more. I lifted the bottle, and said to the painters, “To you, Bourbon. And you, Clutterbuck, for making this choice an easy one.”

Folkoln burst into laughter behind me, and I couldn’t help but grin.

It was quickly wiped out when Sage scampered across my thoughts.

Sorrows building, I drained my glass dry and then moved on to the bottle.

Shadows unraveling around me, I stepped into the quiet throne room, my head as hazy as my thoughts. Sure, I enjoyed a glass of alcohol every once in a while, but it had been a long time since I had abused the substance.

But tonight? Tonight, I'd abused the shit out of it.

All things considered, I had a valid reason.

I looked at the ceiling—taking in the swirling vines and lush white roses that claimed half of it. That, right there, was my reason.

"You've returned at last," said a cold, cruel voice, pitched from high above.

I tilted my head to my right, eyes gazing up the stairs, tracing the voice to my throne. Sitting on it—Saphira. Or rather . . . two versions of her.

Fuck, I was drunk.

If she wanted to get a rise out of me, she would have to try harder.

"You seem to have forgotten your place, once again," I said, shoving a hand into my pocket as I turned to face her.

"I should say the same for you, brother. You seem to have forgotten that you are a king and that you have a duty to your people. People who starve now because you gave up the realms that rightfully belong to us. I never thought you to be a foolish god, but in choosing her, you have proven yourself as such," she said, her manicured fingers wrapping around my throne's arms.

I flashed her a mocking grin. "Ah, but that is where you are wrong. The realms never belonged to you or any of the other Old Gods. They belonged to me and it was my choice to decide what to do with them. Not yours. Not Pertheus's. Mine."

"We went to war for you!" she screamed, the words shredding

their way out of her throat. They echoed off the molten glass walls, bashing against them over and over again. Voice lowering to a trembling whisper, she said, “I went to war for you.”

I exhaled a long breath. “And I am grateful for that, for your loyalty. But what you are doing right now is the furthest thing from it. I have let you act out because I know of the pain you feel for losing Aryx.”

“You know nothing of my pain,” she snarled, a vein popping out of her forehead, threatening to burst through her smooth skin. “My mate died to protect the realm you carelessly traded so that you could have yours.”

“Is that what this is all about?” I had expected it was because of her jealousy, but I did not see the extent of it. Now, it made sense. My voice softened. “Saphira—”

“No!” she growled. “There can be no turning back from this day.”

“What do you mean?” I asked, taking a step forward. My voice darkened. “What have you done?”

“Now!” she shouted.

Hundreds of feet stampeded around me and I rolled my eyes. “You are staging a coup? How original.”

My hand raised. I’d show them all why I was the king of—

Something was thrown over top of my impaired ass—a net of some sort. The weight of it was crushing, knocking me down to the floor. I commanded my shadows to walk me out, but they did not answer. I turned to my power, calling upon my wind to shatter the bones of those who dared to raise arms against me, but nothing happened. I slid my hands beside me, trying to push up, but my immortal strength failed me. My body had never felt so . . . weak.

Damn, it would suck to be a mortal.

Heels clicked beside my head. Black fabric pooled as Saphira crouched down. She ran the tip of her sharpened fingernail along the rope. "Do you know what this net is made from?"

"I don't really care," I told her honestly. I'd done the villain spiel more times than I could possibly count, as if I needed to hear it from my little sister now.

"Well, I'm going to tell you anyway," she said, crimson lips pinching upwards at the corners.

I groaned in response—purposefully exaggerating the sound.

"The rope is made from the hair of the giant—the Ancient One you keep in the lowest tier of the Spirit Realm. As you know, some of the Ancient Ones have the ability to make not only themselves mortal, but others as well, which is why her hair was the perfect choice. Naturally, I could not go down and speak with her, otherwise she would have consumed my soul, so I forced Ithar to go speak with her for me. Of course he was not willing to betray you at first, but with the right . . . persuasion, he realized he didn't have a choice. So I had him go make a deal on my behalf—if she were to aid me in removing you from the throne, I would give her your soul in return. Of course, she agreed."

"I'm not very fond of that idea," I told Saphira. Having my soul devoured by the beastie in my realm's basement was not on today's itinerary—getting drunk and then sleeping for a year or two was more like it.

"Your dry humor isn't going to help you," she said, patting my cheek through the net. She raised to her full height. "Take him to her."

"Saphira, wait," I said as people descended upon me, rolling me up into the net and further locking me in. I imagined this was how mortals felt when they were bagged with a sheet, wrapped in a heavy chain, and then tossed into the depths of the Selenian Sea, never to be seen again.

"I wish things could have been different," she said, turning away from me.

I struggled against my bonds, but it was of no use.

Suddenly, I was feeling very, very tired. And increasingly drunk—to the point the room started spinning.

Damn this fucking net, was the last thing I remembered thinking before I passed out.

Chapter 43
Von

"Wakey-wakey, little god, you've slept long enough," purred a feminine voice, so powerful that the cold, rocky ground trembled beneath me when she spoke. "I do not care to eat my food when it's asleep. I prefer it fully conscious and screaming. Adds to the flavor."

Groggy eyelids opening, I eyed the gigantic female who crouched over top of me. Her skin was a dark gray, her hair, which twirled around her, defying gravity, was a dark purple. Her haunting eyes were the blackest of blacks. Horns protruded from the top of her head, shooting straight up at the roof of the mountainous cave we were in.

Although I was originally a bit foggy about what happened and how I ended up there, seeing the giant female standing before me jogged my memory pretty damn fast—

Saphira had double-crossed me.

I tried to move, but the net wrapped around me would not allow it. The vast power surging through the ropes, woven from the Ancient One's hair, tamped mine down, as well as my immortal strength.

"It has been quite some time since I last saw you. How many centuries would you say it has been?" she chuckled darkly. "Too many to count, perhaps." She pursed her lips in thought, and then hovered her hand over top of me.

I waited to see what she would do, unsure if she was about to squash me like a mosquito or crack my head in two, but what she did was so much worse—

She ran a finger over my body, from head to toe, stroking me like I was some prized new lap dog of hers. And then she did it again.

She was fucking *petting* me. My ego reeled.

Saphira was going to pay for this.

"It is good to see your handsome face," she said, her finger pushing me further into the ground with each blasted stroke.

"I wish I could say the same for you," I grunted, my mouth filling with rock and sediment.

"Oh," she pouted, sticking out her bottom lip as if I had hurt her tender feelings. Her finger stopped. "I had hoped that after all of this time, you might have grown to miss me." The giant leaned in, her movement causing a blast of air to slam against me, followed by her sweet, floral scent. "I'll let you in on a little secret . . . I haven't been able to stop thinking about you," she spoke in my ear, her voice so loud it felt like a nail had been hammered into my head, rupturing my eardrum.

"Fuck," I swore through gritted teeth, pain overriding my senses.

She leaned back on her heels, her voice muffled in my one ear, but not in the other as she said, "I've thought about you every day since you imprisoned me down here. You see, I have traveled to many realms, devoured thousands of souls, and I have never met one such as you—an insignificant god who could best someone like me, and yet, you did." She was quiet for a moment. "I've replayed our battle over and over in my head more times than I can count, and it's still such a mystery to me. Sure, there were other gods who fought against me, but ultimately, you were the one to defeat me. And so here lies the question—how can someone *like you* have *so much* power?"

"I don't know what to tell you," I bit out, warring with my agony but refusing to show it. My voice sounded off—like it was stuck in my head, rattling around with nowhere to go.

She threaded her arms loosely over her chest, one dark brow shooting upwards. "Do you want to know what I think?"

"Not really," I breathed, ear ringing like a Sunday bell.

"Arrogant god," she said in a condescending tone. "I'll tell you anyway. I think that there is more to you than meets the eye. God of Death, king of this pitiful realm . . . I think it's all a charade." A cruel smile curled her lips. "I think you are pretending to be someone you're not. Tell me I'm wrong."

"Fine. Fine. Twist my arm . . . You're wrong."

"You're lying."

"I'm not."

"You are more than what you portray yourself to be. Either you truly have no idea what I'm talking about, or you are desperate to keep your true alias hidden." She tipped her head to the side. "However, there is one way for me to find out." She rotated her wrist, producing a dagger with a thin blade and a sharp, sharp tip.

I eyed it. "That seems a bit aggressive for the job, no?"

She didn't reply as she leaned over top of me, her hair floating around her in rhythmic waves, rippling like water. She unwrapped the net, just enough to uncover my one leg.

I could feel a small trickle of power begin to seep into me, not enough to fight with, but enough to heal. It worked its way to my eardrum, beginning to repair the ruptured tissue and take away some of the pain.

But the feeling was short-lived, because she placed the tip of her dagger against my thigh and pressed it in. I roared in agony as the blade cut into my leather pants, past my skin, muscle, and sinew, stopping when it reached my iron bone.

"That feels promising," she muttered to herself. She moved the dagger up and down, tapping my femur. "I'd like to get a better look at what you're made of, though."

"Fucking bitch," I snarled, reaching for the blade. My fingers curled around the large tip, pitting my tamped-down strength against hers. The knife sawed into my fingers.

She stopped her tapping. “I’d let go if I were you, or else this will become a whole lot worse.”

I didn’t listen, trying to pull the blade out of me.

“Have it your way,” she said as she dragged the dagger forward, cutting off part of my fingers as she slit me all the way down to my ankle.

Pain exploded, my vision flashing white as the remnants of my fingers fell on my chest, a few bouncing off to the side. I moaned in agony.

The beast inside, which I kept under lock and key, rattled against his cage, desperate to take over. But once I let him out, I didn’t know if I would be able to put him back in. I couldn’t give up control—no, not yet.

Clang. The dagger clattered against the ground, a waft of air hitting me as the giant leaned forward, her breath like a tsunami against my skin. Her fingers pulled the bone-deep cut apart and I roared, slurring out a string of profanities.

“I knew there was more to you than what you were letting on.” She cackled in triumph as her fingers released their hold, the two slabs of meat slapping back together.

Before my sliver of freed divinity had a chance to heal my fingers or my leg, she tossed the net back over top of me.

She sat back, a smug grin twisting her lips. “Despite your bloodless veins, your iron bones tell the truth of what you really are, which makes me wonder why you are here and not back home, with the rest of our kin. Either you were banished from the homeland, or . . . you are in hiding. Regardless, when I devour you, your soul will be delivered back to the empress, and then it will be up to her to decide what to do with you."

I struggled against the net, my body writhing in miserable torment.

"Hmm," she said, teetering her head from side to side. "But before I send you on your way, perhaps I should have a bit of *fun* with you. I have been so very lonely over the decades."

I didn't need to ask for further clarification of what her idea of fun was—it was in the way she purred out the word that told me what she had in mind.

The thought curdled the contents of my stomach like rotten milk—regardless of if Sage and I were together or not, I could *never* touch another woman, not now. Not ever. Sage had ruined me. She was the only female that I wanted. Craved. Needed.

On top of that, I had no desire to deep dive in a giant's gloryhole.

No fucking way.

"What do you say, God of Death? Should we have a bit of fun?" she asked, her finger stroking me.

"Over my dead body," I growled through gritted teeth.

She paused her petting, a snarl weaving onto her lips. "I had hoped you would say otherwise, however, your request can be arranged." She plucked the net, tugging me from the ground, lifting me higher, until I was dangling over top of her face. She licked her lips, asking, "Any last—"

A blast of orange and white flames smashed into her throat. She let out a horrible, continuous scream, her fingers releasing me as she clawed at her neck, trying to put out the fire.

I fell roughly forty feet until I hit the ground like a sack of bricks, my head smashing against the rocky ground. Pain erupted in my head, my legs, my back. Everywhere hurt. I wheezed for oxygen—certain my lungs had collapsed.

Damn this net!

"Hold her there, Zahra," Dameon's voice instructed.

"On it," she said, somewhere in the distance.

Dameon appeared over top of me, his wings spread out behind him—they echoed the same vibrant colors of the flames he commanded.

"You're a sight for sore eyes," I grimaced, my finger nubs rubbing at my ribs.

"Wish I could say the same for you. You look terrible," Dameon responded as he began to pull at the net, working on untangling it. "What in the Spirit Realm did she do to your leg?"

"Long story," I grumbled. "Another time."

"Understandable. Let's get out of here first."

I nodded.

"I don't know how much longer I can hold her back," Zahra shouted, her voice nearly swallowed up by the angry screams of the giant. The smell of cooking flesh and burnt hair began to permeate the air.

"I've almost got it," Dameon called out. Grunting, he tossed the last remnants of the net to the side, freeing me from the fucking thing.

And just like that, the dam that had restricted my divinity gave way. Instantly, I was filled with immense, intoxicating power—I breathed it in, welcoming it back. My shadows settled around me, returning to their keeper.

"I'll send you all to the empress for this!" the giant goddess roared so loud that the mountain trembled and the ground shook beneath me.

Dameon's head jerked up, his eyes narrowing, panic slashing across his face. "Zahra!" he growled, his wings flaring out before he shot over top of me.

I jerked upright, my body healing quickly, but not quick enough. The giant's hand was moments from striking Zahra, before Dameon swooped in and scooped up his pregnant mate. He shot upwards, trying to get out of the Ancient One's reach. She leapt up into the air, her hand reaching for them—

I conjured a javelin made of shadow, as strong as the metal bones in my body, and I hurtled it at her with my immortal strength.

She screamed as it impaled her palm, stopping her from grabbing hold of them as they flew into a swirl of black, taking them out of here.

Swearing, she pulled the javelin from her hand, snapping it in two as if it were a toothpick. She tossed it onto the ground, her furious eyes locking on me, nostrils flaring like a bull locking on to a matador's cape. "You!" she yelled, the word ricocheting around us like cannon fire going off. "I should have eaten your soul the moment your sister had you tossed down here."

"You probably should have." I nodded nonchalantly, eyeing my healed fingers. Good as new. Would you look at that.

I flicked my gaze to the giant pissed-off female who looked like she was two seconds away from charging. "But as much as I have not enjoyed this little reunion, I have someone I need to pay a visit to."

I fell into the embrace of my umbra. It swept around me, taking me back to my throne room.

Shooting out like a bow from an arrow, I hurtled through the air, over top of my imprisoned gods, their wrists bound in shackles, straight for one very surprised looking Saphira.

My hand wrapped around her throat as I drove her straight through my throne, past the wall behind it—bits of molten glass spraying out all around us as we fell down the side of the steep mountain.

"Traitor," I snarled in her face, my fury scorching my veins as we smashed through rocks and stones, hitting the mountain and then catapulting back up into the air and then back down.

"You were the one who betrayed us all," she choked out as her fingernails slashed at my wrist, trying to free herself from my hold. Her hand flew towards my stomach, fire shooting out from her palm. I grabbed her wrist, twisting it to the side, before her flame could touch me. Fire scorched the trees in the distance, turning them to ash on the spot.

The wind picked up, hurtling into me, trying to shove me from her.

Mine answered back, shoving hers down.

My wings flared out behind me, catching on the air and lifting us both.

Hers unfurled as she tried to flap them, tried to get away.

"Do not fight me, Saphira," I growled in her face, my voice etched in malice, in fury. "You have made your bed and now you will sleep in it."

"Von, wait!" she cried out, trying everything within her power to break my hold, but her power was no match for mine. And she damn well knew it.

Her pleas fell on deaf ears.

"Submit to me," I commanded of her godly powers, and submit they did, leaving her with little more than tooth and nail to fight me with.

I took her to my dungeon, where I locked her wrists in the diamond bonds I had made for the New Gods and then left her there, sobbing and pleading for me to come back. To have mercy.

But for this betrayal, I would show her none.

She could rot down there for the next century for all I cared.

Let the maggots keep her company.

Chapter 44

Sage

The errant breeze plucked at my hair, twirling the few strands that were not swept into my ponytail. Sitting in the gently swaying branches above me, birds chirped and tweeted in private conversation with one another as the sun set on the horizon, painting the sky in shades of pinks and oranges. From this vantage point, I could see a bit of the sky, but not all of it—that was partly due to the massive brick walls that surrounded the manor's grounds.

The fabric stretched taut over my bent knees was stained with green while my fingernails were filled with earth. I patted the ground beside me, looking for the small shovel I had been using. When I could not find it, I glanced to my left, looking for it. *Not there*. I glanced to my right.

Bingo.

Fingers wrapping around the handle, I plucked it from the ground and began to dig a new hole for the flower I had grown—a vibrant pink lily, its petals etched in white. I gently lifted the plant from the basket and placed it in the ground, then covered it with rich topsoil. After, I raised my hand over top, my fingers rolling rhythmically as I conjured water to rain down from my palm. When the ground was good and soaked, I shifted down and started on the next one.

That was what I had been doing with my time. Planting and growing flowers.

Well, that and—

My stomach rolled.

I lurched over to the side, squeezing my eyes shut as I tried to ride out the waves of nausea. But my stomach clenched like an iron fist and the limited contents came shooting out. Acid burned my esophagus as I vomited on the grass. It wasn't much, considering I couldn't keep a whole lot down these days.

"Dammit," I rasped, lungs rattling in my chest as I wiped the back of my hand against my mouth. I laid down on the lush blanket of nature's green grass, my gaze lifting to the sky. I had thrown up nearly every day since Von brought me here. And although originally, I thought that it might be something to do with the bond, I was now beginning to suspect it might be something else entirely.

That *something else* scared the shit out of me.

And yet—my fingers danced over my stomach—

What if?

Those two little words were all I would allow myself to ask. They were safe. Because *what if* was not set in stone. It was based on a dream, on a possibility. But if I were to change those words into the three that I was too fearful to ask, and if I was given an answer that said yes, well, that would make everything real.

I wasn't sure if I was ready for that kind of realness because I was just barely picking up the pieces of my shattered heart after learning what Von had done. During our time together, I had come to trust him. Love him. But I also thought I loved Aurelius at one time, too, and that turned out to bite me in the ass.

When I left Aurelius, I felt empowered. Excited. Proud.

But all I had felt since Von brought me here was heartbroken and sad.

I could easily stay in bed all day and sob. That's exactly what I had done for the first week I was here. By the second, I knew I needed to do something, to get up, to use my hands.

"Would you like a bit of tea, milady?" asked Eliza, one of the many staff members who worked at the manor as she walked towards me.

Head rolling to the side, my cheek tickled by grass, I looked her way.

Eliza was one of the smallest women I had ever seen. She was tiny, but incredibly strong. I'd seen her carry potato sacks that were bigger than her with ease. Unlike some of the other staff, she lived outside of the manor with her sister, who suffered from some type of brain injury.

She offered me a soft smile, lifting the tray to show me what she had brought.

Abdomen contracting, I lifted from the ground and sat up. "Sure," I said, reasoning that tea would help to remove some of the nasty taste from my mouth.

Eliza walked over to two metal chairs that sat underneath a willow tree, a small table between them. She placed the tray there and then turned to me. "Can I get you anything else, milady?"

Softly, I shook my head. "No, thank you. You are very kind, Eliza."

She looked at the flowers I had planted. They stretched on and on. Had I made it my life's mission to cover the backyard in vibrant-colored plants? Possibly.

"They are all so very lovely," she said with a smile.

"Thank you. You could pick some and take them to your sister. If you think that's something she might like."

Eliza's smile broadened. "She adores flowers. I'm sure she would be very excited if I took her some."

"Then please see that you do." My voice was warm.

"I will. I'll take her some tomorrow." She bowed her head, and then carried on back to the manor, leaving me alone with my rotting guts.

A few days later, I decided I should go see the downtown core of Belamour. Partly because my fingers were nearly raw from all the time I had been spending digging around in the dirt. The other part was because it would give me something to keep my mind busy—other than thinking of Von and my *what if* all day.

Getting ready to leave, I found the cloak that I had purchased all those months ago after I escaped Aurelius. I slung it over my shoulders, feeling its weight soothe my weary bones like a warm cup of tea. The pocketed tin thumped against my leg, reminding me that it was still there. I pulled it out, looking it over.

Von had released me from the deal we made. The tattoo he had given me, his branding bite on my backside, had also disappeared in the process.

"I suppose I won't be needing you any longer," I said as I walked over to a wicker basket used for garbage. I dropped the tin into it. When it struck the bottom of the basket, the lid popped off. My brow lifted—

There wasn't salve in the container after all, which explained why it had felt so light.

In it was a folded white cloth, densely packed.

Bending, I picked up the bottom half of the tin and gently pulled the cloth out. I ran my fingers over top of the soft linen, feeling the small oblong pieces tucked beneath.

"You pee on them," said a familiar voice, young and vibrant.

A smile touched my lips as I looked up, finding Ezra standing in the doorway. with a mischievous twinkle in her eye. "Ezra!" I exclaimed, shaking my head. "What are you doing here?"

She pointed to the tin. "I came to make sure you take a tinkle on those."

I gave her a peculiar look. “Excuse me?”

Ezra walked over to me, her hand gently cupping mine as she unfolded the corner of the linen, revealing a layer of purple seeds.

“In the old language, these are called Neptuah.”

“They look a bit like barley, just longer,” I said, surveying the seeds.

“They are a relative,” she replied with a nod. “They are less nutty in flavor. A bit sweeter. But they also serve another purpose. They will tell you if you are pregnant or not.”

And there it was—*the word* that I had so desperately been trying to steer clear of.

I took a deep breath, felt the air fill my lungs. “How do they work?”

“Traditionally, women would urinate on barley seeds, and if they sprouted within so many days, it meant they were pregnant, but these seeds are a bit different. They work much quicker, or so I’ve been told. So—” she shoved them towards me and then began to shove on me, “—go, go! Get whizzing.”

“Wait a minute.” I pressed on my heels, my feet rooting to the floor. “You gave me this tin months ago. How did you know I would need it?”

“Lucky guess.”

I squinted at her and her ambiguous answer.

“Alright. Fine, fine. The day you showed up at my apothecary, the rocks told me that you would need the grains more than the salve,” she said, as if it explained everything.

It didn’t.

The rocks told her?

I stared at her blankly, deciding at that moment that I would never understand her hokey-pokey ways and continued to the bathing room.

When I was done, I left the grains on the vanity and stepped out into the hallway—fighting the urge to vomit. Not because I felt nauseous, but because I was so incredibly nervous. Like shit-your-pants nervous.

"Now what?" I asked Ezra, who was stretching, her hands above her head.

She dropped her arms, scurried over to my side, and said with a big, vibrant, grin, as she hooked her arm in mine. "Now, we wait."

So that's what we did.

Without a doubt, it was the longest wait of my life.

When it was time, Ezra turned to me. "Do you want me to go look, or do you want to?"

"You go look," I told her as I sat on the end of the bed, my hands twisting uncomfortably in my lap. My heart fluttered in my chest, but that was nothing compared to the acrobatic moves my stomach was currently performing.

What if the seeds sprouted? What would that mean for me? What would I say to Von? What would that mean for us? Would he even want it? What if he didn't? Did I even want it?

My world spun on its axis, threatening to fly off into oblivion as I was bombarded with question after question after question.

Ezra came into the room, the tin in her hand. Her brows were raised as she stared at the grains. She looked . . . shocked.

At that moment, I realized I didn't need her to tell me if the seeds had sprouted or not because judging by the look on her face, that was all I needed to know.

"I'm pregnant, aren't I?" I cried out. I was excited and afraid. My emotions were all over the place.

Ezra's blue eyes lifted from the grains, settling on me. Then she shook her head and showed me them—not one had sprouted. "You are not."

I nearly fell over.

"What?" I scampered off the bed, grabbing hold of the silver container and peering at the seeds, searching for a speck of green, but finding the same answer over and over again—Not pregnant. Not pregnant. Not pregnant.

I didn't understand.

Ezra fished a handful of rocks out of her pocket. "How could you get this wrong?" she asked the mismatched stones, then brought them to her ear.

I blinked.

"You are sure these grains work?" I asked, thrusting them in front of her.

She batted my hand away, as if I was interrupting a private conversation.

"Ezra," I snapped.

She lowered her hand, tucked the rocks back into her pocket, and then said, "The rocks are surprised as well, but they apologize. They said they might have jumped the bow on this one."

I shook my head, unwilling to believe what I was being told. "But my emotions, they have been all over the place. Not to mention I have no interest in food and can't keep anything down," I said, my hand falling over the flat of my stomach.

"Both of those things are easily explained by the bond. It is suffering right now, and so naturally, it is messing with your body as well."

I supposed that made sense. When the bond was newly formed, it made me extremely aroused, as well as emotional. With everything that had transpired between Von and I, now it was affecting me in an entirely different way—it was making me sick.

I took a deep breath, glancing once more at the unsprouted seeds.

On one hand, I felt relieved.

And on the other, I felt, well . . . sad.

Empty.

Chapter 45
Von

I blew out a fiery breath of air from my heated lungs, my bloodless veins boiling beneath my skin. My annoyance was growing by the second. If there was one place I did not want to be, it was here, in the shit-ass company of my squabbling council members. Without Sage, I was miserable enough, let alone having to sit here and listen to all of this.

"I don't know how many times I have to say it for you to understand," Brutus, the God of Logic, said, his person adorned in scholarly black robes trimmed with silver. He was standing, his chair shoved out behind him as he spoke to the redhead sitting across the table from him—Erynna, the Goddess of Fidelity. "Just because

Saphira and the rest of her traitors are locked up in the dungeon, that doesn't mean we've squashed the uprising."

"And for the last time, I understand that," she sighed, lounging casually in her chair, picking at her long nails. "But what you are suggesting would only make matters worse."

"I disagree," Brutus said with a huff. Physically, the man had always reminded me of a bulldog, his wide nose smooshed up into his face.

"Of course you do," she said, hazel eyes flicking up to him.

"So then, what do *you* suggest we do?" Pertheus snarled—a bunch of heads swiveling his way. "Because you haven't given us one single suggestion yet, and we've been discussing this for days."

When Saphira attempted to overthrow me, I had thought that Pertheus would have been chomping at the bit to help her, but he didn't, which surprised me. Something I wasn't used to. In the weeks that followed the rebellion, he had even helped hunt down anyone who had anything to do with it. Yet another surprise.

Erynna dropped her hand and sat up straight as she turned to me. "You remind them who you are—you make an example of their leader. You kill the Goddess of War."

"What?" Zahra hissed. She was seated adjacent to me. Dameon's hand fell on Zahra's forearm, trying to comfort her. Zahra and Saphira used to be friends, a long time ago. She might just be one of the only people in this room who had been able to crack through my sister's cold exterior, gilded in malice and contempt.

"She's right," Brutus decreed, his brows lifting. "Saphira must die. It will set a precedent."

"No!" Zahra shouted, getting up from her chair with some difficulty due to her swollen belly. She was getting close to her due date. "We cannot kill one of our own."

Dameon stood up with her, trying to comfort his mate. "Zahra," he cautioned, looking down at her, then to her belly.

She gave him a fierce look that was enough to make a grown-ass male shrivel up into the fetal position. Still, Dameon held firm at her side, unwavering and loyal.

I had never been jealous of their bond before, but at that moment, I was.

I turned my attention away, eyes fixing on the goddess at the end of the table as she stood up from her chair and declared, "The moment she turned her back on our king, she turned her back on us all."

"Agreed," the god sitting beside her said.

A few more immortals joined in, voicing their approval. Like a tidal wave, it took them over. One by one, people shot up from their chairs, until most of them were calling out for my sister's death.

"How would we do it? Is anyone aware of what the Goddess of War's weakness is?" asked Brutus as he scrubbed at his chin.

"I'm sure Zahra knows," Erynna said, her hands gripping the table.

"I do not," Zahra growled, one hand clenched by her side, the other supporting the base of her stomach. "And even if I did, I would not tell any of you. Have you all gone insane?"

That sparked a great deal of outrage and then the room erupted into shouting and yelling and finger-pointing. My shadows slithered around me, seeping into the room, my anger building and building until—

"Sit down," I commanded in a lethal tone.

Immediately, the room went silent, swiftly followed by the sound of wood creaking as they sat down in their chairs, their lips tightly closed. Not one of them dared to even clear their throat.

I looked around the table, leveling each gaze directed my way. "I will deal with the mess my sister has made."

"What will you do?" Zahra asked, her eyes shining with worry.

"I'm going to make an example of my sister," I said, standing up.

"Von, no," she pleaded with me.

I offered her a sympathetic look before I said to them all, "I do not disagree that a precedent needs to be set, but if I end my sister's life, it will give legitimacy to her claim that I am not fit to lead. It will look like I fear her. And knowing the people, they will make her a martyr. That is the last thing I need." I shook my head. "I won't end my sister's life, but I will show the people of the Spirit Realm what happens to those who rise against me."

I turned to Ismay, who had been quiet for the majority of the meeting. "I want the throne room filled to the brim within fifteen minutes."

She nodded swiftly.

I sat on my throne, overlooking my domain.

Hundreds upon hundreds of souls had filed into the throne room, all of them pulled from different tiers. These people were my witnesses who, in a matter of minutes, would see what happened to those who tried to go against me. They would become my mouthpieces, telling others what they had seen here today.

They just didn't know that that was their purpose.

Because they didn't know, it made for one nervous crowd, made up of weary, suspicious eyes and rigid, trembling bodies. Their expressions became even more severe as they took in what I had placed in front of the stairs that led up to my throne—

A separate dais, high enough for all to see.

Above it, my shadow chains dangled from the ceiling, mirrored by shorter ones that were tethered to the base. Cuffs were attached to them, a set for wrists and a set for ankles.

The doors opened and two sentries dragged my sister into the room. Her feet skittered beneath her as she fought their hold, her hair strewn about haphazardly. Her strapless leather dress was torn. Her skin was covered in deep slits, her body too weak to heal them.

The New Gods preferred iron to suppress divine powers. Here in the Spirit Realm, we had other methods, older methods. Methods that involved depleting the immortal of ichor to dampen their powers. It was a bit more barbaric, sure, but it had been used since the early days of the Three Realms, long before the effects of iron were discovered.

Heads swiveled as she was pulled down the aisle against her will, shouting insults and orders to unhand her—none of which were heard by my shadow sentries. When they reached the dais in front of me, they shoved her onto her knees.

"You'll pay for that," she snarled at them, trying to pull free from their grasp.

I left my throne, appearing in a bit of swirling black, standing before her.

"Brother," she snarled, her green eyes burning hotter than a forge.

For a moment, I held her gaze. That was all I would give her.

Looking at my sentries, I gave my order. "Face her towards the crowd."

They bowed swiftly.

"What are you doing?" she hissed, trying to fight them off as they dragged her up onto the dais. I followed behind them.

I could feel the scabs on her skin as I grasped her forearm, taking her from them. She tried to pull free, but her attempt was futile. I cuffed her wrist and then moved on to the next one. By the time I started on her feet, she was yelling.

"Let your wings out, Saphira," I said.

"No!" she cried out, her body trembling as realization hit her.

"You can do it of your own free will, or I will command it of you," I told her, my voice filled with heavy, heavy smoke.

"I won't," she snarled.

"Then you leave me no choice." Power, ancient and lethal, seeped from my skin, drifting around her as I commanded, "Release your wings."

Saphira yelled as she tried to fight against my control, but it was of no use. The divinity in her was forced to bow to its superior. Sleek, black wings unfurled from her back, the tips draping to the floor. They were the feminine version of my own, a reminder that she and I were kin.

Brother and sister.

At least, we used to be.

I wrapped my hand around the section that connected her wing to her back. The bone was large, covered in the silk of her feathers. With my other hand, I held on to her shoulder. I looked up at the crowd, my voice filling the chamber as I roared, "I will show no mercy to those who raise arms against me."

Muscle, sinew, and flesh popped and tore as I started to rip Saphira's one wing from her back. A bloodcurdling scream slashed its way out of her, so horrific it sent people cowering to their knees. My molars threatened to combust into dust as her wing came off, her warm ichor spraying all over me.

Saphira's body went slack as she sobbed, and sobbed, and sobbed.

I felt her lifeless wing in my hand, dangling there. I looked at it and then to the gaping hole in her back, and I wondered for a moment—would death have been the kinder thing to do for her?

When I glanced up, my gaze immediately met Zahra's. Dameon supported his mate, holding her upright as tears streamed down her face, her mouth open as she wailed. I was reminded of the time when my sister's face had looked very much the same as Zahra's. It was the day she lost her mate—Aryx. A day that would forever be ingrained in my mind.

Just as this one would be.

I dropped her one wing and it landed with a sickening, lifeless *thud*. I reached for the other, my hand locking around it.

"Draevon, no, please," she begged me as she wept, her voice so weak. So broken. The fight in the Goddess of War was gone.

"You left me no choice," I told her. Then I pulled. The joints hissed until they snapped, my arm jerking back from the force as her second wing tore out of its socket, fleshy bits of skin coming along with it.

Saphira slumped, the chains holding her weight.

Her sobs haunted me as I picked up her other ichor-coated wing, the end dipped in ivory flesh. "From this day forth, you are exiled from the Spirit Realm, Saphira," I said over my shoulder, delivering my final blow.

I didn't bother to look back as I walked down the aisle, dragging her wings behind me for all to see.

This was the cost of Saphira's betrayal.

This was the cost of being king.

Chapter 46

Von

Down in my crypt, the spirits whispered with one another as I closed the lid to the glass casket, laying Saphira's wings to rest, as well as the shattered remains of the sibling relationship we once had.

Saphira had not died today, but in so many ways, it felt like she had.

Both she and Folkoln had been with me since the dawn of my creation. We had all been made together, however, Saphira and Folkoln's souls were placed in children's bodies while mine was placed in an adult one. That meant I got to watch them grow up together, and although they were my siblings, I raised them.

For many years, Folkoln was the problematic one, living up to his title—the God of Chaos—but then somewhere along the lines, they switched. Saphira became fixated on finding her mate, and the longer she waited, the colder she became.

Then, when she found Aryx, I saw that same old version of Saphira return, the one I had once known when she was younger, only to watch it be snuffed out again when he died.

A memory flickered free, one that was from many lifetimes ago . . .

"You promised," huffed the young goddess, her black brows thrown together, bottom lip poking out. She gave me that look. The one that told me that I was in deep, deep trouble.

I set down the thin-bladed tool I had made and leaned back in my stool, looking over top of the table to where Saphira stood. Warmly, I said, "I know I did, and I fully intend to keep it, Stargazer."

"How are you going to keep your promise to me if you aren't even here, huh?" she said in her little voice, crossing her pudgy arms over her chest. "Folkoln said that you won't be back for weeks!"

"He is just trying to get a rise out of you. I will make it back in time," I assured her. I leaned forward, propping my forearms on my legs as I brought my hands together. My gaze flicked down to the tiny bones on the table, accompanied by a few black feathers I had plucked from my own wings, then back up to her. "Do you want to see what I'm working on?"

She pursed her lips, thinking it over. Her eyes rolled around, emphasizing just how much thought she was giving it and then she cracked a big smile. "Yeah, I do."

I motioned for her to come around to my side. When she did, I picked her up and set her on my lap. Arms reaching around her, I found the stone slat and showed her the animal I had chiseled into it.

Her small fingers traced the beak, then the head. Looking up to me, she said, "It looks like a bird."

"Correct, but this is a special type of bird," I said, flipping the slat over and showing her what was chiseled into the back side.

She traced the images. "It is a man and a woman."

"It is." I set the slat down. I picked up one of my feathers by the quill and twirled it in front of her. "I'm going to sew a little bit of myself into this new type of species so that they can travel between realms, just as we do."

"Wow. That's neat," she said, her fingers dancing over top of my feather. "But why are you making them?"

"As the mortal species continues to grow, I won't be able to keep up collecting the souls all by myself. Which means I'm going to need some help. That's where these birds will come in. They will collect them for me."

She was quiet for a moment, and then she asked, "Does that mean you will be around more often?" Wide green eyes, framed in long black lashes, looked up at me. Even though Saphira was young, she was incredibly intelligent for her age. She was always thinking.

"Yes," I said with a smile. "I will be."

Her grin widened. "Good, because I miss you when you go away, big brother."

I tapped her nose. "I miss you when I'm away, too, Stargazer."

She smiled up at me and then looked back at the feathers and the small bones placed on the table. "So, what are you going to call them?"

"I haven't really gotten that far," I replied, setting the feather down.

"Well, since you are giving a bit of yourself to make them, you should name them after you," she suggested.

I chuckled. "I appreciate the idea, but I think that might be a bit much, even for me."

"Okay, well, it doesn't have to be your name, but it can be like it. What about something like . . ." She paused, thinking about it for a moment. "Ravens. It's like Draevon but different."

I sat with that for a second.

Nodding my head, I said, "I quite like that. Alright, that's what we'll call them."

"Yay!" she said, swinging her feet excitedly.

I let out a low laugh, giving her a little hug.

Some time passed, and then, "Big brother?"

"Yes?" I asked.

"When I get big enough and have more control over my powers, can we make a species together someday?"

"We can."

"Yeah, but do you promise?" she said, looking up at me again.

"You and these promises are going to get me in trouble someday." I laughed softly, before I agreed. "Alright, I promise."

"Yes!" she exclaimed.

I glanced at the window, finding that night had fallen. "It's dark out."

Those three words were enough to send her scrambling off my lap. Her hand locked around my pointer finger and she began to try to pull me off the stool. "Come on, come on, come on."

"Alright, alright," I breathed through a smile, muscles firing as I stood up.

Moments later, we both were lying on our backs on the lush, green grass, looking up at the sky dotted with twinkling stars. The crescent moon was little more than a sliver tonight, painting the rolling hills in a light, glowing silver.

"That's a lot of bonded mates," Saphira said, attempting a sad, sad whistle. It sounded more like she was pushing air through her lips. Whistling was not something she had quite mastered yet, but knowing how persistent she was, I had little doubt she would eventually.

"It sure is," I replied, my one hand on my stomach, the other beside me, fingers playing with a bit of grass.

"Look!" Saphira pointed to a spot in the sky. "There's the Cat's Ears, but a star is missing from it! Do you see? Do you see?"

I followed where she was pointing. The Cat's Ears was a

formation of stars that looked exactly how it sounded—like a pair of cat ears. But where the top point of the left ear should be, the star was no longer there.

"It was there last night, wasn't it?" I asked, knowing that if anyone would know the answer, it would be her.

"Yes! It was! You know what that means. Two bonded mates are going to be made tonight," she exclaimed, voice chock-full of excitement.

"They will be," I confirmed, peering up at the vacant spot where the star had been before. I couldn't help but wonder . . . once the Creator fractured the star in two, would those halves ever meet again?

A strange sensation formed in my chest, one I tried not to think a whole lot about. Because whenever I did, my thoughts tended to get carried away. I would start hoping and wishing and dreaming of the day when I would be reunited with my other half.

I glanced at the moon, wrapped in the protective embrace of her night sky.

"Big brother?" Saphira asked, her hand tapping my head.

"Yes?" I looked up to find her propped up on her elbows, the top half of her face hovering over mine.

"I hope we both find our bonded someday," she said, small fingers petting my cheeks. "But until then? I'm glad I have you."

"I'm glad I have you, too, Saph," I said, my hand falling over top of her little one.

I slammed my fists against the top of the molten casket, roaring at my reflection in anger. Statues, vases, and paintings exploded around me, decimating the chamber in bits of stone and shreds of canvas. Hundred-year-old treasures, priceless pieces from civilizations long forgotten, were destroyed in seconds, and I couldn't care less.

Because the pain I felt right then, there were no words for it.

I dropped my head into my hands as I leaned over the glass, my world caving in on itself.

And even then, these bastard eyes could not produce a single fucking tear. I could slit every vein in my body open right now and not find a single drop of blood. If I were to carve open my chest, I was certain that all I would find was a frozen, black heart.

What was I missing?

Why couldn't I—

A hand pressed against my back, scattering the noise in my head like ash on the wind.

I turned, my shoulders quaking when I saw her.

"Sage," I breathed her name. I stepped into her, my hand—stained with the truth of what I had done—cradled her wet cheek. Her hand fell over mine as she nuzzled into my touch, cloudy blue eyes, rimmed red, locked with mine.

"Why are you crying?" I asked, brushing away her tears with the rough pads of my thumbs—her skin so soft beneath my touch.

"Because—" her hand fell over my heart, "—I could feel this breaking." She lowered her forehead against my chest, clutching on to my tunic with such desperation. "And I've never felt more scared in my life. I thought something was happening to you. I thought you were—" Her voice cracked, and she started to sob.

I took her into my arms, my hand stroking her hair in a bid to try to soothe her. "I'm alright, Little Goddess. I'm alright."

Was it my pain that she was feeling right now?

Had the barrier that was keeping us apart finally broken and now she was being hit with the brunt of my emotions? On top of her own? She had thought something had happened to me . . . And so, she had come for me.

Because she still *cared* for me.

I rested my chin against the top of her head as I held her, feeling her wet little tears soak through my shirt, dampening my skin below. My little female wasn't just shedding a few tears, she was crying buckets—she was crying the tears I was incapable of producing—both mine and hers.

I lifted her from the floor, carrying her bridal style as blackness swept around us, taking her to our bedchamber. I walked over to the settee and tried to set her down, but she refused to unweave her arms from my neck.

"Let go, little love," I told her softly.

"I cannot," she said through her tears.

I understood what that was like.

From the day I first saw her, I never wanted to let her go.

"I've got you," I said as I repositioned so that she was sitting in my lap.

She nuzzled into my chest, her body holding firmly to mine, unable to spare a single inch. "I thought I might be losing you," she whispered.

"You will never lose me. I can promise you that," I said, rubbing her back.

"Good, because—" She lifted her head, looking up at me with her incredible blue eyes. They were as never-ending as the sea and the sky. I could lose myself to them forever. "I've had a lot of time to think since we've been apart, and I've realized something . . ."

"What?" I asked breathlessly.

"Months ago, I was terrified of coming to the Spirit Realm with you because I feared what might happen if I were to fall for you. I was scared of having my heart shattered again." Her hands pressed softly against my chest, her fingers weaving into the black fabric. Her gaze fell for a moment before she picked it back up, locking it with mine. "I don't know if I would have been able to push past that fear if it weren't for you." She shared a small smile with me. "You were exactly what I needed, Von. You showed me what it's like to be loved by someone . . . *truly* loved." She paused for a moment. "I'm no longer scared of giving someone my heart, because the pain and sadness that I felt while we were apart showed me that I have already done just that. Truth is . . . you've had it for a while now."

My lungs stitched to my chest, frozen by her admission. Gently, I cupped her face, unable to breathe until she spoke again, for she was my oxygen. My reason for living.

"So . . ." Her fingers brushed over my cheek as she said, "I choose you. As my bonded, my lover, my king. My husband."

"I have longed to hear those words from you for so very long." I couldn't stop the smile from pulling at my lips. "Does this mean you will marry me?"

"It does." She laughed softly, her eyes glistening with water. She kissed my lips, whispering against them, "From the Three Realms until the next, I claim you as mine."

Softly, I pressed my forehead against hers, my eyes closing as I vowed to her, "From the Three Realms until the next, Little Goddess."

Dear Reader,

I wish I could tell you that this is where their story
ends, that the God of Death and the Goddess of Life
lived happily ever after, but I cannot.
Because as much as Von and Sage's story is about love,
it is also about loss.

Chapter 47

Sage

One Year Later

Ten seeds. Ten sprouts. As green as my mate's eyes.

I sat in front of my makeup vanity, my heart pounding against my chest like horse hooves against stone. In my clammy hands, I cradled a little wooden bowl. Inside of it, there was a truth that would change my life and Von's forever—

Pregnant.

I was filled with such intense happiness, I couldn't help but laugh softly as tears brimmed on my lower lash line.

We were going to have a baby—*a baby.*

The thought of Von holding our little babe in his strong, tattooed arms made my heart swell with pride. I placed the small bowl on the vanity and my hands fell over the flat of my stomach, my fingers brushing over the exquisite black crystals and intricate rose point lace that adorned the bodice of my gown.

"What will you be, my little love? A boy or a girl?" I asked as I smiled softly. "You are going to have the best daddy. Of that, I have no doubt."

Von and I hadn't been trying to conceive for very long, but I always just had this feeling in my heart that once we tried, his seed would take.

And take it did.

Two nights ago, Ezra had shown up here, at the castle, with a tin in one hand and a tonic in the other. When I opened the metal container, I found a cloth filled with Neptuah seeds. Ezra had said something about the rocks being off a year, but the month and day were right. When I asked her what the tonic was for, she said it was for morning sickness. A few hours later, we were cozied up on a settee, a blanket draped over our laps and a cup of tea in our hands. We proceeded to gab late into the night, until the wee hours of the morning. After she left, I placed the tin and seeds inside my bathroom vanity, not expecting to need to use the grains so soon, but after I vomited up my dinner—and nearly destroyed my dress in the process—priorities quickly shifted.

Now that I knew that the bond wasn't causing my upset stomach, there was one big question left—how and when should I tell Von?

Knowing the territorial alpha male, I knew that the happy news would send him into a protective spiral. My divine feminine didn't mind the thought of it—I adored how much attention Von showed me, how devoted he was to my existence, how protective he was over me . . . how protective he would be over our little one.

But today, of all days, I didn't need him ripping the heads off any of our guests. Crimson blood and gold ichor were not a part of my color scheme—only black and canopy green. The colors that had won my heart.

I decided I would tell him tonight.

A string pulled—a familiar sensation.

I glanced into the reflection of the mirror, finding the incarnate of darkness and sin standing behind me. He was dressed in his regal King of the Spirit Realm attire, a silver skull propped on his shoulder and his crown of flame and bone floating above his raven hair, one side freshly shaven.

Every inch of him was lethal. Deadly.

But best of all? I bit my bottom lip. All of *that* was *mine*.

Striking green eyes, as breathtaking as a forest after it had been rained upon, met mine.

Oh, shit—

Green!

Eyes retracting from his, I looked to the sprouted grains set in front of me. I didn't want to tell him yet.

I felt a bit of warmth come from my belly and suddenly the bowl full of sprouts was gone. I spared a quick glance down. *Was that you, little one?* Apparently, someone had picked up their daddy's party trick of making things disappear.

I couldn't help but grin.

"What are you smiling about, my darling little bride?" Death asked as he swaggered towards me, his incredible power brushing up against me—stroking my divinity, making her purr for him.

My skirts bunched as I rotated on the stool, looking up at the towering male. "I'm smiling because I'm thinking about our future," I answered honestly, knowing that Von would see straight through my lie, so I didn't bother with one. Rising, I closed the last stride of distance between us, my hands falling over his chest as he wrapped me in his strong, muscular arms—arms that would hold our little one in less than nine months.

My heart nearly burst at the thought.

Von's black brows raised as his hand dipped under my chin and he pulled my face to his. "Your happiness tastes different right now, less citrusy and more . . . floral. Like the petals of a daisy on my tongue." His eyes flickered between mine. "What's going on with you?"

Creator above. *This* male was impossible to hide things from.

"Am I not to feel immense joy today, of all days?" I countered as I pulled back from him, stepping over to the cathedral-length veil that hung on the bathroom door. I ran my fingers over the fine black lace, the same floral pattern as my gown. When the veil was pulled out, a crescent moon would show at the bottom of it, nestled among a canopy of twinkling black crystals—a nod to us. I peered at my inquisitive mate over my shoulder. "Besides, *I* should be the one asking what *you* are doing here. Don't you know it's bad luck to see me before we exchange our vows?"

He let out a low, sexy laugh. "What can I say? I'm a greedy bastard. I wanted to be the first to see you like *this*." His eyes raked down my body, taking me and my black wedding gown in, stoking my coals in the process. He walked over to me, his heat kissing my back a breath before his hard body pressed against mine. Starting at my elbow, his ringed fingers brushed up the length of my arm as he purred, "Seeing you wear my colors . . . it makes me feral."

I shivered, committing his words, the way he said them, to memory.

His hand moved beneath my chin, guiding me to look at him. "Do you want to know one of the other reasons why I have come?"

"Why?" I asked, turning towards him.

His lips tipped up at the corners, exposing those incredible fangs. "I want you to feel my seed leaking between your glorious thighs as you walk down the aisle."

"Oh," I said, the word breathy. "But the dress—"

"Will be fine."

"You could easily remove it," I suggested.

"That would defeat the purpose."

"The purpose?"

A wicked, wicked smirk. "Of fucking my bride in her wedding gown."

Like a big, sleek jungle cat, he grabbed me. I squealed as he swept me up from the floor, carrying me with ease—something that was a feat in itself considering how *much* dress there was. His lips met mine as he lowered me onto the soft, black furs that were draped over our big bed.

Von's kiss was molten.

Passionate.

Consuming.

I wrapped my arms around his neck, binding myself to him as he propped himself over top of me, between my arched legs. His hand dipped under the fabric of my dress and his fingers began to trail up my lace stockings. His touch was somewhat muted until he reached my mid-thigh where the stocking ended. His rough fingers brushing against my smooth skin had my legs shaking and my core aching.

And he hadn't even touched me *there* yet.

I think we're doing this backwards, I said through the private pathway that linked us to each other, my lips preoccupied with his. *Aren't we supposed to have sex after the wedding?*

Don't worry, little bride, he mused, fingers hooking my panties, snapping the crotch in two with the swipe of his hand. *I plan to fuck you every chance I get today so that I can fill you with my baby.*

I giggled softly against his lips—unable to help myself. Creator above, it was going to be hard to go the whole day without telling him.

He bit my bottom lip, causing a sting of pain. *You find the thought funny.* At that moment, he inserted a finger into my sex, all the way to the knuckle.

"No," I gasped. His broad finger invaded me so thoroughly. They were always so much better than my own, so much bigger, longer.

Always such a good girl for me, Von praised as he slid his finger in and out. *Keeping this pretty little sex of yours soaked and ready.* He dipped a second finger inside, stretching me even more. The heel of his palm sunk into my clit, rubbing it in circular motions.

Do you know what good brides do on their wedding day? His lips roamed to my neck, his fangs scraping over the sensitive skin—not enough pressure to tear it, but just enough to make it swell.

"What?" I rasped out loud, his powerful fingers exorcising the sound out of me.

They bleed for their grooms. His fangs sliced into my neck. There was a sharp pinch of pain and then euphoria exploded.

"Von." The husky moan fell like a prayer from my trembling lips, my hands weaving into his hair as he drank from me. When his fingers pulled out, I could have cried at the loss of him.

He pulled back, sinking onto his haunches as his shadows swallowed his clothes, revealing the war god's seductive body—built to conquer.

I propped myself onto my elbows, taking view of the monumental cock standing before me—how my body managed to fit *all* of *that,* I would never know. Powerful veins roped around his steely length, a pearl of precum on the slit. My tongue darted over my bottom lip. How badly I wanted to taste him.

With one muscular, tattooed forearm, he stroked himself for my enjoyment. Then he leaned forward and released a mouthful of my ichor onto his cock, drenching his masculinity in my essence.

White-hot liquid heat pooled low in my abdomen.

"Do you like the sight of your blood on my cock, Little Goddess?" he purred, flashing his barbaric fangs, dripping with my ichor.

"Yes," I rasped, the word more plea than answer.

"Tell me why," he demanded softly, heavy, taut muscles flexing as he slid his hand up and down at a slow, easy pace. He was glorious.

I bit my bottom lip, released it. "Because it's like I'm claiming you."

"Now you know how I feel when I see my seed leaking out of you," he said as he crawled over top of me, lowering himself into the cradle of my hips at the same time he aligned himself with my center. "Do you know what that's going to do to me as I watch you come down the aisle?"

I shook my head, recalling that Von could see past clothes, if he wished to. Which meant that was exactly what he would be seeing—my thighs painted in him.

"It's going to make it nearly impossible for me to stand there," he groaned as he pressed himself in, and in, and in—so deep, it felt like the air was being evicted from my lungs.

"Fuck. Von!" I cried out his name, tossing my arms around his neck. With him, it always felt like I was being split in two, but it was a small price to pay for the pleasure he would stitch me back together with, for the ecstasy I would feel.

"I might just have to order everyone to leave, bend you over the altar, and take you right then and there," he mused, his fingers strumming my swollen bud, sparking pleasure with the pain I felt at my entrance from being stretched so thoroughly.

"Yes," I moaned, so completely full of him. It was a fullness unlike any other.

"I want this swollen with my pup." His hand pressed against my lower stomach, over top of my dress. "So that every time I look at you, I'll see the evidence of your submission to me." Slowly, he began to work me in, his tempo increasing. "I want the world to see how pretty you look as you sit on our throne, growing my heir in your belly. I want them to see what a good girl you've been for me, taking my cum."

At that moment, I nearly cracked—I nearly told him—but he picked up his speed and the words never got the chance to leave my lips, because I was too busy crying out for him.

Pleasure intoxicated my veins, making me feel as if I might combust. I channeled that energy into my fingers, running my claws down his back.

Give it to me, love, all of it, he purred as he thrust, and thrust, and thrust.

And so I did. I sunk my nails even deeper as he rode me into oblivion.

I felt pressure against my bladder, making me feel as if I had to pee—making me track towards my orgasm even faster. I looked down. Von's hand was still firmly pressed against my lower stomach—it increased the sensation, it felt incredible.

"Ah, ah, ah." The heavy sighs of pleasure danced from my lips in tune with his thrusts. I looked up at him, my eyes pleading for release.

"Come for me," he purred. Then he leaned forward, his lips parting mine, his tongue slipping into my mouth. It wasn't enough that he could hear the extent of my pleasure—he needed to physically taste it too.

I screamed as I came, the sound muffled by Von's mouth against mine. Stars danced at the back of my vision as my consciousness flickered in and out from the intensity of my release. My body spasmed as I rode out those incredible waves of pure, unparalleled ecstasy.

Von lifted my hips from the bed, angling me as his molten seed pumped inside.

Take every drop, Kitten, he commanded through the bond as he kissed me, working his hips in such a way it felt like he was even deeper than before.

What are you doing? I asked, my hips rolling with his as he continued to do that even after we both had orgasmed.

He smiled against my lips. *Ensuring I plant my baby deep inside of you.*

With his length still in me, he swept two fingers beneath it, gathering the evidence of our joining. He broke our kiss, bringing his fingers to my lips. "Taste us. Taste how good your blood is when it's mixed with my seed."

I opened my mouth and his fingers dipped inside. It was a combination of salty and sweet, and it tasted incredible.

"Mmmm," I moaned, licking us off his fingers.

He groaned, and it was one of the sexiest sounds I'd ever heard. Pulling his fingers out, he looked at me, his eyes renewed with that bright, vivid green I had grown so fond of seeing.

I kissed the tip of his nose, then said, "As much as I'm enjoying being with you like this—" I wiggled my hips, "—we have a wedding to attend, my love."

He raised a black brow, his fingers playing with a lock of my hair. "We could just stay here for the rest of the day. I could have someone officiate on the other side of the door."

"We have guests waiting for us," I reminded him.

"I couldn't care less."

"Von," I warned.

"Fine, little creature. Have it your way," he said, kissing my forehead. Pulling himself from me, he got up.

He offered me a hand standing up, my legs shaky. I hoped that would wear off by the time I started to walk down the aisle.

He glanced down at my dress, a toying smile plucking at his lips.

"Your gown is a mess."

I looked down, eyeing the smears, as well as his massive handprint painted in my ichor, that was placed over my stomach.

"Fix it for me," I told him, my hand itching to touch where he had touched, to connect the three of us, but knowing that maternal move would be a bit of a giveaway, I kept my hand loose at my side.

"So very bossy," he teased before he did as I asked.

In truth, I was sad to see his handprint go. There was something sexy and romantic about seeing it there. First, was the sheer size of Von's hand, which was a turn on itself. But second, it was sweet seeing his large handprint against my stomach, knowing that our tiny babe was already growing on the other side.

After Von left so that I could finish getting ready, I stood in our bathing chamber, my hand circling my stomach as I looked in the full-length mirror, trying to picture myself with a baby bump.

I felt a dark presence standing behind me.

Smirking, I rolled my eyes. *Insufferable male.*

"Von, you have to let me get ready or we'll miss the wedding," I huffed, turning around.

Something scratchy was thrust over my face, painting my world in darkness. I clawed at it, trying to get it off, but a potent, lung-choking scent clogged up my nostrils. I sputtered, breathing the cloth into my mouth with each ragged gasp for untainted air.

Fumbling for my powers, I conjured a barrage of daggers and sent them flying out around me. But they lacked structure, so when they hit my assailant, it sounded like a bucket of water splashed against a wall. Metal screeched, like rusty hinges being pried open, and then something hard was locked around my neck. Long, thin nails drove into my flesh without mercy, and my ichor rose to the surface. I cried out in pain, my nerve endings screaming as if they were being burned.

That potent, acrid smell continued to work on me, causing me to gag.

Causing me to panic.

The baby!

My hands dove to my stomach—my instinct to protect our child at the forefront of my mind as my muscles started to grow weak from the intoxicant.

I needed to protect our baby.

I needed to protect our baby.

I needed to . . .

Chapter 48

Sage

"Welcome back, princess," said a cruel voice.

Pain drilled into my cheeks, like my face was stuck in a vice. But it was nothing compared to the horrific agony I felt around my neck, like dozens of needle-like teeth had sunk into my skin.

Slowly, my eyelids lifted, revealing a silhouette crouched before me. The ominous figure split into two, drifting apart. Eyes focusing, they returned together, merging as one.

Dark-gold eyes met mine, followed by white hair.

Aurelius!

No—not Aurelius.

Nicholas.

I tried to scream, but the hand clamped around my face tightened, his fingernails sinking even deeper into my cheeks, causing ichor to brim. Nicholas raised a finger against his lips. "Shh, princess. We wouldn't want anyone to hear you now, would we? I tell you what. I'll remove my hand from your mouth if you promise not to make a peep." A sadistic smile slithered across his lips. "Does that work for you?"

I nodded, stopping immediately when I felt the torturous pain biting into my neck. My brain was still foggy. Why was I here? What happened?

He released his hand from my mouth, pulling it away.

I went to reach upwards, to try to rub away the ache in my cheeks, but my hands were rendered immobile. With some difficulty, I glanced down—my wrists were bound in iron chains.

"Sorry about those," he said. "And this." He flicked whatever was wrapped around my neck. It made a metal-sounding *tang*.

I winced, realizing what it was. The iron collar. Nails impaled my neck, leeching the power from my divinity, pulling ichor from my veins, weakening me.

Wearily, my eyes flickered around my surroundings. There was no mistaking where we were—the gold-brick walls were a dead giveaway. But it was the dingy look of the unpolished bricks that told me we were somewhere down in the dungeon. Straight ahead, vicious knives hung on a wall, accompanied by spikes and horrific-looking saws. In the middle, a table with shackles hooked up to a wheel. To my left, a trough filled to the brim with water. Chains hung from the ceiling, the iron bonds painted in centuries of spilt blood.

My heart pounded and my palms grew damp with sweat as I realized exactly where I was—I was in a room used for . . . *torture*.

Von! I yelled through the bond.

Nothing.

I tried again and again, finding the same answer with each failed attempt. My stomach filled with lead as I realized that the iron collar had cut us off from one another.

Brows smashing together, I looked at Nicholas and hissed, "Why have you brought me here?"

"Because you, dear sister-in-law, are going to help me," he said, tapping the tip of my nose.

"Help you with what?"

"Help me become king," he said as he stood up.

Become king? I scoffed. "Aurelius will never relinquish his crown. And even if he did, it would go to Arkyn, not you."

"I'm well aware Aurelius won't, which is why I will be taking matters into my own hands. And Arkyn is the least of my concern. He is a measly Demi God and can easily be disposed of." Nicholas turned around and leisurely strolled over to the wall of horrible tools. He plucked a sharp knife from it, eyeing the thin, sinister blade. "Aurelius has not been fit to lead for some time now. Malachai is too blinded by his loyalty to see it, but I am not."

"So what are you going to do?" I asked, an eerie feeling washing over me.

"I'm going to kill him, of course." Nicholas laid the knife down and grabbed another. This one was longer than the last.

"How? No one knows his weakness."

"I do." He grinned with a sinister smile. Then he pointed the blade towards me. "You."

My ichor ran cold.

"Nicholas, I am not the God of Life's weakness."

"I don't believe that," he said, setting the knife down and picking up another. Firelight caught on the blade's edge, emphasizing just how sharp it was. "Let me tell you a little story . . . About five or six months ago, we received word that an Old God was trashing a city in the Living Realm and causing multiple casualties. Aurelius sent me to do his dirty work, as per usual. I ended up tracking the immortal down at a tavern. Do you know who was seated in front of the bar?"

I didn't really care who it was—all I wanted was to get out of here—but I'd play along if it bought me more time. "Who?"

"It was the Goddess of War. She looked terrible, smelt like she hadn't taken a bath in months. I expected her to try to fight or something, but to my surprise, she waved me over. So I decided to see what she had to say. As I sat down beside her, she withdrew a crown from her satchel and placed it on the bar top. It was a strange, white-ish crown woven from something that looked like vines and sharp thorns. I asked her if there was a story behind it. She told me that the God of Death had made it out of the roots of a tree from the Golden Palace, the one that made you horribly sick when you got too close to it. I recalled the tree, remembered that Aurelius suspected it had the ability to end your immortal life. Not that I told her that. Instead, I let her talk. She said that she had stolen the crown from the Blood King's crypt and replaced it with a fake one. Then she went on to tell me that she had led a failed rebellion to try to take over the Spirit Realm because she did not believe her brother was fit to lead. You can imagine my surprise, as I had been having the same thoughts about mine. Naturally, we hit it off over that, and before I knew it, she was helping me come up with a plan of my own. She even gave me an amulet so that I could light walk past the Blood King's wards and into his castle." He pulled a chain from underneath his tunic, showing me the necklace. A dark emerald embossed in a silver bezel hung from it. He dropped it, and the heavy gemstone thumped against his chest.

My heart mirrored the act, landing with a heavy beat . . . That's how he had been able to abduct me from the castle—the amulet.

He continued, "We tossed back a lot of different ideas, but everything we discussed always led back to one person . . . you."

I tried to shake my head, but the nails in my neck reminded me that wasn't a good idea. Wincing, I said, "Saphira has a talent for twisting words. Whatever she led you to believe, I promise, it will get you nowhere. I am not Aurelius's weakness. Of that, I am certain."

"And yet his heart beats in your chest." Nicholas strode over to me, a knife in one hand and a clear vial in the other.

I bristled, trying to back myself further into the wall as he crouched in front of me. Like a snake, his hand shot out, grabbing my shackled hand. I fought against him as he pressed the blade against my skin, but my divine powers were muted by the collar, and in my weakened state, I was no match for him. Still, I fought, trying to keep my fingers clenched shut as he pried them open.

"Hold still," he growled as the steel cut into my palm, slitting it open. I cried out in pain. He held my weeping hand over the vial, letting my golden ichor seep into it.

When the small glass was half full, he let my wrists go and took it over to the counter, grabbing a stopper and shoving it into the end. He placed the vial in a little stand, tapping the side of the glass. "Beautiful," he purred, before he turned back around and strode back over to me. "Do you know what else she said?"

I shook my head, my lips curling at him as he squatted in front of me.

"There is a prophecy that your life is linked to the male you are supposed to kill, or some shit like that. She said that originally, they thought it was about the Blood King, considering you are most definitely *his* weakness." I opened my mouth to say something, but he held up a hand. "Don't waste my time trying to deny that either. I saw the blood seep from his wounds the day you tossed those daggers at us all." He ran the tip of the blade across the metal collar, making an eerie scraping noise. "Now, back to my story. Saphira said that eventually, she didn't believe the prophecy was about the Blood King, because the bond had been forged between the two of you and it would never allow you to raise arms against him, no matter how badly you wanted to. When I questioned who she thought it might be about, she asked me who you hated more than anyone else. Who you would kill if you had the chance, and I knew, immediately—my brother. The god who treated you like a worn-out mat, whose only purpose was for him to wipe his feet on. If I were you, I'd hate him too." He raised a brow in thought. "But the thing is, if your life is linked to his, wouldn't that go both ways?"

He lowered the knife to my chest, placing it over my heart.

"Regardless of how far you plunge that blade in, you and I both know that it will not kill me," I told him.

"No." He glanced at the knife before he tossed it over his shoulder, and it clattered against the floor. He gave me a malicious smile. "The knife won't kill you, but I know something that will."

Horror riddled my bones, stretching my eyes wide—

"Nicholas, wait," I pleaded.

But he didn't. His hands grabbed hold of me as he picked me up from the floor and slung me over his shoulder. I grimaced as I landed with a hard thump, my abdomen taking the brunt of it—

The baby. Our baby.

I became desperate. "Please, Nicholas," I cried out, trying to fight against him. "What do you think Von will do when he finds out what you have done?"

"I'll be ready for him."

"He'll destroy you!"

"Not if I kill him first. Why do you think I collected your ichor just now? It is of you. When I pour it on my sword and decapitate him with it, I'm willing to wager it will end his immortal life."

Internally, I broke at the thought, that my blood would be used against Von like that.

"But he drinks my blood," I argued, hoping I could plant a seed of doubt. "It does not harm him in the least. What makes you so certain that pouring it on a blade will work?"

"Yes, but how many times has he been wounded after he has fed from you?" he retorted.

My heart sank, but I refused to let on. "Once," I lied. "He drank from me in the morning and then was wounded during training. It did nothing to his divine powers and he healed, just as he always does. Your plan will not work."

"You've always been a piss-poor liar, princess. Besides, if it doesn't work, as the new king, I will have an army to defend me."

"You are a fool to believe that an army will be enough."

"I guess we'll find out, now won't we?" he said, his light wrapping around us.

Seconds later, the darkness of the dungeon was replaced with bright daylight and a blue, blue sky. The unwelcome rays of the sun brushed across my skin as I kicked and fought against Nicholas's hold. Adrenaline and panic raced through my veins. My body had gone numb to the feel of the nails in my neck as I thrashed and thrashed and thrashed. I banged my chained wrists against his back, screaming and crying out as he carried me through the courtyard gardens.

I *knew* where he was taking me. *Knew* what it would mean for me and my unborn babe.

Tears welled in my eyes as I continued to try to break free.

Von! I screamed for my mate. I screamed his name repeatedly. Roared it through the bond. Out loud. "Von!"

"I thought you and I had a deal? You agreed to keep quiet if I removed my hand from your mouth and now what are you doing? Going back on our agreement," Nicholas sighed. "Oh, well. I suppose you'll be dead soon enough."

For a fleeting moment, I thought to tell him that I was pregnant, but then—

The hairs on my arms began to rise.

That was all the warning I had before I felt the full force of *it* come crushing down on me.

Like a fist sailing into my gut.

Like a hand wrapping around my throat, my stomach.

Squeezing.

And squeezing.

I could feel my body being pulled, summoned to its destructive embrace.

"Please. No," I choked out, as memories of Aurelius dragging me towards the white-leafed tree began to play out in my mind. Like a tidal wave, those memories swept over me, pulling me under, pulling me into them . . .

"Please," I sobbed desperately. "Please. Please. Please."

But Nicholas did not listen as he shoved me against the tree. The ground shook beneath my feet as roots shot from the mossy floor, cracking it apart as they wove around me, sucking me tight against the trunk.

Von . . .

And then I felt it—

Like glass in my arteries, shredding me apart.

Vein by vein.

Chapter 49

Von

Standing in front of hundreds of people was something I had gotten used to over the eternal span of my life. It didn't matter if I was speaking privately to one person or an army of ten thousand, leading and commanding had always come naturally to me.

That's why I had been made.

With the crown that was bestowed upon my head, I was supposed to be the Creator's iron fist, supposed to bring rule and law to the realms. But when they forged me on their great anvil, they hammered that need to control a little too deeply into my metal-derived bones, and in so many ways, it backfired on them. Because that meant that they could not control me—could not get me to do what they wanted.

I was not like anyone else. I was the bringer of death, and I did as I pleased, while answering to no one. Not even the Creator. And that was how I had lived my life for thousands of years.

But then—I looked up to the dark night sky, up at the moon—*she* was made.

A frightened blue-eyed goddess with hair as white as January and skin that glowed like silver moonlight. She had been so terrified of me back then as she hid behind the God of Life. Everything about her was intoxicating—adrenalizing, arousing. I was like some sick, sadistic animal who wanted to sink my teeth into her and never give her up, despite how much she fought. I wanted nothing more than to take her. To drag her into my darkness. To devour her entirely and never let her go.

I became obsessed with her. Obsessed in ways I didn't understand.

So I cursed her. Cursed her so that she would need me to survive.

Looking back now, it all made sense. Those intense feelings were because my soul knew who she was long before I ever did—shc was my bonded.

I would kill for her. Die for her. Destroy for her.

Anything that she needed from me, I would do.

Including standing at the end of an aisle in the middle of the forest where we were first bonded, under the watch of the moon and her night, waiting for my bride to come to me.

Just as I was doing now.

Sage had been planning this day for months and it showed. I might be a crusty old bastard, but I could appreciate beauty when I saw it, especially when it was presented in a form I could understand.

Large arrangements of moody flowers—all made by her—waterfalled from the trunks of the towering oak trees, spilling out onto the mossy forest floor. A string quartet played a slow, dark melody, lending a sense of intimacy. Thousands of candles were placed along the long expanse of an aisle, lighting her path to me.

On either side, rows and rows of wooden chairs, full of both familiar and unfamiliar faces. Among them, a great deal of Old Gods whom I recognized, the notable ones being Folkoln, Ismay, Zahra, Dameon, and their baby boy, just shy of a year old.

The only request I had for this wedding was the number of people in attendance. I wanted there to be hundreds of them. The more witnesses, the more mouths to spread the word that the Goddess of Life had joined herself to the God of Death.

I wanted it to be known by all—Sage was no longer Aurelius's wife.

She was *mine*.

My wife. My mate. My queen. My everything.

And someday, the mother of my evil little spawns. I smirked at the thought.

A family was something I never really gave a whole lot of thought to, but when she came to me just over a month ago with a pretty plea on her pretty lips to give her a baby, I took her into my lap, kissed her senseless, and told her that I would. Ever since then, I'd taken every opportunity to do just that. To say the least, I was a happy, happy male and—

A bitter sweetness spiked on my tongue, one that swiftly turned acrid—sour and metallic. The potent concoction formed a ball inside my mouth. I tried to swallow it down, but I couldn't. I made a face, my hand going to my stomach, which churned with unease and something else that I could not place.

Fear, unlike anything I had ever felt before, washed over me, but it was not my emotion I was feeling.

Sage! I roared through our bond, desperate to hear her voice. At the same time, I let my shadows sweep around me, taking me to her.

I strode into our bedchamber, back at the castle.

"Sage!" I shouted again, but only an eerie silence answered in reply.

The scent of her ichor filled my nostrils, sending every nerve ending within me burning with fiery rage and intense fear. The beast within roared against its cage, begging to be unleashed, begging to find her. I refused to let it loose. I was no good to Sage if I didn't stay in control right now.

I turned to the tattoos I had given her, trying to use them to track her, but it was of no use—something was blocking them. Whatever it was must have been administered here, which was why I was only able to track her to this point.

I traced the smell of her ichor into the bathing chamber.

My eyes widened as soon as I entered the room.

On the floor and against the walls were small pools of water—

She had tried to defend herself, but something had made it so that she was unable to fully use her power. In the middle of it all, on the floor, were a few droplets of her ichor.

My body ran cold as I rushed over.

I dropped down to my knees, sweeping my fingers over one spot—still wet. I brought it to my tongue—I had fed from her enough times that I knew the chemical makeup of her life's essence like the back of my hand. There were two things different about her blood—the first was something I had begun to detect over the past few weeks, and the second was something . . . metallic. Not the usual copper, but . . . iron.

I ground my teeth together, my molars threatening to combust.

Iron suppressed divine powers, which explained why I couldn't find her through our tattoos. There was one group *well* known for their use of iron collars—

The New Gods.

Aurelius. I was going to kill the fucker.

Roaring, I let my umbra take me to the Immortal Realm.

Wings flared out, I thundered into the throne room of the Golden Palace, full of hundreds of people. My winds tossed them backwards, snapping their pitiful bones as I strode towards the empty throne, the floors shattering beneath my feet.

"Where is your fucking king?" I yelled at them all, my veins threatening to pop out of my neck. Every nerve ending in my body was on fire, heated and ready to explode.

People screamed and cried as they tried to scamper out of my path.

"Where is he?" I shouted, my voice crashing against the gold-bricked walls with such force, they began to form spiderwebbed cracks. I would reduce this place to dust, decimate them all in a bloodbath, if that's what it took to get her back.

I grabbed one of the gods by his collar, my fist clenched as I hoisted him from the ground as I brought my face to his. "Where is the fucker?"

"He, he, he's d-d-dead, my king," sputtered the male, his face a ghostly white.

Dead?

My neck swiveled as I looked at the empty throne, my gaze drifting to the altar that sat at its base, surrounded by flowers. A white sheet was placed over top.

I dropped the male on the ground and reappeared in front of the altar, ripping off the white linen. Beneath it lay the God of Life. His cheeks were hollow, his skin ashen. Not a speck of life to be found on the miserable parasite.

Heavy footsteps sounded behind me.

"What are you doing here?" snarled a familiar voice, riddled with emotion. "Get away from him!"

S*chiiing*. A metal blade was drawn.

I dropped the cloth, not bothering to cover Aurelius up.

My shadows snaked around me as I flashed in front of Arkyn, my hand locking around his blade. I growled over it. “Where is my mate?”

“I do not know *who* you speak of,” Arkyn grunted as he tried to pull his sword from my grasp.

“Sage, you little prick.” I grabbed him by the throat, my fingers slicing into his neck as I cut off his air. His halfling ichor trickled into my hand.

“Blood King,” said another voice, a diplomatic one, steeped in propriety. Malachai. “Release my nephew. He doesn’t know where she is . . . but I do.”

I tossed Arkyn onto the floor, his useless sword clattering beside him. He glowered at me.

“Take me to her,” I demanded, looking to Malachai.

“Alright.” His voice was weary. “But before I do, all I ask is that when you end Nicholas, you do it swiftly.”

“I agree to nothing. Take. Me. To. Her.” I grated out the words, my last nerve ready to snap.

He nodded solemnly and then gestured to an arched doorway. “This way.”

I followed behind him, walking through this hallway and that, my fists clenching and unclenching the entire time as I fought with my rising anger. It was brimming to the surface, seconds away from erupting and consuming everything in its path. I had felt anger before, but it had never been like this.

Never to this extent.

To the point where I craved to destroy everything. And I think if it weren't for her, I would have. She was the only thing tethering me to my sanity right now. There was nothing more that I wanted than to have her tucked safely in my arms, under my protection.

We walked down a spiral of loosely winding stairs that led out into a courtyard. When we reached the bottom, Malachai led me through a grove of trees. As soon as I caught the scent of her ichor hanging heavily on the air, I charged past him, following it until I came to a clearing, and there I saw her—

Roots stretched up from the ground, breaking through the soil, winding around her body, strapping her to the trunk of a tree, a tree with snow-white leaves . . .

When I returned to my castle with my bride's corpse in my arms, the white roses she had made began to fade to black as we passed by them.

They, too, were mourning the loss of her.

Thousands of years had gone by, and my eyes had never produced a single tear, but for her, for my mate, now they were.

Even in death, Sage was still giving me the gift of life.

kath
ART

Epilogue

Von

I ran my fingers over the smooth, oak wood, tracing the detailed ravens and roses that I had carved into it.

What do you think of it, Little Goddess? I asked through our bond.

I waited to hear her voice, waited to hear her soft laugh. The one I had hoped to hear the night of our wedding, when I finally showed her this room—something I had been keeping from her because I had intended for it to be a surprise.

But Sage didn't answer. All that came in reply was deafening silence.

I inhaled a deep breath, blowing it out through my nose as I tipped my head back and looked at the obsidian ceiling. Not one vine or rose to be found. I had imagined that one day, this chamber would be full of them—full of my mate's creations. I glanced down at the soft, small, cotton blanket—full of *our* creation.

Light footsteps sounded behind me, stopping at the doorway.

"You knew . . ." Ezra said, her voice soft.

I nodded once. "I did."

Her feet padded against the floor as she stepped beside me. There was a moment of silence as she ran her fingers over the wood. Then she said, "It is a beautiful crib. As is the rest of the room. She would have loved it."

I didn't say anything in response because really what could I say? Words no longer had any value.

The moment I had tasted the subtle change in Sage's blood, I knew that she was carrying our child. So I got busy, building and carving every piece of furniture in this room—the dresser, the crib, the rocking chair. All of it was for our family. On the day of our wedding, I had tried my hardest to get her to cave and tell me, but the stubborn little goddess held firm. So I decided to play along with her little charade, although it was not an easy thing to do. I had felt the power of our child brim within her womb, and so while we had been joined, I had kept my hand on her abdomen, not only for Sage's pleasure, but because I wanted our little one to feel my touch, to know that I would do anything for them.

If I had any regret, that would have been it . . . leaving her on our wedding day.

I should have stayed.

I should have fucking stayed.

I should have been there to protect them.

I should have—

"Von . . . I know this is hard, but we need to discuss what must be done with Sage's body," Ezra said, unexpectedly pulling me from my thoughts.

I turned towards her, snarling at the Spinner. "*No one* is to touch her."

"So you expect her to lay like *that*? Down in your crypt? Cold and alone?"

My muscles grew taut. "She is not alone. She has me."

"I know you love her deeply, but your grief is blinding you from seeing that that is not what she would want." She paused, took a breath. Her tone softened again. "Because she possesses both mortal and immortal blood, there is no telling how long her reincarnation could take. It could be decades. Centuries. Placing her in your crypt for that long is not fair to her. She should be given to the embrace of the warm earth, planted by the lake or under a tree. She should not be with the dead, Von. She *needs* the living."

I jerked my head away, looking back down at the crib.

She placed her hand on my arm. "The child's soul might be lost, but hers is not. I know you might not see this as such, but you are being given a second chance here. Speaking from experience, when Sage reincarnates, her memories will be gone. She won't know of her history with you, which means that now, you can let her live on her own terms. When she is grown, then you can introduce yourself into her life once more. Don't you see? You can give her the chance to choose you on her own this time."

"She has already chosen me," I grated through clenched teeth, reminding the pushy goddess.

"You stubborn old goat. Would you listen to me for once?" Ezra snipped.

Slowly, I turned my head, looking down at her with a look akin to well—me. Death.

Her pupils narrowed. "Sage spent three hundred years in Aurelius's cage. Three hundred years. Can you imagine what a life, living on her own terms, will do for her? It will heal her. And it will make her stronger for all that she will have to face, once the crushing weight of her memories return. I am telling you, pleading with you to listen. The kindest thing that you can do for Sage is to let her live, just like a mortal in the Living Realm. In Edenvale . . . Let her be free."

I took a step back, my hands still latched onto the crib as I stretched out my torso. My muscles were wound so tight I couldn't think. I stared at the wolf rug, one finger tapping on the wood.

I was silent for a long while, weighing her words.

I hated them. They were asinine. Ridiculous. And yet . . .

A part of me could see the life that Ezra spoke of. I could see Sage growing up, wild and free, among the mortals she cherished so much. I could almost hear her laughter as she ran through the trees of the forest, her fingers sweeping along their bark.

"Who will look after her?" I asked, hardly able to believe that I was entertaining the thought.

"I will."

Skeptically, I looked at Ezra, one brow raising in question. "*You* will?"

She nodded swiftly. *Eagerly.*

I blew out a breath of air as I stood up. "Will you tell me one thing?"

"Ask, and I'll decide if I wish to answer."

"Why are you so invested in my mate?"

She pursed her lips, swishing them from side to side as if she were tasting a mouthful of wine. Then, "You've asked me that question before."

"I did, but you wouldn't tell me."

"Ah, well then, you already have my answer."

"Ezra," I ground out her name.

"Fine. Fine. I will tell you this . . . I genuinely care for her, and I do want what is best for her. Does that help you feel better about my interests in Sage?"

"Not really."

Ezra laughed. When the sound faded, she said, "There is something else you need to know."

"What?" I grumbled.

"Because Sage's life is linked to Aurelius's, when she reincarnates, so will he. As you know, if he dies again, so will she. And so, I'd recommend you grant Arkyn and his father—well . . . his father's corpse—passage through the mist to Edenvale so that he can reincarnate there as well, where he will also be safe."

"Or . . . I could toss him in my dungeon and let him reincarnate there and rot for eternity. Not that the asshole deserves that much from me."

"He would be like a lamb, dangled in front of a den of bloodthirsty lions," Ezra interjected, her eyebrows smashing together. "No one hates Aurelius more than the Old Gods. Sure, they might listen to whatever command you give them not to harm him, but eventually, they will crave his blood and they will want his head on a pike. Then what? What if they succeed? Are you truly willing to gamble with Sage's life like that?"

My lips curled at the thought. No, I wasn't.

"Edenvale will be the safest place for him," she pushed.

"Fine. I'll grant them passage to Edenvale." I hated the idea that both he and Sage would be growing up on the same continent. I didn't want him anywhere near her. But should their paths cross, I would be there to protect her from him.

"Good," Ezra replied. "Now, what are you going to do about Nicholas?"

Molten anger filled my bloodless veins.

"I will hunt him down and teach him the very definition of agony." I looked down at the empty crib. "I will destroy him for taking what is most precious to me."

Ezra took a step back. She held her hands in front of her, palms facing towards the ceiling. In them, a glossy black sword was formed before my very eyes. I recognized it immediately.

"The Blade of Moram," I said with a degree of question, wondering why she was showing it to me.

"Yes," Ezra said as she handed it to me. My fingers wrapped around the handle and I lifted it, my muscle memory recalling its hefty weight. It was like being reunited with an old friend. "When my sisters and I forged this mighty, powerful blade, we vowed that it would go to the protector of the Three Realms. As you know, that was you, at first. Then when Aurelius was made, it went to him. But it was the strangest thing because on the day we gave it to him, it made him appear sickly when he picked it up."

Although not all immortals became ill in the presence of something that could end their immortal lives, most did. I knew what it meant . . . the Blade of Moram was Aurelius's weakness. I shook my head, recalling a memory of him wearing the sword on his hip, tucked neatly into his golden leather scabbard. I had seen it there. Which meant that even though he physically couldn't touch the blade, that didn't mean he couldn't wear it. Somehow, it seemed fitting—the king of lies had worn a blade he couldn't even wield.

"Why give this to me now?" I asked, my gaze lifting to Ezra's.

"Because . . ." The Spinner's eyes twinkled. "Nicholas couldn't touch the blade either."

Acknowlegdements

First and foremost, thank you to my readers, especially the ones who turn the pages and stay up all night to gobble down my stories. For following my journey, for commenting, loving, and sharing my posts, for your endless support and constant cheering. Without you, this seed of a dream would never have had the water and sun it needed to sprout. I cannot thank you all enough.

To my beta readers, thank you so much for reading *Between the Moon and Her Night*. You all have helped to shape it for the better, and without you, BTMAHN wouldn't be what it is today. Not even close.

To my ARC readers, thank you for applying, for supporting, and for reading. Thank you for the reviews—they make a world of difference. Thank you for taking a chance on me.

To Team BTMAHN, the highlight of my day, my cheer squad.

You bring so much support my way. I will never be able to thank you all enough for everything that you have done for me and this story. I adore you all.

To my editor, Jessica McKelden, you bring so much experience, patience, and knowledge to the table. I always look forward to handing my unedited manuscript off to you because I know it will be polished to perfection. I'd be lost without you. Please don't ever leave me.

To my proofreaders, Whitney at New Ink Editing and Vanessa Barbas at Veerie Edits. Whitney and Vanessa, thank you for making BTMAHN sparkle! It is always so wonderful working with you two. Thank you for handling my book baby with love and care.

To my formatter, Amy Kessler at Imagine Ink Designs, it has been so wonderful to work with you on this series. Without you, BTMAHN wouldn't look nearly as pretty as it does. Thank you for being part of my team.

To my cover designer, Gigi at Gigi Creatives. You have swept me off my feet with your incredible skills. Thank you for giving me this beautiful, eye-catching cover! It was a pleasure to work with you, and I can't wait to see what magic you create for the next one!

To my SisterHOOD girls, Cel, Ris, Shay, and Vee, you fineeee ladies have been with me for so long. You all bring so much love and support my way, and for that I can't thank you enough. To see where we all started and where we are now is honestly so amazing. I'm proud of you all for chasing your dreams. <3 Never ever stop.

To Sara Flanagan, my sounding board, my ride or die, and the person who makes me feel sane when I know I'm probably teetering on the edge of insanity. You are the best cheerleader friend a girl could ask for. P.S. everyone, Sara's debut dark fantasy *Wish* is out now! I've read it, and I loved it. Go check it out!

To Kath, my talented darling, our friendship sparked with a giveaway, and look where we are now. I'm so lucky to have you in my life, and I am forever stunned by your incredible talents. Thank you for being so down to earth and for blessing my eyes with your beautiful art.

To Angela van Liempt, my kindred spirit. Thank you for being there for me during my highs and my lows. Being able to talk with you always leaves me feeling better by the end of our deep conversations. I'm so glad we have one another.

To Kai's mama, A.J. Vrana, my fellow Canadian author who comes out swinging for her friends. You were there for me during some of my darkest days, and for that, I can't thank you enough. I'm honored to have a friend like you.

To the AAP chat, y'all be sipping some delectable tea, ladies. So glad to be a part of our little group. I wish all of you every success and a viral, book-selling reel or two. Y'know, for good measure.

To Helyn Wilson, my bestie and proud mama. Congratulations on your darling new babe, my dear. I am in awe of how strong and resilient you are. A warrior through and through. You fought a long, hard battle, but you never gave up. You deserve every ounce of happiness from this world. I love you.

To my mom, my biggest supporter, even though I write some questionable things sometimes. Haha. Thank you for listening to me vent for hours on the phone and for loving me at my worst. I couldn't ask for a better mom. P.S. we're out of sourdough bread, so like, send some over, please.

To my dad and my family, thank you all for being there for me and for cheering me on. I love you all. Bits and pieces of you have gone into the creation of this story and even into some of the characters. This story wouldn't be what it is without each one of you.

To my husband, my soulmate, my love, Tanner. Thank you for your constant support and eternal patience. You constantly show me what it is to be loved by a good man, and I could not imagine doing this thing with anyone but you. Through and through, you are my *bonded*. And I'm so thankful for you and this beautiful life we are building together.

Thank you *all* for giving me the opportunity to tell Sage and Von's story.

<3 Jaclyn

About the Author

Jaclyn Kot is a prairie girl, an avid reader, occasional Netflix binger and a total foodie. She is a proud mama of many chickens, two fabulous kitties and a good doggo. She lives on a farm in Saskatchewan, Canada with her husband.

She writes high fantasy fiction and likes her fantasy served with plot twists, a side of spice and morally grey males with a palate for strong-willed females.

It is her hope that readers will fall in love with Sage and Von's story just as much as she has.

Looking for the latest information on the Between Life and Death Series or wanting to connect with Jaclyn? You can here:

www.instagram.com/jaclyn.kot/

www.tiktok.com/@jaclyn.kot

www.jaclynkotbooks.com

www.ingramcontent.com/pod-product-compliance
Lightning Source LLC
Chambersburg PA
CBHW020504310726
48979CB00016B/2779/J
* 9 7 8 1 7 3 8 7 0 2 2 6 8 *